Love a

Double RITA(R) nominee Kate Clayborn lives in Virginia, where she spends her days reading and talking about all kinds of great books. Kate loves to hear from and connect with readers— follow her on Twitter, on Instagram, and on Facebook. Visit her at www.kateclayborn.com to sign up for her newsletter.

Also by Kate Clayborn

Love at First

Chance of a Lifetime

Beginner's Luck
Luck of the Draw
Best of Luck

Love at First

KATE CLAYBORN

CANELO

First published in the United States in 2021 by Kensington Books, Kensington
Publishing Corp.

This edition published in the United Kingdom in 2023 by

Canelo
Unit 9, 5th Floor
Cargo Works, 1-2 Hatfields
London SE1 9PG
United Kingdom

A CIP catalogue record for this book is available from the British Library.

Print ISBN 978 1 80436 627 1
Ebook ISBN 978 1 80032 681 1

Look for more great books at www.canelo.co

Printed and bound in Great Britain by Clays Ltd, Elcograf S.p.A.

1

For Noni

You were so loved.

You are so missed.

You (and your Romeo) are so alive in our memories.

Prologue

The first time Will Sterling saw Nora Clarke, he could barely see at all.

In the cool shade of the large maple tree he leaned against on that bright summer day, the whole world looked blurry to him—the leaves above him green but shapeless, the patio furniture to his left dull black but soft-edged, the building in front of him tall and sand-colored, the back doors for each apartment little more than dark, smudgy rectangles leading out to wood-built balconies whose slats looked wavy unless he squinted.

He'd gotten used to it, the blurriness, or maybe he'd never really *had* to get used to it. He couldn't quite remember a time when he didn't have to narrow his eyes to bring things into focus, though he knew it'd been getting worse. He knew that sitting in the second row of most of his classes didn't cut it anymore; he knew that last year he sometimes left third period—AP Lit, his only class with Caitlin, who liked to sit way in the back—with a thudding headache. He knew the dull white leather of the baseball had become the most important thing about it, that he saw it best against the bright blue of a clear sky, that he was more likely to get chewed out by Coach on cloudy days.

He knew he couldn't always tell anymore, unless he was really up close to her, whether his mother was smiling.

But... *glasses*? Will Sterling in glasses? Out on the field, in those huge, sweaty-looking sports goggles Brandon Tenney wore?

He couldn't come around to the idea, not yet. So all last year, he'd dodged the school nurse when she did eye exams, took notes off the person next to him instead of from the board or the projector screen, always asking—politely, he hoped charmingly—first. He crossed his fingers for sunny days.

He let his unreliable eyes drift back to the smudgy black rectangle he'd been trying his best to watch most closely, the one from which he'd made his unceremonious exit barely twenty minutes ago.

"Wait outside," his mother had said in a sharp, unfamiliar voice, once it'd been clear that things weren't going according to whatever plan she'd had when the day started. A two-and-a-half-hour drive into Chicago, a city Will had never been to before, a promise not to tell his father, and not a single word of preparation for that moment when they'd stood in the dim first-floor hallway of this apartment building and she'd knocked on the door with a determined insistence that had almost felt rude.

"This is your uncle," his mother had told him when a short, barrel-chested, wholly unfamiliar man answered. Will was close enough, eye level enough, to see the way the man's mouth had dropped open slightly and briefly before he'd closed it and set his jaw against them both.

"My brother," she'd added softly, a crack of emotion in her voice.

You have a brother? he'd thought, confused, blurry in his head, too, but still he'd stuck out his hand for the man—his *uncle*—to shake.

"I'm Will," he'd said automatically, politely, glad that his own voice had mostly stopped cracking over the last few months since he'd turned fifteen. It came out, to his own ears, sounding more grown-up and unsurprised than he felt inside.

But the man—his *uncle*, his uncle he'd *never heard of*—hadn't taken his hand. Hadn't looked at him at all. Instead, he'd stared at Will's mother like she was a ghost, or maybe like she was alive, but back from the dead.

Inside the apartment, which smelled like cigarettes and the same furniture polish his mother used at home, no one had moved to sit down; no one had spoken. His uncle—Donny, his mother had finally supplied, since the man himself had shown no interest in further introductions—stood beside a brown recliner (lumpy but undefined, to Will's unreliable eyes), his hands shoved deep in the pockets of his jeans. His mother had stayed near the door, and so had Will. She'd been waiting, he thought, to be well and truly invited in.

But even Will could see that wasn't going to happen.

"I won't do this with your kid here," Donny had said finally, the first words Will ever heard him say.

Your kid, Will had repeated in his mind. He'd always been a good listener, at least, and he got the message. Maybe this guy Donny was Will's uncle, but he sure didn't intend to be any kind of family, and Will tried to tell himself that was fine by him anyway. After all, he was an only child, and up until this moment he'd thought his parents were only children, too. Other kids in his school had grandparents, cousins, big gatherings at the holidays. But the Sterling household, it was a small unit. Just the three of them. Not even a dog or a cat or a goldfish to complicate things.

Still, Will had felt a flush creep up his neck, a hot fire in his stomach, a tightness in the muscles of his arms. He was quick-tempered lately, easily angered. When he wasn't preoccupied with thoughts of girls—Caitlin, mostly, but if he was honest he had a real wandering eye—he could be moody and distractible and sullen. If all the stuff his health teacher said in class was right, it was all part of growing up, but right then, he felt like there was a purpose to all his confusing, quick-fire emotions. Maybe he was only fifteen, but he was already taller than this Donny person, and he lifted weights for baseball. He didn't like anyone speaking to his mother so sharply.

But that's when she'd given her *Wait outside* directive, and he'd been so surprised to be directed that way, to be... almost *disciplined* that way. At home his parents had always been loose, accommodating, a little absentminded, and if Will thought it was less about a parenting style than it was about wanting some time for the two of them and their constant, sometimes exhausting affection for each other, well... at least he got to stay out later than other kids; at least he didn't have to ask permission for everything, or to show anyone his homework at the end of the night, or to call when he'd be late coming home from practice.

So in his shock—from that moment, from all the moments that had led up to it—he'd gone. Out the back door instead of the front, the same smudgy black rectangle he watched now. He couldn't rely on his eyes or on the bright July sunlight enough to count on being able to see if anything went wrong in there, so he'd left the glass door open behind him when he'd gone, only shutting the screen. He'd turned to the left on the rickety wood beneath his feet and taken the few short, also-rickety steps down from the first-floor balcony. He'd crossed a stretch of sunbaked grass to a leafy, too-large-for-the-yard tree.

And he'd waited.

Tried to focus his eyes and his mind.

What did it mean that he had an uncle he'd never heard of? What did it mean that his mom had come here—and brought Will along—without telling his dad? Come to think of it, what did it mean that things had been quiet at home lately, that his mom and dad sometimes seemed to have sullen moods to match his own, that they seemed to retreat even more often than usual into each other, closing their bedroom door and shutting him out, brushing off his questions when they'd finally emerge?

Maybe someone else would say divorce. A lot of Will's teammates had divorced parents, one of them with a real messy situation that involved court appearances and social workers, the mom and dad constantly trying to out-parent each other, even from the bleachers on game days. But Will knew better than to think his own parents would split. The Sterlings were devoted to each other, devoted enough that in all their secret, usually smiling looks for each other, in the way they sat close all the time, in their touches and kisses and whispers, Will sometimes felt like a complication himself. Like an unwanted dog or cat or goldfish.

An interruption.

"Hey!" interrupted a voice from above.

A girl's voice.

A perfect voice, somehow, even from that short, everyday word. It sounded like a laugh at liftoff.

He turned his head up toward it—on instinct, in anticipation.

And then… a laugh that *did* lift off. It burst into the air above him, then trailed down from one of those balconies above like ivy, making his whole body go still, making his adolescent heart stutter-stop in his chest in a way it never had before. Later, much later, when he allowed himself to think about this day, this day on which almost every single thing in his life had changed, he'd remember that the girl's laugh had been the only thing that had felt familiar to him in that strange backyard, with his never-before-seen uncle inside, with his mother secretive and sad and angry and scared. It'd felt familiar enough, *welcome* enough, that he'd forgotten—for that short space of time—everything else that was confusing about that day. He'd certainly forgotten, however shameful it was, about Caitlin.

"Hey," she repeated, louder this time, another laugh following, and he pushed off the trunk of the tree, took a step forward to the edge of the canopy so that he could see her, or see what he could of her.

Be cool, he told himself, pushing his hair back from his forehead. He hadn't known anyone on those upper floors would be able to see him where he'd been standing, but clearly—

"Get away from there!" she called, right as he stepped from the shade, and he stilled again. Disciplined twice in one day? That was certainly unusual, and this time he was even more confused about what he could've done wrong.

5

But then.

Then, he saw her.

Third floor, right side. She was blurry—of course she was blurry—but the sky was bright blue behind her, and the blurriness seemed as much about her movement as it was about his eyes. Arms waving in front of her, her long, straight ponytail a light brown rope that swung forward over a shoulder covered with a bright white T-shirt. The balcony slats prevented him from seeing anything of her lower half, but he knew it when she jumped up and down—saw her ponytail swing again, heard her feet thud on the wood beneath her feet.

"Get, *get*!" she yelled, and he almost took a step back, feeling his breath leave his body in shock and disappointment at having been so... dismissed. By her, specifically. But when he saw two brown, furry shapes—bushy, curving tails trailing behind—leap from the balcony and onto a power line that crossed the yard, scurrying away, he realized, with relief and happiness, that she hadn't been yelling at him at all.

She'd been yelling at—

"Squirrels, Nonna!" she called over her shoulder, toward the smudgy black rectangle behind her, and he wrinkled his brow, curious at that second word, one he'd never heard before. He took another cautious step forward. He narrowed his eyes, saw that her face was like an oval. Saw her set her hands to her hips, saw her turn her body toward the retreating squirrels, as though to ensure they were really leaving. If his heart stutter-stopped before, now it took on a quick, desperate rhythm.

It wasn't how he felt when he saw Caitlin; it wasn't how he felt when he saw any of the many crushes he'd had over the last couple of years. Something felt so *different*. Different in his head and in his heart.

She made a noise of frustration, a gusty sigh-groan, dropping her hands from her hips and bending forward to look at something. For the first time, Will paid attention to what surrounded her on her balcony, more indistinct greenery peeking out

6

between the slats and above the top railing. He lost sight of her behind it all, cursed it as well as his vision. Would he even know if she looked down toward him? Was it possible she could see him now, through all that wood and all those plants? He should absolutely think of something to say to her. Should he bring up the squirrels? Should he ask her what *nonna* meant? Could he think of *anything* that didn't make him sound like a backyard creeper, which is probably exactly what he was at the moment?

He cleared his throat softly, insurance against any rogue voice cracks, right at the moment she straightened herself again.

Maybe if he just said hello. That wouldn't be creepy, would it?

He opened his mouth to speak, but then something… *pelted* him. Right on top of his head. Even as he reached up, another pelt, and then another. Not painful, not forceful. Like the first big drops of a thunderstorm. Bouncing off him and onto the grass.

Was she *throwing* things at him?

Pelt, pelt, pelt. In his hair, he felt something warm and wet. For the first time since he heard her voice, he looked toward the ground. At his feet, he saw small, bright red globes, and he crouched to pick one up. Perfectly ripe cherry tomatoes, marred by the bites of two intrepid squirrels who'd been chased away by the girl on the balcony. He smiled for the first time in what felt like hours. He gathered a few of them up in his hands, even as she continued to rain half-eaten ones into the yard. He stood, his cupped hands held at his waist, and looked up to see that her face wasn't turned anywhere near his direction. She was throwing these homegrown, city-grown, balcony-grown tomatoes over the railing without even looking, and for some reason, that made him want to meet her, to talk to her, even more now.

He crossed the yard again, back the way he came. He didn't climb the few steps back to his uncle's balcony, but he stood beside it, thinking she might be able to see him better from there, thinking he might be able to see *her* better from there. He'd call up to her. He'd say, *Hey*, just like she'd said not to him. He'd say, *Did you drop something?* and he'd smile and hold up his hands. He hoped *her* vision was sharp enough to see the tomato seeds he was sure were still in his hair.

But then he heard his mother's voice through the screen, through the smudgy black rectangle he'd forgotten he was meant to be watching.

"We need help," she was saying. "My husband and I, both of us… we are begging you for help."

And for the third time that day, Will's heart changed inside his chest.

He made himself listen; he made himself completely still. If the girl saw him now, she might mistake him for a statue. A tomato-catching lawn ornament she'd never noticed before.

But for those long, life-altering minutes while he listened to his mother and to the uncle he'd never met, while he heard a conversation that made his skin turn clammy with shock, he didn't think about the girl at all.

He'd remember later how loudly and abruptly it had ended: his mother raising her voice to tell Donny that he was cruel and stubborn, that he would regret this. That if he let her leave now, he would never see her or Will again.

He'd remember that there was absolute silence in response.

Will had dropped his hands when he'd heard that silence, barely noticing the tomatoes tumbling to the ground. He'd moved to the stairs, moved to get his mother, to make sure they started making good on that ultimatum immediately, but she beat him to it, opening the screen and following his same path out of the apartment, her face pale. When she was close enough, he could see her cheeks were wet with tears. She did not look at him as she passed him by, but somehow, he could tell.

He could tell she knew that he'd heard.

He followed her to the car, for the first time in a long time feeling like he had to make an effort to keep up with her short-legged stride as she crossed the yard—under the tree and out the other side, into the rear alley where they'd parked not even all that long ago.

He was in the passenger seat, watching his mother's hands shake as she fumbled with her keys, before he even thought of the girl. Her voice, her laugh, her nonna and squirrels and spoiled tomatoes. He thought of how silly it was, that he had noticed her. That she had felt so important to notice. Everything about his world felt silly—school, summer, Caitlin, baseball—everything that wasn't this, what he'd heard his mother say and what she and his dad were desperate enough to ask. Everything about *himself* felt silly—his restlessness, his moods, his absurd crushes on tomato-throwing strangers, his stupid fucking *eyes*, and his ridiculous, immature vanity.

He reached out and touched his mother's wrist.

"Mom," he said, and he made a decision right then, right when he heard his own voice again. He decided he would catch up to the way his voice had grown up. He decided that what he had overheard being said in that apartment meant that he had to.

"We're okay," she said, and he thought maybe she said it more to herself than to him, but still she moved to clutch his hand, squeezing it and steadying herself.

"We're okay," she repeated.

He said it back to her. Multiple times, until she was calm enough to start the car.

When she backed out, he wanted—for a desperate, fleeting second—to look back up toward the sky, toward that third-floor balcony. Toward the girl with the lovely voice and the long ponytail. The girl he hadn't really been able to see at all.

But he didn't.

He was done with blurry distractions. He was done with being a kid.

On Monday morning, he called an eye doctor with an office in a strip mall close enough that he could ride his bike to it and made an appointment, knowing already he'd fail every single test they'd surely give him. That same afternoon, he showed up for summer practice only so he could quit the team, and he ignored every one of Coach's shocked, confused protests, the same way he ignored Caitlin's when he broke up with her only a few hours later.

He didn't let himself think about the girl on the balcony at all.

He was seeing clearly now.

Chapter 1

Sixteen years later

For Eleanora DeAngelo Clarke, the best time of day was, many people would argue, not daytime at all.

The best time of day was before dawn.

It was a fairly recent development, this fondness for 4:00 a.m. When she'd first come back, it hadn't been so much a choice as a necessity, the demand of days that started early and stretched long, the fallout from frequently disrupted sleep. During those times, 4:00 a.m. had felt indistinguishable from every other hour of the day: darker in quality but not really in character, another part of the grim, human process of saying goodbye that she hadn't felt—wouldn't have ever felt—prepared to go through.

When it had been over, though, when the daylight hours became busier and more bureaucratic, when the reality of her new life had started to sink in—4:00 a.m. had started to transform for her. Sometimes, she'd do little more than sit and stare, a mug of hot coffee cupped in her palms, steaming straight into her puffy, tear-stained face. Sometimes, she rose from a restless, unsatisfying sleep and walked to the back door, sliding it open and taking a single step onto the balcony, breathing in the crisp, cold autumn air like it was medicine. Sometimes, she'd sit at the old rolltop desk in the living room, making lists to help her move through the day, to help her feel in control in this place where she'd never once, not in her whole life, had to be in control before.

But day by day, 4:00 a.m. took on a softer rhythm, and Nora moved to its beats with some improved version of those early, impulsive behaviors. In the pitch dark and perfect quiet, she sipped at her coffee and stayed inside when it was cold, letting her body and brain wake up slowly, softly. She left the lists to later, letting herself breathe. She let herself think and not think, remember and not remember. She let herself *be*.

Eight months on and 4:00 a.m. had become habit, a secret practice she'd even put a name to. At night, when she got in bed, she'd open the clock app on her phone and toggle on the alarm she'd titled "Golden Hour." She'd close her eyes and look forward to it, to the reset it always seemed to provide her, to the gentle welcome it always seemed to give her to the day ahead.

Four in the morning, she'd started to think, could fix pretty much anything.

Except.

Except for this.

It'd been two and a half weeks since it'd happened, and every day since, Nora had spent 4:00 a.m. exactly like she was right now: sitting on the balcony, still in her pajamas, fretting.

And it was all Donny Pasternak's fault.

Nora knew it was a terrible thing to think, a terrible thing to *feel*. Who could blame a man for dying, after all, especially a man so quiet and kind as Donny? Who could sit in judgment of someone—a neighbor, a friend, practically a family member—who'd left this world so suddenly, so unexpectedly, so prematurely? Who could be so... so *angry*?

Well, the answer was Nora.

Nora could.

You're not angry at Donny, she scolded herself. *You know that's not it.*

She took a sip of her coffee, trying to get that golden hour feeling again. It was a perfect not-quite-morning, warm and dry and pleasant, the kind she'd waited for all through her first dark, brutal Chicago winter.

But it didn't work.

She *was* angry. She was angry and stressed and scared, because quiet, kind Donny Pasternak was gone, and that was bad enough, especially so soon after Nonna. But beyond that—beyond that, there was the terrible realization that being Donny's neighbor and friend and *almost* family member turned out to mean exactly nothing when it came to finding out what would happen to his apartment.

Nora had never been naive about how outsiders judged the old, brick, blocky six-flat that was, for the first time in her adult life, her full-time home, though the precise nature of the judgments had changed over the years. When she'd first come to visit, her parents had spent the whole drive from the airport speaking quietly—well, not *that* quietly—to each other about Nonna wasting years of money and effort on this "little building" when she could've stayed in her perfectly nice, paid-off house in the suburbs after her husband, Nora's grandfather, passed. Two decades later and the judgments were different: Wasn't it the most dated-looking building on the block? Shouldn't it try to do a little better to keep up? Hadn't anyone considered making it brighter, more modern? Was that striped wallpaper in the hallways made of... *velvet*?

The problem was, people didn't appreciate a classic. People had no loyalty!

Nonna had always been saying that.

Nora closed her eyes, thinking of what Nonna might say now. She probably would say that Donny wasn't *people*. She would say that she trusted Donny—that Donny, like everyone else in the building who had been her neighbor, her *family* (no almost about it!), for years and years, would've made sure the apartment would be left in good hands, left to someone who understood what it was all about here. In fact, that's what everyone else in the building seemed to think, too. Nonna, after all, had left her apartment to Nora, because she'd known that Nora would take extra care. She'd known that Nora loved the building as much as she did.

"Maybe he'll have left it to one of us," Jonah had said only the week before, during their first building meeting since Donny's passing. Nora had stood at the front of the room, the concrete floor of the basement laundry room a hard press of reality against the soles of her sneakers. She watched the faces of her neighbors light in hope, and she'd thought of the three unreturned phone calls she'd made to Donny's attorney.

I think we would've already heard, she'd thought. *I think we would've heard if it was one of us.*

But she hadn't said that. She'd pasted on a smile and said, "I guess we'll have to wait and see," clutching the building bylaws in her hand with a sense of impending doom. If it wasn't one of them, she didn't know who it could be, because in addition to being quiet and kind, Donny was also, for as long as she'd known him, alone. No girlfriend, no boyfriend, no friends or family outside these walls.

Was 4:00 a.m. too early to try calling that attorney again?

She let out a gusty sigh, rippling the surface of her still mostly undrunk dark roast. The fact of the matter was, it was long past time to stop her 4:00 a.m. fretting. Maybe she needed to go back to list-making for a while, because those unreturned phone calls almost certainly meant something bad was in the offing: some faceless property investment firm was probably combing through Cook County death records even as she ruminated, looking for opportunities to do one of those quick turnaround "flips." They'd show up and park a dumpster out front and toss all of quiet, kind Donny Pasternak's things, and they would absolutely complain about the hallway wallpaper (*No* loyalty! Nonna sniffed, from somewhere). A month later there'd be a "For Sale" sign for Donny's apartment in the front courtyard with a sticker price that'd start spelling the end for this building that Nonna had made a second life in, this building that had—with a bit of fate and a lot of effort—become a family all its own.

She sighed again—it was a real *woe is me* situation during this particular golden hour—untucked her feet, and stood from her chair, stretching into a posture that was stiff, upright, preparatory. There had to be something she could do other than simply... *waiting* like this.

But right then, she heard a door slide open somewhere below her.

Nora knew 4:00 a.m.

Nora knew 4:00 a.m. *in this building*.

And she knew no one—besides her—ever came out onto their balcony at this hour.

No one except.

No one except... someone new.

–

Nora realized that it would be, by all accounts, extremely inappropriate to rush to her balcony railing, hang her head over the side, and ask whomever was down there how they felt about vintage wallpaper. First of all, the sun wasn't even up yet. Second of all, she was not wearing a bra beneath her pajamas. Third of all, if wallpaper was the only conversation opener she could think of at that moment, it was truly time to make good on her intentions to start getting out more.

Maybe it was the attorney with questionable phone etiquette? Or worse! The actual face of the faceless property investment firm? Sure it was early, but maybe these people needed the whole twenty-four hours in any given day to carry out their terrible, wallpaper-hating plans? She was absolutely not prepared to have this confrontation, not without a bra and a PowerPoint presentation about the mercenary nature of real estate trends.

Bra first, she told herself, reaching a hand toward the door handle before pausing again.

What if it's not one of those two people?

She couldn't really explain it, the feeling she had—the feeling that she shouldn't go inside quite yet, the feeling that the person who'd slid open that door was someone she should meet.

15

Of course, there remained the problem of the early hour, and her lack of supporting undergarments, and also her apparently limited ideas for what she might actually *say*, so she decided that, at least for the time being, she'd try to make this meeting one-sided. Carefully, she set down her coffee on the small patio table beside her chair, and—grateful for the quiet of her bare feet against the wood and her long-honed awareness of which boards were likeliest to creak—silently stepped toward the railing, tucking herself into one of the empty spaces between her many potted plants.

And then she peeked over the edge, down and across to Donny's balcony.

She saw him first as a dark outline, limned by the lights left on in the apartment, her perspective from above him giving her only an impression of his body—hands gripping the railing that jutted out slightly farther than her own; long arms spread wide, triangles of empty space between them and the lean waist that fanned out into a broad, curving back; head bowed low between the tense set of his shoulders.

It was like looking at a sculpture, a piece of art, something that took all of your attention. Something that insisted you stay right in the moment you were in, something that told you to memorize what you were seeing. She could've looked and looked. Until the sun came up. Until the golden hour was over for real.

But then, it hit her.

This was not the posture of a property man who needed a PowerPoint presentation.

This curved-back, bowed-head balcony lean was the posture of a man who was… grieving?

She sucked in a surprised breath and, too quickly, stepped away from her railing.

And knocked over one of her plants.

The sound of the terra-cotta hitting the wood, the sound of a clump of dirt scattering in its wake, the sound of the waxy leaves swishing in the trembling aftermath of their fall—all of it, Nora thought, sounded like the actual loudest noise that had ever been released in the entire history of the known universe.

She squeezed her eyes shut tight. She tried to make herself completely still, the way he had been. If she pulled it off, maybe the man on the balcony would think a rogue, third-floor-exclusive wind had knocked over the pot. Or some kind of critter? Yes, that made sense. A raccoon, or a particularly forceful sq—

"Hello?"

His voice was deep, but he spoke the word quietly, cautiously, and Nora supposed she could ignore it, keep on with the whole sculpture-posture idea until he went back inside. Later (*with* bra), she could go down and introduce herself, express her genuine condolences, and keep secret her nascent, selfish sense of hope that Donny may have done right by them after all.

It felt a little mean to ignore him, though, after she'd been spying and all, and also after she'd spent the past half hour being unjustifiably angry in the general direction of his recently deceased possible relative. A quick hello, then. An apology for disturbing him. No questions about his feelings regarding classic wall coverings.

She stepped back toward the railing, at the last second remembering to cross her arms over her chest.

This time, when she peeked over the edge, he was looking up at her.

He was tall; she could tell even from high above, and that was down to how well she knew this building, how every person in it looked in relation to its various structures—its railings, its overhangs, its doorways. Standing upright, his shoulders still looked broad, but overall, he seemed leaner to her outside of that bent-over posture she'd first seen him in. Maybe it was something about the clothes he wore—too dark to see him well, but they seemed to fit him loosely, pajama-like, and she liked that, thinking that they might both be out on their balconies, still in their sleepwear.

But it was what she could see of his face—bathed in the warm, golden light from the apartment—that made her breath catch, that made time stop. He was clean-shaven, his jaw square, his brow lowered in an expression to match the question that had been in his voice. Those sharp outlines might have been attractive all on their own, but they were improved—they were made stunning, really—by the soft curves that complemented them. Thick, wavy hair, messy in a way that made Nora wonder if there was perhaps an extremely flattering first-floor-exclusive wind. Full lips, slightly parted. She could only assume about his eyes, because they were hidden from her by the glare off his dark-rimmed glasses.

She swallowed.

"Hey," she finally whispered back to him.

For a few seconds, he didn't move at all, and she thought he seemed so good at that, staying still. Like, professionally good at it. *Maybe he's a mime*, said the extremely stunned part of her brain. *No, a castle guard*, she amended. Still stunned, obviously, given the absolute dearth of castles in, you know, Illinois.

But then he lifted his right hand. Slowly, he raised it to the center of his chest, his broad palm rubbing once across his sternum, toward his heart.

"You..." he said, his hand resting there, right over his heart, and Nora had the wild urge to count the beats of her own. *One-two, one-two.*

"Startled me," he finished, though nothing about his tone, or his still-quiet voice, suggested that he'd been startled at all. He shifted, finally letting his hand fall back to his side. There was still that glare shielding his eyes, but she could feel his gaze on her all the same.

"I'm so sorry," she said, inching closer to the railing, resting her still-crossed arms against it. "I didn't mean—"

"No, I'm—" he began, and then paused. When he spoke again, his voice was quieter. "I'm sorry if I woke you, coming out here."

"It's okay," she said, nodding her head toward the building. It felt like they were in a conspiracy of two out here, whispering in the dark. "You won't wake anyone."

Three of the six units in this apartment were occupied by people with hearing that was... not sharp, to put it mildly. And Benny, in the apartment below hers, waxed poetic about his white noise machine at the barest provocation, so he certainly wouldn't hear them.

"And I'm always up at this time," she added, then promptly pressed her lips together. Why had she told him that? It was a *secret*.

He cocked his head to the side, and it was like everything expressive about his face tipped with it—one eyebrow raised, one side of his mouth quirked. Something about it—something about this expression of genuine interest, of curiosity—hit Nora in such a vulnerable, neglected place.

It had felt like such a long time—months and months, really—since she'd felt interesting. Since she'd met anyone new.

Her cheeks warmed with pleasure.

"You are?" he said.

"Yeah." She meant to leave it at that, especially because it'd come out decidedly more... breathy than she'd intended. But before she could stop herself, she added, "It's the golden hour."

Nora! her brain shouted (not breathily). *What! Are! You! Saying!*

She had a fleeting hope he might not have heard her. Like, over the sound of his first-floor-exclusive hair breeze.

"Golden hour?"

Okay, well. He'd heard her.

She cleared her throat. She would answer this, briefly, not weirdly (or breathily). Then she would somehow find a way to bring up Donny, offer the condolences that she was sure were necessary.

"It's what I call this time of day… or, I guess, sort of not quite day?" *Brilliant*, she thought, inwardly rolling her eyes at herself. "It's peaceful, I've always thought."

He was unmoving again, nothing but his brow furrowing, as though he had to consider the definition. Then he sent her a lopsided grin that managed, somehow, to be both self-confident and self-deprecating.

"Not so peaceful now," he said, taking a step closer to the railing, and she tried not to notice how his smile, his still-soft voice, made her feel. Specifically, in the area beneath her crossed arms.

Yikes, she thought. *Better do something about that.*

She tucked them tighter against her chest.

"It's okay," she repeated, feeling her own lips curve into a smile.

"It means something different in my line of work. The golden hour, I mean."

"You're a photographer?" That was the only other context in which she'd heard the phrase—something about the light at a specific time of day. A time of day that was not, of course, 4:00 a.m.

The grin—and the confidence—faded. "Uh. No. Never mind. It's not… very pleasant."

Now it was Nora's turn to tilt her head in interest. What could be unpleasant about a phrase like *the golden hour*, in any context?

"What do you mean?"

Definitely after this she would find a way to bring up Donny. Absolutely she would.

His chest rose on an inhale before he spoke again. When he finally did, he seemed almost sheepish. Apologetic.

"It's what we call the hour after someone's been injured. Uh, traumatically injured. It's the time where you have… it's the best window you have to treat them."

"Oh." She lowered her eyes from his face, took in a detail that made more sense to her now. Those weren't pajamas he was wearing; they were hospital scrubs. "You're a doctor?"

"Yeah."

Wow, good thing Mrs. Salas from 2B wasn't up. Nora could practically hear her now. *A doctor, Nora!* she would say. *Wouldn't you like to marry a doctor?*

Nora cleared her throat again, course-corrected that train of thought. She should bring up Donny. Now was as good a time as any.

Instead, she said, "Do you work nights?"

"I work whenever," he said, and she thought she could *hear* the exhaustion in his voice. "I work all the time."

He sounded so... defeated, the way he said that. So weary. She opened her mouth to say something—that she was sorry, that it sounded difficult. But he spoke before she could.

"Do you?"

"Do I work all the time?"

He smiled up at her, a different one, this time. She thought it looked like a sunrise, this smile, for all that it was still dark around them. It shined out every other thought in her head: Donny, the apartment, the building.

"Do you work nights?" he clarified.

"Oh, no. I'm an early riser, I guess. I work during the day. From home."

He hadn't asked that, had he? But suddenly, to Nora, this conversation had taken a golden-hour quality all its own. Secret and special and hers alone.

"Oh yeah?" he said, that delicious note of interest in his voice. He reached up and adjusted his glasses, and in that second Nora let herself be absurdly, giddily attracted to him. She almost missed it when he asked his next question.

"What do you do?"

She smiled down at him, shifting her feet against the wood in something like anticipation. She hadn't had an opportunity to talk about, *really* talk about, her work, with someone who wasn't an actual coworker, in a long time. She liked what she did, for all the headaches it had given her recently, what with her new situation and all. All right. She would answer this one question, *then* she would bring up Donny.

"I design w—"

But before she could finish, a scream rent the air.

"What the hell?" the man said, his head snapping to the side, out toward the inky-black no-longer night.

Nora couldn't help it.

She laughed.

He looked back up at her, his hand coming to his chest again, that same gentle rub over his heart. Easily startled, this tall, handsome, bespectacled man, and she was so... *delighted* by that. So thoroughly, completely charmed.

"It's a cat," she said, the laugh still in her voice. "A stray. Probably one of the big toms."

Her laughter faded as she realized something. She hadn't heard them in a couple of weeks, not since...

"Donny," she blurted.

The man on the balcony dropped his hand away from his heart.

There was a long, awkward pause, during which Nora's soul certainly left her body. *Not sticking around for this!* it probably said, adding a cheerful wave as it went.

She cleared her throat. "He—um. He used to put food out for them."

The pause that followed was even longer. Even awkward-er. What a terrible way to bring up the condolences conversation.

The man turned his head again, out toward the yard, out toward where the frustrated feline scream had come from, his hands curling around the balcony railing again, as though he needed to ground himself. She was desperate to say something, *anything*, but she also wanted to give him a minute, if he needed it. God knows she'd needed a lot of minutes, over the last few months. That's what 4:00 a.m. was good for, wasn't it? The poor guy.

It nagged at her, a little, that she'd never seen him before, never heard Donny mention him. But that didn't necessarily mean anything. Donny wasn't a talker, wasn't a sharer, not even with Jonah, whom he'd known the longest. And he'd worked up until the day he died, leaving every weekday morning at seven and not returning until five thirty. He had a whole life away from here that Nora didn't know about. Maybe he knew tons of people, but just never brought any of them to the building.

"Did there used to be a tree out there?" the man on the balcony said, interrupting her thoughts.

"Yeah," she said automatically, her eyes going immediately out to its former spot. "We had to have it removed a couple of months after I moved in last year."

She'd been devastated, getting that tree cut down. Her first official act as the building's association president, and it'd felt foreboding, damning, especially so soon after Nonna had passed. *I don't want to do it*, she'd told everyone, afraid of what they'd think. *I wish I could keep it exactly as it is.* But it'd been rotten to the core, that tree, and frankly they'd been lucky it hadn't fallen on its own. In the end, she'd watched it come down—a whole day of chain saws running, men in truck lifts, wood shavings in the air like snowfall. She hadn't cried, but she'd really, really wanted to.

"Wait," she said, realizing that she'd neglected the most important part of what he'd said. She looked back down, found him watching her. "You've been here before?"

"Once. When I was a kid." Something had changed in his voice, though she wasn't sure she could've said what. Maybe it was that the *air* was changing all around them—the sky lightening, the predawn pitch transforming into a velvet blue-black. She knew it well enough to know: golden hour, almost over.

He cleared his throat. "He was my uncle."

Nora blinked down at him, shock and relief coursing through her. So it *was* a relative, then. *Loyalty!* Nonna was saying smugly, from somewhere, but it also wasn't really the time to be counting chickens.

"I'm so sorry," Nora said. "I'm so sorry for your loss."

The man dropped his head, something like a nod of acknowledgment, or maybe some kind of bow of respect for the mention of Donny. Inside her chest, she felt her heart squeeze in sympathy, in recognition.

I hate that I'm all the way up here, she thought, though definitely being down there would be weird. What would she do, hug him? Without a bra on? Disastrous. Extremely inappropriate! Nonna, obviously, would never.

"I didn't know him very well," he said, and *there*… there she could've said what. His voice sounded a little clipped. A little frustrated.

A little… disloyal.

No, Nora, she told herself. *That's only your 4:00 a.m. fretting talking. He's probably still in shock, same as you.*

Below her, the man reached up, scratched at that same spot on his chest. He cleared his throat again. "Do you like it here?"

Did she… *like* it?

What a question. This place held the best memories of her childhood, her adolescence. And now, she'd happily moved her whole life here for it. She could talk all morning about this building, thus her PowerPoint idea. Maybe *this* was an opportunity to bring up the wallpaper! Though probably it made more sense to talk about the people first, and—

They were interrupted again, this time by a shrill, urgent beeping, and the man quickly patted his leg.

"Shit," he said. "Sorry." Within seconds, what she could see of his face was being lit by the bluish screen of his phone. The hand that wasn't holding it rubbed absentmindedly through his hair, and she watched, transfixed. He had lovely hair, which was a compliment she absolutely would not offer out loud.

"I gotta run," he added. "Other type of golden hour, I guess."

"Right." She felt suddenly, overwhelmingly flustered. She hadn't had time to say that *she* had known Donny. She hadn't had the chance to ask him so many things—what he knew about the apartment, for one, but also the small matter of his actual *name*. And she hadn't had time to answer his question, which seemed like the most important thing of all.

She *loved* it here.

"Wait," she began, wanting to say this one last thing before 4:00 a.m. was finished.

It was clear he hadn't heard her, though. He was already moving toward his door.

Before he ducked inside, he looked up at her one last time, the glare still winking off his glasses.

"I'll see you," he said.

But he didn't stick around for her answer to that, either.

Chapter 2

Well, he figured he already knew the answer.

You couldn't like it there.

First of all, there was a smell. Not a terrible smell, Will had to admit, but not the kind of smell you'd want greeting you every time you walked through the front door. It was sort of like opening a musty wooden box and sticking your face inside it. The only thing in the box would be dust bunnies and maybe a handful of old pennies.

Second of all, there were the lights. Like any person who spent the majority of his days (and often nights) under the grim, fluorescent tray lighting inside most hospitals, Will appreciated a good old-fashioned incandescent, or even a modern-day LED. What he did not appreciate, however, was a bronze chandelier—hung low and made lower by a bunch of dangly glass things—that he hit his head on in the entryway, or a series of also-bronze wall sconces where round-cheeked cherubs seemed to watch his entire journey down the hallway.

And speaking of the hallway: the wallpaper. It was… gold, or at least it'd once been gold, though under the lights from the (dangerous) chandelier and the (creepy) wall sconces, the color looked more faded mustard than fancy metallic. Every six inches or so, the texture changed, and Will had set his palm on it and thought, *It couldn't be.*

But it was. It was *velvet* wallpaper. Striped velvet wallpaper.

Who could like that?

It couldn't be, he thought again, but this time, he wasn't thinking about the wallpaper.

It could not be her.

The girl on the balcony from sixteen years ago, and the woman he met this morning. That... could not be.

She'd said so, after all, or at least she'd said as much. Last year, that's when she'd moved in.

So it couldn't be clearer, obviously.

It could not be her.

It was only that... there had been something about her. Something about her voice when she'd said *Hey*, something about the sound of her laugh, something about the ponytail that had slipped over her shoulder as they'd talked. Something about the way she'd *looked* up there on that balcony, no matter that she'd been far away, no matter that it'd been dark. Something about the way his heart had moved when he'd seen her, like a hiccup in his chest.

But he could not let himself think about that.

"Could I, uh——?"

A voice interrupted, and Will blinked up to see the familiar barista he'd given his order to reaching gently for the travel mug he held in one hand. She gave him an understanding smile, used to seeing staff from all corners of the hospital space out in front of her while they waited for their next fix, while they recovered from whatever made them require it.

"Yeah, sorry, Janine," Will said, handing it over. "I'll take an IV bag of the same, if you've got it," he added, which was a bad joke, the coffee shop equivalent of *Hot enough for ya?*, but it was the best he could do under the circumstances, and the circumstances were that he'd been up since three o'clock in the morning, he'd seen about twenty patients since he'd shown up here four hours ago, and he also could not stop thinking about the woman on the balcony.

No, not the woman. He could not stand around thinking about the woman.

He would think about the *apartment*.

He moved down the counter to wait for his order, willing himself to focus his attention on where it should be, at least for however many minutes he had until he got paged again.

The apartment, okay. He had to unload it. As soon as possible.

Which was in twelve months.

Fucking Donny.

It was a phrase he'd been repeating to himself with a fair bit of regularity since he'd gotten the attorney's call last week. Donny had apparently already been gone for several days by then, and Will had tried to take the news of his death in the only spirit his uncle really deserved: neutrally, and with the detachment of a person who dealt with death on a fairly regular basis. What did it have to do with him, after all, that Donny was dead? Exactly nothing, that's what, which is what he'd tried to politely tell the attorney.

But as it turned out, when you were both the sole executor and sole beneficiary of said uncle's estate, it actually had a lot to do with you. And when that estate was tied to a petty, passive-aggressive, hostage-holding last will and testament, it was going to *keep* having a lot to do with you.

Twelve months before he could sell the apartment. Twelve months of musty-smelling hallways, must-avoid light fixtures, and mustard wallpaper.

Twelve months of the woman on the balcony, he thought, then clenched his jaw against it.

Focus, Will.

"Here you go, Dr. Sterling," Janine said, saving him from himself.

Any other day, he'd probably correct her. *You can call me Will*, he'd say, same as he always did, because almost six years out of medical school and he still didn't much like being called "Doctor" outside the bay, and even there he sometimes—when he thought it'd make a difference, when he thought it'd make someone more comfortable—led with his first name.

Today, though. Today he only smiled and said thanks. Today he'd get Dr. Sterling—ed all day if it kept his head on straight, if it helped give him the kind of distance he wanted: the distance between the man he was here in this hospital cafeteria, and the boy he'd felt like early this morning. First, when he stepped inside that stuffy, stale-smelling apartment he hadn't seen in sixteen years.

And then when he'd stood outside on that cool, dark balcony and seen the woman look down at him.

He'd actually been *nervous*.

"Fucking Donny," he muttered.

"And who is Donny?" said a voice from beside him, and he let his eyes close briefly.

Of course. Of course it would be the person in this hospital most likely to make him nervous.

"Good morning, Dr. Abraham," he said, hating himself a little for the way he pitched his voice lower. He already had a pretty deep voice; when he talked to Gerald Abraham he sounded like he was auditioning to play Darth Vader. He'd never wanted to get paged so bad in his life, but unless he heard the chime on his phone, he knew he was well and truly stuck. Dr. Abraham was his direct superior in the emergency department, but even if he wasn't, pretty much everyone in this hospital knew what Will had learned in the eight months since he'd been hired out of his fellowship as an attending physician at this hospital: you could not walk away from this guy, not when he asked you a question. He was five foot six of fifty-six-year-old dead seriousness, with an encyclopedic knowledge of hospital policy and absolutely zero sense of humor.

"A person called Donny, you mentioned?"

Will turned to look down at his boss, but the man was doing what he was usually doing when they stood anywhere together, which is to say: not looking back at him. Unless Will was seated and Dr. Abraham was standing, eye contact in general was a no-go, though Will had learned not to take it personally. Right now

Dr. Abraham was staring at the coffee counter with absolutely fixed concentration, but Will knew the truth.

He was waiting on an answer.

"No one important," Will tried.

"I certainly hope you are not referring to a patient."

"Certainly not."

Will drank a too-hot gulp of coffee instead of wincing. In addition to the Vader voice, he also hated the way he always ended up weirdly mimicking Dr. Abraham's formalities. *A lately deceased kinsman*, his Abraham-infected brain said, and out of sheer annoyance at his inner voice he blurted, "My dead uncle."

That almost got the man to turn his head. Instead, he cleared his throat, rocked back on his heels in that way he had. If he did this while you were on the floor, giving orders for meds or settling on a diagnosis, you knew you'd done something he didn't like, something he'd tell you later was an "unusual choice" or a "departure from our normal procedures."

Will waited.

"I assume he's done something pre- or postmortem to deserve this language?"

Where to begin? Will thought. But he only took another sip of his coffee and said, "He left me his apartment."

Everything in it, too. Near as he could tell, the same brown recliner was still there. It *smelled* the same, a fact that flooded him with terrible memories of that terrible day. Getting out of there, it's what had sent him onto the balcony in the first place. Where he'd met the—

"An unusual reason to curse someone," Abraham said. Janine was handing him his coffee across the counter. Frankly, she looked nervous, too, so Will sent her what he hoped was an *I get it* smile when Dr. Abraham stepped forward to take it, briefly nodding his thanks. Abraham wasn't just a know-it-all; he was also bare-minimum polite, a fact that was confirmed when he turned to leave the cafeteria, clearly intending for Will to follow.

And since the man wrote his performance reviews, Will did.

"The apartment is here?" Abraham said, once Will was in step with him again.

Will felt himself clenching his jaw again, his back teeth grinding together, a knee-jerk instinct to shut down this conversation. This was the problem, really. Since he'd gotten the call he'd known he *should* be thinking about this, the situation with Donny's estate—paperwork, probate, everything— but instead he'd stayed busy, stayed moving. He stayed late here, or he took an extra shift at the clinic where he worked as a doc-in-the-box on his off days, crowding out the noise that kicked up in his head every time he thought about Donny and his damned apartment. Last night, lying wide awake in his bed, counting the hours until his alarm went off, he'd decided he'd had enough of the ruminating, ridiculous avoidance. He'd taken the shortest of showers, thrown on his scrubs, and made his way to the address he'd been staring at on legal paperwork for more than a week.

He'd been determined to do the practical thing. The responsible thing.

But then there had been that bolting desperation to get out onto the balcony, away from Donny's things. And ever since, this unruly instinct to keep his mind fixated on a woman whose *name* he didn't even know, instead of on the problem at hand. And now, this pressured impulse to shut down a completely innocuous conversation about it?

He was being a fucking *child*.

"North," he answered, determinedly. "Up around Logan Square."

"That would add considerable commuting time each day, but—"

"I can't live there," Will said, more sharply than he intended. He thought of the mustard wallpaper, the unnerving, possibly haunted wall sconces, the messy detritus of Donny's life. "I need to get rid of it."

"My sister is a Realtor," Abraham said, clearly unfazed by Will's tone. Probably because ninety-three percent of his own sentences were delivered sharply. Once Will had seen Dr. Abraham tell a crying, concussed twelve-year-old that football was a "fool's sport."

"The terms of the will say I need to keep it for a year."

Abraham cocked his head, his brow furrowing. "Odd, that. Is it legal? You know, my brother is a lawyer."

How many conveniently employed siblings did this man have? Will figured he'd better not bring up his recent insomnia, or else he'd be learning about a sleep therapist sister next. He also better not mention the fact that he'd briefly entertained the idea that the woman he'd had a conversation with at four thirty this morning had also been the girl who'd thrown tomatoes at his head one summer day sixteen years ago.

That'd mean a regular therapist sister, probably.

"I spoke to a lawyer. He said I could contest it while it's in probate, but that might end up delaying things even more."

I'll bet you a hundred bucks you end up keeping it the twelve months, the attorney had said, blustering and genial. *Donny loved that apartment*. Will was pretty sure that couldn't be true, and that was before he'd even seen the place.

It couldn't be true because he didn't think Donny could love anything.

He thought of the stray cats, felt another spike of anger. What an insult.

They turned a corner down the long hallway that would lead them back to the ED, and out of habit, Will's pace increased. The ED was like that, sort of a speed vortex, even when not all that much was going on. You got close to it, you moved faster, your attention necessarily pulled to whatever problem was right in front of you. Will had always liked that about it.

But then Dr. Abraham stopped.

So Will stopped, too. They were, obviously, still standing, so no eye contact allowed. They both simply stared at those double doors, like they were preparing to storm a castle.

"My ex-wife," Abraham began, and Will almost, almost laughed. Another relative, Jesus. This was an extremely unrelatable area for Will personally.

"She owns three apartments in this city."

Will raised his eyebrows. Must be nice. Up until a few days ago, he owned exactly zero apartments, and hadn't planned to until he'd paid off some more of his truly astronomical student loan debt. Before he'd learned about this twelve-month condition, the best thing he could say about inheriting Donny's apartment was that selling it would at least help him put a sizable dent in his monthly bill from the federal government. It still would, he guessed, but not soon enough.

"Short-term rentals, all of them. She's quite successful."

Will looked over then, something about Abraham's tone less pedantic than usual. The man was smoothing the lapel of his white coat, and for one second—not even one second, probably not even half a second—he looked entirely unsure of himself.

Odd, that, Will thought, Abraham-echoing. He took another sip of coffee, wondered if Janine had accidentally given him decaf.

"That's—" he began, once he'd swallowed, but it was clear this was the kind of conversation where he was not supposed to participate with actual replies, because Abraham talked over him.

"She uses a website. It seems that once one gets the units up and running, they rather pay for themselves. And they must require very little intervention. She travels a lot."

There was that lapel-smoothing again. Abraham was the only doctor in the ED who even wore the white coat with any regularity, which up until this minute Will had always chalked up to the man's pathological insistence on something he called "professional rectitude." But clearly there was also a lapel-smoothing pathology happening, too.

It was a good idea, a short-term rental. He'd stayed in a few during his fourth year of med school, four weeks at a time at various programs where he'd done his acting internships. But those places had been bland and sterile, the furniture inside neutral and inoffensive, the hallways outside entirely absent of dangly chandeliers and cherubic sconces and textured wallpaper.

He thought of the woman on the balcony again, felt that stubborn hiccup in his heart.

"I'll call her for you," Abraham said.

Will blinked. "Wait, who?"

Abraham broke the no eye-contact rule to look over and up at him, his expression annoyed. "My ex-wife," he snapped.

"Right," Will said, the back of his neck heating. "My apologies."

My apologies, Christ. He pushed up his glasses. It *was* a good idea, the short-term rental. Maybe exactly the right idea. It was absolutely more productive than insomnia, or than thinking compulsively about ten minutes of conversation with a woman who'd made him feel like a teenager.

"It couldn't hurt to take a phone call," Abraham said. He was using his full-on "professional rectitude" voice, which meant Will was taking too long to answer.

"No," he said finally. "It couldn't."

A phone call was the least of it.

At the end of his shift, Will was back in the cafeteria, sitting across from a small, brightly clothed woman who'd introduced herself as "Sally no-longer-Abraham" and who preferred hugs to handshakes as a form of greeting. She was a day and a half away from a two-week Caribbean vacation, and despite Will's insistence in their initial phone call—during which Dr. Abraham had stayed unnervingly close—that there was nothing urgent about his situation, she'd insisted on an in-person meeting.

"Time is money!" she'd said, assuring Will that she loved nothing more than "talking about the biz."

And based on the way this meeting had gone so far, that was... absolutely true.

She had not stopped.

Sally's three units were all in Wicker Park: a basement apartment on North Elk Grove, quiet but close to a bunch of shops on Milwaukee; one on West Le Moyne; a "problem child" for its window AC and its unreliable building elevator; and finally, her prized showpiece, a loft on Western Avenue with free parking and a per-night price that soared in the summertime. She had pictures of each one on her tablet, queued up on the rental website she used and ready for Will's inspection, and as he swiped through, she provided commentary that could only be described as *thorough*. Will now knew where she'd gotten every carefully chosen area rug; he also now knew, incidentally, about the incredibly detailed thought processes Sally had for placement of said area rugs. He might not have needed to know about the area rug placement, but he appreciated it, all the detail. Already he felt invested in this idea, focused on it.

But he was still harboring some doubts, especially when Sally handed the tablet over so that he could scroll through the truly impressive number of five-star reviews she'd racked up on each unit, even the window AC one. As Will scanned the all-caps parade of them ("AMAZING!" "CHARMING!" "STEPS FROM THE BLUE LINE!"), he started to feel guilty, as though it was his fault that there was such a gigantic, insurmountable gap between Donny's apartment and the ones Sally was so deservedly proud to show him.

He felt like he was about to break bad news to a patient.

He set down the tablet, cleared his throat.

"The thing is," he said, while she paged through a neon-pink three-ring binder she'd brought along, "the place I have... it's not in as good of shape as what you're showing me here. It needs a lot of work."

Sally waved a hand, used the other to reach over the binder to take the tablet back. "That's easy. I've got names of contractors out the wazoo, and they're loyal to me. You could have it fixed up before I get back from sunning myself in paradise!"

He shifted in his chair, the bad-news-breaking feeling even heavier now.

"That's probably not in the cards," he said, trying to keep his voice light. He couldn't blame her for thinking that hiring a bunch of contractors to do speedy work would be easy for him. A lot of people thought doctors wiped their asses with money, and Will guessed some of them probably did. But that was so far from his own experience it was almost comical. "I wouldn't have a lot of start-up costs for something like this."

Sally looked up at him, fixed him with a problem-solving stare. Will thought the contractors were probably a little afraid of her, in addition to being loyal. He almost wished Dr. Abraham had come down to this meeting, too. It might've been nice to see the guy get put in his place, for once.

"Do you have time? Because time is almost as good as money when it comes to something like this. My places"—she tapped at the tablet with her index finger—"they look sharp now, but they didn't always."

She turned the tablet, showing a picture from her personal photo gallery—the cluttered living room of what he thought was the North Elk Grove place. It looked dark and neglected, the furniture sagging and the walls stained. It looked… not all that different from Donny's place.

Sally swiped once, revealed the same room, freshly painted, light-colored furniture in a different arrangement.

"Bright walls and sturdy slipcovers did a lot for this one. After a while I started to turn enough profit that I could do more, but at first it was only me and my elbow grease."

"It's impressive," Will said, focusing on the photo, imagining the truly outrageous elbow grease this must've taken. He didn't even know what a slipcover was. Well, he didn't mind hard work. And not minding it meant he was basically a workaholic, so he had a lot of personal leave stacked up. He could probably swing two full weeks. Maybe not before Sally's vacation was over, but still. He could get the job done.

He reached out a finger, swiped back, and then forward again. He liked it, seeing this transformation. He absolutely didn't relish spending two weeks in Donny's apartment, going through all his things, but something about this—the stripping of it, the sanitizing of it, the starting-over feel of it—appealed to him. Two weeks to everything in that apartment boxed up and out of sight, out of mind. Two weeks to money in his pocket and a countdown started to this ridiculous condition's end date. Two weeks to Donny being nearly nothing to him.

Two weeks was so much more manageable than twelve months.

"What about the registration?" he asked, intent now. He'd done a little reading when he had lulls in the action today. The site Sally used was locally owned, Chicago-specific, and for that reason it had a better reputation around here than the huge, international short-term rental sites that had run afoul of pretty much every building code in this city. But Will had skimmed a few *Trib* articles that'd suggested there'd been no shortage of attempts to block their licensing process, too.

"I've got an in on that, too," she said, shrugging. "And if the association hasn't already put itself on the prohibited-buildings list, they can't do it once you've put in for the registration."

She tapped her chin, her brow furrowing. "You said your place needs a lot of work, but what about the rest of the building? Has it been fixed up?"

Will snorted, thinking of the wallpaper. "God, no."

But as soon as he said it, he felt oddly guilty. Not unlike the feeling of being watched by sentient, cherubic wall sconces.

Or by a woman on a third-floor balcony.

He shifted in his seat, frustrated. He'd been doing so well the past few hours, putting her out of his head, focusing on the right thing about this whole disaster. He did not have the time or inclination to be distracted. He did not have the time to be who he'd been this morning. He had to be responsible. To focus.

"That's good, in terms of bylaws," Sally said. "If the building's neglected, their documents probably are, too."

"I wouldn't say neglected, exactly," he said, for no good reason. He had no idea about the bylaws; they were in the same pile as all the other documents he'd taken with him from the attorney's office. But still, he had that guilty feeling again.

Sally ignored him, picking up the tablet again.

"What's the address?"

He rattled it off without thinking, then furrowed his brow as she tapped away. "What are you looking up there?"

"I'm seeing if any LLCs are already listed as unit owners. If so, it's almost certain you won't be the first to do a short-term rental."

"You can see that?"

"Cook County website," she said, *tap tap tapping*. She frowned. "Hmm."

That didn't sound great.

"Privately owned, all of them. That's a bummer, but it's not the worst thing. My place on Western was like that when I bought in. You'll probably have to do some campaigning."

Campaigning. He had a vision of himself in the now-treeless backyard, staring up at that third-floor balcony. His heart hiccupping, his hands full of half-eaten tomatoes.

But that was ridiculous, because he wasn't that kid anymore. And anyway: *It. Wasn't. Her.*

"Have you had any contact with anyone in the building?" Sally asked.

He coughed. "Uh. Briefly. I spoke to a woman on the third floor this morning." *During the golden hour,* his brain supplied, unhelpfully.

"Hey, no," Will said, once he realized Sally had gone back to typing. Looking for an LLC, that was one thing. It didn't feel right to get details about individual people who lived in the building this way, let alone about the woman on the balcony. "You don't have to—"

"Eleanora DeAngelo Clarke," Sally said, before Will could finish.

His heart hiccupped; his hands twitched. He would not do the chest-rubbing thing.

That was a beautiful name, though. *Eleanora.*

Sally barreled right on, which was for the best. What did her name matter, after all?

"I mean, I'm assuming. The other third-floor resident is a guy called Jonah. Eleanora, she's probably the one."

God*damn* these hiccups. Medicine had really never found a cure for them, not that his were the typical kind.

"Anyway," Sally said, "Gerald told me—grudgingly, if I'm being honest, but you know how he is—that everyone here thinks you're *real* charming. You gotta translate some of that famous bedside manner into this job! Some smiles and reassurances while you clean up the place, and you could have this whole thing sewn up quick."

Will cleared his throat, straightened in his chair. Right. Two weeks, basically. He could do that. And he *was* charming! Witness his coffee jokes, or the way he always got called in for crying kids. Or crying adults, frankly. He could do this. Get some goodwill, get the apartment into shape, get money, get Donny out of his head. The woman on the balcony had nothing to do with it.

He just had to stay focused.

Sally snapped the tablet shut, smiled across the table at him as though they'd shaken hands on a deal. "If I were you," she said cheerfully, "I'd start with Eleanora."

Chapter 3

"He called you *Ms. Clarke*!"

Nora pursed her lips and prayed for strength as murmurs of disapproval spread through the assembled group. This building meeting was really, really not going well.

That made two in a row, not that Nora was counting, and since the last one had been what basically amounted to a collectively devastated debrief over Donny's death, that was really saying something. But this morning—called together hastily once again—Nora's neighbors seemed almost as shocked, almost as shaken as they were during that last meeting. Their regular business—maintenance reports, budget updates, event calendars—all of it shunted to some other day.

All because of the man on the balcony, and his awful letter. His *letter*!

"Marian," Nora said, trying to keep the exclamations that were in her head out of her voice. "Why don't you let me have that back for now?"

"*Ms.!*" Marian repeated, drawing it out, fully exclamated—*Mizzzzzzz!*—obviously not ready to let Nora have the letter back. She was staring down at it through the lenses of her glasses like she could make it catch fire with her eyes. "I give him points for making no assumptions about you, Nora, but this whole thing doesn't seem very *neighborly*!"

"Right," Nora said, reaching a hand out from her spot by the washing machines. "If I could—"

"Strangers," Emily said quietly, shaking her head. "Staying *here*."

"Don't see as how it'll work," said Jonah, his arms crossed over his skinny chest. "People coming in and out like that. What is it, like a hotel?"

"Yep," said Benny, also arms crossed. He and Jonah always sat together, the younger, quieter Benny having long ago developed an abiding admiration for eighty-year-old Jonah's extremely loud pronouncements.

"A hotel!" Emily gasped, and Marian reached over, gently patting her wife's hand. At present, however, her attention was divided between comfort and outrage, because she was still looking down at the letter.

"He's already filed for the registration!" she cried, affronted, and Nora definitely knew the feeling.

The man from the other morning wasn't loyal, after all.

In the days after she'd first met him, Nora had spent her golden hours back out on her balcony, listening for some sound of him below. At first she'd convinced herself that she'd only been waiting for an opportunity to finish their conversation, to tell him all the reasons he would surely come to love the building as much as she did. But the truth was, in the shadowy quiet of the predawn, she'd been waiting for something else—a chance to see his soft smile, to hear his golden-hour whisper.

She'd thought for sure he'd come back.

But he hadn't.

He'd sent a *letter*.

She stepped forward, propelled by a fresh feeling of betrayal, pulling the letter from Marian's fingers and hoping that it'd lost some of its power since she'd first opened it last night. She'd stood at the kitchen counter, a red-alarm fire in her brain, realizing that while she'd been lapsing into some kind of balcony-induced, clearly-not-meeting-enough-men-her-age hypnosis, the guy who had charmed her so completely had been making plans: the registration with the city, sure, but also a set of what he'd described in his letter as "modest upgrades" that would be "minimally disruptive" to other "tenants" (tenants! Nora's head had almost blown off). He *planned* to start on Monday. He *planned* to take no longer than two weeks. He *planned* to have his "unit" (*unit!* Enraging) ready for short-term renters by the beginning of June.

So far, all she'd planned was this emergency meeting.

She cleared her throat. "I've printed out some fact sheets from the website he's planning to use," she announced, reaching for the small stack of papers on top of the washing machine. It was not the most edifying thing, using a washing machine as a podium, but needs must, for this emergency. "As you'll see, their minimum rental term is three days; the maximum is six weeks."

At that, Nora caught sight of Emily's small face paling as she clutched her newly acquired fact sheet. Emily had always been sensitive, prone to worrying, but a mild heart attack a couple of years ago—one that had prompted an earlier-than-planned retirement—had dialed it all up, and that was even before Nonna and Donny. Nora left her desk two days a week at lunch to go down and eat with Emily, folding into a rotation she shared with Mr. and Mrs. Salas. She was pretty sure Emily ought to be talking to a therapist, but so far, Nora's gentle suggestions had been met with sharp resistance.

"Three days is bad news," said Mr. Salas. "That's weekenders. People who'll come in and make a mess and leave, and I doubt this guy is going to run his place like a *nice* hotel."

Emily shuddered, and Nora cringed inwardly at Mr. Salas making things worse, but he wasn't wrong. Nora had seen the return address on that envelope. Will Sterling (another betrayal: his last name wasn't even Pasternak! Instead, he had a name like a doctor on *General Hospital*, which Nora found extremely insulting) lived far south enough that coming up to this part of the city regularly would be a massive hassle, particularly given what he'd said about the way he worked. So he'd either neglect it or hire people to maintain it, which would mean more traffic in and out, more disruption.

Disruption was not the business of this building. Or at least it hadn't been, not until lately.

"Can we stop this, Nora?" asked Mrs. Salas. "Do something about the bylaws?"

Nora swallowed, feeling shamed. If she'd been better about all this, she would've studied the bylaws right after Nonna had died. She would have paid more attention to the fact that they basically hadn't been updated since the year Nonna had led the effort to take the building condo. She would've done whatever cleanup and updates were necessary while Donny was still alive, to make sure she prevented anything like this from happening.

But she hadn't been better, at least not about this. She'd been figuring out her move and her work; she'd been dealing with paperwork from Nonna's estate; she'd been grieving.

She cleared her throat. "We can't, not really. When you all went in on this together, you made sure every decision about the building had to be made unanimously."

Nora had always loved this part of the building's story—a commitment they'd made to each other all these years ago, a seal on this found family they'd made together. Now, though— with Will Sterling out there, making *plans*—Nora had to admit that it was, as Nonna might have put it, *very* inconvenient!

"And so now we'd need Donny's nephew," said Mrs. Salas, shaking her head.

For a few seconds, the room was quiet, and Nora's heart clenched. They'd all been so shocked to find it out—all this time, Donny had someone, and he'd never said a word. That, she knew, felt like a betrayal all its own.

"Terrible of him to do this," said Jonah, his voice rough, and it wasn't until he spoke again that she realized he wasn't making the accusation against his longtime friend. "Turning that place into a hotel room."

Emily sniffled, and Marian patted her hand again.

Mrs. Salas said, "How could he do this to Donny?"

Everyone fell quiet again, this silence more about sadness than shock, and Nora felt a surge of protectiveness for her assembled neighbors, for Nonna, for Donny. If Will Sterling had bothered to stick around the other morning (*I'll see you*, he'd said!), *this* is what she would've gotten around to telling him. *This* is what she loved about it here—people who weren't *technically* family taking care of one another like they were.

She sensed something in the room changing, everyone looking up to where she stood, as though all of a sudden, they'd decided Mrs. Salas's question wasn't really rhetorical at all. Well, what did it matter *how*? The fact of the matter was, no matter the how of Will Sterling's betrayal, Nora owed it to Nonna and to her neighbors to try her best to stop this rental-property plan. After all, no one here had even batted an eye at the end, when Nonna had said she wanted Nora to take over for her. No one had questioned it, because they'd always trusted Nonna, and they'd always, always believed in Nora.

She straightened, letting that belief bolster her.

She would absolutely fix this. She had to.

"He *won't* do this to Donny," she said firmly. "I won't let him."

But that's when she realized that no one, in fact, had been looking up at her at all.

"Hello," said a voice from behind her.

—

She recognized it right away.

It was a different sort of *Hello*, this one, not the soft, tentative inquisition that he'd spoken from his—no, *Donny's*; on principle, she would keep thinking of it as Donny's—balcony. This *Hello* was full-throated, confident, and even without turning she could tell that the person who'd said it was smiling. Or maybe *smirking*. It was the kind of *Hello* that told her he'd been *standing. right. there.* for the exact moment she'd made an extremely confident promise about his future prospects in this building.

It was the kind of *Hello* that made her dread turning around.

For a half second of stunned embarrassment she assumed the previous plant-dropping posture: statue-still and squeezed-shut eyes, a breath caught in her throat. It was so like that morning from a few days ago that she had to drag her attention to the details that made it different: the dusty smell of the laundry room, the letter in her hand, Benny's late but pointed throat-clearing, and also the fact that she was wearing a full set of clothing.

She opened her eyes, and turned to face him.

And—well.

Well!

Taller and leaner than she'd thought initially, her perspective obviously distorted during her first high-above sight of him. Straight on like this, he seemed to take up the whole doorway, the definition of his chest more apparent in the long-sleeved T-shirt he wore, sleeves pushed up, and neither of his hands lifting to his not-startled heart. Instead, they stayed tucked into the front pockets of his loose, faded jeans, everything about his body as casual and comfortable as could be.

She decided that he was, in fact, smirking, a smirk to match his stance, and also a smirk that went obnoxiously nicely with his still very attractive face: wind-machine hair, thick and deep brown to complement dark eyebrows and lashes that would probably cost her at least a hundred and fifty bucks at Sephora, because there was no justice for women in this world. Maybe she would've noticed the color of his eyes, but the fact was, she was too preoccupied by the final betrayal in this balcony-to-basement transformation:

He wasn't wearing his glasses.

She'd really liked those glasses.

"You," she said without thinking, her face heating immediately at the way it sounded to her own ears: a monosyllable that didn't so much express her disdain as it did her sense of injury, of heart-piercing disappointment. The letter in her hands felt heavy, outsized.

He didn't respond, other than a slight falter to his smirk, and before she could think of anything else to say, he was moving past her, his arm outstretched, his expression transforming into a full, disarming, totally charming smile, and she almost groaned when she realized he'd known exactly where to aim it for maximum tension-diffusing effect.

"Hi," he said to Mrs. Salas, offering his hand. "I'm Will Sterling."

"Oh my," she said, taking it. *General Hospital* was her favorite show.

"You must've been hearing about me," he said, with a self-deprecating chuckle. He'd somehow managed to shape his body toward her, a curve in his spine that Nora could tell was natural to him, a bedside-manner bend that reminded her of the care workers who'd come at the very end for Nonna.

When he shifted to Mr. Salas, he both maintained it and made it look different; he said, "Hey, I'm Will," and raised his eyebrows *just so* at Mr. Salas's firm handshake, who might as well have said *Oh my* himself for all the flattered surprise he seemed to take in Will's reaction.

Nora had to concentrate on not rolling her eyes.

He started to move toward Marian and Emily, and Nora finally found her voice. "I've pretty much already introduced you, via your letter," she said, her voice like ice, and it seemed to blow over the room—all at once her neighbors seemed to remember her and themselves, shaking off their distraction at the new arrival.

Will straightened, apparently feeling the chill, and when he looked over at her, the smile dropped from his lips. In the crowded space, he only had to take a step back from the arc of hastily arranged folding chairs to be beside her, so now it was like they were awkward partners in one of those awful group project assignments from school, the ones where you had to get up in front of the whole class and pretend like one of you wasn't harboring a terrible bitterness about the uneven work distribution.

46

Nora cleared her throat, determined to demonstrate—however false it was—that she was the prepared one. "We—"

"I don't intend to cause any of you trouble," he said, before she could really begin, and when she shot him an annoyed look she saw the way he'd put his hands up, a gentle, deferential surrender that looked obnoxiously earnest. "In fact I feel lucky I came by to find you all here, because I'd like to—"

"You'd like to explain that you're taking advantage of a loophole?" Nora snapped, holding up his letter.

Marian made a little *hmm!* noise, like Nora had scored a point. She would've liked to feel encouraged by it, but the way Will turned to Nora—with his eyebrows raised in something like amusement, with his posture still so calm—it made her feel like *he* was the one winning. He knew he'd caught her flat-footed on those bylaws.

"Doesn't strike me as much of a loophole," he said, shrugging. "There's no prohibition on owners operating short-term rentals. And I'm an owner."

If she didn't dislike him so much, she might've winced for him. Boy, he'd stepped in it there, acting like Donny had never existed.

"Listen here," said Jonah. His voice was commanding, but he also weighed 130 pounds and was pointing at Will with one of his knobby, arthritic hands, so the effect was somewhat dulled. "I don't think you need to be speaking to her that way. She's in charge here."

"Yes, sir," Will said. "I understand she's your association president, which is why I wrote to her first. But seeing as all of you have lived here for so much longer—"

"What's that supposed to mean?" Marian nearly shouted. "Nora's been with us for twenty years!"

Even without looking over at him, Nora could feel that Will had turned to look at her. Her whole right side felt hot with his gaze.

For long seconds, no one said a word, and that's because everyone was waiting for Will to respond. That's how it worked when it came to Marian Goodnight: if she asked you a question, you answered it, and quick, too. Everyone knew that.

Everyone but Will Sterling.

"I thought you said you moved in last year," he said, to Nora's very hot right side.

"Last year!" shouted Jonah. "She lived here when she was in diapers!"

"She never lived here in diapers," said Mrs. Salas. "You're thinking of Benny."

Jonah scratched his head, looked over at Benny, who had, in fact, lived here for a good portion of his childhood. Which was over forty years ago.

"She came when she was nine, Jonah, remember?" said Mr. Salas. "She had a bowl cut."

Jonah furrowed his thin, white eyebrows, and then he laughed, slapping his knee. "Right! Called her Ringo that first summer."

Beside him, Benny snorted. "Good thing you grew that out."

Right *and* left side—all sides, really—now hot with embarrassment. It was a Herculean task not to touch her ponytail, just to reassure herself it was still there. At the moment, she felt about as awkward as she had when she was nine, standing outside with her parents on the hot-concrete cracked sidewalk with a brand-new suitcase and a whole lot of anxiety.

"You've lived here since you were nine?" Will said, and this time—it wasn't quite a golden-hour echo, but it was softer, quieter. She looked his way.

Brown eyes. He had brown eyes, a shade or two lighter than his hair and eyebrows. It was so easy to notice them now, what with how focused they were on her.

"Uh. It's complicated."

"Complicated," he repeated. She felt pinned by his gaze, by this softly spoken word, and for a second, she forgot about their audience. About what they were doing there in the first place.

48

But then Jonah shouted, "What'd they say?"

She looked away from Will, back to her neighbors. "Nothing. It doesn't matter."

Out of the corner of her eye, she saw Will move, but she didn't look over to investigate. *He's leaving*, she thought, and tried to be relieved about it. If nothing else, at least she'd stopped his charm offensive before it could get started. He'd be gone for now, and she could get back to figuring out how to fix this.

She waited, eyes ahead, for him to offer at least a cursory goodbye to her neighbors.

But he didn't.

"Ms. Clarke," he said instead, exactly like his awful letter. "Can I see you outside?"

He hadn't waited to see if she would follow.

No, he'd left the basement in an upright stride that was the exact opposite of the lanky, casual charm with which he'd walked in, and when Nora made her way up the musty rear stairwell, her palms still sweaty, she half expected him to be gone already.

It had taken a few minutes to disentangle herself from the cacophonous aftermath of his departure, her neighbors bursting with various assessments of Will Sterling ("Rude!" according to Marian, agreed upon by Jonah and Benny; "Seems a bit moody," offered Mr. Salas, countered by Mrs. Salas's more generous "Maybe he was nervous!"; and, finally, "Very tall!" per Emily, who seemed not to mean this as a compliment). After that, there'd been a sweeping instructional impulse: everyone wanted to remind Nora of their own particular grievance with the short-term rental idea. As she took the steps up to the yard, she could hear their various pleas and insistences:

You've got to tell him, Nora—

What he needs to know is—

He has to understand that—

When she pushed open the back door and walked into the bright, warm afternoon sunshine, Will was there waiting. Middle of the yard, arms crossed, staring down at the black, wrought-iron tabletop of their collectively held patio furniture.

He hardly seemed to notice her approach, didn't move when she came to stand even with him. He kept his eyes on the table, his brows furrowed, as though he was expecting to find something there. Weirdly, she felt compelled to stare at it, too. They probably looked like they were solemnly standing over a casket, or a headstone, rather than over the spot where Benny and Jonah had an extremely regrettable potato-skin-eating contest last week.

"You said last year," he finally said, and she looked over at him, though he didn't return the gesture. He was really focused on this table, and also an incredibly specific thing about her life timeline that extremely didn't matter.

"That's not untrue. I moved back here last year. As a kid I used to... I lived here every summer, with my grandmother. And I came for a lot of holidays. That's what Jonah meant, about twenty years."

The arms he had crossed over his chest shifted, tightened. But he didn't say a word.

She chafed under what felt like an admonishing silence. What did he expect, that she'd give him her whole life story in a few minutes of golden-hour conversation? Anyway it's not like *he'd* given her a full accounting of his terrible rental-property scheme. She should be admonishing him! She would start with his behavior in the basement. No matter that she'd wanted him gone; it'd been rude, the way he'd walked out. She would say that. She would tell him about his manners! Nonna definitely would have done that.

But when she turned to him and opened her mouth, the admonishment that came out was, "I thought you wore glasses."

And then she promptly looked back down at the table, which she very much would have liked to crawl under. It could conveniently serve as the headstone for her oncoming death from embarrassment.

Beside her, Will cleared his throat. When he spoke there was possibly another smirk behind it, but she wouldn't know, what with all the attention she was paying to her new backyard tomb.

"I do, sometimes. I also have contacts."

"Right, of course. That must be very convenient."

There was a long silence. Surely he was using it to suppress his laughter.

"Ms. Clarke," he said finally, and the best thing she could say about that as a reopener was that it at least made her angry enough to feel like speaking again; it at least reminded her of his letter, and what they were here for in the first place.

They turned to face each other again, Will dropping his arms and returning his hands to his pockets. Whatever frowning, frustrated countenance he'd left the basement with, he'd smoothed it. Obviously he'd been helped along by her ridiculous comment about his glasses, and she kicked herself for giving him the upper hand.

"You don't need to call me Ms. Clarke," she said, though the stiffness in her voice suggested she was exactly the kind of person who would prefer to be called Ms. Clarke. "You can call me Nora."

"Nora, then," he said after a beat, and as it turned out, she didn't like that much better, primarily because she immediately liked it way too much—the way he said it, the way he looked at her when he said it.

Like he *knew* her.

Beneath her shirt, she felt warm with… annoyance? Yes, she would definitely settle on annoyance. No other feelings options allowed.

"What you need to know," she began, because thinking about her neighbors' instructions absolutely made her feel less… annoyed, "is that this building can't really accommodate what you've outlined in your letter."

"I don't see why not. I have a unit I don't intend to live in. I have a permit to rent it on a short-term basis. It's accommodated."

Okay, now she was *genuinely* annoyed, not lying-to-herself annoyed. "It's not about your... your *unit*." Her cheeks heated. Why did *unit* sound so off-color when she said it? A mystery! She rushed on. "It's about the people who live here. *We* can't accommodate it."

"It's not for you to accommodate. As I said in the letter, I'll maintain the unit, and I'll do my best to make sure—"

"You won't be able to do that. You live all the way across town, and you work all the time. You said it yourself."

Something ticked in his jaw. "I'm not here to make trouble for anyone."

"You *are*, though. You have to understand"—*Good*, she thought, *remember your lines*—"you have to understand that this building is really unique. Everyone who lives here has lived here for a long time, and we—"

"Right. Twenty years for you, was it?"

She narrowed her eyes. "Whatever, yes! Twenty years, though I don't see why it matters so much to you. In any case, I know everything you don't about this place, and I'm telling you, you'll be causing a lot of difficulty for the people who live here."

"But you don't."

She blinked. "I don't what?"

"You don't know everything. For example, you clearly didn't know that it's not on the prohibited-buildings list for short-term rentals."

Okay, that was at least two points to him, if she wanted to update Marian on the score later. He was right; that was the worst of it. He was completely right.

But still. Still, twenty years! She had to remember that she knew lots of things he didn't.

And she intended to use them.

"I know you said you didn't know your uncle well," she said, and almost immediately the look in his eyes changed—all that confidence gone with a blink, replaced at first with something cautious and vulnerable, and then, when she finished her sentence, something determined and hard.

"But I did. And he wouldn't have wanted this. He really loved that apartment."

He stared at her. Nothing like the starlit gaze from the other morning.

Nothing like that at all.

"I've heard," he said flatly.

"It's only that," she said, not really minding the note of pleading in her voice, "we're a *family*."

For a second, she thought it might've worked. He dropped his eyes to the grass and shifted his feet. She thought he might've even nodded his head.

But if he did, it wasn't in agreement.

"Well, Nora," he said (she *did! not! like it!*), raising his glasses-free, sympathy-free eyes to hers. "I'm not really a member of your family. So."

So?

That *so*—it sounded to Nora like a declaration. Whatever soft conversation they'd started with on their balconies, there was no going back to that. They were on different sides now.

Around them, the backyard seemed unusually still, unusually quiet, and she had the sense that they were being watched—that everyone had gone back to their apartments, pressing their curious, concerned faces against their back doors to see how Nora would handle this.

So, she thought, making it a declaration of her own. She would not break first. She would stand here where it felt like the air got thinner and thinner between them, where it felt like her body buzzed with strange, stifling confusion: a cocktail of anger and attraction, disappointment and excitement.

She would not break first.

When his phone beeped again, she held herself still. But when he moved to pull it from his pocket, looking at the screen, she let herself breathe a sigh of relief. A win by default was still a win.

"I need to go," he said, but she could tell it cost him, to be the one who had to walk away.

Good, she thought, relishing the thought that her neighbors would see him retreat. When he turned from her and started making his way toward the back fence, she felt a surge of reckless, unearned confidence.

"I won't make it easy for you!" she called toward him.

He stilled in place. When he turned around, he seemed to look past her, toward the building, toward its balconies. She wondered if he could see her neighbors there, watching them both. That smile—no, *smirk*—played again on his mouth, and she thought (she couldn't believe she thought!) that she'd like to kiss that expression right off his face.

"It's a good thing, then," he called back, his voice carrying across the yard. "It's a good thing I'm not used to easy."

Chapter 4

It was easier, frankly, to think of her as an enemy.

Will had a lot of experience with enemies. Not people, not exactly, though he guessed if he thought about it hard enough, the man in whose apartment he was standing would probably qualify. No, Will's enemies had always been bigger, more... institutional. School systems, government programs, billing departments, that sort of thing. Becoming a doctor meant that he'd managed to keep these deep-seated blood feuds from his adolescence alive into his adulthood, though he supposed he had a more experienced perspective now. Still, when he'd been younger, full of fear and sadness and anger, having adversaries had helped him focus, helped him survive. Nothing was complicated when you had an enemy. It was you versus them, and you versus them stopped you thinking about the other problem, which was usually something more like: you versus you.

You versus your fear. You versus your sadness. You versus your anger.

So with Nora—the girl on the balcony after all, it seemed— it would have to be him versus her, and not him versus his memory of her. Not him versus his attraction to her. Not him versus his boyish, reckless feelings for her.

In the two days since he'd walked away from her, he'd worked on it, this perspective. Instead of thinking about the way she'd looked up close—that long ponytail and those light blue eyes—he'd gone to big-box hardware stores, buying paint and trays and rollers. Instead of thinking about what she'd said—about protecting Donny, about this godforsaken pile of bricks being some kind of "family"—he researched haul-away companies and mattress deliveries and cleaning services. Instead of thinking about how he'd felt in that basement—unsure, unbalanced, unwanted—he'd scrolled through pages of similar-sized rentals in the neighborhood, drafting three different versions of the unit description he'd post when the time came. He got invested.

And getting invested made it possible to think of her and her neighbors as an institution all on their own. An easy enemy, then. Nothing personal about it.

When he'd arrived back at the building this morning, he'd prepared himself for confrontation, half expecting that there'd be some kind of notice taped on Donny's door. A cease-and-desist, maybe, or at least a hastily scrawled "KEEP OUT" sign. But nothing greeted him, not even the flick of curtains in the front windows as he'd walked up, a stack of flattened boxes tucked under his arm. In the hall, even the cherub sconces seemed indifferent, not that it was healthy for him to imagine otherwise. And now, inside Donny's apartment, the silence was deafening—he couldn't even hear footsteps in the unit above him.

Well, fine, then, a freeze-out. That made it even easier.

He started in the kitchen, because he figured that would be easy, too—he doubted he'd find anything too personal there, and he had a good list from Sally's binder about what essentials he'd need to have for renters. He put on an emergency-medicine podcast he liked, an episode about compartment syndrome he'd been meaning to listen to, and started sorting. Keep, donate, toss.

Easy.

Until there was a knock on his door.

He almost missed it, what with the sound of pots and pans shifting and also the voice of a woman through his phone speaker describing—in great, gory detail—the right technique for a fasciotomy. But when he raised his head he heard it again, a definite knock, and also the sound of murmured, feminine voices.

The institution arrives, he thought, controlling his breathing as he stepped around various piles of junk. *Don't think of her as Nora.*

When he opened the door, the doctor on the podcast was saying "infected surgical bulge" and there were two familiar faces—neither of them Nora's—staring up at him from the threshold, each holding dishes covered in aluminum foil.

"Uh," he said, over the podcast host's commentary on pus color. "Let me—" He stepped back and shut it off. Whatever they were carrying smelled like bacon and carbohydrates, which meant he *was* getting an institution, of a sort: the Midwestern welcome and/or bereavement wagon. It didn't look all that much like an enemy cavalry had arrived, unless there were laxatives baked into those dishes.

"Sorry about that," he said, adding an embarrassed smile, because if this was a peacekeeping mission, he was going to turn the charm offensive back on. Easy enough, when it wasn't Nora standing there.

"We've brought you some dishes!" one of the women said, the one whose hand he shook in the basement. She was wearing lipstick so bright red he could almost hear it. "I'm your upstairs neighbor, Corrine Salas, and—" She paused, nudging the woman beside her with an elbow. When that produced nothing in the way of a reaction, she spoke again. "And this is Marian Goodnight, who lives across the hall from you." Another nudge.

"Not sure if you'll have much of an appetite," Mrs. Goodnight said abruptly, holding out her dish and nodding toward his phone. "If that's the kind of thing you're listening to."

"That must be an occupational hazard," said Mrs. Salas excitedly. "Nora mentioned you're a *doctor*! Now if I could scoot right by you here to set this dish down..."

And before he could say anything, that's exactly what she'd done—moved past him in a cloud of perfume and chatter, her companion silently (and unscentedly) following her lead into the kitchen, pushing aside his Keep, Donate, and Toss boxes. It took a minute to realize that the two covered dishes were only the start, that each of them had also been carrying bags over their shoulders, and were now also unpacking those.

"Now these things will keep nicely," Mrs. Salas said, not really to him, not really to anyone, so far as he could tell. Her eyes and hands were busy on the absolutely insane amount of food that was being stacked up onto Donny's stained laminate countertops. "So I'll pop them in your freezer. As for this Tupperware, the red tops can stay on the counter, and the blue should be refrigerated, though I suppose if you're not going to eat the red tops within a couple of days, you could refrigerate them, too."

He cleared his throat, confused. What the hell was happening? Could *all* this food be laced with laxatives? "This is very—"

"Oh, shoot," she said, her hands on her hips. "I forgot the shortbread! If you could give me one minute." She was already shuffling his way, moving in the same path around Donny's things that he'd taken, only she didn't seem to have to think about it at all. "I'll be right back. Marian, start telling him about the bathroom faucet!"

Then it was quiet again, he and a stranger named Marian Goodnight staring at each other across a countertop of casseroles and the width of an apartment he thought no one wanted him in.

"Mrs. Goodnight," he said. "It's nice to mee—"

"I'd sure like to know how you got that permit so fast," she said, abandoning the fussing she'd been doing with the food. She had a voice like his third-grade teacher—loud, insistent, permanently disappointed. She crossed her arms and raised her eyebrows over the gold frames of her glasses.

For a second, he raised his hand to his face, as though to push up his own, but then he remembered he hadn't worn them.

Which was a choice that had nothing to do with Nora.

Honestly, the look Marian Goodnight was giving him was pretty intimidating, but it was at least less confusing than the meal delivery. Clearly there was a good cop/bad cop situation playing out here, so he relaxed his shoulders, tucked his hands into his pockets, and prepared for battle.

"I know someone," he said, smiling.

Marian narrowed her eyes. "Well, that's Chicago for you, isn't it? Who'd you have to murder?"

He blinked. "What? No one."

She looked him up and down, her lip curling. "It'd be easy for you, probably. You and all your... *medicines.*"

Man! This lady was mean. He sort of liked it.

"I have not murdered anyone."

She sniffed. "We'll see."

He pressed his lips together, though he wasn't sure why being accused of a felony made him want to laugh for the first time today. Either way, whatever Mrs. Salas had meant about the bathroom faucet was information that was not going to be forthcoming, because Mrs. Goodnight went back to completely ignoring him, opening Donny's fridge and refilling shelves that Will had only finished cleaning out a half hour ago.

Within minutes it was perfume and chat again, Mrs. Salas back with a tin of what she told him were mantecaditos, the lid already off when she'd walked back through the door. "Have one," she'd said, practically shoving a cookie into his face, and he wondered if maybe he was about to get murdered.

But as he chewed it—crisp and buttery, and not a bad way to go, if it came to it—he started to realize something else was afoot.

Mrs. Salas didn't just have ten thousand pounds of food; she also had ten thousand questions and ten thousand topics of conversation. She had to know what kind of doctor he was and what hospital he worked at and whether he'd ever watched a show about a dermatologist who pops pimples all day. She had to show him the leaky bathroom faucet, the one Donny had reported at the last building meeting he'd been to, and the one that Will would need to reschedule the plumber for. She had to tell him about the tiny storage door in the front bedroom closet, in case he hadn't found it himself yet. She had to ask if he'd found a pair of red-handled scissors she'd let Donny borrow last month, or if he'd want a box of Donny's mail she'd been keeping.

No, this wasn't murder.

This was something more... complicated.

This was filling up Donny's apartment with things, when he'd come to clean it out.

This was filling up Will's time with conversation, when he'd come to be quick.

This wasn't easy.

This was sabotage.

-

It didn't stop with the food.

Barely a half hour after his first guests left, there was a knock at the door, and this time, it was drink.

Homemade drink, to be specific, made by a middle-aged man named Benny who lived on the second floor and had a small home-brew operation. He brought Will a growler of something called American Wheat Ale, along with a special glass for Will to try it in. Food eventually got involved again, because Benny had heard that Marian made a potato casserole, and would Will mind if he had a few bites? Ten minutes later Benny was sitting in Donny's brown recliner with a plate of cheesy bacon potatoes and then the husband of Mrs. Salas arrived, and wouldn't you know he'd like a few of those mantecaditos? But he also had something to drop off, a handheld vacuum cleaner of Donny's that he'd repaired, and sorry for Will's loss, a real shame for everyone, but this handheld was now as good as new, and he'd leave it right there on the coffee table if that was all right.

Will thought he caught a break in the late afternoon, a lull that lasted almost a whole hour, but when there was another soft tap on the door he had to bite his cheek so he wouldn't shout in frustration. For once, there was no one on the threshold, but there were three houseplants, one with a note tucked between its fat, bright green leaves. *Dear Dr. Sterling*, it read, in a tiny, neat cursive. *I took these from your uncle's apartment after he passed and have looked after them since. I have written instruction cards for each one, and taped them to the pots. I hope they will thrive in your care. In sympathy, Emily Goodnight.*

A third-string player, obviously, since she could've taken up a ton of his time delivering those instructions with the same kind of robust, detail-driven attack all the other residents had arrived with. He'd never had a houseplant in his life, and also took ludicrous offense at the fact that Donny had. He was already thinking about people at work he could hand them off to, but before he'd gotten the last one inside he heard the sound of footsteps in the stairwell.

He felt like he was on the longest shift of his life.

It was the man who'd scolded him in the basement the other day, short and surprisingly fast-moving for his age as he descended the final steps carrying a cardboard box that looked a little unsteady in his wiry arms.

"Can I help you with that?" Will said, stepping forward, already frustrated with himself. Damn his instincts. What good did it do him to make their sabotage plans easier? To let them stay, to indulge all their chatter, to walk each of them to the door like they'd been invited?

The man squinted at him over the top of his box. "I don't need your help," he said, overloud, his voice echoing off the hallway walls, probably scaring the decorative cherubs. "I could bench-press you, Beanpole."

Jeez, all right. No one had ever called Will a beanpole. But also no one had ever accused him of killing someone for a rental permit, or given him three houseplants, so. It was a day for firsts. He sighed as the man moved past him, walking into Donny's place like he owned it.

The box went onto the seat of the recliner, and the old man stuck out his hand for Will to shake. "I'm Jonah Hajduk. I'm eighty years old, and I've lived here longer than anyone, which means I like you and what you're doing the least, I suspect."

"Okay," Will said, returning Jonah's strong grip. At this point, the honesty was refreshing. At least he wouldn't have to feed this guy cheesy potatoes and make conversation.

When they dropped hands, Jonah gestured toward the box. "These are a few of your uncle's things, mostly tools he lent me, but also a couple of books I never got around to reading."

"Sure. Thanks for bringing them by." *Now please go*, he thought, but he couldn't bring himself to match Jonah's frankness.

"You don't look anything like him."

Will shrugged. "I wouldn't really know." He hadn't gotten a good look, that day.

"And he never mentioned you. Not once."

Will ignored the pang he felt at that. He moved toward the recliner, pretending to look at the contents of the box. But really, he saw nothing.

"That's not a surprise to me, if that's what you're aiming for. He fell out with my mother a long time ago."

As near as he could tell from the few bits of information he'd been able to pry out of his mom in the weeks after their ill-fated trip here, the feud between her and Donny had mostly been about the trouble she'd caused when she'd gotten involved with Will's father—sneaking out, lying, big fights with her mom. Maybe that all would have been regular teenage stuff, but eventually, she'd also run away, and taken a good deal of Donny's and her mother's money with her. She'd told it all simply, and without shame. Maybe even with a bit of pride.

He reached into the box, shuffled some of its contents around, trying to look busy.

"All's I'm saying is, none of *us* knew you exis—"

"Jonah," came a voice from the doorway, and like everything else having to do with Nora Clarke, he couldn't really explain it, the relief he felt. Out of all his visitors today, she was the enemy he should be dreading the most; she was the most dangerous to him. Frankly, she was probably here to finish him off.

But he didn't think any of that, at first. He looked up and saw her there and all he could think was: *Finally*.

Finally, she came.

Her hair was up again, that sleek, straight ponytail he had an absolutely deranged urge to tug on, and she was dressed casually, like she'd been the other day—a loose, long-sleeved gray shirt, dark leggings that stopped above her ankles, and a pair of sneakers that looked like they'd never been worn outside.

She was so pretty.

It doesn't matter, you knob, he told himself. *She's the enemy.*

"Your ride's here," she said to Jonah.

"Already!" He reached up to smooth his tufts of white hair, then patted his pockets. "She's early." He looked over at Will. "I'm watching you, pal," he said gruffly, before heading toward the door.

"No wine," Nora said to Jonah when he got close, a warning note in her voice.

"Sure, sure." He looked over at Will and proclaimed that he was "on the dating apps!" and then waved as he passed by Nora, saying something to her Will didn't catch.

Will felt a tide of annoyance sweep through him. He didn't want any more of this *We're a family* performance-art shit these people had been doing all day, distracting him and slowing him down. He finally looked away from Nora, his eyes sweeping over the room. It'd started a mess, and now it was more of a mess, and he figured he knew who'd given the marching orders.

"I see you came empty-handed," he said, turning toward the kitchen. "That's new."

Out of the corner of his eye, he could see her, still in the doorway, a more tentative approach than any of her neighbors had taken, and for some reason, that annoyed him even more. He wanted her to come in; that was the hell of it.

"Can I offer you something?" he added. "A casserole, or a small appliance? Maybe a potted fern?"

She took a step inside, and he and his heart had a firm, silent communication about its recent behavior. This visit wasn't anything special. She was the last neighbor in the building, and obviously he wouldn't be left in peace until they all came through. It was like ticking a box; that was all. Easy.

"So," she said, casting her eyes around the space. She didn't seem quite as familiar with the place as Jonah had been, and that was strangely comforting to him. "Now you've met everyone."

"Everyone but Emily," he said, gesturing toward the plants.

Nora shrugged, reaching out a hand to gently touch one of the largest one's leaves. "She's shy."

"I'll give you credit," he said, bending down to pick up his still nearly-empty Toss box. "It was a good idea."

"I'm sure I don't know what you mean by that."

He held up the box. "Would you like to see how far I've gotten with cleaning out the kitchen? Or if that doesn't appeal, I could tell you about Benny's starter wort, which slowed me down quite a bit. That's wort with an *o*, if you weren't aware." He hadn't been, and for a good ten minutes he'd thought Benny was asking him for his professional opinion. "It's got to do with beer. I learned a lot today."

Her face flushed. "It wasn't really—" She cleared her throat. "We only thought it might be nice to welcome you to the building."

There was absolutely nothing so interesting about that plant. She was avoiding his eyes.

"I'm not sure it worked as you intended," he said, and her mouth pulled to the side.

"Jonah's manners are a little rough, that's all."

"It wasn't just Jonah. Marian thinks I use my medical license for bribery-related poisonings."

64

She finally looked up at him, her mouth curving into a closemouthed smile that she was clearly trying to keep from spreading further. Watching her wrestle it under control—full, pink lips, a small dent in her left cheek—was not easy.

It was a goddamned impossible delight.

"Marian likes a conspiracy theory," she finally said.

"I gathered. She thinks I did something illegal for the permit."

The almost-smile dropped from her lips. "Did you?"

"No. I had some help. A friend of mine keeps a few properties like this." He wasn't exactly sure if it was fair to call Sally a friend, but last night when she'd texted to ask him whether he'd gotten started yet, she had included a selfie with the hotel's buffet spread as a backdrop. That seemed friendly.

Nora rolled her eyes. "Of course. Is that your plan, to make a business out of this? Any other property-related inheritances you're expecting?"

"No. I didn't expect this one. I told you, I didn't know him well. I'm as surprised as you all apparently are about it."

She furrowed her brow, crossed her arms over her chest, looking around again. She'd talked a good game the other day, about Donny being a member of this family she kept talking about, but seeing her now, he had to wonder. Her eyes kept landing on things—that box on the recliner, the stack of newspapers beside it, the black-and-white photograph of Wrigley Field hung above the flat-screen television—like she was looking for answers.

"Aren't you curious?" she asked, her eyes coming back to him. "I mean… if you didn't know him. Aren't you curious why he left it to you?"

He shoved a grubby set of dish towels into the Toss box, keeping his head down. *Curious* wasn't the right word. He was frustrated, full of resentment. Being curious about Donny felt like a concession, and he didn't want to concede anything.

"Not really. And even if I were, he's not here to answer my questions. Not much use dwelling on the past, I've always thought."

She wrinkled her brow. "That's going to be pretty impossible, for a while."

"What's that mean?"

She took a step forward, peered into the box Jonah had dropped off, then moved again, past the recliner and closer to where he stood, by the long kitchen counter that overlooked the living area. Her eyes ran over the space—the pots and pans he'd pulled from the cupboards below, the few stacks of dishes he'd managed to take down from the ones above.

"It means you're surrounded by the past. His past, specifically."

He swallowed, his neck heating. He thought of the haul-away companies, the cost of their most comprehensive packages. If he could've afforded it, he would have had them in here sorting through all this, leaving him well out of whatever was in Donny's past. He didn't want any part of it.

"I'll move quickly," he said gruffly, and then he looked up at her. "If you'll let me."

She turned her face from him, looking back over the living room, toward the door that led to the balcony. He liked it, seeing her profile—the slope of her nose, the angle of her jaw, but also the curve at the back of her neck, exposed to him thanks to that ponytail.

"I thought you might change your mind."

Her voice was quiet, like she was telling him a secret. Like he was on that balcony again, waiting for her voice to filter down to him. The truth was, he was probably at great risk for changing his mind, if only she kept talking to him this exact way. If it was dark and they were alone. If Donny had nothing to do with it.

She cleared her throat, and when she spoke again, she'd stripped the softness from her voice. *Easier*, he told himself.

66

"After, you know. You met everyone. It's real people here, in this building. It's not an investment property."

"Real people have investment properties. I'm a real person."

She looked back at him, her eyes narrowed. "You're missing my point."

"Am I? What's your point, then, Nora?"

She made a noise—a quick, frustrated exhale that was almost this side of a groan, and... yeah. It made him the exact opposite of easy. He caught one side of his cheek between his teeth and bit down. He said it like a chant in his head—*easy easy easy*—and tried to feel a sense of victory when she gave up, dropping her eyes and turning to go.

He couldn't really explain what happened next, except to say that once again, his instincts failed him. If she was going, he'd walk her to the door.

But either she hadn't expected him to be behind her, or she'd thought of something else to say to him. She turned, suddenly, right next to that brown recliner he hated so much, the back of her foot catching on the sloppy stack of newspapers. In a split second, she reeled backward, one of her arms going out to restore her balance, and he could've let her ass hit the arm of the chair, an unplanned sit-down that might've jostled Jonah's box but certainly wouldn't have hurt her.

He didn't, though.

He reached out and caught her hand.

Palm to palm. A clap as they both curled their fingers to grip each other.

A seal.

He was bent slightly over her, and up close like this he could see everything: the fine, wispy hairs that quivered along her hairline. The impossibly small flecks of gold hiding like a secret in her blue eyes. The irregularity he'd seen before in her left cheek—not a dimple, but a thin, straight scar, barely visible. The flash of white from her slightly crooked bottom teeth when her lips parted in surprise.

The thudding pulse in her neck.

Holy shit, he thought. *Holy shit, the palm of her hand.*

It felt like an electric shock. All the way up his left arm. All the way through to his heart.

Let go, some distant part of his brain said. *This is dangerous to you.*

But he wasn't really listening to his brain. He was listening to his heart, which had been shocked right out of its hiccup, beating in time with her pulse. He watched as she watched him—as she looked up at all the up-close things she could see about him, too. He thought it would be the easiest thing, to pull her closer. She only had to say, and he'd do it. He'd catch her full bottom lip with his own; he'd—

"Is there someone else?"

He blinked, and straightened. Barely realized that their hands were still clasped, even though they were both fully upright now. Her voice had been low, almost a whisper.

No, he wanted to say. *There isn't.*

But he actually had no idea what she was asking, what with his brain having jumped ship. So instead he said, "Someone else?"

Along her neck, he could still see her pulse. "I—um."

She cleared her throat and took the smallest step away from him, dropping her eyes. He immediately loosened his hand, opening his mouth to apologize—what had he been *doing*, holding on to her like that?—but she rushed out the next part of her sentence.

"I only thought—listen, you obviously don't have any interest in this place. But don't you think someone else in your family might? Maybe they could buy it off of—"

Like that, his brain came fully back online. Easy: she was the enemy again.

"I'm an orphan," he snapped, cutting her off. "And Donny was, too, eventually, so I guess we had that in common. No siblings, no cousins. So no, Nora. There's no one else."

Everything he could see of her flushed. From her wispy-haired hairline all the way down to the place where the pulse beat along her neck.

He almost regretted it, almost wished he could take it back. As best he could, he tried not to bring it up with people; it was nearly always embarrassing for everyone involved. It wasn't so much that it was hard for him to say it—he'd had a lot of time to get used it, after all. It was more that it was hard for people to hear it. They'd stumble through some kind of apology, or worse, ask questions he didn't want to answer. Bringing it up now—when she was still standing close enough that she could've taken his hand again, if she'd wanted to—it felt like a cheap shot.

But it was a cheap shot that saved him, because for a second there, he'd almost forgotten why Nora Clarke was not for him.

"I'm sorry," she said, and to her credit, she didn't stumble at all. "I really, really am."

He shrugged, and he hoped he made it look casual. Unaffected. "I'd like to get back to it, if you don't mind."

"Right, of course," she said, carefully taking a step to the side, avoiding the newspapers. This time, he didn't even try following her to the door.

But when she got there, she paused and turned back toward him. "I'll see you," she said, but he didn't really notice that particular echo.

Instead, what he noticed—what he thought about long after she left—was how she'd been using the thumb of one of her hands to rub the palm of the other.

The palm that had been pressed to his.

Chapter 5

"He's not happy."

Nora looked past Deepa's shoulder to the conference room door. Maybe Austin would come back after a few minutes, but honestly, she doubted it. The guy wasn't known for showy displays of temper, so even a slight frown followed by a request to "pick this up later"—before their meeting timer had even sounded!—meant he'd well and truly had it. By now he was probably back at his ruthlessly tidy desk, squeezing the Verdant Media–branded stress ball he kept in a box on the upper-right corner.

"Well, we're doing our best," said Nora, trying to keep up the breezy, unbothered tone she'd maintained through the last forty-five minutes of this video call. It was her "business-as-usual" tactic, the one she'd been honing since Austin had grudgingly agreed to let her work remotely. As long as she acted like nothing important for her had changed, she figured, there'd be no reason for him to second-guess his decision. "It's not like the client is making it easy."

"Ugh," Deepa said, rolling her eyes. "You don't know the half of it. At dinner last week she asked whether we should consider building a game app. She showed me the bitmoji she uses of herself as an 'inspiration pic.'"

Nora shifted in her uncomfortable desk chair, suppressing a wince. Some of her discomfort was definitely about this bitmoji story, but most of it was about the *you don't know the half of it*. She *didn't* know the half of it, because she never went to client dinners or lunches or coffees or juices now. She herself didn't miss them—they'd always been the worst part of the gig—but she knew that Austin missed her *at* them. More than once, Austin had privately lamented to Nora about Deepa's F-grade poker face. That eye roll Nora had just watched through the screen of her laptop probably made an appearance at the dinner table, too.

"What if we try redoing the color scheme?" Nora offered, trying to stop herself from wading into this particular tide pool of guilt. She lived here now, and that was all there was to it. Austin needed to get used to not having her in San Diego, and the only way to make that happen was to keep doing what she was good at, and showing him how indispensable she was. "She's always seemed lukewarm ab—"

"She's not a good fit for us," said Deepa. "She's going to henpeck us to death before she realizes that she wants to be a celebrity more than she wants to save the world."

Nora sighed, knowing Dee was right. When Austin had first started Verdant Media, his mission had been crystal clear: to become the premier digital design and marketing agency for sustainability-focused brands. Ten years ago, it'd been boutique, but now it was pretty much booming—Nora herself was currently maintaining thirty-five different major websites and had seven projects in the queue for build-out. Most of her accounts were corporate, but recently Austin had started bringing in clients like this one—"eco-influencers," he called them, people who did things like stage Instagram photos of homemade cleaning products in pretty spray bottles.

Nora didn't love this new trend, but it was Austin's company, and Austin had given Nora her first shot as an intern when she was only twenty years old. Because of Austin, she was one of only a handful of people who'd had a job in hand when she graduated. Because of Austin, she'd gotten to have a front-row seat to the small firm's success for almost ten years. And because of Austin, she got to keep doing what she loved, what she was good at, even though she wanted to do it from all the way across the country.

"I'll talk to him," Nora said, closing out all the eco-influencer-related windows she'd had up on her second, larger monitor, and blinked in relief. She still hadn't gotten the setup right in here, still felt like everything was too close to her face when she worked.

Over on her laptop screen, Deepa went out of frame for a second, and then came back in, resettling in her chair with a small metallic pouch in front of her. Nora smiled at this new version of an old routine. When she'd still worked in the office, she and Dee would often debrief in the office building's third-floor bathroom, which was almost always deserted. Dee would touch up her makeup and they'd chat about work or life or whatever. They did the same now, only with the video-call app serving as the makeup mirror. Nora supposed it was a little odd, talking to someone who was doing an extreme close-up of her mascara or lipstick application, but then again, Dee was really good at makeup.

"Okay," Deepa said. "Give me the update. What happened with the new guy?"

This time, Nora didn't even bother suppressing her wince. What *happened* was that she'd made an absolute mess of it, and so she'd been hiding out in her apartment for a day and a half, trying to recover—not only from what she'd pushed him into revealing about himself, but also from what touching him had revealed about *her*self. This morning, for the first time in months, she'd done 4:00 a.m. from her bed, her covers caught up around her legs and her eyes staring up at the ceiling, trying desperately to blink away the memory of an incredibly vivid, incredibly inappropriate dream she'd had about Will Sterling and what he might be able to do with the palm of his hand.

"Uh," Nora said.

"Let me guess. Your 'kill him with kindness' plan backfired. I told you, hide a whole fish somewhere in there. You've got a key. The smell will be *unreal*."

Nora shook her head firmly while Dee did something with a highlighter brush that deserved a YouTube tutorial. "No, we're not doing stuff like that. We're not criminals."

She got another eye roll for that, but Nora knew that Deepa wouldn't really go through with fish-hiding, either. Probably.

"Then you're not going to stop him, I hate to tell you. You know my building has like twenty Airbnb units now? And I'll bet at least a few of my other neighbors rent out their places during Comic-Con this year." She paused mid-highlight. "Wait, should I do that?"

"No," Nora snapped, annoyed, even though Deepa lived in a twelve-story building with a rooftop pool that bore no meaningful relationship to Nora and her neighbors' beloved six-flat.

Dee shrugged, rooting around in her bag. "Good money, though." When Nora didn't respond, she looked up, a brushed gold tube of lipstick in her hand and her eyes narrowed. "Why are you acting so strange?"

"I'm not!" Shoot, she'd said it too loud. Deepa's eyes narrowed even more.

"You are. Your face has that look about it. It's the same face you had the whole time we worked on the—"

"Don't say it," Nora interrupted, her face heating automatically. Only a few months before she'd moved to Chicago, she and Deepa had been collaborating on the launch of a sustainable sex toy brand's digital platform. Nora had never quite recovered from having to say the word *dildo* during a work presentation.

"Eleanora!" Deepa said, her formerly narrowed eyes now wide as saucers. "Did you *do something* with this man?!"

"What? No! He's not even my *type*." This was a lie, because Nora didn't really have a type. If you went solely by her largely disappointing dating history, her type was probably something like "men who talk about themselves too much." That described the type for a lot of women out here in the twenty-first century, she figured.

Dee was still staring through the laptop screen like she could see straight into Nora's dirty dreams, though, so she absolutely had to correct this misimpression.

"We had this little—I don't know. I caught the edge of my foot on some stuff in the apartment and tripped, and then we…"

"*Had sex?*"

"No! Keep your voice down; we're at work!"

"*I'm* at work. You're at home."

Nora ignored that. "We didn't have sex. He—he grabbed my hand, and then… I don't know. We stayed like that. For a few seconds."

Deepa blinked. "You… held hands." She tipped back her head and laughed. "This is the most you story. So then what?"

Nora did not want to do the *then what*. Thinking of the look on Will's face when he'd said *I'm an orphan* was already one of the top ten moments in life she did not want to relive, just ahead of talking about dildos in a conference room. She'd never heard someone call themselves an orphan. It was a little Dickensian, to be honest, but then again, Nora had always liked to read.

Though judging by the look on Will's face, he'd closed the book.

Firmly.

She shrugged. "Nothing. I think it was a blip. We both remembered ourselves, I guess. I tried to get him to reconsider, and he assured me that he won't."

"Hide. The. Fish." Dee was mid-lipstick application, so it sounded more like *Ide. Uh. Ish.*

"I don't want to ruin his life," she said, although what she really meant was *I don't want to hurt his feelings.* She'd had the sense she'd done that, somehow. When he'd dropped her hand, she'd felt it in her stomach. Like a tiny stone of regret had lodged itself there.

Then again, what about the feelings of her neighbors? What about sitting with Emily yesterday, encouraging her to stop reading articles online about problems with short-term rentals?

What about the way Marian had looked at her with expectation by the mailboxes, or the way Jonah had shaken a small fist at her and said, "We'll get him next time!"

What about what Nonna would want?

"I only want him to… I need him to understand why this won't work here."

Deepa made a humming noise as she put the lipstick away and pulled out a setting spray. In the third-floor bathroom, if they were working out some design problem, this is the point at which Deepa usually got ideas. It was like all the touch-ups were brain calisthenics for her.

"No offense, Nora, but since you've moved back there you have told me no fewer than six things that your neighbors do that would absolutely have me packing a go bag and fleeing back to the wide world of living with people my own age."

"That's rude. They're—"

Dee waved a hand, twisting her fresh-painted lips. "They're your family. And they're great, I know. I'm sure he got the sense of that with the food drop-off, or whatever it was. But you need this guy to see the stuff that his future renters would find absolutely bizarre. The stuff you hardly even recognize as unusual."

Nora furrowed her brow, thinking. The fact that nothing came immediately to mind probably proved Deepa's point, but then she looked down to the desk calendar and saw what she had written on it for tomorrow night. If she flipped the page, she'd see the same entry again, on the next month. And the next and the next.

"Like a monthly poetry reading?" she said, not even really to Deepa.

"There's a monthly poetry reading at your apartment building? Uh, yes. I'd say that's weird."

Nora's mind was already racing with ideas. Where this kind of creativity download had been when Austin had been in the room and they'd been trying to figure out this situation with the eco-influencer from hell, she wished she knew, but it didn't really matter now.

"It's not weird," she muttered. Then she looked up and smiled through the screen at her friend. "But I'm about to make it a whole lot weirder."

—

At first, there was no doubt in Nora's mind that she had Nonna's full support.

In the first place, there was the weather, which could be nothing less than a gift from above: warm but not humid, not a cloud in the dusky, early-evening sky, a light breeze fluttering the colorful line of paper lanterns strung up from one corner of the fence to the other. It'd seemed so unbelievably perfect, in fact, that Nora had even pulled up a radar app on her phone, double-checking to confirm there wasn't some freak, fast-moving rainstorm on its way.

But no—for the next six hours at least, it was nothing but clear skies ahead.

And that was plenty of time for a poetry reading.

It wasn't the weather alone, though, that had Nora feeling confident. When she'd hung up the phone with Deepa yesterday, she'd set about making a list, and it'd been a long one—impossibly long, really—and when she'd made her way down to Marian and Emily's afterward, nervous about how Marian would take a request to alter her monthly plans, she wasn't actually sure she could get it all done.

But like the weather, everything had fallen *exactly* into place. Marian hadn't only been on board, she'd also—in the spirit of the great public school teacher she'd been for decades— set immediately to work on the evening's... uh, *elevated*... agenda, while Nora and her other neighbors got to work on the logistics. Oh, nearly everyone they called last-minute could come? Great. The florist over on West Fullerton happened to have a whole bunch of flower crowns from a canceled event on deep discount? Terrific. Benny was looking to unload a bunch of that same American Wheat Ale he'd offered to Will a couple of days ago? Perfect. Hey, a guy two buildings down had a microphone and amplifier they could borrow? Well, why *not*?

By seven, the backyard was packed, the air thick with conversation and the smell of the grilled meat Mr. Salas was proudly in charge of, having agreed to participate only if he had no poetry-related responsibilities.

So really, the night only wanted for one thing.

An appearance by the suddenly scarce Will Sterling.

From her spot near the back fence, standing behind a "welcome" table she and Benny had set up earlier, Nora reached up to adjust the crown of daisies perched on top of her head, then moved her hand down to tug at the elastic band across the top of the off-the-shoulder cotton dress she'd chosen, a long, flowy thing that she thought matched the Late-in-May-Day theme they'd gone with. Beneath it, her feet were bare on the cool, dry blades of grass, and she tried to let the feeling ground her, keep her in the moment, but she kept fidgeting, kept looking up to see whether Will's car would come rumbling down the back alley.

He'd been around this morning, Emily had said; she'd seen him carrying two cans of paint into Donny's place, but within a couple of hours she'd noticed his car was gone again, and he hadn't made another appearance, not during all the time they'd been setting up. Nora had been under the assumption that he'd taken time off work, that his plan was to be at the building every day, every night. If he didn't show, Marian would still have a great poetry reading, sure.

But Nora would definitely have egg on her face.

She was starting to give up hope, the prettily decorated box in front of her nearly empty of its contents, when Nonna came through again—Will's car crackling along the gravel, pulling in to his spot—and she had to clasp her hands together to keep from raising them in victory.

She felt a thrill of satisfaction when he didn't get out immediately. Since she couldn't see him well through his windshield, she imagined the expression she most wanted him to have: eyes wide, jaw agape. She hoped she had him on the run already.

But when he stepped out of his car and stood to his full height, closing his door behind him, he didn't look like he was on the run.

He looked calm and in control and extra handsome, because he had his terrible (terrific) glasses on. He was dressed less casually than she'd seen him before—not in scrubs or jeans or a faded T-shirt. Instead, he wore a pair of slim-cut, dark blue pants, a crisp, lighter blue button-up tucked into them, the sleeves rolled back neatly, almost to his elbows.

She suppressed a sigh. Not a swooning sigh! An exasperation sigh, for sure.

She tugged again at the elastic of her suddenly too-bohemian-seeming dress as she watched him approach. *No need to be nervous*, she scolded herself. *You're prepared for this.*

"Hi," she said cheerfully. "Perfect timing!"

But she *was* a little nervous, because for a second, when he stood in front of her, his eyes seemed to take her in, flower crown and then down, his gaze slipping briefly—so briefly, she might've imagined it—over the bare skin of her shoulders.

He cleared his throat, reached up to adjust his glasses, and Nora thought: *There. Right there is your type.*

"Whose party?"

Nora shrugged, definitely *not* thinking about whether doing so made her shoulders look nice. "Everyone's. The whole building! So glad you could make it."

"I'm pretty sure you know I didn't have any intention of making it." He looked around, his eyes snagging on the microphone across the yard. His brow lowered. "Whatever *it* is."

Nora smiled up at him. "It's Marian's monthly poetry reading!" She swept an arm out, gesturing to the whole setup. "Isn't it great? It can get sort of loud, but it's fun. Anyway, it's good you're here, to get a sense of it. Maybe you can leave a note for your... tenants, or whatever. So they know what to expect."

He looked down at her, one of his eyebrows rising. "I can't imagine how you got a permit for a gathering like this."

She tried not to do anything lying-related. "You're awfully into permits," she said.

"So is the city of Chicago."

She straightened things on her welcome table that did not need straightening. Chances were low that a poetry reading full of people mostly over sixty would get too loud, she figured. What was most important was that Will thought all this was business as usual.

"Well, like I said. This one happens every month, so."

"This one?"

She nodded. "This one's the biggest one. But there's other things we do here and there."

"Is that right?"

Nora looked up and narrowed her eyes at him. This was probably the tone of voice he used on kids in the emergency room who said they had no idea how that raisin or penny or LEGO piece got stuck up their nose. Fine, if he wanted a whole accounting, she'd give it to him. He could make that doubtful doctor face at her all he wanted.

"Well, every other Sunday there's—"

"Dr. Sterling!" Mrs. Salas called across the yard, hoisting the basket she was holding in a sort of party-prop wave. She adjusted and shuffled over with it hooked over her forearm, a cup of Benny's beer in her other hand. Mrs. Salas knew how to party, even if it only took one cup of not-strong beer to make it happen.

"I saved you a crown!" she said to Will, once she got close.

"Let me tell you about the discount Nora and I got on these. They were actually from a—"

"A store that we order from every month!" Nora interjected quickly. She gave Mrs. Salas a warning, reminding look before glancing up at Will. "Sort of a *thanks for your business* discount. You know how it is."

"Sure," he said, but Nora could tell he meant that he definitely *didn't* know how it was. He looked away from Nora, smiled down at Mrs. Salas, who now stared at Will like she was drunk-watching *General Hospital*. "That's all right, Mrs. Salas. I probably don't need a crown."

She laughed and patted his arm, the basket hooked over her wrist swinging between them.

"Now, don't worry! The one I put aside for you is very masculine! If you're worried about that sort of thing! Most men are. Nora, hold my beer."

Nora followed the order, bit her lip to hide her smile. If Will thought the poetry reading was intense, she couldn't wait until Will got a load of Mr. Salas's robotics club meeting. Unfortunately that was only every three months, though Nora would definitely be making a request for him to schedule something sooner.

"I'm not so worried about it," Will said, still smiling his obnoxious, not-bothered-about-gender-norms smile down at her.

"Mrs. Salas," Nora prompted, to get her out of her apparent trance.

She blinked. "Sure, yes! Here it is. More of a laurel wreath, this one." Will gave a sidelong glance to Nora, then dutifully bent his knees and tipped his head down toward Mrs. Salas so she could settle the crown on his head. Nora very much objected to how his thick mass of hair gently curled around the edges of the leaves. Honestly she also objected to Mrs. Salas getting to touch it, but she shoved that thought away as quickly as she could.

When he stood again, Mrs. Salas set a hand against her chest. "You look like an Olympian! Nora, doesn't he look like an Olympian?"

"Corrine!" Mr. Salas called, from over by the grill, and Mrs. Salas rolled her eyes. "He never knows how to put things on a plate, I swear. Anyway, I'll see you soon, Dr. Sterling!"

She swanned off, and Will reached up to straighten his laurel wreath.

"I don't look like an Olympian," he muttered.

Nora snorted. "You look like you won the gold medal in being uncomfortable."

"I don't really have the time for this."

"Suit yourself, though good luck getting past Marian." She directed her gaze over to where Marian stood near the microphone, then tapped a finger on her chin, trying to look thoughtful. "I guess maybe you could open your back door, listen from your balcony. That's what Donny always did."

Will turned his head toward her, his crown going crooked, his jaw setting firmly.

Got him, she thought.

"I can stay out here for a while," he ground out.

"Oh, *great*! Now, since you've got your crown and everything, you'll need one of these." She picked up one of the rolled pieces of paper from the table and held it out to him, and for a too-long second, he stared down at it. Nora felt it—a little pulse of energy in her hand, like it was anticipating getting close to his.

This is the most you story, she heard Deepa saying.

But when he finally reached out, he did so carefully. He made sure he didn't touch her at all.

"What's this?" he asked, and she tried to ignore the pang of disappointment she felt.

"That's your poem. I'll try to get Marian to call you up early, so you can get back to—"

"My poem?"

"Yeah. Everyone reads a poem, unless they've written their own. I'm guessing you didn't write your own! Though a few people here will improvise, probably."

"Everyone. Reads. A Poem."

She beamed out at the crowd. This was going to take *forever*. "Yep."

"Is this... always how many people come?"

She didn't look over at him to answer. She kept her eyes focused on her neighbors, on the five to ten extra guests each she'd asked them to call.

"In the spring and summer months, yeah. Now in the colder months, it's in Marian and Emily's apartment, so it's smaller, but not *that* much smaller." She looked back toward him. "Sometimes it kind of—you know. Spills out into the hallway. I'm sure that won't be a problem for you." She paused meaningfully, adding a smile. "Or your tenants."

For a second, she felt fully like she'd already won the evening—her smile, her snark, her surprise poetry reading. No fish-hiding necessary. He'd been caught completely off guard, and Deepa had been exactly right—she hadn't needed to *tell* him what this building was all about in the day-to-day. She'd needed to *show* him. This wasn't the kind of place some weekender could find peace in. This wasn't the kind of place where people came and went.

But then he lifted the scroll of paper he held in one hand and slowly—meaningfully, *teasingly*, she thought—tapped the edge of it against the palm of his other hand. His dark gaze locked on to her, the corner of his mouth crooking up to match the tilt of his laurel wreath.

She wanted to snatch the poem back. She wanted to cut her own hand off, for all she could feel it vibrating with the memory of touching his.

He took a step back, the curve of his smile widening. Like he knew exactly what she'd been thinking—about his poem, about his palm and hers.

"I'd better get over there and see it for myself, then," he said.

And when he turned to walk away, to weave his way into the crowd, she had the strangest feeling.

She had the feeling that Nonna's plans for this night weren't so simple after all.

Chapter 6

Maybe she thought he wouldn't be good in a crowd.

But he was *great* in a crowd.

Under the lights of colorful paper lanterns he kept having to duck beneath, Will stood with his poem tucked into his back pocket and a beer in his hand, nodding along to a story one of Marian Goodnight's former students (he *knew* she was a teacher; no one could fake a voice like that) was telling him about the time he'd gotten caught sticking gum underneath his desk in her classroom. Will laughed at all the funny parts, asked all the right follow-up questions, same as he had through what by now felt like dozens of similar stories—not only about Marian, but about everyone at this party. Who they knew, where they worked, what neighborhood they grew up in, why they were at a backyard poetry reading on a Saturday night.

This was how Will worked a crowd—be pleasant, interested, self-effacing. Shake hands, laugh easily, stay curious. In life, this kept him where he was comfortable: a place where he was unlikely to have to answer questions about himself, a place where he could keep people at a safe distance. And in his profession, in the hospitals and clinics where he'd trained and worked, it had always served him well as a bedside style, too. As best as he could, he tried to help people feel better about being in a place that had the word *emergency* in the title, even when he was talking to them about their chest pains or the bone sticking out of their shin. Tonight, he put his mind in the manner of work. This building was the bay, and to Nora and her neighbors, his plan for Donny's apartment might as well be a heart attack or a compound fracture.

But out here at this backyard party, with his calm, ready smile and his willingness to listen—nobody, for the moment, seemed to feel all that bad about it.

Not even Nora.

Even from all the way across the yard, it was like he could feel her—like his body knew where hers was at all times. When gum-beneath-the-desk guy stopped talking, shaking Will's hand a final time and telling him he was going to take a seat, Will only had to raise his eyes to find her, his gaze tracking automatically to where she stood. Up near the microphone, she and Marian and a smaller woman Will was almost certain was Emily Goodnight bent their heads together over a sheet of paper Marian held, Nora pointing down at it and nodding. When Emily leaned in and pointed at something else, Nora stood straighter and tipped her head back to laugh, one hand coming up to hold on to the flowers in her hair, and suddenly, Will remembered his own sporadic, Nora-specific chest pains. In that dress, with the smooth, somewhat-freckled skin of her shoulders showing, her ponytail foregone in favor of a thick, loosely woven braid...

Don't, he told himself, remembering the smug way she'd greeted him, her smiling show about this big crowd and these ridiculous flower crowns. Maybe these people did hold a monthly poetry reading, but if it was this involved every time he'd eat this laurel wreath that kept tugging irritatingly on his hair. If Nora thought he was spooked, scared off his plans—well, she had another think coming. They were out here tonight in an *I'm Enjoying Myself* smile-off, and he was determined to win.

Right then, she looked his way. There was no point in pretending he hadn't been watching her, so he simply raised his cup toward her, tipping it in what he thought was a toast to this not-so-friendly competition. She didn't have a drink, so she couldn't return the gesture, but he thought she might've raised her chin in acknowledgment.

Everyone was going the way of gum-guy, finding seats in the rows of folding chairs lined up in front of the microphone or standing around the perimeter, so Will did the same, taking a spot behind the back line of chairs near a group of younger guests he figured had been Marian Goodnight's students in more recent years. Up toward the front, Nora and her neighbors sat together, all except for Marian herself, who stood behind the microphone in a bright yellow dress, a matching patterned scarf woven high on her head.

"Welcome," she said, her voice oddly less teacher-y when projected through a microphone. She spoke without notes, a brief introduction to the night's schedule: first up, readings—chosen randomly—from anyone who picked a poem from the box ("*Picked*"? he thought, remembering the way Nora had handed one to him like it was a ticket for admission), followed by anyone who wanted to read an original composition. Marian had rules, too—you could get more food or drink, but not in the middle of anyone's reading. You could clap, but she preferred snaps. You could use the restroom, but only the one in Marian and Emily's apartment, and only if you had the good sense to wash your hands after.

When Marian finished speaking, Nora joined her at the mic, holding another basket. Will could tell by the anticipatory energy in the crowd that whatever was coming next was something familiar to most everyone here, or at least they'd been given a better primer upon arrival. He saw people taking out their small scrolls of paper, so he did the same.

"Now remember," Marian said, "you'll find your number right at the top edge of your paper. You can say *pass*, but I sure don't know why you'd want to."

Will looked down, then held up his scroll to get it closer to one of the lantern lights. Number sixteen, fine. He tucked it back into his pocket and took a sip of his beer, hoping they'd decide to move on to the original compositions before his number got called. But when he looked up back toward the mic, his gaze tangled with Nora's again, right as Marian reached into the basket, and he could tell by the look on her face; he *knew* she must've checked his—

"Number sixteen!" Marian called, and Nora Clarke's face fairly broke open with the force of her smile.

Fuck, Will thought, but he didn't show it, because he wasn't going to let *poetry* sabotage him, for Christ's sake. He raised a hand, though he didn't so much know why it was even necessary, since he had a feeling every single piece of paper in that basket had been, since shortly after his arrival, marked with the number sixteen.

"Well!" said Marian, as Will made his way up. "Wouldn't you know, it's a brand-new guest who'll be starting us off?" There was a ripple of snapping, a smattering of applause, and he waved a hand in casual, embarrassed greeting.

"This here is Dr. Sterling," said Marian, who obviously had compiled a file on the way he would least like to be introduced, though it was frankly nothing compared to what she said next, right as he pulled up even with her and Nora. "He's recently moved in to our beautiful building, after we said farewell to our beloved Donny, who was Dr. Sterling's uncle. We welcome him."

Will gritted his teeth, tipped his chin in a nod, a feigned gesture of gratitude to the murmur of sympathy that went through the crowd. He almost said "Pass," or at least "I didn't move in!" but when Marian moved past him toward her front-row seat, Nora waited half a beat, leaning in close enough that he could smell the crisp scent of flowers in her hair. The very edge of her braid touched lightly, briefly, against his forearm.

"I didn't tell her to say that," she whispered quickly.

He tipped his head down, putting his mouth closer to her ear, and he thought he could win the smile-off right then, if he let himself have his honest reaction to the way she shuddered, ever so slightly, at his proximity.

"But did you tell her to call my number first?" he whispered back before pulling away, turning toward the crowd like being

87

at a poetry reading was the most natural thing in the world to him.

He waited until Nora was in her seat to take out his scroll again, could feel her eyes on him, but he wasn't going to look back. He was going to work this crowd; he was going to do the best goddamn poetry reading they had ever seen.

He gently tugged at the ribbon keeping the scroll closed, said a silent prayer that Nora's scheming hadn't also involved making sure he got something extra-long or ultra-weird. It'd be trickier for him to sell that, though he'd do it if he had to.

Unrolling the scroll, he tried to temper his first genuine smile of the night as he read a name he recognized at the top. He let his eyes scan over the not-too-many lines, let the audience wait it out for a second or two longer than was comfortable. He hoped he had Nora on the edge of her seat.

Then he stepped up to the microphone and cleared his throat.

"I'm Will," he said, and maybe then he *did* smile. "And funnily enough, I got Shakespeare."

–

"Nice going, Beanpole," said Jonah, coming to stand beside Will in the back-row spot he'd returned to after his reading. Side by side like this, it was a bit like standing somewhere with Dr. Abraham, and for a second Will wasn't sure where to look.

"You got a good voice for poetry."

Okay, he'd look. Only to see if Jonah was making fun of him.

But the man seemed serious, and Will decided to take the compliment, since it tracked with what he'd heard from most of the guests since he'd finished. He got a loud round of snaps, a few backslaps from the standing gallery, and in between the various other readings he'd even had the chance to chat up a few of the guests, dropping in a couple of mentions of his short-term rental plans, in case any of them had Marian's ear and could put in a good word for him. Nora had been steering well clear of him, but he was counting that a victory. He knew she'd thought he would bolt during this, thought it would scare him off his plans.

"Thanks," Will said. "You did pretty good up there, too."

"I'm an old pro at these things. Pretty sad one you got stuck with."

Will blinked, confused. "What's sad about it?"

The truth was, he didn't really give much thought to *what* he'd been reading—he'd focused on getting through it, sounding calm and unbothered. He remembered stuff about spring and summer and the names of a whole bunch of flowers. Poetry shit: the usual.

Jonah made a noise of disapproval. "Doctors. Something wrong with the lot of you."

Will shifted on his feet. What *was* that poem about? Oh well; it didn't matter. He was pretty sure he'd put in enough of an appearance at this thing. Maybe he'd duck away soon, get back to work on Donny's unit, definitely with the back door closed. He'd lost time, getting called in to the very short-staffed clinic today, but he planned on working at the apartment overnight tonight.

"Easy for you to say," he countered to Jonah. "You got to read a poem about baseball."

Jonah looked up at him. "You a fan?"

"Used to be." *Used to play*, he thought, for the first time in ages. He hadn't thought about baseball all that much since… well. Probably since the last time he stood for any length of time in this backyard.

It was really time to go inside.

"What's that mean, 'used to be'?"

"Don't have much time to watch these days."

"We put games on out here sometimes. Nora hangs a sheet over there between Donny's balcony and Marian and Emily's. She gets her computer and some projector thing out."

There's other things we do here and there, he remembered her saying. Probably projector-supported viewing of ball games counted. That sounded nice, sure, but he'd have to talk to her about continuing to use his balcony. He couldn't imagine renters would like that. Maybe he'd find her now, before he went in for the night. Maybe—

"Next up is number nine!" called Marian, interrupting his thoughts, and he figured he ought to take his chance to go now, before the next reader got started. He'd catch Nora some other time, could even try waiting for her out on his balcony early tomorrow morning, once he'd gotten some work done.

But then he saw her rise from her seat, waving her scroll sheepishly. Number nine, then.

"Darling Nora," Marian said, welcoming her to the mic with an arm around her shoulders. "Nora read her first poem here when she was ten years old!"

Everyone snapped for that, and even though he was far away, Will had the feeling that Nora was blushing. She lowered her head, pulling her braid over her shoulder, and smiled at Marian. When the older woman took her seat, Nora stepped up to the mic, using one hand to straighten the neckline of that pretty, bare-shouldered dress.

She looks like summer, he thought, which meant he was probably full up on poetry shit for the night.

Jonah made another one of those snorting noises. Either he had a mild upper-respiratory problem or he could read Will's mind.

"First one she's done by herself in a while," Jonah said.

"What?"

Jonah tipped his chin toward the mic. "Last few years she visited, she always read with Lidia. Her grandmother."

"Ah," Will said, but now he watched Nora more closely— the way she fumbled a little with the ribbon on her scroll, the way the bottom edge of her dress fluttered erratically along the ground, as though her feet shuffled beneath it.

She was nervous.

He reached up, rubbed a hand across his chest. Shot a glance at Jonah when the man snorted again.

"Let's see," Nora said into the microphone as she unrolled her page, her voice soft. "Oh."

There was a long pause, and Will looked over at Jonah, then at the back of Marian Goodnight's head, way up in the front row. Did she usually take this long to get started?

Nora cleared her throat, the sound too loud over the mic. "Whoops," she said, and a few people snapped in encouragement.

"Say *pass*," Will muttered under his breath, then looked over at Jonah to make sure the old man hadn't heard him.

Nora looked up, and because he'd been watching her smile all night in this petty little game they'd been playing, he could tell something different about this one. He could tell it was brittle, a little wobbly at the edges. *Say pass*, he thought again, almost desperately, because he hated that smile on her face.

"My poem is by Mary Oliver," she said finally. "It's called 'The Summer Day.'"

She started reading after taking a deep breath, and Will felt like he was holding his own. He may not have made a lick of sense of his own poem while he was up there, but when Nora read, he paid attention to every word; he listened to her read about watching a grasshopper, about kneeling in the grass and being idle, about everything dying at last, and too soon.

When she finished, she gave that brittle smile again, did a funny little curtsy that made a few people laugh amid their snapping, and Will blew out a breath. She seemed fine, ushering Marian back to the mic, patting Emily's shoulder, taking something from a tray Mrs. Salas handed to her.

But she also didn't go back to her seat.

She stood off to the side for a few seconds, but she kept that same tense, fragile smile on her face. She seemed to be waiting for something, and when Marian started speaking again,

announcing the changeover to the evening's original compositions, he could tell what it was.

She was waiting for everyone to have their attention
diverted. She was waiting for the right moment to leave. When
Marian called up the first poet for the night, Nora found her
opportunity.

And Will barely waited a minute before following her.

—

She hadn't gone far.

He found her in the vestibule at the front of the building,
where the small, silver mailboxes were dotted with glinting light
from the too-low chandelier, where the wallpaper—he had to
give it credit—looked more metallic than mustard at this time
of night. She was looking out the front door, her back to him,
her bare shoulders slightly slumped, and her flower crown off
her head, held loosely at her side. But even in a posture that
looked a little defeated, there was still something so vivid about
her standing there—her dress summer green in this dull, old-
fashioned vestibule, the flowers at her side an antidote to the
musty smell.

"Hey," he said softly, not wanting to startle her.

Her shoulders straightened immediately, one of her hands
lifting, and he shifted his gaze to her reflection in the glass door,
saw the dimmer, smaller version of her swipe gently beneath her
eye.

He took a step forward.

But when she turned around to face him, she was all smiles
again, raising her chin and swinging her flower crown softly by
her side.

He *hated* it. He'd had enough of smiling for one night, and
he didn't want to think too hard about how, with Nora, not
smiling would've somehow felt like a truce.

"Oh, hi!" she said, that same high, false note of cheer that'd been in her voice when he'd first shown up tonight. "I needed some air."

Will stayed silent, watching as she realized what she'd said: a pause, a blink… a minute, nearly undetectable cringe.

"Uh, inside air, I meant." She reached up, fidgeting again with that band holding her dress up. "Are you having fun?"

Once again, he didn't answer, because he didn't really know how. He kind of *had* been having fun, until he saw her up there, looking small and smiling and fragile.

She cleared her throat. "Okay, I can see you're mad. But I didn't tell Marian to call your number first, I promise." She paused again, looking down. At some point, she'd slipped into a pair of sandals, and she shuffled her feet now, pulling the hem of her dress from beneath the sole of one. "That was a coincidence."

"I don't care about the number. I did fine up there."

She swung her crown again, her lips pursing and pulling to the side, the dent in her cheek showing. "You *were* pretty good. Kind of a sad poem you got, though."

Now he was the one shifting in his shoes. Jesus, he was really going to have to read that poem later. Still, this was the first thing she'd said to him that didn't feel like it was part of the show, and it was easy enough to bluff this one, given what had made him come after her in the first place.

"Same for you, it seemed like."

She met his eyes briefly, then lowered her gaze again. Another fake, brittle smile, a shaky laugh. "Who knew so many poems about summer were sad?"

"Nora." He didn't know why he said her name, especially like that. Like he was scolding her. Like he could see right through her.

She waved a hand. "It's silly."

"I doubt it."

She raised her head and her eyes met his, and like a punch right to his hiccupping heart, he could see that they were shiny, wet with a new rush of tears.

"Nora," he said again, but this time, it wasn't a scold.

"I don't—I don't want to talk about this." She put up a hand, and that's when he realized he'd stepped forward again. "Especially with you."

Ouch.

He stepped back, clearing his throat, embarrassed. How many ways did he need to be shown that this woman did not *want* him here? Well, he should be grateful. What a good reminder. He needed to turn around and walk down the cherub-surveilled hallway and get back to fucking work.

"No, wait," she said, stopping him. "I'm sorry. I meant— um. Because of what you told me. About being an..." She trailed off, obviously uncomfortable saying the word he'd basic- ally grenaded at her the other night. She switched the flower crown to her other hand, shaking loose some of its petals in the process. "It's not the same... losing a grandmother, I mean."

He stilled, relaxing his posture. So it wasn't that she didn't want him there, at least not for now. He still should go; he still should get back to work.

But he didn't go. He leaned a shoulder against the wall, right at one end of the line of mailboxes, and tucked his hands in his pockets. He thought about that tear he suspected she'd been wiping away, and he could not for the life of him bring himself to turn around and go back to Donny's place.

"I don't really think grief cares so much about titles. It sounds like you were close."

She tipped her chin down in a nod. "She was ninety-two years old. It's really... I'm fine, you know? She had a good, long life, and she wasn't well, right there at the end. So it's..."

She trailed off again, and then she gave a shrug that was so, so familiar to him. He'd given that shrug to people for what had felt like his whole entire seventeenth year of life. *He'd been sick for a while*, he remembered saying to people. *It's good he doesn't have to suffer anymore*, he remembered people saying to him.

"It's still awful," he said. "No matter what way it happens. No matter when." He thought of the poem she'd read. *Doesn't everything die at last, and too soon?*

Now that, he thought, was a sad poem.

She nodded, and then she moved to the side, mimicking his posture—leaning a shoulder against the wall, right at the other end of the line of mailboxes. She didn't smile, and he breathed a sigh of relief.

"Probably I shouldn't have said 'orphan,' before," he said, honoring this unsmiling honesty with an offering of his own. "My dad passed when I was seventeen, my mom about a year later. I was an adult by then."

She looked at him for a long time. "That's not… really an adult."

What was there to do, except offer that trusty, shared shrug? "Adult enough," he added, and then he promptly changed the subject. "Jonah said you and your grandmother used to read together at these things."

She hesitated before answering, her eyes on him soft and seeking, and for a second, he thought she might press him, might ask him what "adult enough" meant.

But she must've seen something forbidding in his expression, because she eventually relented, rolling so that both her shoulders rested against the wall, her legs stretched out in front of her, one foot crossed over the other. The soft fabric of the loose, flowing part of her dress draped close over her front— her stomach, her thighs, the sharp line of her top shin—and everything in his body heated. Once he realized he'd been staring, he jerked his eyes back to her face, but she didn't seem to be watching him, anyway. She was looking up toward the chandelier and all its dangling crystals.

"It was strange tonight," she said. "I kept feeling like—I don't know. I guess I kept feeling like she was around. Not in a creepy way, but sort of a nice way. A watching-over way."

He thought of the moment he'd first arrived, Nora's sharp interruption of Mrs. Salas. He reached up, touched the edge of his laurel wreath. "A discount-on-flower-crowns way?"

She laughed—a quiet, breathy sound that for once didn't go right to his heart. Somewhere else, sure—to all those heated-up places in his body—but with a little concentration he could deal with that. He inhaled through his nose, curled his fingers into his palms. Cooled himself.

"Yeah, maybe. But also the weather, and everyone we called—" She stopped herself, looked at him from the side of her eyes, her expression stricken.

Now it was his turn to laugh. "I figured it was a bigger-than-usual crowd," he said. "For my benefit." At the moment, alone with her in this weird, wallpapered vestibule, he couldn't work up much anger about this whole charade, not if it gave her some comfort. He'd be up all night, making up for lost time, but he'd manage. "Maybe she got me called up to the mic first, too."

Nora smiled—a real one, this time. "I admit, I wondered."

She was quiet for a few seconds, lifting her crown, making small adjustments to cover some bare spots.

"That Mary Oliver poem I read," she said, when she finally spoke again. "That was one of her favorites." He noticed that her expression had changed—her brow furrowed, her mouth set more firmly. "I guess it made me a little emotional, to read it."

"I don't think anyone noticed, if you're worried about it."

She looked over at him. "You noticed."

"Well," he said, which was not an answer. But the real answer—that he noticed nearly everything about Nora Clarke—wouldn't do him or her any good at all.

"Do you ever feel like that?"

"Like what?"

"Like the feeling I had tonight. Like Nonna was *with* me. Do you ever feel like that, about your parents?"

"Not really. They weren't all that with me when they were alive."

As soon as it was out of his mouth—loose, thoughtless, immediate—he regretted it. He clamped his mouth shut and ground his teeth together. He did not do this. He did not talk about his parents to anyone, not beyond the barest, shallowest facts. What they did for a living, when they'd died. Anything more ended up reflecting poorly on them, and probably on him, too. And now, to Nora—to a woman who, by virtue of her association with Donny, was already too close for comfort when it came to his messy family history—he'd made his mom and dad sound selfish or negligent or something worse. He'd made himself sound grudging, resentful, petty.

Childish.

Why hadn't he said something blandly comforting, something vaguely commiserating? He did it all the time at work. He had all kinds of canned answers, stacked up inside him like they were on pantry shelves.

But with Nora, it seemed like he could never quite reach for one when he needed to. With Nora, it seemed like he didn't have those answers at all.

She turned her shoulders again so she faced him, that look of gentle invitation in her eyes, and that's when he realized that she hadn't really agreed to the subject change after all. She'd simply found another way in. Part of him admired her for it, same as the way he admired her for this poetry reading, no matter that it was making his life damned inconvenient. It was sly and soft and strangely disarming.

But another part of him wanted far, far away from it.

Away from her, and the things she made him feel, and what those feelings made him fear.

He should've never followed her in here.

"Do you—" she began, but he cut her off.

"I should go," he said, maybe a bit more sharply than he intended. "I have a dumpster being delivered tomorrow."

She blinked. "A… dumpster?"

He reached up, pulled the laurel wreath off his head. "Getting rid of some things," he said. *Most everything*, he thought.

This feeling, he thought.

He held out the laurel wreath to her, and she looked down at it, then back up at him. This look, it was worse than any of the smiles he'd seen on her face tonight. It was part confusion, part embarrassment, and all disappointment. He almost wished he didn't have his glasses on.

He concentrated on keeping his hand steady while he waited for her to take the wreath from him, but eventually, it became clear she wouldn't. Instead, she lifted her own crown of flowers back onto her head, smoothed the front of her summer green dress. When she met his eyes again, her own were perfectly, icily dry.

"Keep it," she finally said.

And she didn't smile as she moved past him.

Chapter 7

After poetry night, Nora made a decision.

She didn't need to see Will Sterling to sabotage him.

She didn't need to see his windswept hair or his terrific spectacles or the dark, watchful eyes behind them. She didn't need to see his smile or his frown or the little furrow he got in his brow. She definitely did not need to see the way he moved his body—strolls and leans and hands-in-his-pockets postures—and she did not need to see how quickly he could move that body when he so clearly wanted to get away from her.

No, Nora could do what she needed to do without interacting with Will Sterling at all, and she'd started by making it difficult for him to find a place to put that dumpster.

It hadn't been any sort of challenge, not really—a few calls to neighbors in the surrounding buildings, a few requests to park in pretty specific places. The good thing about being loyal—about being neighborly!—was that you could make requests like this, and you could always count on enough people to help you out. By 6:00 a.m. on dumpster day, there was a line of cars right out front, and every spot in the back alley parking was taken. If Will had been hoping for a short back-and-forth trip to trash poor Donny's things, he'd show up to find those hopes well and truly dashed.

Of course it'd ended up being more complicated than all that, since Will had either changed his mind or misrepresented what he'd meant by "dumpster." What had actually shown up, in the end, was a charity service and a locally owned waste-and-recycling company, and according to Emily—truly, the ideal watchwoman, homebody that she was—the charity service had taken the lion's share. That had definitely put a damper on Nora's petty satisfaction over making things complicated, but also Emily and Mrs. Salas had both cried over seeing Donny's recliner being taken away, and Marian had gone glumly, unusually quiet, so in general she still had a whole lot of anger to spare.

Since not-really-a-dumpster day, Nora's efforts had been mostly email-based, and she was working on an idea that she thought was somewhere between poetry night and Deepa's dead-fish plot. So far, doing the outreach had meant some disruption to her daily schedule, and she was feeling more than a little guilty about how distracted she'd been during the hours she was supposed to be working on the continuing-to-be-a-nightmare eco-influencer site. But every once in a while, passing by a window or heading out to run an errand for herself or one of her neighbors, she'd get a glimpse of Will Sterling's car. He was here and he was taking apart Donny's apartment, and that meant she was running out of time.

It also meant, she thought, that the last few days had been an exercise in mutual avoidance.

From her cramped desk space, she resisted the urge to stand, to peer out the front window to look for some sign of him. The fact that she even *had* such an urge was the whole problem, frankly. It seemed like every time she saw Will Sterling, she forgot herself. Not for the first time since poetry night, her stomach fluttered with the memory of their conversation downstairs—how he watched her, how he listened to her.

How he turned away from her, when she got too close.

They weren't all that with me when they were alive.

He hadn't meant to say it; that much had been clear in the seconds after she'd turned to face him. And it wasn't only that he'd bolted, with his sloppy dumpster-based exit strategy. It was the way he'd looked at her before he'd gone—some combination of anger and betrayal and confusion. Like she'd tricked him somehow, when he'd been the one to follow her in the first place.

The only comfort in that, she figured, was that at least he seemed to forget himself, too, every time they talked. When they were in each other's orbit, nothing ever seemed to go to plan. After all, she hadn't meant to say anything to him about Nonna, or about Mary Oliver, or about how she'd souped up poetry night for him. But one look from Will—one simple, soft use of her name—and it'd been the golden hour all over again.

That feeling that she could've talked and talked.

And that she could've listened and listened.

All she'd wanted, in that brief, loaded moment of silence after he'd said it, was to stay with him, to keep the conversation going. There was no comparing their situations, of course—Nora's parents were alive and well, probably right now covered head to toe in dust at some faraway dig site without a reliable cell signal—but still, Nora couldn't help it. She'd wanted to know if Will's parents hadn't been with him in the same ways Nora's parents hadn't been with her.

A chime from her computer snapped her attention back to her email screen, where an unread message sat waiting, a name she'd been watching for. A confirmation, she was sure of it, and she should've felt excitement, or relief. But so quick on the heels of her thoughts about Will and his past and what they might have in common, she hesitated to open it.

Forgetting yourself, she thought, frustrated.

Still, instead of clicking, she stood from her desk to stretch, closing her eyes to resist the persistent window-watching instinct. What she needed to do was focus, to get right in her head before she clicked on that email and proceeded with her new, not-seeing Will Sterling plan. The other night had been a mistake, trying to… *bond* with him, in some way. She needed to keep her mind on the bonds that mattered; she needed to—

Answer the door.

Nothing about that knock that rattled through the apartment indicated that it was one of her neighbors coming to call; in fact, more than once, Mrs. Salas hadn't bothered knocking at all, though fortunately, Nora had always been dressed and decent on those occasions. And anyway, knocking wasn't often the way of it around here, not when everyone knew each other's routines so well, when it was easy enough to know when your neighbor checked the mail, or went for a weekly grocery shop. So a *sharp* knock? That was even more—

It sounded again before she'd made it halfway down the hall, and she called out an agitated "I'm coming!" in response.

A brief look through her peephole confirmed her quickly-forming suspicion, and she took a deep breath before finally pulling open her door to the man she did not need to be seeing, who was standing there with his loosely-fisted hand already raised, ready to knock again. His hair was a typically delightful mess and his mouth was set in a firm line, and no, she did not *need* to see him again, but damn if it didn't make her heart beat a little faster when she did. She crossed her arms over her chest and prepared to pretend like she was entirely unaffected.

"Can I hel—"

"Did you do something to my unit?"

Once again, Nora's brain went directly to the most adolescent possible thing for a good two and a half seconds before she was able to blink herself back to sanity. To decency!

"Pardon me?" she said, because sounding stuffy seemed like good insurance against further thoughts regarding Will's unit. *Do not look down*, Nora thought, with the determination of a person standing on a very narrow ledge of a very tall building.

"Did you put something in there? Something that would smell?"

Her eyes widened, and his narrowed.

"You did," he said flatly.

"No!" she said, but it was a too-quick *no*. A guilty *no*. The *no* of a person who definitely had *discussed* the dead-fish idea at least once. But she hadn't actually *done* it.

"I promise I didn't," she added, which was also probably a hit man's first line of defense. It sounded unconvincing even to her own ears.

"Your face got all red. As soon as I said it."

She resisted the urge to uncross her arms, to press her palms to her hot cheeks. "It's probably a stress rash. From your aggressive knocking."

"Just tell me where you put it, and quick. I don't get the sense that it's the kind of smell that stays local, if you know what I mean."

Yikes, that didn't sound great. She hoped to God it wasn't something with the building's septic system. She had a sudden and unpleasant memory of the details Nonna had provided—during one of their regular Sunday night phone calls—about a street-wide issue involving sewers about five years ago.

"I didn't put it anywhere, because I didn't do it." But already she was shoving her feet into the sneakers she had by the door, because if there was a smell seeping its way through this building, it was her responsibility, even if she hadn't made it happen. "What's it smell like?"

"Like hell's toilet bowl."

Yikes yikes. That *did* sound septic in nature. She straightened, grabbing for her phone and shoving it in her back pocket. There was a whole corner in her contact list related to building maintenance, and also a whole corner in her brain that was well aware of how much it cost to get repair people to come on short notice.

"A poetry reading is one thing," he said.

"Will," she snapped, pushing past him and closing the door behind her. "I did not put anything in your apartment. I wouldn't do that." She could feel the heat of his body beside her, and the reaction of her own—a gut-deep desire to lean into him—was so sharp, so acute, that she practically flung herself down the hall to get away from it.

"Would anyone else?"

She stopped at the staircase railing, turned back to face him. It was one thing to suspect her of something like this, but she'd bet her life no one else in this building had ever done a dead-fish teleconference. She was ready to scold him with a passionate defense of her neighbors' upright standards of conduct, but when she saw his face, she realized that his mask of tight, impatient frustration had temporarily slipped. He looked almost... chastened.

"No," she said, more gently than she'd originally intended. She was helpless against that look. "They wouldn't."

He cleared his throat, dropped his eyes briefly, then nodded toward the door across from Nora's. "I ran into Jonah the other day. After I had the dumpster here. He seemed pretty pissed."

"It wasn't really a dumpster," she blurted. *God!* What was she, his attorney? It was as *good as* a dumpster. Sort of. Either way, she was already doing exactly what she'd been chastising herself for only a few minutes ago—forgetting herself.

She turned back toward the stairs, eager to get out of this hallway. At the very least, she couldn't get moony-eyed around a man who was meant to be her enemy while she was inside of hell's toilet bowl.

"Come on," she said as she descended, but the truth was, she was talking to herself as much as to him.

–

"I don't smell anything," she said, standing inside the shockingly bright, shockingly clean space formerly known as Donny's apartment. It hadn't been that long since she'd last been in here, piles of Donny's things everywhere, the apartment messy and stale-smelling in a way that'd been hard for her to confront. For all the boasting she'd been doing to Will Sterling about the community-mindedness of the building, the inside of Donny's apartment had not, on first sight, suggested the surroundings of a community-supported man.

But now, the place looked sunny and felt fresh—the sliding door, open to the balcony, casting bright light over the newly painted walls, the floor mostly clear of debris except for a few boxes stacked tidily against one of the walls. Even with its old cabinets and countertops, she could see that the kitchen practically gleamed. Sure, it was still too bare to seem welcoming, but already it was a massive improvement.

Will had obviously put in a ton of work.

And he was obviously really, really close to finishing.

"I smell paint and bleach," she added, because she had a feeling her stunned silence was noticeable.

Beside her, Will tipped his head to the right. "We gotta go down the hall."

She nodded and took a nervous breath, indicating to him that she'd follow his lead. She could've made her own way, certainly—every apartment in the building was the same, with bedrooms toward the front of the building and the living areas toward the rear, all of the rooms stacked up single file in the long, narrow arrangement of countless other Chicago apartments. But letting Will go ahead of her at least allowed her the opportunity to openly gawk at the changes without his notice. Even the hallway seemed brighter, and when she tipped her head back to see that two modern-looking light fixtures had been installed, she felt... well! She felt almost envious.

But then, she smelled it.

"Oh," she said, stopping past the first bedroom, right before the apartment's bathroom door. It wasn't quite so bad as Will had made it sound, but it sure wasn't great, either. "I got it now."

"Yeah. So far as I can tell, nothing in the bathroom, though. No leaks, nothing in the cabinets."

She edged forward and peeked in, found it as gleaming as the kitchen—nothing on the countertop other than a full bottle of hand soap, a crisp white curtain hanging bright and smooth across the shower. There were fluffy white hand towels to match, hung from a shiny chrome rod on the wall. Hey, she didn't have one of those! She had to use this annoying freestanding thing that took up extra space on her countertop and made it hard for her to blow-dry her hair without the cord getting caught. Twice she'd almost broken a toe because of it falling down. Also, had he put a new faucet in? That one looked nice, more functional than her—

"I think it's coming from in here," he said.

He gestured toward the apartment's biggest bedroom, the one at the very front of the building with the large picture window. It was the copy of the room she'd been in inside her own apartment—the room that had once been Nonna's. Seeing Will's version of it—nothing much more than a (*gulp*) crisply made bed and a couple of nightstands—was a reminder of how big it really was when it wasn't crowded with the furniture of Nonna's that Nora had stubbornly kept even as she'd tried to fit in the things she needed to make her own life here work.

Thankfully, there was no time to dwell on that, not with the reason for her visit becoming immediately more pungent. It still wasn't quite as bad as she'd been imagining—it reminded her a little of the way the basement had smelled in the shared house she'd lived in for her last year of college—but it certainly wasn't the kind of odor anyone would want hanging around or spreading.

"You already checked under the furniture?" she asked.

From the doorway, Will nodded. She followed his eyes toward where two vent covers had been lifted from where they were usually set into the hardwood floors, and she furrowed her brow in curiosity.

"I didn't know if—" he began, then cleared his throat again. "I thought maybe you'd put something in the vents."

Her eyes snapped to his. "For God's sake!" she said. "What kind of person do you think I am?" (The kind of person who has definitely thought about it once!)

He shrugged. "I didn't—"

"Wait," she interrupted. "Did you hear that?"

She waved a hand to shush him before he could answer, turning her head. Silence. But she could've sworn she'd heard something a second ago, a barely audible, high-pitched...

"There!" she said, waving him over to where she stood. "Did you hear that?"

Slight miscalculation to usher him over, since once he was beside her she again felt compelled to move closer, to lean her body into his. If she pressed her face against his chest, if she breathed in the scent of his soft-looking T-shirt, she wouldn't have to smell the—

"I heard that," he said, and she nearly jumped.

Forgetting yourself, she scolded.

"Right?" she said, even though she'd missed whatever he'd heard by virtue of her inappropriate olfactory fantasies about a rude man's T-shirt. "It sounds like a—"

"Oh, Christ. Is there an animal in here?"

"*Shh.*" She tiptoed in the direction of the closet. After a few seconds of renewed silence, she looked back at him and whispered, "Did you already look in here?"

He nodded, stepping forward to follow her. And then, like they'd choreographed it, Nora slipped her phone from her back pocket and flicked on its flashlight, and Will reached his arm out to slide open the closet door.

Despite not-dumpster day, this hadn't been emptied yet, and immediately, Nora felt a wave of sadness to see a line of Donny's faded flannel shirts, so familiar to her.

"This stuff still has to go to Goodwill," Will murmured.

Nora ignored that, stretching to her tiptoes and shining the light on the shelf above.

"I said I already—" he said, but quieted when they heard the noise again, coming from somewhere lower, and before he could stop her, Nora dropped to her knees, bending forward to stick her whole head inside the closet. Will made a noise behind her, maybe some kind of cough-warning, and at that moment she realized both her awkward position and her suddenly increased risk of getting bitten or spit on by a rabid animal that was about to have its hiding place discovered.

But from her spot on the floor, she could hear the noise clearly when it came again, and it was only because she knew this closet as well as she knew her own that she could tell immediately where it had come from. She thought of that bad-smelling basement from college, remembered the roommate who had an old and recalcitrant cat that had a sad habit of missing the litter box.

She knew what that sound was.

She moved her flashlight so it wouldn't beam directly on to the small storage door she already knew she'd find partway open.

And when she gently pulled it the rest of the way, two sets of wide, frightened eyes peered back at her.

"Congratulations," she said to Will, a smile spreading across her face. "You've got kittens."

"The storage door," Will said, for probably the fourth time in the last hour. "In the *closet*."

Nora suppressed a smile. "Mrs. Salas tried to tell you about it," she said, only a little smug.

"*Kittens*," he said, that stunned quality still in his voice.

Nora hoped he couldn't feel her shoulders tremble with suppressed laughter, but honestly, she doubted he could miss it. Inside what had to be the tiniest treatment room of an otherwise spacious veterinary clinic, Nora and Will sat, side by side, on a small vinyl-covered cushioned bench, waiting for the vet to return. Probably during any other time, Will would be leaning casually against the door, looking annoyingly unbothered while he kept his distance from her, but Nora had the feeling he was so shocked his legs wouldn't support him anymore. It was pretty funny, but at the same time, now she definitely had her suspicions about the texture of his T-shirt confirmed (soft, indeed!), and she also was newly privy to what his skin and muscles felt like (soft and *not* soft, respectively) when they grazed against her, so some things about this were not a laughing matter.

She had not, in fact, laughed until they'd gotten here, a sort of spontaneous, half-stifled giggle that came out every time Will tried to explain something to a veterinary professional about finding two kittens inside a secret compartment in the closet of his not-apartment. Before, she'd managed to maintain at least a veneer of seriousness as they dealt with the practicalities—donning latex gloves Will had in his car before handling the kittens, setting them gently inside a plastic hamper they'd borrowed from Marian and stuffed with some of Donny's shirts. Nora had called the vet while Will had dealt with some of the most immediate cleaning-related tasks associated with finding live animals in one's closet, and then—without ever really addressing the weirdness of it—they'd gotten into Will's car and driven to the vet's office together.

"How'd they get *in* there?"

"Now, don't start this again," Nora said, rolling her eyes.

"I believe you. I'm saying, how?"

This was really taxing Will's man brain. She took a sidelong glance at him and he was staring into the middle distance like he'd gotten punched in the face by those kittens.

"My guess is, they came in through the back door you seem to be leaving open while you work." She didn't want to talk about her additional guess, which was that they had probably been led there by one of the strays who'd come looking for Donny's regular handouts.

He turned to look at her, blinking. He didn't have his glasses on but it didn't really matter, not when he was up close like this. She thought he might've been the most attractive man she'd ever sat next to. Along the strong, stubbled line of his jaw, he had a hair-thin pink scratch from where one of the kittens had caught him during hamper transport. That was a version of getting punched in the face, she supposed.

And because she was still in the habit of forgetting herself, it took everything she had in her not to reach up and touch it.

"Right," he said, but honestly he still seemed a little dazed. Was he... looking at her mouth? Or did she also have kitten scratches somewhere on her face? "That's probably it."

"What're you going to do?"

"Keep the door shut, I guess," he said automatically, and this time, she didn't bother stifling her laughter. It came out in a surprised burst, the moment—the entire *situation*—so ludicrous and unexpected, and Will's answer so bland and matter-of-fact and unsuited to the moment. She laughed so hard she had to tip her head back against the wall behind them; she had to reach up to wipe tears from the corners of her eyes. She laughed so hard that she had to sigh when she was done, to catch her breath, and the best part was, Will laughed along with her—a quieter, more constrained version of her own, but enough that it made the ends of his messy hair tremble.

When they'd finished—when they both seemed to remember that laughing wasn't really something they did together—an awkward silence fell, the muffled sounds of ringing phones and barking dogs coming from the lobby outside their treatment room. Nora shifted on the bench, trying not to notice the way their thighs had come to press against each other during their shared outburst.

"I meant about the kittens," she finally said, because now, after the laughter, the quiet between them was killing her.

"Oh. Well. I—I don't know. I can't keep them."

She looked over at him, saw that his face had gone all serious again.

"Cats are very self-sufficient. Probably great pets for a work-aholic doctor to have."

He quirked an eyebrow at her. "Probably even better for someone who works from home."

"Oh, *I* can't keep them," she said cheerfully. "Pets are against the bylaws. I'm sure you know that!" Truthfully, getting rid of the no-pets clause was something else she could've done after Nonna had passed; the main reason it was there was because

Nonna had always had terrible allergies, and asthma, to boot. But she didn't need Will to know that.

"Listen, Nora—"

The door to the treatment room opened, and there was Dr. Taylor again, holding two wide-eyed, freshly washed black-and-white kittens in the crook of each arm.

Nora did the sensible thing, which was to make an unintelligible noise in a high octave range. Will stood from the bench, and immediately, she missed the warm strength of his body beside her.

"You lucked out on the flea situation, so far as my techs could tell," said Dr. Taylor, setting each kitten gently onto the exam table. "We had a good look over with a comb, and gave them each a little bath back there in our sink. Good sports, these two."

He scratched one of them gently under the chin with his index finger, and Nora cocked her head to the side. Dr. Taylor was pretty cute, actually, which she might've noticed earlier on any given day that she was not running an errand with her very attractive sworn adversary.

"They're healthy?" Will said, which was a better thing to be focused on than Dr. Taylor's handsomeness in comparative terms. Nora stood, smoothing the front of her denim shirt.

Dr. Taylor nodded, pulling a small tablet out of the pocket of his white coat and swiping his finger across it. "They both look good, though we'll need a bit of time before we get results back on the tests we ran. Now in this apartment you two share, where do—"

"Oh," Nora said quickly, "we don't… we definitely don't share it."

Dr. Taylor looked up, moved his eyes back and forth between them, before settling his… interested…? gaze briefly back on Nora. Well! That was nice, to be noticed. Especially when she was covered in kitten hair. Possible presence of other kitten detritus, but best not to think of it at the moment.

"Will's my neighbor," she said pointedly. "He has a very sensitive sense of smell but not very good detective skills, I guess. So I helped him—"

"I'm sure he doesn't need the full story," said Will, tightly. She looked over at him and he was giving Dr. Taylor a pretty annoyed look! She recognized it, having been on the receiving end of many of Will's annoyed looks.

"I don't mind," said Dr. Taylor, winking at Nora. A wink, that was a little much. Probably he would talk about himself a lot on a first date. "Now will you be keeping the kittens, or...?"

"You know what, Dr. Taylor," Nora said, leaning in, "Will and I were *just* talking about that! I suggested that *he* might want to keep them. On the way over here they kept wanting to crawl right out of that hamper to get to him."

"They didn't," Will said, his voice clipped. "Listen, do you have ideas for a rescue organization? Rules say we can't have them in the building."

Nora pursed her lips, looked back at Dr. Taylor, who furrowed his brow and made a noise of concern. "Well, I have to say, that's not the best news. Do you think your landlord could make an exception for a temporary period?"

"Probably not," Will said. "She's kind of a stickler."

Nora rolled her eyes and nudged his side (muscles: still hard!) with her elbow. "Why a temporary period?" she asked.

"Kittens this young—I'd say the mother's nearby, somewhere. Maybe they all got in when you were out one day, but I wouldn't be surprised if she comes around looking for these little guys. We have a program here for spaying feral cats, so we might be able to help her if she does."

"Oh," Nora said, looking down to where the kittens playfully swatted at each other. Well, this was terrible. What if the mom cat *had* gone back to Donny's, or what if she was nervously pacing outside somewhere, looking for her babies? The truth was, Nora didn't even really like cats all that much, but this was sounding worse by the minute. She had a sudden, unbidden memory of the first morning she'd met Will, out on the balcony. She'd thought that loud, feline scream had come from a tomcat, but what if even then there'd been a mother cat in trouble? What if there was some kind of community cat crisis, all because of Donny's sudden passing?

She didn't want to be responsible for piling onto that.

"I'll find a way to keep the kittens for a while," she blurted. "Should I call here if I see the mom? Or—"

"I could give you my personal number," said Dr. Taylor, and she really hoped he didn't wink again. It felt like a wink was close. An imminent wink. "She probably comes around at night. If you see her, you can call me, anyti—"

"I'll keep them," interrupted Will.

Nora and Dr. Taylor both looked at him. Nora was pretty sure her mouth was hanging open. One of the kittens made a squeaky (celebratory!) *mew* noise.

"If the, uh, mom"—he said *mom* like it had a question mark at the end—"comes back, it'll be to my unit. I might as well keep them there."

Keep them there? Nora thought back to the bright walls, the mostly clean, impersonal spaces that now made up Donny's apartment. You couldn't keep kittens in an apartment you were *renting* out. You couldn't watch for a possibly angry adult cat if you didn't even *live* in the place you thought it might show up.

What was he *doing*?

He looked down at her, all stubble-faced and kitten-scratched and unwinking, and he may have had a serious expression on his face, but she felt oddly like their shared laughter still lived between them, same as the way their weeks-gone golden hour always did.

"It's temporary," he said, and he sounded so full of conviction—so full of something like a warning—that she really tried to take his word for it.

But deep down, she had a feeling she was about to be seeing a whole lot more of Will Sterling.

Chapter 8

He was starting to feel like he'd never again see the outside of this apartment.

In the four days since Nora Clarke had, once again, turned all his plans upside down, Will had found himself existing in a strange, outside-of-time universe where his daily tasks revolved around two small animals whose appetite for attention was matched only by their appetite for attempted destruction of every effort he'd made to ready Donny's apartment for rental. During the day, he felt like he mostly worked at containment efforts—how to set them up in the room where he needed to work on completing a painting or cleaning or rearranging task, how to keep them entertained while he did. At night, he slept fitfully on the functional but deeply uncomfortable couch that'd been delivered only a few days ago, cold from the back door he left open, one ear always trained on the outside, waiting for some sound of the cat he'd done all this for.

Fool, he'd think to himself as he tossed and turned. *You didn't do it for the fucking cat.*

The problem was, Dr. Taylor didn't really care about any mother cat. He cared about finding some reason to come over at night to see Nora, probably so he could try to look down her top again, which Will had definitely caught him doing in that exam room, and then it was like his whole entire brain had turned to static. Will figured that agreeing to take the kittens was, on balance, a better static-brained outcome than punching Dr. Taylor in the throat and carrying Nora out of that room like he had some sort of claim on her.

Then again, he had also spent the last fifteen minutes cleaning up a kitten-shredded roll of toilet paper and he hadn't seen Nora for days, so.

So it didn't seem like any of his instincts were all that great.

"Now," he said sternly, setting the kittens inside the stuffed-shirt hamper they still preferred as a resting spot, "you gotta behave if you want treats."

Three days ago he might've chastised himself for engaging in the absolutely ridiculous process of negotiating with these two tiny terrorists, but by this point he'd abandoned all pretense of normalcy within these walls. This wasn't even that high on the list of weird shit he'd done over the last few days. Other examples included: borrowing two shallow dishes (decorated with the painted faces of characters from *The Wizard of Oz*) from Mr. and Mrs. Salas to help the kittens eat more comfortably; accepting a gift of three PVC pipe scraps from Jonah, who'd been right on in assuming that the kittens would like to crawl through and climb over them; drinking craft beer with Benny in the backyard while putting out carefully spaced out "food incentives" for the deadbeat mom cat; and following the directions provided in another note—this one, hand-delivered, with a shy smile—from Emily Goodnight, who had advice on which of his three plants should be kept out of reach with cats in the house.

This didn't even count all the times he'd thought about going up to Nora's apartment.

Go up there and knock, the static part of his brain would think. *Take the kittens. Make her laugh like that again.*

Ask her why she's stayed away.

Ask her why she's given up.

Of course that had to be the static talking, because what did he care if she'd given up? In fact, her giving up—no sabotage, no scheming, no *nothing*—was great. Her giving up meant he was getting back to normal. This morning, in fact, he'd called up the pervert veterinarian himself, who'd all but owned up to blowing smoke the other day—the mother cat coming back had always been a long shot, especially since the kittens had obviously been weaned early, even before Nora and Will had found them. Probably, Dr. Taylor had said, she'd simply moved on, and that meant Will could do the same, rehoming the kittens or placing them with any one of the area rescue operations he'd already spent a bunch of time looking up.

With that done, there'd only be the apartment left. Any minute now, Sally no-longer-Abraham—who'd checked on Will's progress every few days, even on her vacation—would arrive to look over his almost-finished product, and once she gave him the thumbs-up, he'd list the unit for rent. In two days he'd be back at work, a newly free man, and he wouldn't have the time to think about these kittens or Donny or his neighbors or Nora Clarke.

It would be so *normal*.

"I'm serious now," he said to the wide-eyed kittens, when Sally's knock came. "Don't embarrass me."

When he opened the door it took his brain a few seconds to process to the truly outrageous tan Sally was sporting; it looked like she'd spent her entire trip with a foil-covered trifold of cardboard under her face. She beamed her extra-white-looking smile at him and went in for a hug like they were long-lost friends, but abandoned him quickly with a shriek of delight once she caught sight of the hamper.

Will sighed, because he knew what was coming. Even Marian Goodnight had cooed and cuddled over those kittens for a good twenty minutes when she'd made an excuse to drop off a package he'd missed in the vestibule. The fact of the matter was, the fucking things were cute, even when they were trying to tear holes in his new slipcovers.

Not that it seemed to matter to Nor—

"What did you name them?" said Sally, who had turned the bottom of her oversized T-shirt into a hammock and was now settling the kittens into it.

Will cleared his throat. "I didn't name them anything."

Sally looked up at him with wide eyes, the whites of which, like her teeth, seemed newly bright against her tan. Will hoped for her sake Dr. Abraham hadn't seen this; he felt very strongly about sun-protection factors.

"How could you not *name* them?"

"I'm not keeping them. Probably the shelter will name them."

Sally gasped. "My ex-husband must be rubbing off on you!" she exclaimed.

"I found three good ones," he said quickly, because *God*. He was not getting to be like Gerald Abraham, was he? "No-kill. Lots of volunteers. Foster homes, that kind of thing."

"You should be called Quincy," Sally said to one of the cats, as though Will had not spoken. "And you, you look like a Francis."

"Would you like to have a look around?" asked Will.

Sally stared dreamily at the kittens and nodded.

Once they got started, Sally rallied. The kittens sat quietly inside her makeshift hammock while Sally praised his progress, asking the kinds of questions that let him explain exactly how much work he'd been doing for all the days and nights he'd been stuck in here. He'd taken all her advice; he'd focused on making it clean, on making it neutral, on making it simple. He could hardly believe the transformation, even though he'd made it happen himself.

"Now in here," he said, gesturing for Sally to go ahead into the front bedroom, "I still have to empty out the closet, but it's mostly—"

"Oh, this is where you found these babies, right?" She swung her T-shirt hammock gently.

Will nodded, a dangerous, filthy static-signal kicking up at the edges of his brain as he remembered what it'd looked like, to see Nora get on all fours to investigate. He sent a silent, grudging apology to Dr. Taylor. Who was he to judge?

"My neighbor found them," Will said. "The one from the third floor."

"Oh, right. What was her name? Esther?"

"Eleanora," Will said, and did not rub his chest. "She goes by Nora."

"She's the one that's been giving you trouble?" Sally peeked into the closet, obviously checking out its size. It wasn't like he'd been able to explain to her over text what a potato casserole or a poetry reading had to do with anything, so mostly he'd stuck to giving her bland, uncomplicated updates about getting "pushback" from the building residents.

"Not so much the last few days," he said, trying not to wince as Sally gently unfurled her T-shirt to let the kittens onto the recently purchased comforter. "I think I got some goodwill, having the kittens around. Lots of the neighbors came by."

Not Nora, though.

"Humanized you, probably!" said Sally, cheerfully. "Who hates a man who rescues kittens? No one, that's who."

"I didn't rescue them," he began, but Sally had become distracted, moving toward the picture window with her brow lowered. Will had hung up those room-darkening curtains only the day before. He'd read that those were good, and when they were pushed to the side like they were now they still let a lot of light in, but maybe he'd made the wrong call there. Or maybe she was noticing some of the claw-related damage caused by Quincy (*What! Was! He! Saying!*) climbing up one this morning, hanging on to it with all his tiny legs spread, a deranged look in his eyes.

"Hmm," Sally said, so she'd definitely noticed the damage. Well, who cared? Certainly short-term renters wouldn't. But then he realized Sally wasn't looking at the curtains.

She was looking right out the window.

"You said goodwill, huh?" she said, the lowered brow now rising with curiosity.

Will had a sudden, not-entirely-sinking feeling about why Nora Clarke hadn't come around. It was a feeling more like… relief?

More like anticipation.

He didn't take a step toward the window, and deep down he knew it was because he didn't want to be disappointed if it didn't turn out to be her after all.

"What's she done now?" he asked, hoping it didn't sound hopeful.

"I hate to tell you, Will," Sally said, crossing her arms over her chest. "But I think she's gone and called the press on you."

—

Sally had overstated it.

But not by much.

When Will got outside, a short, dark-haired woman with a handheld voice recorder and small microphone was standing next to a guy with a high-quality camera, and every tenant in this building—with the exception of Nora—was gathered around, seeming like they were waiting their turn to speak.

Damn, Will thought.

"Don't worry," said Sally, from behind him. "I brought Quincy and Francis!"

Will had no idea how this would help, but he didn't have time to ask, because Benny was raising a hand to gesture him over. Honestly it was difficult not to feel a little betrayed; he'd sort of thought he and Benny were becoming friends, what with the beer-drinking and cat-incentivizing.

Could be that he was overreacting, though. Maybe this lady and her companion photographer were doing some kind of story that had nothing to do with—

"Is this him?" the reporter asked, as soon as he approached.

Damn, he thought again, and pasted a smile on his face. "Hey there," he said easily. "I'm Will. Big news day around here?"

The reporter—Yael, her name was—was a freelancer for a monthly community newspaper, the kind you picked up inside of restaurants or coffee shops if you wanted to know what neighborhood festival or concert series or museum exhibit you might be missing. You also picked them up, he was now finding out, if you wanted to read a heartwarming story about a close-knit group of neighbors who'd lived together for decades, constant over the course of years of change, stalwart even against the most recent tide of rising prices and building-wide renovations all around this block.

"We've only just gotten started, but of course we'd love to get the newcomer's perspective, too!" Yael said. "Now as I understand it, despite inheriting your apartment from a family member—"

"I told her that," said Jonah. "Hope you don't mind."

"It's the facts," said Will. "Where's Nora?" Strangely, nothing about what he'd learned in the last five minutes had dulled his sense of anticipation about seeing her; if anything, it was only heightened. This had to be her doing. This had to be why she'd been avoiding him. A *newspaper* article.

This woman never ran out of ideas. Why'd he *like* that so much?

"She'll be down," said Marian, but Will thought there was something funny about the way she'd said it.

"We oughta get a picture," said the photographer. "Light's good at this hour. Golden."

Will clenched his teeth.

"Oh, all right. Picture first, and then we can talk more?"

"Is Will going to be in the picture?" said Sally, who Will had forgotten about. "If so, he should have Quincy and Francis with him."

"Who're Quincy and Francis?" said Marian. "Who are *you*?"

Sally shifted the kitten hamper to one hip, stuck out her hand. "I'm Sally! I'm helping Will get his place ready for rental."

"Golly, she's tan," Jonah said in a tone he maybe *thought* was a whisper.

Benny stifled a laugh, and Sally beamed.

"I just got back from vacation!" she said, seemingly delighted that he'd noticed.

"You want to be in the picture?" asked the photographer.

"Oh!" said Sally. And Will said, "We don't need to be in the picture."

"We should wait for Nora," said Mrs. Salas, but when Will heard the building's front door open and turned to see the woman they'd all been waiting for there, he could tell she wasn't camera ready.

He could tell something was wrong.

She paused as soon as she saw him, a brief but noticeable stiffening that made him think she was contemplating turning around to go right back inside. In spite of the warm weather, she wore a bulky, cream-colored sweater, stretched out around the collar and falling to the tops of her thighs, the frayed, cropped jeans she wore, faded and loose-fitting. Maybe he would've been able to tell more by the expression on her face, but it was hidden from him by the brim of her ball cap, faded blue with a familiar, embroidered red *C*.

"Oh, is that her? I thought she'd be older," said Sally.

Will ignored her and took a step toward Nora.

"Don't," she said sharply, and backed toward the door.

He felt it like a slap across the face.

"Marian," she called across the length of the front courtyard. "Can you please…?"

"I'll handle it," Marian called back, and Will turned to her.

"What's wrong with her?" he said, and there was nothing easy to his tone, absolutely *nothing*. The static was back, snowier than ever.

"I don't think that's your business," said Marian, but she still had that funny look on her face, and Will saw Emily nudge her lightly.

Mrs. Salas made a *tsking* noise. Well, this was bullshit, this little cabal of people blockading him. Will turned away from them, moved past Yael and the photographer.

"Nora," he said sharply, when she took another step back. "I need to speak to you."

"No!" she said, overloud, and *Jesus*, this was getting embarrassing. She made a vague gesture over her shoulder. "I… I'm actually in the middle of something."

Something was wrong with her voice. Something didn't sound the same.

"It's an emergency," he said, an exaggeration he delivered practically through his teeth, but then he got close enough to see her.

And all of a sudden, it *was* an emergency. It was an emergency to him.

The first thing he noticed was the skin he could see on her chest, flushed pink and flaring all the way up the column of her neck, fading to the sickly pallor of her cheeks. The brim of her hat cast a dark shadow over her eyes, but he could still see her nose, red at the edges and oh *man*, big, swollen at the tip and across the bridge, and he knew without even looking what kind of shape her eyes would be in.

But he still took a step forward and gently tipped the brim of her hat back.

"Nora," he breathed, because it was worse than he expected. Puffy as all hell, red-rimmed, glassy. He had to get her *out* of here.

She jerked her head back and tugged down the hat. "It's fine!" she said, bumping against the door. "It is."

"You're sick."

She looked up at him, squinting against sunlight that wasn't even that bright, as though it was a struggle to keep her eyes open, her head upright.

"It's a cold. It's fine," she repeated.

"You have a fever."

She reached a hand up, touched her neck. "I don't. It's hot out here."

"Then why are you shivering?"

She stiffened, pushing her shoulders back from their hunched posture. "You're imagining things. You work too much, that's your problem. Probably you see sick people everywhere."

"No. I see a sick person here. Right in front of my face."

She sighed, but he thought maybe she didn't expect that sigh to sound so weak. So... wheezing. He felt panicked, half-crazed, sweat dewing his back like he was staring down a full-on crisis. He couldn't think of any of the usual things; he couldn't think of thermometers or throat cultures or drug names or IV drips. He could only think of picking her up and carrying her upstairs. Of setting his hand against her overwarm brow, of telling her to lie back on a bed he'd arranged, of bringing her water and medicine and whisper-coaxing her to take it. Of staying and staying, until she was better again.

"Let me take you inside. Look you over." He winced inwardly. Why didn't he add a Dr. Taylor wink, to really creep her out? "Or I'll take you somewhere. A doc-in-the-box, or wherever you want to go."

She shook her head miserably, her shoulders sagging.

Baby, he wanted to say, which made no *sense*.

"Nora," he said instead, injecting every ounce of sternness he could into her name.

She looked up at him, her swollen eyes even wetter than before. "I can't," she said. "I can't go anywhere with you."

Her chin quivered, and his heart cracked.

"I think I'm allergic to the kittens," she said, and then she burst into tears.

–

When Will was in his third year of medical school, he spent four weeks on a family medicine rotation in small-town Wisconsin, long days stuffing himself in the same exam room over and over again with the physician, the patient, and whatever family members had come along. The office had one nurse and no receptionist, minimal equipment, and temperamental internet service, and while he was there, he learned more about medicine than he had from any classroom or clinical experience before or after. Over the course of her days—most of which clocked in at around eleven hours—Dr. Calhoun saw everything from pink eye to prostate cancer. She didn't just know everyone's health history; she also knew the names of their kids and their pets. Her tiny office constantly looked like a bomb full of paper had gone off in it, she never had a pen when she needed it, and the maddest she ever got at Will was on a day three weeks in—right when he was starting to feel loose, confident—after he'd seen a patient for a minor cooking burn.

"Never heard somebody whine so much," he'd said, when the guy had finally left the office, a bandage around his arm that was more about placation than treatment.

Dr. Calhoun had turned on him with the kind of speed he'd started to think, from the slow way she moved throughout the day, was impossible.

"I know you did not say a patient *whined*," she'd snapped, and then she'd read him a riot act he'd never really forgotten: about pain and perspective, about fear and loneliness, about respect and empathy and kindness. At the time, Will had thought he'd already known all about those things, had thought that losing his parents the way he had had taught him what he needed to know.

But Dr. Calhoun had taught him that every patient—even the ones with minor cooking burns and a penchant for exaggeration—deserved the same kind of empathetic care as someone with a traumatic injury, or a chronic illness, or a life-threatening condition.

Nora Clarke, though. Will thought Nora Clarke with an acute sinus infection brought on by allergies might even test the limits of Dr. Calhoun's patience.

"I don't *want* to," she said from her fussy, flower-upholstered couch, her legs tucked up underneath her.

Will ignored her, because this was about the tenth time he'd heard her say a version of this sentence in the half hour since he'd come up to her place, out of breath from the frantic, terrified twenty minutes he'd spent after she'd covered her tear-streaked face and fled from him. A few barked instructions—for someone to go up and check on her, for Sally to take the kittens, for the photographer to put his goddamned camera away—had been followed by the hottest, most aggressively scrubbing shower Will could stand, a change into an extra, cat-danderless set of clothes he'd had in his car, and a dead run up the steps to Nora's apartment.

"I don't want you to come in," she'd said, at first, her voice still tear-soaked, but Marian, for once, had taken Will's side and opened the door to him, and then she'd shouted at Nora that she'd needed a doctor for two days, and "this one's probably as good as any."

Once he was in, Nora had given him a whole host of pouting *do not wants*—to get checked over, by either him or someone else, to have her temperature taken, to have her nasal passages examined, to take Tylenol, to drink water, to sit down. Every time, it was pretty toothless; he could tell that she was the kind of sick where simply every single thing felt bad, even the things that were meant to make her better. Between him and Marian—who'd only left a few minutes ago to start an aggressive group vacuuming project—they'd at least gotten her to do the basics.

"Come on, then," he said to her now, setting a metal bowl of steaming water onto the coffee table. "Lean forward."

She made a noise of protest, and Will bit his cheek to keep from smiling. An hour ago, with his heart pounding in his throat and his whole body gripped with irrational panic, a smile would've felt impossible, but now that he was here, close to her—being of some use to her—he'd calmed down. It was still straight misery, seeing her like this, but at least he was seeing her. At least he was helping her.

With exaggerated effort, she leaned forward, turning her still-swollen eyes up to where he stood. "This is all pretty embarrassing, Dr. Sterling."

"Don't call me that," he said. "Put your head down."

She sighed, then coughed, then finally put her head over the bowl.

"I'm going to set the towel over your head, okay? This is going to help with some of the pressure behind your face, until I can go get you a strong decongestant."

She nodded, and he took the same quiet breath that he had when he'd set his fingers against her neck, checking for swelling. He was staying *professional*, even if in draping a towel over her head he had to concentrate on not staring at the long, straight curtain of her hair that was spread across her back—the first time he'd ever seen it down.

Nora made another noise, a moan of relief that prompted another professional failure on his part. Will took a step away from the couch, cleared his throat. "I'll run over to the pharmacy."

She lifted her head. "You don't have to."

"Head down," he said, and she made a face at him.

"Your bedside manner is terrible." But she put her head down again, shifting even farther forward on the couch. The next time she spoke, it was so muffled by her closeness to the bowl that he had to step closer to hear her.

"I didn't want you to have to get rid of the kittens," she said.

"That's why I didn't say anything. I didn't even know I was allergic, I swear. I never have been, before."

She sounded so miserable that he got even closer, moved around so he could sit on the coffee table, right beside the big bowl of water. "Allergies sometimes come on late."

The towel rocked in a sad, short nod.

"I wasn't ever going to keep them, Nora," he said, because he thought it would make her feel better to know it. It wasn't her fault that he wasn't cut out to have pets, even if Quincy and

Francis (*sigh*) weren't so bad. "My friend Sally, you might have seen her down there, I think she's going to keep them, and she's great, so you shouldn't worr—"

"You stayed so many days," she interrupted. "You stayed so many days, I thought maybe you'd changed your mind."

Oh.

He swallowed, unsure of how to respond. He hadn't changed his mind, of course he hadn't. He was still on track to getting back to normal; he was still going to list the unit and go back to work. These last four days, it's all he'd been trying to think about, no matter that he hadn't always succeeded.

But he didn't even want to try to succeed right now.

"That interview today," she said, and he waved a hand in dismissal, but she probably couldn't see it.

"Forget about it," he said, because that's what he wanted. While he was here, sitting with her like this, caring for her like this, he didn't want to talk about this thing between them—this feud they'd been carrying on. The one that he was, whether she liked it or not, about to win with a few clicks on his laptop and a return to his regular life.

"I was going to cancel it," she said. "I didn't really want to do it anymore, not after we found the kittens, but then I felt so sick, and I lost track of the day, and then today I—"

"Nora," he said. "Let's leave it for now, okay?"

She pulled the towel back, her face pink and dewy, her eyes still puffy, and her mouth tugged down at the corners in the saddest, sweetest pout he thought he'd ever seen.

"I feel awful," she said, and for sure, she was whining.

"I know, baby," he said, and for sure, it was the static talking. They stared at each other, steam from the bowl between them, and in those silent seconds, it seemed like they were agreeing to something. For as long as she was like this, they weren't going to be feuding neighbors. Nora wasn't going to cheerfully smile, and Will wasn't going to charm. She was going to admit that she felt bad, and Will was going to call her *baby* when she did.

It wasn't going to be normal at all.

She slumped against the back of the couch. "I'm probably gonna fall asleep," she murmured, already sounding halfway there.

"Good." He grabbed at a faded, crocheted throw that hung over one end of the couch, waited for her to put her feet up before he draped it over her legs.

"Only for a little bit. I only sleep for a little bit at a time, since this started."

"Sure," Will said, but he hoped she would sleep good and long; he could tell she needed it. And while she did he'd go pick up a scrip for her, and then he'd sanitize every cat-dandered surface in this building, even if it took him all night. He'd barely slept the last four; what was one more?

"I'll go pick you up some meds, okay?"

Her swollen eyes flickered open, and her brow furrowed. "You'll come back?"

He nodded. "Yeah, of course. I'll leave it on the—"

"And then you'll stay?" she said.

He stared down at her. Everything he saw when he looked at Nora, it was still a problem: his weaknesses, his past, his fear for how he figured he was destined to turn out, if he let himself get too close to her.

But he knew she didn't mean *stay forever*. He knew she meant *for now*, for while she felt like this, for the term of that silent deal they'd made only a moment ago. And he figured that was safe enough. He figured he was strong enough for that.

One night, and then he'd go back to normal.

"Yeah," he said, bending down and tucking the blanket around her, barely stopping himself from setting his lips against her brow. *Not that*, he warned himself, before straightening again. "I'll stay."

Chapter 9

The first time Nora woke up, he was in her kitchen.

He'd been to the pharmacy, a small white paper bag tipped on its side on the counter, but he'd also stopped by the grocery, picking up a small crate of clementines and a loaf of bread and three different kinds of ready-made soup, one of which she found him heating on the stovetop. When she shuffled into the kitchen, she could tell by the notch between his eyebrows and the tense set of his jaw that she looked about as good as she felt (which was to say: hideous!), and so when he set the bottle of Tylenol in front of her and uncapped her new prescription decongestant, she took it with the full glass of water he said she had to drink and she didn't complain at all. She ate a bowl of soup, and they talked about her work and his, anything that wouldn't get them talking about the building. When she'd finished eating, Will had pointed her back to the couch and told her to put something entertaining on TV for them to watch, but she'd fallen asleep again before he'd finished clearing plates.

The second time, he was out in the hallway.

It was mostly dark in the living room, a soft glow from the light left on above the oven, and when Nora first sat up, sweaty from her obviously broken fever, she thought at first—with no small sense of wholly unjustified disappointment—that he'd gone. But when she'd rubbed at her eyes and brought more of her senses back online, she'd heard the familiar sound of Jonah's absurdly loud TV and noticed that the soft glow wasn't only from the oven light; it was also coming through the narrow crack of Nora's partially open front door. She'd hauled herself up from the couch, leaving behind the now too-warm blanket, and tiptoed toward it, peeking out to see Will's broad back as he leaned against Jonah's open doorway, the light from that huge TV flashing as Jonah shouted at him about the guy on first base. She could've stood and watched like that for a long time— Will watching baseball with one of Nora's favorite people in the world, a member of this family she'd been trying so hard to get him to recognize—but when she reached up to scratch her head she made contact with the sweaty, sticking-up side of her hair, and so instead she crept into her bathroom to shower and brush her teeth. When she came out, dressed in a fresh set of pajamas, her wet hair twisted into a loose bun on top of her head, he was back inside again, folding up the blanket she'd left behind and looking like he was getting ready to leave.

The third time, he was in her bed.

It took her a few sleepy seconds to remember how he'd ended up there, and once she did, she squeezed her eyes shut in embarrassment. It'd started with his insistence on her taking another dose of Tylenol and drinking another full glass of water (the whole thing! He was so bossy about water. She did *not* reflect on how bossy he might be in other contexts; she did *not*!), and then a pretty effective scolding (no other contexts, *none*!) when she suggested she might go catch up on some of the work she'd missed during the day. She'd sighed and agreed that yes, she was, in fact, pretty tired, but maybe she'd sleep on the couch, because she had to change the sheets on her bed, and the couch was fine anyway, and—

And he'd said, "Okay, let's go change them," and marched past her, and five minutes later they were smoothing clean linens across the mattress and not making eye contact, but it was all fine; she'd get in bed and he'd go, and that was fine and good and normal; it was silly that she'd asked him to stay before.

But then—oh *God*, this was the embarrassing part—she'd asked him to stay again. She'd crawled into her cool, perfect bed and curled onto her side and asked him if he'd heard from Sally about the kittens, and he'd shown her his phone, three videos of the newly named Quincy and Francis happily exploring a cat tree and a small scratching post, and then she'd gotten sleepy again, *real* sleepy, talking-nonsense sleepy, and she'd said, "Sit right there for a minute," and pointed to her mattress, and then she'd held his phone close to her face and watched the videos again, maybe even twice, feeling a little wistful about her stupid late-developing cat allergy, but not wistful enough, she guessed, to keep from falling asleep again.

It was still pitch dark, so maybe it hadn't been all that long, but judging by how rested she felt, and judging by how dry her hair was, she'd been out for a while. She even had a mean crick in her neck, which was weird, because her pillows were usually...

Oh no. Oh no no no.

She was not sleeping on her pillow.

She was sleeping on Will Sterling's lap.

Her cheek on his thigh, rising and falling slightly from the long, even breaths that suggested Will had fallen asleep, too, sitting up in the same position she last remembered seeing him in, his back against her headboard, one of his feet still on the floor.

She gently—so, so gently—pulled her cheek away, and with mortifying clarity realized that it was damp.

Because she'd *drooled* on him.

Please don't wake up, she thought.

"Hey," he said, his voice low and rough, because of course she'd fall asleep on the lightest sleeper alive.

Please don't notice your leg, she thought.

He unfolded his crossed arms and set a hand on his drooled-upon thigh, and Nora put her face in her hands and groaned.

He chuckled. "Hey, now. Two nights ago a kitten crawled out of a hamper, peed on my torso, and screamed in my face. This is nothing." He shifted, rolled his neck. "How're you feeling?"

That was nice, how he did that. How he moved right on, from the humiliating thing. Probably she ought to take back what she'd said about his bedside manner. On the scale of things, the *I've seen worse* approach worked pretty well, actually.

She sniffed tentatively, relieved to find it was, for the first time in three days, possible to get some air through her nose. "Pretty good, compared to... yesterday? Is now... tomorrow?"

He shifted again, patted the bed for his phone, which he found in the folds of her comforter. When it lit up she could see more of his face, the handsome, charming curve of his smile. She clutched uselessly at the sheets tangled around her, remembered the way it'd sounded when he'd called her *baby*.

"Wouldn't you know," he said, and turned the phone screen toward her.

She smiled back.

4:14 a.m., it read.

The golden hour.

—

For what felt like long seconds, neither of them said a word— long enough that the phone screen went dark again, long enough that Nora began to feel a nervous anticipation set in. The truth was, no matter what had happened between her and Will since that first morning, pretty much every golden hour since, she'd thought of him: of him and her on their respective balconies, whispering to each other before they knew they'd be enemies.

She wanted, desperately, to believe that he'd thought about it, too.

But if he left now—now that he was assured the worst of her illness was over, or now that she'd removed her drooling face from his lap—she'd know she was alone in clinging to that memory.

"Even on your sick days, you're an early riser," he finally said, his voice quieter, almost a whisper, almost like he had on that morning outside, and she breathed what she hoped was a silent sigh of relief, sinking back onto the pillows she'd apparently never slept on. She tried to imagine the space between them as fresh, cool, early-morning summer air.

He was staying.

"Guess so," she said, reaching up to uncoil the bun from the top of her head, feeling the crick in her neck ease and more of her embarrassment fall away as the heavy weight of it came down on her shoulder. She moved, leaning against her headboard to mimic his position. Like this, it was civilized, normal. It might as well be a couch. It was sitting and talking, nothing more.

"It's kind of funny, to be sick," she said, once she'd gotten comfortable.

A volley! A normal, conversational volley.

"What's funny about it?" he returned, and she smiled in relief.

"Well, it's my first summer back, since Nonna passed. And I only ever used to get sick when I came here in the summers. It was like, the school year would end, and a few days later I'd come. And always, within the first month, I'd get sick."

Even with the space between them, she could feel something about his body change, become more tense. "Maybe you're not allergic to the cats. Maybe there's something in this building, a—"

Nora snorted a laugh. "No, no. It was never one thing. Sometimes it was a cold, or a stomach bug. Two summers in a row I got a bad flu, the worst fevers I ever had."

"Surprised you have so many good memories here, if that was the pattern."

She smoothed the comforter, suddenly feeling cautious. Talking about this—it felt like a risk, given how their conversation on poetry night had gone. But he was as good as asking, wasn't he? It's what he'd been like on that first morning. Curious about her. Interested in her.

"I never got sick during the school year, not ever," she said, leaning into that interest, settling into it like it was another cozy bed to climb into. "I got perfect attendance from second grade on. In first grade I broke my arm during a field trip, so I missed half a day for that."

"You only got half a day for a broken arm?"

She shrugged. "I liked school. But also, my parents were really into their work." She took a sidelong glance at him. The darkness around them was already changing, or her eyes were already accommodating it, because she could see that he'd tipped his head toward her.

"Yeah? What'd they do?"

"They're professors. Both in archaeology."

"Shit, really? Like Indiana Jones?"

She laughed quietly, the sound somehow so intimate. What else could it be, really, to laugh with someone in your bed? It felt like the most secret, private, special thing. It felt like a fever dream. She gave up on thinking there was anything normal or casual about it.

"More boring than Indiana Jones. Anyway, that's how they met, in graduate school. They work a lot during the school year, teaching their classes, but also writing all these papers and stuff. They're actually pretty famous."

"Not Indiana Jones famous."

"No. Like… nerd famous. PBS documentaries famous."

"Huh," he said, then paused. "So they didn't get summers off, or… ?"

"They do their field work in the summer. Digs all over the place. They're on one now, actually." As they got older, it bothered Nora more, but she didn't suppose that mattered much. Once her dad had told her he hoped he was lucky enough to die on a dig. *Doing what I love*, he'd said, and Nora— who'd been twelve at the time—had felt almost breathless with hurt.

"They never took you along?"

She shook her head. "It would've gotten in the way with their work, I think."

Now that—*that* was straight out of her mom's script. *Nora, it's simply not practical for me to come to Nonna's with you this year. Nora, it wouldn't be worth it for you to travel all the way to Greece, not with the schedule your father and I have planned.*

"And anyway, I liked coming here. There were always people around."

Beside her, Will laughed again, a soft, knowing sound. Probably he was thinking of all the kitten visits she didn't get to come over for.

"Always," he said, a trace of indulgent sarcasm in his voice.

She smiled over at him. "I think maybe my body knew this was an okay place to be sick? A safe place. My parents, they weren't really… nurturers. They didn't have time for that."

She paused, caught herself tugging on the ends of her hair, an old habit that had been, in her younger years, a constant source of frustration to her mother, and also the reason for the infamous Ringo haircut she'd had for her first summer here. But she was probably being unfair to her parents. They still called her, still checked on her. They'd made sure she'd had what she needed, growing up. They were smart and interesting and worldly. They told her they loved her all the time, and she believed them.

But… they hadn't been like Nonna. They had never been like Nonna. They had never taught her about the things they loved; they had never cooked with her or stayed up late to do old jigsaw puzzles with her or planted pots of vegetables with her. They had never asked her what she was reading or told her about what they were reading; they had never regaled her with long, winding stories about their lives, full of the names of people she'd never met and never would.

She shut her eyes against a wave of golden hour grief, the kind that had kept her company all through the winter.

"That's probably not how sickness works, I know," she added, when she felt like she could speak again.

135

The mattress shifted as he moved, lifting the leg he'd had on the floor up to stretch beside the one on the bed. "I only ever got sick during my residency when I had a run of days off, it seemed like. The body does all kinds of things, in response to stress."

"Oh," she rushed out, embarrassed by the comparison. "I don't want to act like it was stressful, with my parents."

It *was*, though. It was stressful to spend so much time alone. It was stressful that it wasn't easy to make friends, that most of her socialization came from people who were way older than her. It was stressful to feel small and inconvenient, to feel like you spent nine months of your year looking forward to three, to come back at the end of them and feel like you had to get used to life all over again. It was still stressful, all these years later.

Will was quiet, and Nora felt a sinking sense of embarrassment, of disappointment. That had been a bad volley, and now it was poetry night, all over again: this was not something he wanted to talk to her about. To bond with her about. No matter that she thought they might have this in common.

"My parents, they were kind of like yours."

She stilled, desperate not to move, or to speak, to do anything that would break this brand-new early-morning spell.

"Not about work, but about—" He broke off, ran a hand through his hair. When he spoke again, he rushed the words out, so quick that Nora couldn't even be sure she heard him right. "About each other."

"Each other?"

He cleared his throat, scratched at a spot on his chest. "Yeah. They were... they met pretty young, when they were teenagers. They were tied up in each other, always. Obsessed with each other. They never wanted to be apart."

Nora swallowed, a sick feeling that had nothing to do with her sinus infection settling into her stomach. Another memory from poetry night: *My dad passed when I was seventeen, my mom about a year later.*

"That sounds intense," she said. She wouldn't say—wouldn't *ask*—anything else.

He didn't speak for a long time, and all Nora could do was lie there beside him, that not-balcony space between them feeling like floors and floors of distance. What would it be like, she wondered, to close it? To scoot her body across that space and lie right next to him, and to *mean* to, this time? To not fall asleep on accident, but to say with her body that she could tell he'd said something painful, something honest?

"It was isolating," he said, and then shrugged. "I had buddies from school, but then I—well, I had a lot of responsibilities at home that kept me pretty busy. I'm not even sure I ever learned how to be a good friend. And obviously, I didn't have any..."

He trailed off and made a gesture toward the air around them, to the structure around them, and Nora had to swallow around the shock of sadness she felt, seeing him do that. Exactly what she'd been trying to get him to see about this place, and it was the hollowest sort of victory.

"Family," she whispered, not even really meaning to. Once she realized she had uttered the word, she thought that would be the end of it, frankly. Mentioning his parents, that had been huge, she figured. There was no way he'd bring up—

"Donny and my mom," he said, and Nora held her breath. Easy enough, what with the sinuses. "They'd stopped speaking, a long time before. Back when my parents first got together and then when my mom left home for good. I never met him until we came here, the once."

She wanted to ask a hundred questions. She'd start with: *What year, what month, what day?*

But all she said was, "Why did you come?"

"My mom had found out my dad was sick. She was pretty desperate for help."

Nora thought about Donny—how he'd been good at hanging pictures and at fixing the dryer hoses in the basement when they got clogged. How he'd always been the one to put in everyone's window AC units, back before they'd gotten central air, a huge, expensive project that Nonna had said he'd done all the legwork for. How he always hosed off all the outdoor furniture when it got dirty in the spring and summer, even though he himself never really used it. How he'd fed all those cats, for God's sake. They weren't even *his*.

"And Donny...?"

"Didn't help," Will said grimly.

Nora could only really blame her loyalty for what she said next—her desperate instinct to bridge the gap between the Donny she'd known and the Donny this man in her bed was describing.

"Donny never really seemed to have much money," she said quickly. "Maybe he—"

Will made a noise, something too flat to be called a laugh. "She didn't ask him for money."

"Oh." It was barely a sound, barely a breath. She felt cold again, almost like the fever was back, but she knew that wasn't it. She knew that wasn't it at all.

"She asked him to take me."

—

Part of her wanted to turn on a light.

The one on her nightstand would do—it was small and shaded; it gave off the kind of soft glow that was perfect for the in-betweens of her day: when she was waking up, when she was winding down. This moment, with Will—it felt like both, somehow. It felt like the beginning and the end of something, all at once, and so maybe that's why the other part of her didn't want to turn on any light at all.

"For the summer?" she whispered.

"No," he said, in that same flat, matter-of-fact tone. "For good."

She swallowed, scratchiness in her throat reasserting itself. It was probably time for more medicine, or maybe for another shift over that hot bowl Will had made her use yesterday, but she wouldn't have moved for all the decongestants and hot bowls in the whole entire world.

"Could be that she didn't mean it," Will said, and Nora felt such terrible certainty about where he'd learned his *I've seen worse* bedside manner. Maybe he'd been *I've seen worse*-ing himself his whole life, only to feel better about this one awful moment.

"Or that she would've changed her mind, eventually. I don't really know. But Donny, he didn't want to have anything to do with me."

"Why would she... why would she take you to someone you didn't even *know*?" Nora had always known Nonna, even before the summer stays started. There wasn't a week of Nora's life that hadn't included some interaction with her—a phone call, a card in the mail, the occasional visit.

"She wanted to be with my dad, for the time he had. The two of them."

If he'd said it in any other way, in any other tone of voice, Nora might've figured something else—that Will's mom wanted to shield him from his dad's sickness, whatever it had been. But she could tell that's not what it had been, or at least that's not what it had been to Will.

"Did she ask you first? I mean... if you wanted to go?"

Everything about him was a silhouette, but she could still see him shake his head.

"She didn't tell me where we were going. A couple days after we got home, I kept not being able to find some of my stuff—my favorite T-shirt, a ball cap I wore a lot. Eventually I realized they were out in the car, in a suitcase she'd packed. She'd forgotten to bring it back in."

Nora had really never been much one for name-calling. Nonna had always told her that calling someone a bad name was a symptom of a small mind and an even smaller imagination. When someone was rude to Nonna she would say things like,

Well, he seemed to be having a bad day! or *She must have misplaced her manners this morning!*

But right at this moment, Nora felt like she had the smallest mind, the most minuscule imagination. The only available capability of both was to come up with names for Will Sterling's mother.

"What a—" she began, but at the last, loyal second her long years of Nonna training took over, and she recalibrated. "What about your dad?"

"I don't know if my dad knew. We never talked about it."

My parents, they were kind of like yours, he'd said, but for all her desperation to believe it, to bond over it, now she thought that wasn't so true. Nora's parents, they'd talked *constantly*. Months before her first summer here, they'd talked to her about independence and resilience and trying new things; they'd talked to her about how she was "practically" a teenager, about how her dad had gone to summer camps far from home, about how Nora needed to learn to let go of the rigid routines she seemed to cling to. Sometimes Nora thought that all her parents knew how to do was talk.

She'd probably been pretty wrong, to get annoyed with them for that. All families were messy, but Will's… Will's really *did* sound like a Dickens novel, or worse.

"When my mother died," Will said, his voice rough, cautious, and she knew he was about to confess another painful part of this story. "I sent a copy of her obituary here. But he didn't… I never heard from him. I don't really know why I did it."

I do, thought Nora, and it felt like her heart broke into a million pieces, thinking of Will, a kid himself, without both of his parents. Reaching out to the person who'd been, apparently, the only family he had, and getting nothing in return.

"Nora," he said quietly, and she swallowed again, knowing already they'd gone too far with this conversation. She could feel the way it'd led them right back to what they'd been trying to avoid, all through this temporary, allergy-prompted truce.

"Yeah?" she whispered, knowing already what he was about to say.

"I haven't changed my mind. About the apartment."

She nodded, wondering if he was watching her silhouette, too.

"I believe everything you say about this place. Everything you showed me."

She meant to nod again, to stay propped up. But there was a stinging pressure in her head—behind her nose, behind her eyes—and she started sinking, by degrees, back into her pillows. *It's your sinuses*, she lied to herself. *You probably need more medicine.*

"But I can't be here," he said, and she closed her eyes against a wave of something so potent, so recognizable, something no medicine could fix. Grief, again. For Nonna. For this place, and the way it would inevitably be different now. For Will.

"This is a place where a lot of things changed for me," he continued. "And not for the better."

It was hard to hear it. To hear that her experience of this place—the exact opposite of his, really—wasn't anything sacred, or anything universal. It was hard to face that something she loved so much, something she'd tried to preserve so much, could be something so painful to someone else. She felt small and naive. She felt chastened.

"Right, of course," she said. "I get it."

He cleared his throat, and the mattress shifted again, because—yeah. His confession—it *had* been the end of something. It was right for him to leave. It was right for them to move on from this, to call off this feud. When he stood, he stayed by the bed, and she regretted letting herself lie down again. Whatever he said next, it would probably feel like instructions. Maybe that's what he'd do. *Drink water, take your pill every four hours, watch your fever.* Doctor-patient, and nothing else between them at all.

"I'd appreciate if you don't tell anyone else," he said, which might as well have been instructions. "About Donny. It doesn't do any good for them to know."

"I wouldn't," she said. "I won't."

Embarrassingly, she hadn't even really been thinking about her neighbors, about what she'd say to them. But of course she'd have to find some way to explain, and she would be a model patient; she would do exactly what the doctor ordered. She'd deal with her own feelings about Donny—and what she'd learned about him—privately.

"I meant what I said before, back at the start of this. I don't mean to cause you any trouble. Or anyone who lives here. I'm a responsible person. I'm a practical person."

The way he said it—she got the sense that he really needed to believe it. Like he had some reason to doubt it, even though for the whole time she'd known him, he'd always seemed like both. That hot bowl had been *real* practical, for example. Drinking water, that was something responsible people were always into.

Her face heated with memories—welcome-wagon schemes and flower crowns and poetry scrolls, emails to reporters and crying over kittens and *drooling* on this poor, beleaguered man. She felt like the most irresponsible, impractical person alive.

"I know that," she said. "And I'm sorry about… everything. All the food, and the poetry. I'll stop. And I'll—I'll get that article canceled, I promise."

He was quiet for a long time, and then he said, his voice soft again, "So far as sabotage goes, it was all pretty clever, Nora. I might even miss it."

She had to bite her lip to keep from another irresponsible bout of tears. Maybe that decongestant gave her PMS. That was definitely it, she decided (impractically).

He moved then, came around to her side of the bed and lifted her water glass. "I'll go get you some more before I go. You should take another dose of medicine, too. But better if you do it with breakfast."

"No, that's okay," she said, too quickly, finally finding the energy to halfway sit up. "You don't have to do anything else. I'm going to get up for the day. Early riser, and all that."

He set down the water glass, a clink of finality. "You're sure?"

"Definitely sure. I feel loads better." *False*, she thought. *Now you feel worse. Differently worse.*

"All right. I'll…" He paused, seemed to rethink whatever he was going to say. "I'll see you," he finished, exactly like his first golden-hour goodbye.

He turned to go, and she held herself still, waiting. She definitely wasn't going to get up, not yet. Four a.m. could honestly go fuck itself. She was *done* with it. She was going to lie back down as soon as she heard her front door shut behind him and sleep for as long as she could.

But he didn't go.

Instead, he turned back around and held out his hand.

She blinked at it, then up at him. Did he… want to *shake her hand*, to end this? Like a professional goodbye, or maybe some kind of weird gentleman's agreement that would remind her not to get any more ideas about wrecking his rental property? Honestly, after everything they'd talked about, it felt insulting enough that she almost wanted to take a pass.

Instead, to get it over with, she put her hand in his.

But it wasn't a handshake he wanted.

As soon as they touched, he tilted his palm; he pressed his against hers, wrapping his warm, strong fingers around the edge of her hand, the same as he had that night in Donny's apartment, to keep her from falling. She knew he could hear her sharp intake of breath but hoped he couldn't hear the way her heart thudded in response to his touch, his nearness. Even through her still-stuffy nose, she could tell that he smelled like sleep and her sheets and something else, something clean and spicy, and without thinking, she tipped her face up to get closer to it.

He leaned down, and set his lips against her forehead. Soft, sweet, and somehow sad.

A goodbye.

Still, the best medicine she'd ever had, for the seconds he stayed there. She felt—rather than heard—him murmur something against her skin, but before she could ask what he'd said, he straightened, loosening his hold on her hand.

This time, when he turned to go, he didn't change his mind.

Chapter 10

Two weeks and two days since he'd seen her.

Not that he was counting.

But he was counting.

He stared down at the stack of call sheets where he'd been scribbling notes all day, half-formed words about patients he'd seen over the course of his shift. The fragments, they were part of the job, or at least they were part of the way he'd always done it: nothing that'd make sense to anyone else, but that made perfect sense to him when he finally sat down to do notes in between rushes or at the end of his shift. Sometimes he'd write things like *pudding cup*, and that would remind him that the woman in treatment three who'd fainted in the middle of her daughter's piano recital had taken a bite of her orderly offered chocolate pudding right before she mentioned to Will that her jaw bothered her, *only a little, really*, but it was the jaw pain that made him put in the orders for an MI workup, and once he saw the words *pudding cup* he could somehow remember it all for the patient note.

Tonight, though—sitting in one of the uncomfortable chairs at a messy workstation right in the center of the ED—he was struggling with his own scribbled clues, frustrated with the way his brain was slow to jog and to focus, to remember what a phrase like *sock history/hamster???* meant, especially when for two weeks and two days his mind had teemed with all sorts of useless fragments, memories he didn't want or need, things that made him think of Donny and his mom and, most of all, of Nora.

Of Nora and what he'd done to her, the morning he'd last seen her.

You think I'd take your kid?, he could hear Donny saying, each time the memories would come back to him. It was clear like day, Donny's voice, no matter when Will heard it. Clear like the afternoon sky when he'd stood beneath Donny's balcony for the first time. *He's probably turned out like you*, he'd hear, and then the real hits would come.

Rash.

Reckless.

Selfish.

Will had hated Donny for saying those things about his mother, and by extension, about him. But he couldn't deny the effect they'd had on him; he couldn't deny that he'd heard something true in them. Everything about his life that felt chaotic to him—his moods, his temper, his intensity over his baseball games and his frivolous crushes—he'd ended it, after that day. In his house, he was half ghost, half manager. He ducked in and out of rooms, bringing things to his mom and dad, disappearing again when he'd done whatever service was required of him. He'd use the phone he'd brought into his room to make the calls his mother couldn't bear to. He wrote checks from his bed, his biology textbook a lap desk, the imitation of his father's signature practically a work of art. He studied. He cleaned. He counted pills. He planned burials: first, his father's, long expected, and ten and a half months later, his mother's—not expected but still somehow not shocking—when an aneurysm took her in her sleep. He got loans. He got into college, then medical school, then residency. He focused.

I'm a responsible person. I'm a practical person.

His own words now, the ones he'd used to win with Nora, to stop the feud over the apartment. He'd meant them, of course he had. They were the same words he repeated to himself, every day for years until he'd believed them, until he'd *become* them: Will who works late, Will who stays even-tempered, Will who puts everyone else at ease.

146

But once it was all over—once she'd quietly agreed, once she'd promised to keep his confidence, once she'd apologized—he'd felt heavy with guilt, because he hadn't told her the full truth. He hadn't told her what else he'd heard that day—her laugh and her voice, high above. He hadn't told her about his heart, that the way she made it beat felt like the last relic of who he'd been before everything changed.

He hadn't told her that it wasn't only the memory of Donny he was afraid of.

It was the memory of her back then, and it was the reality of her now.

It was the way she made him feel. *Rash, reckless, selfish*. Like the most intense version of himself.

And it was that version who'd struggled to go—who'd bent back over her bed, who'd taken one last chance to touch her. Who'd *kissed* her. Soft skin, soft hair. Everything about her smelled good. He'd said *I'm sorry*, right against her skin, but he knew he was being a coward. He knew she wouldn't hear him, and then he'd gone.

Two weeks and two days ago.

"Dr. Sterling."

"Yeah," he said, irritated, and then he looked up to see who else but Gerald goddamn Abraham looking down at him, standing at the workstation with his white coat and his permanent look of judgment.

He suppressed a heavy sigh.

"Yes," Will corrected.

"Dr. Viswanath started his shift an hour and a half ago. You're meant to be off." If Will was meant to be off, then so was Abraham. But he supposed it wasn't worth it to point it out.

"I'm doing notes."

Except that he wasn't. In fact, at some point, the screen saver had come on. He nudged the mouse with the edge of his hand. "This computer is broken."

Amara, the nurse in the chair beside him, made a noise. He looked over at her, and she stuck the straw of her water bottle

147

into her mouth and raised her eyebrows while she took a big drink. She'd already told him to clear out twice because she said he typed so slow it made her want to murder him.

Will sighed and stood up. "Fine," he muttered, patting at the chest pocket of his scrubs, then at the waistband. His favorite pen, check. His badge, check. Amara's smirk of victory, check.

"I'll walk you out," said Dr. Abraham, and Amara chuckled quietly.

"I need to stop by the workroom, get changed."

"I'll wait."

Will hustled down the hall and into the workroom, changing out of his scrubs as quickly as possible, wanting to get whatever Abraham had in store for him over with. When he walked out, bag over his shoulder and bike helmet under his arm, the man was there waiting, paging through the small leather notebook he always kept in the pocket of his white coat. Probably he never wrote anything like *sock history/hamster???* in there.

They fell into step silently, Will altering his strides to accommodate Dr. Abraham's. He was going to get a lecture; he could *sense* it. He knew he'd been off since he'd been back, but surely that was normal after such a long break. Surely he hadn't done anything to warrant—

"You gave my wife two kittens."

Will almost missed a step. He *had* done that.

"My ex-wife," Dr. Abraham corrected.

"It wasn't so much that I *gave* them to her," Will said.

"She's very taken with them. She's named them—"

"Quincy and Francis," Will finished. "I know." She'd sent him a few more videos, all received while he'd been at the hospital. He'd saved every single one and thought about sending them to Nora.

But thought better of it every time.

"Sally often lobbied for a pet, during the time we were married."

Oh, *Jesus.* What kind of mess had he stepped into here? A month ago, walking these halls with Abraham, he'd had the sense that there was something different about his boss when he talked about his ex, but back then, Will was still his mostly normal self, and that meant he didn't get near anyone's sloppy romantic problems. Unfortunately, Will was currently his mostly abnormal self, with a head full of memories he didn't want and a heart in his chest that felt like it was made of cracked glass.

"You didn't want pets?" Will said, abnormally.

Abraham cleared his throat. "Sally and I had different ideas about what made for a comfortable home."

Even from the brief time Will had spent with Sally, he could tell that *what made for a comfortable home* was probably only one item on a very long list of things she and Dr. Abraham had different ideas about. The truth was, Will couldn't imagine how they'd gotten together in the first place. And that was the hell of it, wasn't it? People did all kinds of wild shit for love, and this was only one of the bad ways it could turn out: getting divorced and then trying to initiate an awkward conversation with a colleague about your ex-wife's adopted kittens and your disparate household management preferences.

Rash, reckless, selfish, he thought, with renewed conviction. Enough of counting days, of staring blankly at scribbled notes and computer screens, enough of thinking about Nora's skin and her smell. He didn't *want* mess like this; he never had. Up ahead, the exit doors promised a colorful sunset, and that was a time of day he ought to celebrate, because it didn't make him think of Nora at all.

"Would it be odd, do you think," Abraham said, which is right about when Will realized he hadn't ever responded. "If I also gave her one?"

Will stopped in front of the exit doors, turned and blinked down at Abraham, breaking the long-unspoken eye contact rules. "If you… gave her a kitten?"

Abraham smoothed his lapel. "Yes. As a gesture."

A gesture of what, Abraham didn't say, but despite the *sock history /hamster???* brain sluggishness, Will had enough of his

149

wits about this to see it for what it was. Gerald Abraham was trying to reconcile with his ex-wife, and wanted Will's advice. Truly a reckless move. What did Will know about reconciliation? He'd never tried such a thing in his life, because it'd never been necessary. You never needed to have a breakup if you never let things go beyond a night or two, if you only shared those nights with people who also weren't looking for anything more.

Still, that lapel-smoothing. It got right in there, up against that cracked glass in Will's chest. He took a breath and thought about Quincy and Francis, who were in fact enjoyable to look at on a phone screen but a lot of work outside of that.

"Two is enough," he said, and Abraham nodded gravely, looking toward the doors Will was about to go out.

"You could maybe get her something from a pet store," he added. "Supplies. A gift card."

"I often bought her gift cards. During our marriage."

Will winced. "Don't do that, then."

A memory of two weeks, two days ago came back to him, something he'd said to Nora in the dark, confessional solace of her bedroom: *I'm not even sure I ever learned how to be a good friend.* Definitely he and Gerald Abraham weren't friends, and definitely Will would never be finding himself in this particular situation—broken up, lonely enough to be coming up with cat-purchasing schemes, looking for advice from the nearest person you knew the name of.

But that didn't mean he couldn't offer *something*.

"You ought to go see her," he said, putting his hand on the door handle. He'd help, but then he had to get the hell out of here. This was uncomfortable enough that he thought he might be blushing. "If you—if pets weren't your thing, I mean. Going to see hers, that would be a nice gesture."

Abraham tucked his hands in the pockets of his white coat, and Will wondered if he was going to get out his notebook and write this down. Maybe he would, once Will left, but for now he simply looked at Will, gave him a curt nod, and said, "Very good," as though Will had offered up a satisfactory diagnosis and treatment plan. He added a brief, "Enjoy your evening," and then turned and walked away.

Will shook his head, pushing out the door. In spite of himself, he felt a smile tug at his lips, thinking about Gerald Abraham getting climbed all over by Quincy and Francis. A rogue urination and follow-up face scream wouldn't be the worst thing. But as he stepped into the evening air, the smile faded. *You ought to go see her*, his rash, reckless, cracked-glass heart told him, and he was so *tired* of it. Tired of wanting what he shouldn't want. Tired of missing what he shouldn't miss.

Tired enough that when he looked up, he thought he might be dreaming.

Because that was Nora Clarke, standing there waiting for him.

—

"I was pretty sure I missed you."

It was the first thing she said to him once he'd crossed the parking lot to get to where she stood, her cheeks flushed pink and her hair in that loose braid he liked, the one that made his forearm prickle in remembered awareness. She said it with the kind of frazzled, slightly out-of-breath frustration of a person who'd been dealing with traffic for a while, but he heard it all wrong, of course, and for long seconds all he could think was, *I'm sure I missed you.*

"I remembered you said you sometimes worked six to six," she rushed out, obviously discomfited by the long silence, "And so I took a chance on showing up a little after that, but then… the truth is, I got lost! I've never come down to this side of the city, and"—she broke off, shook her head—"it doesn't matter. I figured I'd missed you, being so late getting here and all, but then I called and got transferred to a nurse who said you'd left a few minutes ago, and anyway that's why I'm here! I wasn't, uh. It's not like I've been standing out here for a long time or anything."

For the first time, he noticed she was holding something— a thin, square package that seemed to be wrapped in quilting material. She thrust it forward, holding it out to him, her face turning even pinker. "This is still warm, see?"

He looked down at it, shifting to tuck his bike helmet under his arm so he could take it from her. But as soon as he moved, she pulled it back toward her stomach. "Oh! I can hold it! I didn't… if you ride a bike, you won't be able to—"

"Nora," he said, because he knew this about her now. That if he said her name this way, she would slow down. She would look up at him.

When she finally did—her lips pressing together, her flush deepening—he could not help his smile.

"You look like you feel better," he said, which was an under-statement. She looked like the best thing he'd ever seen. Fresh and pretty and painted with the pink-orange light of the setting sun. *How* had he not gone to see her? That was the real question.

"You left me all the food that was in your freezer," she blurted, and that quick, everything between them shifted. Now it was his turn to flush, her turn to smile teasingly— knowingly—at him.

"You told Benny to send me text message reminders for when to take my medicine."

Benny, Will thought, dropping his eyes to the concrete. *A traitor, through and through*. Still, Will wondered if he'd been able to get that starter wort going.

"You told Marian I shouldn't go out for three days, and she basically set up a security checkpoint."

Marian! Dammit. Though the security checkpoint, that was a good idea. He knew he could count on her. He hoped at least Mrs. Salas had been more dis—

"Mrs. Salas made me mantecaditos."

Will suppressed a sigh. He hadn't *told* Mrs. Salas to make the cookies. He'd maybe mentioned, when he was bringing up the food he hadn't eaten from his freezer, that he didn't have any of them left. Mrs. Salas was the one who'd insisted.

"And I can only assume you asked Jonah to put his air purifier in the hallway for a few days."

He cleared his throat. "I... no."

That had been the worst, asking for a favor from Jonah. Even after the ball game they'd watched together, Jonah still looked at Will through narrowed eyes. He still called Will "Beanpole," even when Will was giving him doctor's orders.

"No?" Nora said.

He scraped the toe of his shoe against the concrete.

"Fine, yes."

He didn't need to look up to know she was smiling even bigger now.

"Neighborly of you," she said, and he couldn't just *hear* the grin in her voice. It was like he could feel it, like she had her mouth pressed right against his chest.

It wasn't neighborly of me, he wanted to say. *It was something else of me.* Not rash, not reckless, not selfish. But not neighborly, either.

"It was nothing," he said, finally working up the courage to look at her again.

She rolled her eyes, flicked her braid over her shoulder. "I brought a thank-you gift. It's only one serving, because I didn't want it to seem like a threat."

He breathed out a laugh. "Is it more of those cheesy bacon potatoes?"

Her face fell. "Oh. No. This is something I made."

His eyes dropped to the package again. He had no guesses as to what could be in there, didn't even really know if Nora was any kind of cook, but suddenly he felt hungrier than he had all day.

Than he had in two weeks, two days.

"I didn't really like those potatoes," which was half a lie. He liked them fine, when there weren't ten pounds of them. He just wanted to know what Nora had made him.

"It's manicotti. Homemade sauce. My nonna—"

He held out his hand, beckoned for the dish. "Lemme try it," he said impatiently.

She clutched it tighter. "You can't eat in a *parking lot*."

He furrowed his brow. He'd eaten a lot of food in this parking lot. Last night when he'd gotten off his shift he'd shoved an entire hunk of stale corn bread from the cafeteria into his mouth before unlocking his bike. He was still chewing when he'd pedaled away. He hadn't even tasted it.

"This is my best dish. You can't disrespect it like that! This is a tablecloth kind of meal."

She had this look in her eyes, one he recognized—the *what a nice houseplant, here's a laurel wreath, I found you some kittens* look. Part mischief, part triumph. He'd missed that look. If he had a lapel, he'd probably be smoothing it.

"Is that right?" he said, then shrugged. "I don't have a table-cloth."

She traced the tip of her finger over the loopy, colorful fabric of the package, and that—that was even more dangerous than the grin. He felt that finger's path in the kind of way that was going to make for a very uncomfortable bike ride home, unless he got control over himself.

She blew out a gusty, exaggerated sigh. "Well I don't know what to tell you then," she said. "It's a shame you won't be able to en—"

"I've got an idea," he interrupted, and she practically *beamed* at him.

Rash, reckless, selfish, that stubborn voice said to him, but he was so hungry—for her food, for that smile, for *her*—that at the moment, he couldn't make himself care. And anyway, it's not like his idea was to take her back to the building. This was different; this was separate.

This was safe.

"Let's go," he said.

In a pinch, the jacket he had stuffed in his backpack made for a fine tablecloth.

It wasn't the first time he'd had an impromptu sort of picnic in this spot, one of his favorites in the city—a stretch of beach that only took him about twenty-five minutes to get to on his bike, a route along Lakefront Trail that made for a good workout. Every once in a while, he'd stop here, sweaty and pleasantly out of breath from his ride, lock up his bike, and walk to one of the expanses of smooth, tiered concrete. He'd sit and unwrap some half-smashed sandwich he'd forgotten to eat during the day, staring out at a spot on the horizon and letting his mind empty and his belly fill before riding the rest of the way home.

But with Nora here, everything felt different.

In the first place, there was no need to lock up his bike—it was stowed away in the back of Nora's car, the front wheel off to make it fit. In the second, Nora had no use for tiered concrete, not when she saw the open stretches of pale sand, warm from a day beneath the bright sun. And in the third, Nora—the maker of the best meal Will had ever tasted, sauce like a religious experience—liked to look at *everything*. The whole expanse of water, the city skyline, the boat slips, the sparse pockets of people gathered in different spots along the beach.

And because Will liked to look at Nora, he saw it all anew.

In between bites of food, that is.

"You really only brought one serving?" he said morosely, once he'd finished his last bite. The glass dish in his lap still had sauce in the bottom, and he was waging a desperate battle with himself not to stick his face into it like a dog.

She shrugged, smiling over at him. "It's like I said. I didn't want it to seem like a threat."

He pointed at the dish. "You can threaten me all you want, if you bring me more of this."

This teasing about their shared history—the little sabotages of the last several weeks—it was the closest they'd gotten to the subject of the building since they'd arrived, like a bruise they were both avoiding, save this occasional, soft-touch reminder that it was still there. He knew it couldn't last; he knew there was some reason beyond a single dish of food that she'd come all the way here.

He even had a good guess what it was.

But right now, his stubborn, sated brain wouldn't give over to thinking about it. Instead, he watched her wave her hand, saw her make a small noise of self-deprecating dismissal while the flush in her cheeks deepened. His mind prodded him with one compliment after another. *You look pretty in this light. I could listen to you talk about making sauce all night. Your voice carries like a song out here.*

He picked up the lid for the container, pressed it back on with more vigor than was necessary. *Quiet,* he thought, as if he was lidding his own brain. Once he had it on, he set it down and shifted to mimic her posture—facing the water, knees up, elbows resting on top of them. Between them, the jacket-tablecloth had wrinkled up, a dozing chaperone.

He was trying to concentrate on being responsible, practical, when Nora's laugh broke the silence—a bright, lilting thing, the grown-up version of the laugh he'd heard all those years ago. It was hard to feel responsible in the face of that.

He looked over, glad he wasn't two floors beneath her. "What?"

She was still looking toward the water, big smile broadcast in its direction. "It's… this is so *neat*, that there's this whole beach here!"

He smiled, shaking his head. Sometimes, when he was around Nora, he could sense—even though he'd never met her—the way her grandmother must have shaped her. She said words like *neat* with total sincerity. When someone cut her off in traffic on the way here, her only exclamation had been a quiet, surprised "Well!" The night he stayed with her, he noticed all kinds of funny contradictions about her space—the sleek, top-of-the-line laptop set beside an old corded phone on the heavy, ornate console table in her living room. The complicated chrome coffee machine sitting in crowded formation on the countertop next to an almond-colored toaster oven that looked like it'd seen better days. Her fluffy, bright white comforter and pillows, and the flat, frayed quilt that she had folded over an old rocking chair in the corner of her bedroom.

"Wait," he said, a thought striking him. "Have you... never been to the beach here? In Chicago?"

She looked down at her knees, gently digging her heels into the sand, her bare toes wriggling with the effort. "I haven't. I'm sure that sounds silly."

"It doesn't," he said, but also, it sort of did. He didn't get here as often as he should, but to his mind, the whole world slept on Chicago beaches. They thought of the city and pictured that shiny silver bean or the Sears Tower or the sign outside of Wrigley Field, maybe the fussy, lit-up Ferris wheel on Navy Pier. But Chicago beaches, they were something else. All through the winter they'd punish you with possibility— gray-beige and iced-over and unwelcoming, and then a sunny day would come and the water would look unreal, blue like you were in the tropics even as the wind was cold enough to make your eyes water, your tears freeze. You felt like the whole world opened up when it turned warm again and you could see it up close.

"Nonna didn't drive much, not even when I was younger. She stuck close to what she knew, and I stuck close to her."

"Too bad," he said. "It would've been fun to come, as a kid."

He'd grown up landlocked, had learned to swim in the rectangular chlorinated pools of the Indiana suburbs. If he'd been a kid in this city, he would've wanted to go to the beach all the time, and it's not like his parents would've stopped him. He had a rash, reckless thought: *If Donny had taken me. If Donny had taken me, I would have brought Nora here. Every summer she came, I would have.*

I would have counted the days.

He was going to need a bigger brain lid, with those kinds of thoughts.

"I've been thinking about the apartment," she said.

So, she'd brought her own lid, then. He looked away from her, out to some spot on the horizon. They were getting to it, then, her real reason for coming all this way. He hated how disappointed he felt, having his suspicions about it confirmed. He'd been having such a nice time.

"I haven't changed my mind," he said, and hoped the breeze off the lake softened his tone. He felt hard all over, frustrated more with himself than with her. He should've finished this in the parking lot. Now sunset was going to be all fucked up for him, too.

"I was waiting until—"

"Until I wasn't sick anymore," she finished for him. "I know."

He dropped his eyes to his hands, embarrassed again. He hadn't told any of the neighbors—when he was making his rounds—that he planned to wait. He hadn't even really known himself, not until he'd gotten back to his own place. He'd sat on his couch and pulled his computer onto his lap and thought about what he'd said to Nora. He'd thought about her puffy eyes and quivering chin, the soft, stuffy snore that had lulled him into an unplanned sleep in her bed.

Give her a couple of weeks, he'd told himself, pushing the computer aside again. *You can list it in a couple of weeks.*

But it was more than a couple of weeks now. He'd left it too long, and look what had happened. She'd shown up with a great meal and a gleam in her eyes, because he'd given her some kind of false hope about his plans. *Reckless*, he thought. He needed to get it up on the site tomorrow, first thing. Tonight, maybe, if he could get his head on straight.

"That was nice of you," she said. "Not necessary, but nice."

Wait—*not necessary?* His brow lowered. Maybe she hadn't gotten her hopes up, or maybe—

"I actually meant my apartment," she said.

He turned to look at her, could feel the surprise that was surely registering on his face. "Your apartment?" he repeated, confused.

She nodded, her eyes still out on the water, and he watched her chest lift on a deep inhale. He couldn't quite see her eyes, but he had a feeling.

He had a feeling she was about to say something rash.

"I want to make mine like yours."

Chapter 11

So, she'd said it.

Will was quiet beside her, and at first she was grateful. It meant that she could spend the first few seconds following her confession—was it too much to call it a confession?—with her eyes ahead, out on the sunset waters of this place she'd never seen, letting the feeling of her words wash over her. She hadn't *quite* planned to say them, or at least she hadn't fully decided yet, but now that she had—

"You want to rent your unit?" he broke in.

"What!" Nora exclaimed, snapping her head toward him so quickly that she nearly lost her balance. She shifted, turning to face him. "Not *rent* it!"

He looked at her from behind his glasses (of course he was wearing his glasses; that's probably why she'd made the confession! There was no telling the power of those spectacles), the dark mass of his hair blowing gently across his forehead. He looked like he could be in a calendar—twelve months of men looking terrific by a lake—but also the expression on his face suggested he thought Nora could be in a monthly calendar featuring people who made absolutely no sense.

"*Not* rent it?" he repeated.

"No!" She lowered her voice from outrage volume, then narrowed her eyes at him. "And don't call it a unit."

He pressed his lips together in a way she recognized, holding up his hands in mock surrender. Silence fell between them again, and she could tell he was waiting for her to explain herself. But even the suggestion, the misunderstanding—that she would *ever* rent Nonna's apartment!—was so rattling to her that she barely knew how to start again.

"Want to walk a bit?" he said after a minute, tipping his chin up toward the shoreline.

She nodded, grateful for the suggestion, and they both stood—Nora brushing her sand-coated palms across the front of her jeans, Will shaking out his jacket. She was still thinking over what to say when they reached the shoreline, a cool wind blowing off the water that had her crossing her arms over her chest.

"Here," Will said, and settled his jacket over her shoulders.

And like that—with that warm and perfect weight enveloping her, Will's scent close and soothing—something inside her eased, shook free. It felt like that night two weeks ago, in her bed: the golden-hour perfection of those first few minutes of conversation they'd had, before things had turned so fraught and sad.

Before he'd gone, and before she'd got to thinking.

"Mostly it's about the towel rod," she blurted, which was maybe not that ideal thought to have shake free first. Then again, maybe it was. The towel rod was simple, specific. A change, but nothing drastic. Nonna, she was sure, would support it.

"The... what?"

She cleared her throat, reaching up to gather Will's jacket tighter around her. There, that was better. "The towel rod that you put in your bathroom?"

"Yeah, I remember. But why—?"

"I want one of those. It'd be nice to have one, so I'm going to put one in."

Even to her own ears, it sounded overly sharp, full of the same strained, nervous conviction she'd needed to get herself to come here today. *You're going to put the address into your phone*, she'd told herself. *You're going to drive there*, without *getting lost, and you're going to say thank you*.

He stopped, and after a step she did, too, turning back to face him. When they'd gotten here, the light was a bright, stunning pink-orange, but now it was nearly dark, the planes of Will's face lit by the harbor lights in the distance.

"Is this really about the towel rod?" he asked, with his doubtful doctor face on.

It's about you, she thought, blinking down at the sand, at the soft lapping of the water that stopped short of her feet. *It's about what you told me, and how it made me see things differently. Donny's apartment, Nonna's apartment.*

Instead, she shrugged and said, "It's about settling in, I guess. I've lived there for a while now, and I've been so busy. I think I'm starting to notice that there's a few things I could do to make things more—"

Mine, her brain supplied automatically, but it felt wrong to say it. Disloyal.

"Convenient," she finished.

He tucked his hands into his pockets, his brow furrowing. They stared at each other across the stretch of sand and she knew he could tell she wasn't telling him the full story. But the full story—the story of how she'd spent the last two weeks—felt too complicated, too tentative. Nora wasn't even sure she understood it herself, really. All she knew was that after Will had gone, she'd waited, caught between some strange feeling of anxiety and anticipation, for someone new to show up downstairs. And when it'd been clear that no one was coming yet—that Will's quiet efforts at caretaking via her neighbors had extended to his delay with listing Donny's apartment—she'd almost felt... well.

She'd almost felt disappointed.

It wasn't really that she'd come around to the idea; in fact, breaking the news to her neighbors—in a lousy, impromptu backyard building meeting during which she was still battling her sinuses—had been stressful enough to make her consider bricking over all of Donny's doors and windows in the hopes that by some miracle everyone would forget it had ever existed.

But beneath all that knee-jerk resistance had been something else, too. She *understood* something about Will now, about how he related to Donny's apartment, to the building. And losing the battle over the rental—or maybe accepting that she'd lost it to a worthy enemy, for good reasons—had made her think differently about herself and how she related to Nonna's apartment. If the rental was going forward, she needed to find some way to stay true to Nonna and to her neighbors that didn't involve keeping every single thing exactly the same. She needed to take control of this new normal.

And maybe, *maybe*, the right place to start was in the apartment.

Minor changes. Adding a towel rod, and… that sort of thing.

"I could help," he said.

At some point, she must've dropped her eyes from his, because now she had to raise her head to look back at him. His posture was exactly the same, but the expression on his face had eased into something more practiced, more casual, and for some reason, it soothed her. That's how she wanted this to be. A towel rod! Very casual. No real disruptions there.

"You're probably too busy." Even as she said it, she hoped he'd put up a fight. Sure, she could make measurements and operate a drill—uh, once she bought one—but for some reason, no matter how nondisruptive a towel rod was, she didn't quite feel up to doing it alone.

"Won't take but a minute. I've done it once recently." He added a small, crooked smile. Probably that would've looked like a smirk to her, only a few weeks ago. But now it looked like the most gentle, welcome encouragement. "I'll have to be coming by anyway. I need to put a lockbox on the uni—um. Apartment."

"Right." She shifted on her feet, newly uneasy. Would her neighbors think of it as a betrayal, Will coming in and out of her apartment? Their reaction to the news of the rental going forward hadn't been as extreme as she'd anticipated, but still— their memory of Donny was unchanged, this plan of Will's seemingly as disrespectful as it was disruptive. To them, she and Will were still on different sides of this thing.

But like always, he seemed to see right through her.

"We can keep it between us," he said. "It's not as if we both don't keep weird hours."

She couldn't help her smile, the flutter of excitement in her stomach. "That's true."

"One condition," he said, and the flutter faded. If he asked her for some favor about his rental, she—

"You gotta let me have more of that sauce."

She narrowed her eyes, pursed her lips in feigned, joking contemplation. *He's coming back*, she thought, inwardly thrilled, and eventually—right when she thought he might be starting to sweat it—she let her smile break free once again.

She held out her hand. An agreement, not a farewell. Her palm tingled in anticipation.

"Okay, Will," she said. "You've got a deal."

Nora had always thought of herself as a patient person.

The art of waiting had been instilled in her early, and unlike most of the qualities she considered to be her best, she could mostly credit this one to her parents. In practical terms, honing this skill had been an essential part of her childhood days: waiting quietly outside her mom's or dad's office on campus after school, eavesdropping on the excited or concerned conversations they'd have with their research students. Waiting at the kitchen table, where she did her homework each night, for one of her parents to put together or bring home dinner, at least until she got old enough to handle the occasional dinner for herself. Waiting for her mom to have a few free afternoons to teach Nora how to drive when she got her learner's permit; waiting for her dad to read over her college application essays.

But in philosophical terms, too, waiting had been an important part of her parents' ethic. Their projects took a long time; they sometimes took years to get access to important dig sites, or to make a breakthrough on even the smallest, most banal part of a research argument. As a result, they seemed almost preternaturally calm about delays of any kind. They treated waiting like it was opportunity, like it wasn't really waiting at all. When Nora was eight, she'd gone with her dad to a meeting he had with a colleague at UC Riverside, and on the way back they'd gotten caught in a twelve-mile-long traffic backup. Outside her window, Nora could see drivers on every side getting frustrated—slapping at their steering wheels, rolling their eyes, craning their necks to try to see what was up ahead. But Nora's dad had barely been bothered. He'd put the old Volvo in park and said, "Well, we'll get there eventually." For two hours he'd helped Nora practice her spelling, picking out words he chose at random from the sonorous sentences of whatever NPR program was on.

To this day, Nora was a really good speller.

But her patience?

It was starting to wear thin.

It'd been three days since she'd shaken on their deal and set tonight as the date for Will to come by, and while she'd done fine for the first two—working and reworking the eco-influencer site into something she thought was finally bulletproof, having her regular lunch with Emily, driving Mrs. Salas to an appointment with the eye doctor—today had felt *interminable*.

Of course part of the problem had been that it started early—golden-hour early, because her body was trained for it. Out on her balcony, she'd watched the sky go from dark to light, already fairly twitching with awareness that the sun had a long way to go before it would set again. In her office, she'd readied herself for the remote presentation she'd be making later that afternoon, frustrated each time she bumped an elbow against something on her desk or accidentally backed her chair into the side of Nonna's old dresser. When her stomach had growled for lunch, she'd stood and stretched before she realized it was only 9:30 a.m. Second breakfast, then, *fine*, but she sure would've liked things to move faster.

By the time her presentation came around, she'd somewhat recovered her sense of being in the moment: she'd done good work, and she was looking forward to showing it off. But the meeting, too, had been filled with tedious, aimless questions from the client—questions that barely related to the site at all, and in the end, she hadn't even given her final approval for launch. Deepa had practically slammed her notebook shut; Austin had gone coolly silent, and Nora half considered bringing up the sustainable dildos, if only to get a conversation going.

If there'd been a bright spot, it'd been her post-meeting debrief with Dee, who had to retouch her brows after a rare moment of rubbing them in frustration when the client had brought up the bitmoji again. Dee fully expected to leave that conference room and get treated to Austin's bad mood for the rest of the afternoon, so Nora—with no small amount of remote-work survivor's guilt—did her best to fill her friend's time, even if it did mean she had to answer fourteen questions about what Will Sterling looked like.

When the workday was over, that's when the real waiting set in. She and Will had decided that he'd come by around 10:00 p.m., when her neighbors would almost certainly have turned in for the night, especially since the Cubs weren't playing, and that had seemed like an exciting, clandestine idea during their lakeside rendezvous. But getting up before dawn made 10:00 p.m. a dim prospect on normal days, and so Nora had to fill her remaining waiting hours with keeping herself awake: a strong coffee; a shower; at one particularly low point, a few light slaps on her cheeks as she stood in front of the bathroom mirror.

Come on, she told herself, or told the setting sun, or possibly told the yet-to-arrive Will. Dimly she was aware that nothing about her impatience suggested a casual engagement with their planned project. But as the sky turned dark again, as the building quieted and the clock ticked down the minutes, she accepted the excitement that coursed through her body as her due.

It felt good to be excited.

At 9:59, there was a soft knock at the door, and the secret-keeping nature of their meeting meant that Nora didn't even have to stall before answering. She opened the door and hoped the waiting didn't show all over her face, and Will Sterling stood there in his glasses, one hand holding a toolbox and the other holding two bags from the hardware store, and he looked so easy and unbothered that for a second she had the sinking feeling he hadn't been waiting at all.

Still, she smiled (unbothered!) in greeting, stepping back so he could come inside. He set down his stuff and then held up a finger and retreated into the hallway again. When he came back, he was bearing the biggest towel rod Nora had ever seen.

"Uh," she said, once she'd closed the door behind him. "That—"

"It's for a shower curtain," he clarified immediately, setting it onto the floor. "Like the one I put in downstairs. It's got this curve to it, see, so when you're in the shower it feels bigger in there. It matches the towel rod I picked up, and they're pretty much right next to each other in the aisle, and..."

He carried on, something about his friend Sally's advice, and also a sale at the hardware store, and the returns policy if Nora didn't need anything new when it came to the shower curtain situation, and as he talked Nora realized, with a delighted sense of relief, that he *had* been waiting. Maybe as much as she had been.

Suddenly that shower curtain rod looked like the best thing she'd ever seen.

"Will," she interrupted. He looked up at her, and maybe she was imagining the faint touch of color high on his cheeks, but she liked it all the same. "That was a good idea, thanks. You'll let me know how much I owe you?"

He waved a hand. "We can figure that out after."

"Okay."

So this was it, the thing she'd been waiting for. Three days, or maybe—probably—even longer. Minor changes, and now she had the supplies. She had the will, and she had... well.

She had Will.

It was time to do this.

"Let's get to work."

–

"My God, you were right! It feels *huge* in here!"

In her bare feet, Nora stood inside her shower, curtain pulled closed, and admired the view. Above her hung her newly installed rod, sitting slightly higher than the previous one and bowing gently outward. She couldn't quite account for how such a small change could make such a big difference, but it really, really did. She turned to the side, mimicking her hair-washing posture, exaggeratedly sticking out her elbows as she raised her hands to her head.

"I'm not even *touching* the curtain!" she exclaimed.

From the other side, she heard Will's soft laugh, the clink of a tool being set down, and for a second, she relished this small moment of something like privacy. In all the time she'd been waiting these past three days, she hadn't really given much thought to what it would be like to work with Will in a space as small as her bathroom, but over the last hour and a half or so she'd gotten a *real* clear sense, and the fact was, Will's body was... *effective*. Effective at doing things like holding tools and fixtures, yes. But also effective at looking fantastic while doing such things. Thirty minutes ago, Nora had stood on the edge of this shower with a drill in her hand (Will was also effective at power-tool-use instruction, and at letting Nora do things herself), her partner-in-home-improvement holding up the rod that was destined to change her shower experience forever. One stray glance and Nora had caught sight of the narrow strip of skin exposed at his waist—the curve of his lean, strong hips, the line of dark hair above the button of his jeans.

She'd almost fallen right into the tub.

"Whoa, there," Will had said, dropping one arm to steady her. So, another point for his hands in the *effective* column, especially since she was pretty sure she could still feel the spot on her waist where he'd touched her.

She lowered her arms, taking the occasion to use her own decidedly less effective hands to fan her face. She needed to look normal when she reopened this shower curtain, and not like a woman who was wondering about what it would be like to fit a (specific) man into this newly expanded space.

But also, in here, would he be able to—?

"You ever coming out?" he said.

"I might stay in here," she said, relieved to sound like she was joking, and not like she was halfway to a full set of deeply inappropriate fantasies. "There's so much new ground to explore!"

Another chuckle, some more tool clinking, and Nora took a few deep breaths before finally settling herself enough to face him. She pulled back the curtain, smiling broadly (innocently!).

He straightened from where he'd bent to close the lid of his toolbox. "Happy?" he asked tipping his chin up toward the rod.

He asked it lightly, casually. But she knew Will better now— not only from the time she'd spent with him over the last couple of hours, but from the weeks she'd watched him and talked to him while they'd been feuding—and she had the sense that things weren't always what they seemed, even when they seemed effortless. During their first project—the hand-towel fixture—Nora had had a brief but embarrassing moment of pause, and Will had done his best to act entirely unfazed.

"I don't know why this feels so weird, to do this," she'd said, Will's drill resting heavily on her thigh. "It's like... this wall has always looked *exactly* the same."

"We don't have to," Will had said, shrugging. "You've still got that thing over on your counter."

Nora had looked over at the cord-tangling, toe-crushing towel rack and had taken a deep breath. "Nope," she'd muttered, and held up the drill. But after that, she could tell Will had been cautious, almost as if he worried that she'd blame him if she ended up regretting any of the changes.

"Still good?" he'd ask, every time they entered some new phase of it. He wouldn't even look at her as he said it; he'd ask it like it was all part of the checklist. But behind it was something serious, something focused.

Something kind.

Now, Nora stepped over the lip of the shower, determined to alleviate any of his concern over their shared project. She reached out and grabbed the old towel rack from the counter. "I'm thrilled," she said, holding it up. "Thrilled enough to send this thing to the garbage."

Probably she wouldn't actually send it to the garbage; Nonna would hate that. But she didn't want to say so to Will. She set it gently down on the floor between the vanity and the toilet, promising herself that she'd deal with it later. Surely someone else had need for a deeply annoying, vaguely threatening household accessory.

When she looked back up, Will's glasses caught the light from overhead, and she couldn't help but laugh at the lenses.

"What?"

"You've got... uh." She pointed in the direction of her own eyes, and Will furrowed his brow, then turned toward the mirror, leaning in.

"Oh, Jesus," he said, and she liked the laugh that came out— part amusement, part embarrassment. "It's drywall dust. Let me clean them off real quick."

When he pulled them away from his face, Nora could see— small bathroom, striking again!—the pink indentations left on either side of his nose, and for some reason that felt so tender and so tempting that she moved quietly past him, stepping into the hall, conscious of her every breath as she went.

After a few seconds he came to the doorway, leaning against the jamb with his freshly cleaned glasses back on, his hands tucked into the pockets of his jeans. Behind him, the leavings of their work—his toolbox, discarded packages and tags—sat tidily, ready to be taken out, and she felt absurdly disappointed that the night was almost over.

Will cleared his throat.

"So," he said, something tentative in his voice. She hoped he felt the same disappointment, but then she remembered their conversation from back when he'd first arrived.

She slapped a hand to her forehead. "Right, jeez. Let me get the money I owe you."

"No, no," he said quickly. "I mean, I didn't mean that. I wanted to mention…" He trailed off, dropped his eyes. "You know, never mind. I could send you an email. It's official building business."

Ah, Nora thought, bracing instinctively for the shudder of anxiety she was used to feeling when they talked about the rental.

It still came, but it wasn't nearly as… shuddery. Anxious-y.

"You listed your place?" she guessed.

"Yeah. The day after we went to the beach. But it's actually—" He broke off, cleared his throat again.

She smiled across the short space of hallway, encouraging. "Might as well tell me now. I'm in such a great mood about blow-drying my hair later that I can take it."

He smiled back, and a different sort of shudder tried to take up residence in her body.

But after a second, he turned serious again.

"I didn't expect to get so much interest so quickly, but… uh. I've got someone booked starting Tuesday."

Tuesday. That was so soon. She swallowed, nodded. Did not make eye contact with either of those new bathroom rods.

"She'll be staying for about four and a half weeks. I know the real short-term stuff isn't the best thing. For everyone here,

I mean. So I'm going to try to keep it to longer-term renters, as best I can."

She blinked up at him, grateful for this concession. She hoped it wasn't four and a half weeks of a total nightmare, but it *had* been good of him to consider everyone.

"The woman who'll be staying, she and her daughter—the daughter's about ten, I think—they need a place to stay while their condo gets some big repairs done. She's been a homeowner for about fifteen years, so she'll be responsible. She owns her own business, too. Consulting work, I'm pretty sure."

Nora cocked her head, confused. She'd been on the rental site an awful lot since Will Sterling had shown up in her life, and she knew for a fact that owners didn't have to bother getting a bunch of information about their tenants before finalizing an arrangement. That was pretty much the whole point for property owners, so far as she could tell: to collect their money, without much inconvenience or involvement.

Had Will... *interviewed* people?

"After her, I think it's possible I can get people who are doing rotations over at Northwestern. It wouldn't be the most convenient location, but as it turns out, Sally knows the placement coordinator there, and she said she'd direct people my way. And those people, they work so much it's likely you won't ever see them. They probably won't even care if you do that projector thing using the balcony down there."

She raised her eyebrows. "How did you—"

"Jonah told me about it. At poetry night."

I believe everything you say about this place, she remembered him saying, that night in her bedroom, and back then, she didn't know if she really, truly believed it. She believed Will when he said he was practical, responsible. She believed him when he said this building meant something different to him, something painful and permanently scarring.

But she hadn't really believed that he was capable of seeing it her way, too. She hadn't really known that he'd been watching and listening so well. It made her feel warm and soft all over.

"Thank you," she said. "For doing that for us."

He looked down, and she thought he might've shaken his head, but the movement was so slight, she couldn't be sure.

"I did it for you," he said, and her breath caught in her chest.

For long seconds, she couldn't speak—couldn't think of anything at all to say. She could only watch him, the memory of the first time she'd ever seen him coming back to her. That morning, it had been from above, outlined by the light from the apartment he never even wanted. She'd seen him like this: tall and lean, his body curved, his head bowed.

He'd looked so far away, so alone.

So untouchable.

She didn't even realize she'd taken a step forward until he raised his head, and she found herself only inches away, her own face tipped up to meet his gaze. He wasn't untouchable now: he was flesh and blood and right in front of her. But that—*oh*, that was too much, wasn't it? To touch him? That was so forward; that was no way to return a favor.

"Thank you," she said again, almost a whisper, and had he moved closer, too? Despite her first sight of him, she *had* been close to him before; she knew she had. She'd been in her *bed* with him before. He'd touched her in her *shower* before.

But this was nothing like any *before*. This was quiet and certain and perfect and *new*, everything new; her whole body felt new.

"Nora," he said, a whisper to match her own, and this, too, was novelty, unlike any time he'd said it in all the weeks she'd known him: not a scold or sympathy or a *slow down*, not anything other than the pure pleasure of saying it. It was the way you said your lover's name, the way you sometimes softly asserted the fact of their being there, of their being yours.

Mine, she thought, and this time, nothing felt wrong or disloyal about it. She thought about the small steps she'd taken tonight, fixing up this bathroom that had been exactly the same forever, and it was great; of course it was great. It was convenient and helpful for hair-washing and hair-drying and towel-hanging and whatever, but it wasn't making this place well and truly hers, not in the way that really mattered.

And at the moment, the only way that really mattered felt like it had something to do with the man right in front of her. A claim on this space that she would make entirely for herself.

She moved again. A small step that didn't feel small at all. She could see the pulse beat along the line of his throat, could see his chest rising and falling with his quickened breaths.

"Will," she said, something like a question, and felt it like an echo in her heart:

Will

Will

Will

And with barely a hesitation, he gave her his wordless answer. He bent his head, and set his mouth to hers.

Chapter 12

Oh, he would surely see hell for this.

But god, she felt like heaven.

Only her lips right now—soft, full, giving, perfect—but he knew deep down this one touch was temporary; he knew with heart-hiccupping intensity that he didn't want to stop there, that if she let him, he'd get his hands and mouth all over her. It felt good to fully acknowledge it, like loosening the cord in his body that had been coiling tighter and tighter since that night on the beach, since that morning on the balcony.

Since before, some voice in his head taunted, and he clenched his fists in his pockets. He didn't want to think about how far back this went, about how far forward it could go. He didn't want to spend tonight like he'd spent the past three days, half angry at himself for offering to come back to this place that he knew meant trouble for him, and half hopeful that once he did, this exact thing would happen.

So he silenced the voice, himself, everything, by sinking further into Nora, parting her lips with his own, and when she made a quiet noise of pleasure and slipped her tongue across his bottom lip, it wasn't like having the cord loosened.

It was like having it cut clean through.

He might've groaned in relief as he brought her closer—one hand at the curve of her waist, one tucked into the cool, smooth strands of the hair she still had up—and she came to him like she'd been waiting, putting her arms around him and pressing her whole body against his. All at once it was hunger and heat, Will's hands firm where they held her, Nora's fisting at the back of his T-shirt as she pushed up onto her toes, opening her mouth against his, her tongue sweet and seeking. She tasted like something—mint, maybe coffee, too, like first thing in the morning even though it was the dead of night, and he could not get enough of it, could not stop kissing her, could not get over the way she tasted him back.

When she used her teeth to tug at his lower lip he practically jolted away from the doorframe, had to clutch at her in desperate, frantic restraint—not to lift her up, not to press her against the wall, not to thrust against her. But in his haste he'd clutched at what was close, at what felt natural—that long rope of hair that was so easy to grip, that tipped her head back, and as soon as he did it she gasped, and then moaned, her hips rolling against him.

"*God*," she said, between kisses, her voice rougher and breathier than he'd ever heard it sound, and it felt like fitting a key to a lock, knowing this—that touching her this way made her move that way, *sound* that way, and so he left his hand where it was, gripping her hair a little tighter before he used it to tug her head back gently.

Another pulse of her hips as he bent his head to the line of her exposed throat, and he missed her lips but he wanted his mouth on this too. The lip that still tingled from her bite, he dragged it up the side of her neck and felt her body shudder, imagined her skin flushing beneath her clothes, her nipples pebbling beneath her bra. He paid her back in kind, nipping at her skin, soothing it with his tongue, and then he started all over on the other side. Her hands were in his hair, holding him to her, and it felt so good and perfect that he didn't care that his glasses were probably fogging up, worse and more embarrassing than having them coated in drywall dust. Up close like this it didn't matter anyway; he could see everything he wanted to see, could see her by touching her and tasting her like this, by hearing her whimper when he sucked gently at the soft patch of skin behind her ear.

"*Oh.*" Her exhalation rippled over his skin, and he got impossibly harder. Would she mind if he walked her back, if he pressed her against that wall, if he—

"This is so…" she began, trailing off when he moved his lips again, back to taste her mouth; it had been a while since he tasted her mouth.

"You're really good at this," she finished, when she had a second to speak again.

He didn't answer, couldn't think enough to answer. He bent his head again, using the hand that wasn't in her hair to tug at the hem of her shirt, tucking his lips against the newly exposed skin at the base of her throat, breathing her in.

"Like," she whispered, her breaths coming in quick, frustrated pants now, "*Really* good. Have you done this a lot? Kissing like this, I mean. It's—you are… have you done this a lot?"

He lifted his head again, capturing her mouth and kissing her hard, stalling for time while his poor, blood-deprived brain tried to catch up enough to process her question.

"I don't remember," he said, when he finally came up for air. He caught her answering laugh with his lips, but he wasn't really joking. At the moment he didn't remember any kiss he'd ever had before this one, certainly couldn't remember any kiss *like* this one. He couldn't remember ever being with a woman and feeling this focused and this frantic all at once: even as he noticed, in clear, crystalline detail, every single place where he touched Nora and where Nora touched him, his mind rushed ahead, blurry images of being above her, beneath her, however she wanted it, their clothes off and their bodies intertwined.

Something inside him seemed to strain, to twist, like the two loose ends of that cord were trying to find their way back to each other, trying to wrap their way around his chest and remind him of what he'd known about Nora all along: that he felt rash and reckless when he was around her, that she made him feel close to a part of himself he'd long kept hidden away.

How could it feel this *good*?

"Because," she said, and for a split second he wondered if he'd said it all aloud. But then she leaned in to him, mimicked him, dragged her mouth up the side of his neck, pulling herself up higher on his body as she went.

"Because I haven't," she whispered, when she got to his ear.

He stilled, both his hands coming to her waist, and for the first time since this started they separated, at least enough to keep their lips off each other.

"You haven't what?"

"Been with—been like this. With many people."

Don't think about other people, he thought, instinctively tightening his hold on her. *Not while you're with me.*

But almost immediately he loosened his fingers. It wasn't the right instinct, to be selfish like that, to be possessive like that. She was trying to tell him something, and he needed to keep his head together enough to listen.

"I've only slept with two men. Only ever kissed three."

"Okay," he said, even though he knew he would privately and thoroughly hate every one of them, forever. He still wasn't sure why it was any of his business. But if she thought he cared about this number, if she thought he'd care if it was twelve or twenty or two hundred or none at all, he needed to correct that impression.

"Nora, it doesn't—"

"What I mean is," she said, before he could finish, "it's never felt like this. To kiss. To—" She broke off and dragged her hands down his shoulders. His head tipped down to watch as they moved lower, over his chest, and when they stilled on his abdomen he wanted to finish the sentence for her. He wanted her to act it out.

Touch, touch, touch, he wanted to say.

But then he looked up and found her watching him, saw the question in her eyes. And he knew what she was asking; he knew that she wanted to know if it was the same for him. This was Nora, after all—careful, particular, protective. She would want to know. She would want to know if a man she was with like this was worthy of her feelings. If he returned her feelings.

Focus, Will, he told himself, putting his hands over hers, pressing her palms flat against him. *Touch*, those were the feelings she was talking about. Not backyards and balconies and whole entire hearts. She was talking about how it felt to touch him, how it felt to be touched by him. And that was good; that was perfect.

Touch, he could handle.

So he did what he'd been holding himself back from doing and walked her backward, steadying her as he went, until the wall behind her did his work for him. Beneath his hands her fingertips curled against the cotton of his shirt, tugging him closer, fitting their bodies together. He let her feel it, that aching hardness beneath his jeans, and when she gasped he answered her.

"For me, either," he said honestly, and he watched the relieved smile spread over her kiss-swollen lips. He lowered his mouth so he could speak this next part, this truest part, right against them. "This is a first."

Then they were kissing again, harder now that they'd agreed on this, and it was long minutes of roaming hands and tangling tongues before she spoke again.

"Stay tonight."

—

He would've stayed in the hallway, if that's the way she'd wanted it.

In fact they got halfway there—desperate, mismatched undressing, Nora pushing Will's shirt up while he shoved her pants down, Nora pulling at his belt while his hands smoothed beneath her top to get to the clasp of her bra. He had her legs wrapped around his hips before he even realized the impossibility of it, before he smiled against her mouth and tucked two teasing fingers beneath the waist of her underwear, tugging to remind her of their presence. She leaned her head against the wall with a soft thud, inhaling through her nose before she breathed out the word *bedroom*, in a voice laced with the same quiet sort of command she'd used to tell him to stay, and it made his body turn unexpectedly harder.

When she slid down his front and stepped away he had a brief, panicked moment of insecurity—that losing her touch would mean losing his focus, that the cut cord would reconnect and remind him why this was all a dangerous idea. But then she walked by him, her legs bare, the back of one thigh pink from where his hand had been holding her, and to him it might as well have been another command. That looked the same as having the words *follow me* whispered right into his ear. He'd never really thought of himself as a man who liked to be bossed around during sex, but damn if he didn't walk toward the cool, dark quiet of Nora's bedroom and want her to tell him every single thing she wanted him to do, exactly how she wanted him to do it.

And Nora—perfect, particular Nora—she gave him exactly what he craved.

As soon as he crossed the threshold she set her hands back on his chest, guiding him to the foot of her bed before pressing his shoulders down.

"Stay there," she said, smiling as she stepped out of reach of his grasping hands, all at once pulling her shirt and already-unhooked bra over her head. She stood, backlit by the light that spilled into the hallway from the bathroom, and he thought he'd never seen something as beautiful as that—every curve and angle of Nora's body shown to him, mostly in silhouette, with small, intimate details coming clearer as his eyes adjusted. When she hooked her thumbs at the sides of her underwear and pushed them down, he thought he might've stopped breathing, seeing the movement of her body while she bared herself to him. All those blurry images from before got sharper, more distinct: his tongue licking across the rosy tip of her nipple, his teeth set against the slope of her shoulder, his thumbs smoothing their way up the inside of her thighs.

"Not yet," she said, another whispered command, and only then did he realize he'd been reaching for her. He pulled his hands back, setting his palms flat on the bed and trying not to clutch too obviously at her comforter. But then she reached up and took down her hair, and he stopped trying; he took two whole fistfuls of her bedding as he watched it fall over her shoulders, her breasts, the full, straight length of it hitting right at the top of her rib cage.

"Nora," he said. "You're beautiful."

She stepped between the V of his thighs and reached up, gently pulling his glasses from his face, and when she moved to set them down on the dresser behind her, he made a demand of his own, catching at her hips roughly and stilling her. "Stay close," he said, low and serious, because it *felt* so serious.

He did not want to lose sight of her. Not even for a second.

She made quick work of coming back to him, setting her hands against the stubbled skin along his jaw before bending to kiss him, and the next thing he knew they were both on the bed, Nora's warm, soft skin running the length of him. It took all his concentration to let her explore first: her mouth on his neck, down the center of his chest, across his abdomen as she worked the button and zipper on his jeans. He could tell something about the way she moved over him, the way she straddled him, the way she touched and tasted him—it was an assertion, a claiming, the demands she was making as much about herself as they were about him.

I can give her that, he thought, clenching his jaw tightly as she took down his jeans and boxer briefs and socks all at once, as she climbed back over him, the damp heat between her legs pressed against one of his thighs. He breathed out his frantic impatience, his desperation to tug at her again, to set her where he wanted her. He breathed in his focus, and for the first time in his life it felt truly easy, truly natural to sharpen his attention.

It was easy because it was all for her.

To give her this, whatever she wanted. Whatever kept making this feel like a first for her.

She lifted his hands from where they rested in readiness on her waist, moving them up, giving him permission, and when he cupped her breasts in his palms she moaned, dropping her head back, and oh, *fuck*, when she did that, the ends of her hair grazed against his thigh, his knee, his shin—all places, apparently, that had a direct line to his balls. He levered himself up, his hands on her not enough, and set his mouth to work—soft kisses first, a teasing stroke of his tongue along the edge of her nipple, and when she rocked her hips and clutched at the back of his head he gave her more, sucking at one breast while groping the other roughly, moving his free hand to that fall of hair, giving her the tight, tense hold he already knew she liked.

He did it for so long that the movements of her hips got more rhythmic, more insistent, her breathing quick. A revelation, a first: somehow satisfying Nora with what amounted to a dry hump against his leg was already the best sex he'd ever had. *But if you could only—*

Once the thought intruded, it was so vivid he had to pull his mouth from her breast, to rest his damp forehead against the flushed skin of her chest. He was speaking before he could stop it, before he could regain his focus. "Nora," he whispered, a plea. "Let me taste it."

She made a small noise, part gasp, part grunt, and his thigh got wetter. If she came from this, he certainly wouldn't blame her, and he definitely wouldn't be far behind. She hadn't even touched his cock yet and he was *close*. Edge-of-a-cliff close. He breathed in, smelling her sex, his mouth fairly watering for it.

"Not yet," she said again, and then she moved off of him, crawling toward her nightstand and pulling out a still-sealed box of condoms.

"I want this first," she said, so bold and gorgeous, and thank God she let him take the box from her; thank God she let him rip it open and grit his teeth and put one on himself, because he wouldn't have survived her touch, not right that second. But what she *did* do was almost as arousing, her body easing onto its side, her elbow propping her up, her eyes on his hand, on the hardness between his legs. She watched him roll the condom on like she'd never paid attention to a man doing this particular task before.

When he was done he moved to lie beside her, waiting for her to tell him, to show him, what she wanted. Given what they'd been doing he half expected her to push him over, to straddle him so that they could pick up where they'd left off, but instead she gripped his shoulders and rolled onto her back, and he didn't know how it could be so perfectly done, how this first time they could line up like this—her legs spread beneath him, her sex rubbing so exactly *right* against his.

Focus, he told himself, bending to kiss her, to whisper against her mouth and ask if she was sure. She gave it to him three ways: her nod, her *yes*, her hand on his ass, guiding him toward her. But the second he pushed inside her—the barest inch—he had to drop his head to the mattress with a groan and reach back for her gripping hand. He would not last with her touch like that, urging him on, and he had to make this last, to make it so good for her. So he made another silent demand, catching up that hand first and then her other, intertwining their fingers and raising their pressed-together palms above her head.

"*Yes*," she said, before he could ask if it was okay. "Yes, like *that*."

So, like that. Like that he pushed all the way inside her, her clutching heat breath-stealing. Like that he gave his first, slow thrust, and he closed his eyes, wondering if he'd actually seen stars. Like that he knew he'd never felt anything close to this— Nora beneath him, breathing out her pleasure and rolling her hips to intensify it, her grasp around his fingers tightening as they found the perfect pace together, as he went deeper.

Like that he knew he would never be the same.

But he couldn't think of that now, not with Nora getting closer and closer. At some point, they'd lost their shared patience for keeping their hands out of it; when his focus came back, she had one on his back and one on his ass; he had one pressed flat on the bed and the other on the back of her thigh, holding her open for the thrusts that had gotten harder, more insistent. He bit the inside of his cheek, not making the demand he wanted, not telling her to come, but as it turned out he didn't need to, because Nora's hips sped up beneath him, her nails scratching perfectly against his back as she bit down on her lip to quiet her moaning cry.

Don't come, he commanded himself, wanting to see her all the way through it, wanting to feel fully every clutching pulse along his length. But it had been so long; he had waited so long to feel this with her, since the very—

"Will," she said, lifting her head to lick up the side of his neck, dewy with the sweat of his exertion, and that did it; that was all it took. He groaned and stilled above her, grateful for her arms around him, grateful for the way she held him tight as he came apart. It was better, more intense, more complete than seeing stars; it was like becoming them, cut-up pieces of him scattered to the night. He said her name, once and then again, because nothing else would come to him, no other thought or feeling available. No pressure, no practicality, no responsibility. Nothing but Nora.

A perfect, unforgettable first.

-

Well, he didn't see hell.

But he sure slept like the dead.

When he first woke, Nora was against him, not far from the spot she'd been in when she'd fallen asleep. Then, she'd tucked herself against his side, her head growing heavier against his shoulder and chest as she'd drifted off, the small muscles in her hands and feet occasionally twitching out whatever tension they'd held over the course of the day. Now, she'd shifted enough so that her head rested on his stomach, the smooth, straight strands of her hair draped across his bare chest, and without thinking he lifted a hand to them, stroking sleepily, barely conscious.

It wasn't so unusual for Will to sleep hard, not after years of chaotic hospital schedules, long stretches of time where he wasn't simply awake but also *urgently* awake, dealing-with-something-serious awake. A blank, consuming sleep after that wasn't so much a pleasure as it was a necessity, his body simply giving out on him and going pitch dark with fatigue. But this waking up... *this* was different. Hesitant, when it almost always felt like he sat straight up; fuzzy, when he nearly always had the day's schedule clear in his head. His eyes stayed closed and his mind stayed slow, not working through much of anything other than the soft tangles he found in Nora's hair.

In fact it might have been that he... drifted off again? That seemed almost unreal, impossible, but the next thing he was aware of was Nora stirring against him, her soft cheek moving across his abdomen, her lips pressing into his skin before she half settled again, making a sleepy, frustrated noise.

"What time?" she mumbled, and he kept his eyes closed, still dozing, his lips curving.

"Dunno," he said, or maybe just thought.

After a second her arm reached across him, her head coming up and her hair tickling across his skin. Well, one part of him was awake, at least. Nora slapped at the nightstand where she'd plugged in her phone last night, part of a routine—their one-after-the-other trips to the bathroom, their teasing arguments about which side of the bed he'd sleep on—that had felt, despite the first-time circumstances of it all, strangely normal.

When she lit up the screen he threw an arm over his eyes but then changed his mind when he realized he was missing an opportunity. He squinted one eye open, then the second, Nora's profile lit in white-blue light, her face scrunched and sleepy and still goddamned sexy. He moved his hand, traced a finger along her spine.

"Four fifty-seven," she said, setting the phone back down with a clatter before dropping her forehead to his skin. "Late."

"No," he protested lazily, stroking outward from her spine, running his fingertips up her side, over the curve formed by the side of her breast. "Early. Not even morning, really."

She made a funny, disbelieving half snort but then shuddered when he stroked her again. Pretty much it was only his hands and his dick that were fully online, but he could work with that. *She* could work with that, if she'd only—

"Let me—" She broke off when he got his finger close to her nipple, then sighed, dropping her head to kiss his stomach again. "Let me run to the bathroom first."

He laughed softly in satisfaction, knowing he had her, and when she slapped playfully at his chest as she climbed out of bed he caught her hand, pressing a kiss in the center of her palm. When she started to walk away he did a small, simple thing, a thing the sleepy part of his brain told him was most natural: he held on to her loosely, a move that was less about keeping her than it was about touching her right up until the last possible second, and she laughed, squeezing his fingers back before letting them trail lightly away from his.

But when she let go, he realized why it seemed so natural.

Where he'd seen it before.

That was what his dad used to do.

Every time his mom left the dinner table, or her spot beside him on the couch. Every time they were out, and she'd walk away from him, only ever for a minute or two. Even when he was sick, his most sick—in bed, in the hospital—he did it. Any time she left his side.

Oh, he was awake now.

He pushed himself up when Nora left the room, then blinked at the brightness cast his way when she flicked on the bathroom light. But as he heard the door creak shut, he was slowly sent into darkness again, a catch in his breath as he tried to shake off that brief, ill-timed trip to his own personal underworld. Waking up this way, that had been a mistake.

With Nora, he had to be more careful.

He swallowed, rubbing a hand across his chest and then reaching for his own phone beside Nora's. *4:59*, not that he needed to check again, but this time, with his brain back in the game, he could remember the practicalities. Last night, what they'd agreed to was sex; what they'd agreed on was that they were good together—for this, and in secret. But this morning, he had to remember: it would cause trouble for Nora, him being here too late. It would cause trouble for him, too—for the apartment down below, for the business he was basically running out of a place everyone else here called home.

For his heart.

Right, yeah—should he get up? No, that would be a coward's way out, getting up and getting himself dressed when he'd all but told her to come back to him. The least he could do was wait, and anyway, he ought to let this erection settle down before he even attempted pants. He rubbed his palms down his thighs, attempting some semblance of focus: later today he had a shift at the clinic; tomorrow he should probably deal with bills. The tenant that was coming on Tuesday, did he owe her an email? He ought to—

He heard the bathroom door opening, light sneaking into the room again, and he suddenly felt more sheepish than he might've if she'd found him already dressed. It was probably weirder to be sitting up like this, halfway to going, but not really committing to it.

"So," she said, a smile in her voice as she came into the room. "*Now* you think it's morning."

She came to stand in front of him, and when he raised his head, she surprised him, gently settling his glasses on his face. He swallowed, looking her over—a long, silky robe tied loosely at her waist, sheer where the soft light hit it. Nothing about him was settling down now.

"No," he lied, reaching out to catch at the delicate tie at her waist. Safe to hold on to that, at least.

"I'm sorry to say, I really think you'll have to go now," she teased, and he groaned, dropping his head to rest against her stomach. "What if Marian has her checkpoint set up?"

He laughed miserably. He *should* go. He knew he should; he'd *decided*. But for long seconds, he rested like that in silence, utterly stymied. He couldn't stay this morning; he knew all the reasons he had to be careful. But he didn't want last night's first to be the last, not yet.

And he didn't think Nora did, either.

He looked up, a delicious practicality hitting him. A reason to come back.

"Nora," he said, and she *hmm*ed? in response, her hand stroking softly, absently, through his hair. "When you were in your bathroom just now... did you happen to notice anything about your faucet?"

Her hand stilled in his hair, and then she took a step back. *Damn*, he thought, his stomach sinking.

But when he looked up at her, he was grateful she'd brought his glasses, grateful he could see the fullness of her expression: her hands on her hips, a look on her face that was deliberately, comically determined.

"As a matter of fact," she said, giving him that big, break-of-day smile. "I *did*."

Chapter 13

"So what you're saying is," Deepa said, her chin resting in one hand, a lipstick-printed glass of wine held loosely in the other, "you're trading your sexual favors for bathroom fixtures."

Nora laughed and blushed, taking a sip from her own glass and blinking away from the screen of her laptop, which she'd set up on a stack of cookbooks on her kitchen counter. It was the first time in almost two weeks she and Dee had been able to talk outside of work, and while Nora hadn't necessarily *planned* to get into what had been going on with Will these last couple weeks, she also knew that Dee could read her so well, even through a computer screen. This conversation had been a long time coming, and before Nora had even finished her practiced, prudent explanation of her arrangement with Will, Dee had shouted, "I *knew* it!" in laughing victory.

"You're making it sound awful," Nora finally said, setting down her wine and moving toward the stove, stirring gently at the sauce she had heating.

And it is the opposite of awful, she silently added, staring down at the pot and blinking away images that rose up before her with the steam: Will above and beneath her in her bed; Will on his knees in her shower; Will—her cheeks flamed at the thought of this one—behind her while her hands clutched at the counter of the bathroom sink. Everything so brand-new.

Four times, he'd come over: always late at night, always leaving before dawn, never once since that first time getting so close to breaking the boundary she was still keeping for this. So far, in addition to the towel and shower curtain rods, they'd put in new faucets for her sink and tub, and replaced the old, speckled-at-the-edges mirror that Nora was pretty sure was original to this place. *Look how clearly you can see yourself in this new one*, Will had said that night from behind her, moving her hair to the side. *Look*, he'd repeated, again and again, as he'd touched her.

Stubborn image, that one.

"I think tonight we're putting in a new light," she said, all anticipation. By now she was used to being up late like this, waiting for him. She stirred once more, composing herself before turning back to the screen.

"Your face looks like a tomato," Dee said.

"I'm cooking."

Dee narrowed her eyes but relented. "We'll come back to this."

Nora took a relieved sip of wine. A great thing about Deepa was that for all her teasing, prying curiosity, she always knew when to stop. A joke about Nora's chronic prudishness in the face of a sustainable dildo was one thing, but for the things Nora needed privacy for—or time for—Dee was always discreet, always patient.

And anyway, they both knew there was an elephant in the room.

"So how bad was it?" Nora said, bracing herself.

Dee rolled her eyes but took another big drink of her wine before settling further into her couch. "Bad," she said.

They'd lost the eco-influencer today.

The email—hardly two lines, signed with an *xoxox*—had come through to the whole team around noon, Pacific time, which meant almost everyone at Verdant had their lunch hour interrupted or entirely canceled. Nora had been picking up her phone to text Deepa when it had chimed in her hand.

I called it, Dee had texted.

And she had. Weeks ago, of course, but more recently, at last Thursday's staff meeting. "She's going to bolt," she'd told

190

Austin, voice surprisingly sharp. "Cut her loose first and save everyone from wasting any more hours on this. We're not what she wants."

But Austin—a real *the customer is always right* type—hadn't listened. In fact, for the last week he'd had Nora chasing down freelance game-app designers, even though that was absolutely not in her job description.

"I honestly don't know what the big deal is," said Nora, ignoring the pang of guilt she felt over her annoyance at Austin. "It wasn't like she was a huge account for us. *Why* was he so insistent about this?"

"Because he hates to lose. They're all the same." Nora knew Dee well enough to know that this meant either men in general or men who were in charge of things. Probably both.

"Was it the silent treatment all afternoon?"

"He slammed a door."

Nora raised her eyebrows. Slamming doors, that was serious business.

"Honestly, Nora, I really think I'm almost done there."

A pit opened in Nora's stomach. "What?"

"I'm going to start putting out feelers. I don't know what direction Austin thinks he's going in, but I'm not interested in it."

Nora blinked at the screen, stunned. But she shouldn't be, should she? For months she and Deepa both had been unhappy with some of the new projects being onboarded; their debriefs so often consisted of frustrated disbelief about some new ask, some new plan. And Dee was brilliant, talented, driven, networked.

If she put out feelers, she'd be... well, getting felt. Immediately.

But Verdant without Deepa? Nora's job without Deepa?

She hated to think of it, even though they weren't working in the same office or time zone anymore.

"Wow," she managed. "Do you... would it help if I talked to him?"

Dee waved a hand. "You're sweet, and honestly, you're like one of the only people he listens to, but no. Even if he got his shit together, which he definitely won't, I still need a change. Maybe I'll move back to Berkeley, who knows. My parents would love it."

"Wow," Nora repeated. "This is... a lot."

"You did it, right? I mean, I know it wasn't for the same reasons, and yes, those poetry readings still sound completely bananas, but now you're with your family there, and you're also dating a hot, handy doctor."

Nora laughed, but something about it rang false to her own ears. First of all, she was still catching up to the thought of Deepa leaving Verdant. Second of all, something about what Dee had said about Will—about Nora and Will, together—settled uncomfortably in her stomach.

What they were doing, it couldn't really be called *dating*.

She took another drink of her wine, wanting to shake off the thought. For now, this was working; this was what she'd wanted. It was what she wanted even though the rental situation downstairs had been surprisingly unproblematic so far—the responsible, quiet mother and daughter Will had promised, who so far had mostly kept to themselves, and her neighbors for the most part politely resigned, even once or twice complimentary toward Will's judgment in choosing them. Once, while they'd been out for a walk, Nora had thought of mentioning something about Will to Mrs. Salas—maybe a test run, with talk of towel rods—but she'd lost her nerve at the last minute, a nagging feeling that she'd be doing something disloyal. To her neighbors, to Nonna.

But even more than that, she *liked* it, having this secret.

She liked having this thing for herself, in this place where she'd always shared everything.

And she knew Will had his limits, too. She'd seen the look on his face that first morning, when she'd come back from the bathroom, and it was familiar to her: faraway and pained. He'd looked like that once before in her bedroom, the night she'd been sick, and she hadn't wanted to see that look again.

So she kept it light, kept it specific. A project, an interlude. Each time, a casual, no-promises goodbye.

It was working for both of them.

Wasn't it?

She cleared her throat, setting down her glass and folding her arms across her chest. On-screen, Dee looked as put together as she always did, but Nora could still see strain from the day in her eyes.

"Dee," she said, her tone serious. "You know if you go, I'm one hundred percent in your corner. Whatever you need, you have it from me."

Deepa had done the same for her, all those months ago, when Nora had decided to come back to Chicago for good. She'd never missed a beat: helped Nora pack the things she was taking, helped her sell what she wasn't, helped her plan what to say to Austin about telework. Made promises about staying in touch that she'd always, always kept, even though the truth was, Dee's friend circle had always been much bigger than Nora's.

"I know," Dee said, tapping the side of her glass with one polished nail. "I'd miss you, of course. But I miss you now, and we handle it."

Nora smiled. "I miss you, too. Thank goodness for these cameras, huh?" She uncrossed her arms, picking up her glass again and raising it to Dee, to technology, to their long-distance friendship.

Dee toasted her back, then smiled wickedly. "Now tell me real quick before he gets there. What do you trade a man for putting a new light in your bathroom?"

—

"Please tell me I can have more of this."

Will and Nora sat at two ends of the old couch, his faded jeans and worn blue-gray T-shirt a hilariously monochrome contrast to the loud floral pattern of the upholstery. In his hands he held the empty, shallow bowl that had, only moments ago, been pretty full up with the pasta Nora had made, a promise from that night on the beach that she was overdue in fulfilling. She hadn't quite planned to serve it fresh—she'd thought it would be too late for a meal, that Will would want to take it with him when he left. But only seconds after she'd opened the door to him, he'd turned his head toward the kitchen, his eyes going adorably wide.

"Is that your sauce?" he'd said, abandoning the box with the new light fixture right there on the floor of the entryway.

"At this time of night?" Nora teased now, clucking her tongue. "You'll get indigestion." That sounded exactly like something Nonna would say, and Nora felt her heart squeeze happily at the memory, the echo. The way she kept Nonna alive.

Will dropped his head back, making a funny, frustrated *hmph* noise, and Nora admired the line of his throat, the ridge of his Adam's apple. The desire she felt stir within her was both familiar and different—no less intense, but somehow less insistent. Maybe it was the change to their routine—their project not yet started, their interlude postponed. Maybe it was the glass of wine she'd had, always likely to make her a little sleepy.

Or maybe it was the mood that had descended upon her when she'd closed her laptop screen after signing off with Dee. It wasn't that the call ended badly—in fact, it'd ended with Nora clamping a hand over her laughing mouth at a particularly vulgar suggestion Dee had made for tonight's trade-off (*not* pasta-related!). But almost immediately, Nora had felt the full weight of having had a very bad day at work, followed by having heard the wholly justified, but still upsetting, plans of her friend.

So now, when she looked over at Will, what she wanted most was to crawl closer to him, to put her head on his shoulder or against his thigh, to have him stroke her back or put his hands in her hair. *I know, baby*, she remembered him saying, that day when she was sick, and it wasn't that she *wanted* to be called that, but also…

Also, she definitely did.

"I don't think I ate since breakfast," Will said, snapping her out of her thoughts. Good job, thinking about infantilizing, problematic pet names when Will had been *saving lives* and *starving himself* all day.

She held out her hand. "I'll get you more."

He shook his head, which was still tipped back. "You're right. Probably too late to eat seconds." His eyelids drooped and he smiled. "Man, these carbs."

She laughed. "We can skip the light tonight."

He looked over at her. "I don't want to," he said, his voice somehow both serious and playful, and she knew he wasn't talking about the light. He leaned forward to set his dish on the coffee table, then collapsed back into his former posture, eyes drooping again almost immediately.

"I'll sit here for five minutes," he asserted. Practical, responsible Will.

But he didn't look like he'd be awake in five minutes.

"It was a busy day?" she asked.

He gusted out a sigh. "The usual." He shifted, locking his fingers together to rest over the flat, firm expanse of his abdomen. *Four minutes*, she thought. *If he fights for it.*

"How's it going downstairs?" he said, his voice low and sleepy. That was a guard-down question, to ask about the rental. For the most part, they avoided it during his visits. But already this visit was like no other one: not exactly light. Not exactly specific.

"Never mind," he said. "I shouldn't have asked. It's not your—"

"It's okay," she rushed out, strangely eager to keep the guard-down mood of it all. It was nice, this way. It felt… not even like dating, really. It felt like something else, something more. "It's fine. Everything's been fine."

He nodded once, and quieted again. But after a pause, he said, "Emily is okay?"

Nora blinked over at him, surprised, but he kept his eyes low, away from hers. She tried to think of a time when she'd mentioned Emily specifically to Will, but she couldn't think of a single thing.

"Marian mentioned she had some… anxiety. About this," he said.

"*Marian* told you that?"

Now he looked over, probably shocked into it by the sharp increase in the volume of her voice. "She might have mentioned," he said, his lips curving, "That you weren't the only person in the building who sometimes fought going to see a doctor."

Nora had a feeling she was gaping.

"I gave Marian a few suggestions. For providers who might be good for Emily. I think they were going to make some calls."

Now she *knew* she was gaping. What about *her* suggestions! She had definitely made a few.

He laughed softly at her expression, rolling his head back. "You're so surprised. It took me a while with this crowd, but I've got a way with people, you know."

"You're not Marian's type," she said, and he snorted.

Two minutes, she thought. She leaned the side of her head against the sofa cushion, watching him. He *did* have a way with people, even with people who ought to, by all rights, be suspicious of him. She supposed his job helped with that. He probably spent all day around people who were wary of him, people who thought he was coming to deliver bad news, or to make something worse before it started to get better.

"I'm your type," he said, opening one eye and then closing it again once he'd caught her. "If this staring you're doing is any indication."

"Hmm," she said, noncommittal, but she didn't really stop staring. For all the images she'd been storing up over the last two weeks, she had a feeling this one might be stubborn, too: Will's long, lean body in profile, his expression entirely relaxed. She felt her own body sinking into something similar, a drowsy comfort that made her wish the lights were lower. This was a sort of claiming, too. A kind of intimacy she'd never experienced here.

But almost as soon as her eyes slid closed, her phone sounded—a familiar tone assigned to a very specific contact—and she sat up, grabbing it from the table as Will raised his head.

She winced. "I'm sorry. It's my boss calling."

"Your boss calls you this late?"

Not usually, she thought. But she said, "It's not that late for him. Only eight thirty there."

Will frowned, and she had a feeling she knew exactly what he was thinking. *What should matter is that it's late for you*, that frown said.

"We had a rough go today at work. I'll—" She stood, gestured down the hall to indicate where she'd take it.

Will nodded and stood, and she had a moment of disappointment when she thought he might be leaving, but he only bent to pick up his dish, moving around the coffee table to take it into the kitchen. When she was halfway down the hall, swiping her thumb across the phone, she heard the clink of dishes, the sound of the faucet being turned on.

Her phone was on the fourth ring before she sat and flicked on the small light that cast a harsh glow over her desk space, the leavings of her workday in the same messy arrangement she'd left them in, because she'd been so eager to get away from it all, and to get ready for the night ahead. Now, with Austin waiting for her on the line, she felt weirdly embarrassed by it, as though he could sense through the still-unconnected phone her disorganization.

"Austin, hi," she said, trying not to sound… disorganized.

"Sorry to be calling so late," he said, but he didn't really sound all that sorry.

"Well, it was a difficult day." Nora wasn't really sure that getting dropped by a nightmare client via email (*xoxox!*) counted as difficult enough for an after 10:00 p.m. phone call, but whatever.

"Obviously we have a lot to go over," he said, and she could hear the tapping of his keyboard in the background. She felt another guilty pang for her gut instinct, which was to tell him that this time of night was really no time to go over anything, and also, that the whole second half of the workday had been a process of "going over." That from her and Dee's point of view, it'd been getting "gone over" for weeks before this day even happened.

She thought of Will out there, washing dishes, and couldn't decide who she was being more unfair to.

She cleared her throat. "Okay, are we——"

He cut her off before she could finish.

"But I think the first thing is, we need to talk about getting you back here."

—

When the call ended twenty minutes later, Nora tossed her phone onto her desk with a clatter, shoved her chair back, and hit her elbow on Nonna's dresser.

"Damn," she said, clutching it.

"Nora?"

She closed her eyes, absolutely knowing now who she'd been unfair to. "In here," she called. "I'm so, so sorry."

Seconds later Will came to the doorway, tucking his hands into his pockets and leaning against the frame. Will excelled in doorways, frankly. Excellent standing, leaning, kissing, touching. A+ in all those subjects, and now he was adding a fourth: looking.

First he looked at her, where she held her elbow, furrowed his brow and said, "Are you okay?"

Then, when she nodded, he looked up again and let his eyes pass over the one room in her apartment he'd not yet been in. Her grandmother's most personal things, plus Nora's tiny workspace. When his eyes landed back on her again, he maintained the furrow. He said, "What happened?" and it felt like he was asking her about so much more than the phone call.

She sighed and swiveled her chair toward him, this time concentrating enough not to run into anything.

"Austin—that's my boss—he wants me to come back to San Diego next month."

For the briefest of seconds, something about Will's body changed, even though his posture remained exactly the same. But Nora saw it—a tightening. A tension.

"What for?" he said, his voice light.

She sighed, overwhelmed. Will knew a bit about her work (and rework) for the influencer, but now, everything went beyond today's loss of the account. Everything was so much more complicated.

"A week of meetings, I guess. A few new pitches he wants me there in person for, and"—she shook her head, still in shock about this part—"some talk of moving the whole business to Los Angeles."

This is between us for now, Austin had said, which Nora knew meant something specific: she was not meant to tell Deepa about it.

"Is that a problem for you?"

Nora tilted her head, thinking about it. "It would have been, I guess, a year ago—I wouldn't have wanted to go to LA. Now that I'm here I guess it won't matter so much for me in the everyday, except I think what it means is that Austin is changing direction, and it's... I don't know. These pitches are going to be a lot of work."

More of the same—a celebrity who was starting an ecotourism foundation. A retired pro surfer getting into documentary film production. A vegan home chef who'd recently gone viral on social media. There was nothing wrong with the work, but it certainly wasn't what she was used to. And Austin wasn't giving her much time to pivot. She stared morosely at the mess in front of her, the open notebook where she'd hastily taken notes on what Austin was saying.

"You don't have much space of your own in here," Will said, and she looked up at him.

Only a few weeks ago, this comment might have made her feel flustered, angry. But by now—from the bathroom projects alone—she knew Will understood that every change she made in this apartment was significant to her. And by now she knew that he—even in spite of his own apparent lack of sentiment when it came to family heirlooms—didn't judge her for it. A few days ago, he'd indulged her dozens of back-and-forth texts about the new sink faucet for the bathroom, Nora hesitant to pick anything too modern. *Whatever you want*, he'd text back, and every time, she liked it. Every time, she felt like he saw her.

"This room would be hard to change," she said, casting her eyes around. Nonna's bed and dresser, both from the year she'd been married: 1944, when she'd only been nineteen years old. Her lace coverlet, yellowed with age, purchased the year she'd moved to this building: 1990, when she was a widow of barely a year. A jeweled hairbrush and hand mirror, resting atop a silver tray that Nora dusted every week. Old pictures in elaborate frames. An infant Jesus of Prague statue on a small, delicate-looking table over in the corner. None of it was to Nora's taste, really, but she loved it all the same, because Nonna had loved it.

And this is Nonna's place.

She looked down at her lap, discomfited at the intruding thought. She had a familiar sense of being tugged in all directions. San Diego, Chicago. Austin, Deepa. Nonna, herself.

"You ever think about one of those coworking spaces?" Will asked, and their eyes met again.

"Like where you rent an office?"

"Yeah. My tenant downstairs uses one. You could ask her about it."

"Oh, I—" Her own brow furrowed, considering. At first, not so much about the idea itself, but about the thought of going down two flights of stairs and knocking on the door of a person Will called a *tenant*. In Donny's old apartment! She felt tangled up with the tugging sensation, tried to ignore it.

Anyway, a coworking space, that was definitely out of the question, no matter who she knew or didn't know who used one.

"Austin wouldn't pay for that," Nora said. "It was already a leap to get him to agree to the telework."

Will dropped his head in a nod. "Right, yeah."

They fell into silence, and Nora felt ludicrously disappointed: everything good between them tonight ground to a halt with this additional disruption to their routine. *See, Dee?* she telegraphed, to her long-distance friend, a friend she'd just been asked to keep a secret from. *We're definitely* not *dating.*

Will cleared his throat. "Is he—" He shifted against the doorframe. "Is he all right to you, though? Your boss?"

She opened her mouth to answer—a quick, uncomplicated yes. But that Will had asked at all made her close it again before frowning down at her hands and thinking. Even if her answer was basically going to be the same, she wanted to at least consider the question.

"He is, yeah. He's going through something, I think, which probably has to do with whatever this move idea is about. But he's a good boss. I owe him a lot."

His answer was a quiet noise: not quite assent, not quite disagreement. Acknowledgment, and nothing more.

"I'm sorry," she said again. "I left you sitting out there for so long."

He shrugged. "I did the dishes. Started reading the instruction manual for the light fixture."

God, she did not feel like installing a light fixture tonight. Not now, not after everything. In fact at the moment she felt like building a time machine and going back to the minutes before her phone had started ringing. If she could do it again, she probably would ask him to call her *baby*, no matter how guilty it would make her feel later.

"I'll be honest," he said. "I doubt I've got the hand-eye coordination for working with electricity tonight."

Given her own feelings about the whole thing, she should have been relieved. But instead she was unaccountably disappointed now that there wasn't a reason for him to stay.

"Yeah, of course. It's so late."

She turned to her desk, closed her notebook, fished her phone out from the space it'd fallen into behind her keyboard. When she swiveled back so she could stand, though, she found Will had taken a step into the room and now held out a hand to her.

She looked at it, then up at him, returning his soft, inside-joke smile. When she slid her palm against his, he grabbed hold of her and pulled her up to him. *This*, she thought, when she landed against his body, his other arm steadying her around the waist. *This is the direction you want to be tugged in.*

He kept tugging, in fact—kept hold of her hand while he walked her down the hall, past the bathroom and to the doorway of her bedroom. She halted him at the threshold, confused. "You're not going?"

He looked down at her. "Do you want me to?"

"No," she said quickly. "But I wasn't sure if—"

Another tug, this one bringing their bodies flush, and then he released her hand to put both his arms around her instead. He ducked his head, put his lips close to her ear.

"Nora," he whispered, and a delicious shiver went through her body, everything tense from the day and night somehow falling away. "I think we both know I'm not just coming over to deal with your bathroom fixtures."

She pressed her secret smile against his chest.

"You're not?" she said, feigning innocent surprise. "What're you good for, then?"

He laughed and lifted her, walking a few steps and dropping her onto the bed. "Other things."

"*Psssht*," she teased, but she was already scooting backward, making room for him to climb between her legs. "I heard what you said about your hand-eye coordination."

He paused, one knee on the edge of the mattress, one palm pressed flat beside her hip, and smiled wickedly down at her. Then he ducked his head, nudged up the hem of her shirt, and pressed a hot, openmouthed kiss low on her stomach. *Good direction*, she thought, reaching to tug her waistband down, and he followed it, licking along each new stretch of exposed skin. *Best direction*.

"Maybe I can practice another kind tonight," he said, his voice low, his breath warm.

And for the next little while, Nora only had to lie back in her bed, and go to the places Will took her.

Chapter 14

"It's your turn, Dr. Sterling."

Will looked up from his phone screen, where he'd been staring down at a little gray bubble that told him Nora was currently replying to his last message. He cleared his throat, embarrassed, shoving the phone back into the front pocket of his scrubs before stepping up to the counter.

"Sorry about that, Janine," he said to the familiar barista. "I was…" He trailed off, waving a hand. Wouldn't do any good to lie to her, and telling her the truth—that he was waiting for a text message from a woman whose bed he'd left only a few hours ago—didn't make any sort of sense, either.

When his phone chimed with a notification a second later, though, he had to force himself not to reach for it again. He stared up at the menu, but basically only saw a big stretch of gray text bubbles in his brain.

"How about I keep it simple today?" he said, smiling across the counter at Janine. "Large black coffee, no sugar."

This time he at least remembered to hand over his mug before he stepped to the side to wait for his order. Once he was out of the way, he gave up resisting, pulling out his phone again.

Paint makes total sense, it read, and he smiled, relieved.

That was settled, then—another occasion to see her, and soon, too.

Last week, on the night they'd both bypassed the light fixture project, Will wondered whether they'd simply go forward and drop the pretense—if he wasn't only coming over for these increasingly simple household projects, why bother continuing to come up with them? Even after they'd finally gotten that light fixture installed, though, Nora had stuck to their script: the next afternoon, she'd sent him a link to a massaging shower head, and obviously he was not going to argue with that as an idea.

It had been a good night, when that shower head got installed. And tested. Twice.

Still, there was a border to his relief—a hard line that felt like it kept him from breathing easy about seeing her again under these conditions they'd both decided were safe. Painting, after all, felt like a final frontier: the last real effort they could make without doing things that involved contractors, or at least more time, equipment, and know-how. And for Nora, he knew, that bathroom was a border of its own—the only place in that apartment, other than her bedroom, that she seemed willing to really change.

Not for the first time since that night, he thought of coming to find her in that cramped, sad excuse for an office she sat in every day. Dark, heavy furniture surrounding her. Curtains that very nearly shared a pattern with that awful wallpaper in the common hallways. Her computer equipment pressed up against her, looming and claustrophobic. That chair that made her look huddled, stressed.

He didn't like that at all.

He also didn't like that the home office clearly wasn't the only problem: that Nora's voice changed when she talked about this trip she was going to have to take, that lately she chewed on the inside of her lip when she checked email on her phone, that she'd gotten at least one more of those late-night calls from her boss, this one coming when Will had one hand beneath Nora's shirt and she had one hand inside his unbuttoned pants. Nora had ignored it at first, keeping her determined lips against his, but when it quieted and rang again almost immediately, she'd huffed in apologetic frustration and pulled away.

Frankly, Nora's boss seemed pretty—

"Dr. Sterling."

Will cursed inwardly.

"I see you're rather absorbed in your telephone," Abraham said, coming to stand beside him.

No one calls it a telephone, Will thought, but he still tucked it away as though he'd been caught out at something. Besides, he figured he knew why Abraham was here. Two hours ago Will had taken over for him in dealing with the very anxious mother of a patient who'd been in the bay, an eleven-year-old who was probably right now up on the general surgery floor, getting his appendix taken out. Will knew his boss well enough to know that he wouldn't get a thank-you, but he would get a request to debrief the entire situation.

"Have you spoken to Sally recently?" Abraham said instead, and Will's eyes—pointed straight ahead—widened. There had been no talk of Sally since Abraham's ill-conceived cat-gifting scheme, and since that was a few weeks ago, Will figured that things had stalled in the reconciliation department.

He cleared his throat, in preparation for Vader voice. "I— uh." His eyes went pleadingly to Janine and her coworker, who were clearly a bit backed up today. Nothing for it, then. He'd have to answer.

"I believe I spoke to her yesterday," he said, which was a lie. He didn't believe it; he knew it. But feigning a vague memory about it seemed like the right move, especially because beside him, Gerald Abraham had the energy of a coiled spring.

"Hmm," Abraham said, but that definitely wasn't going to be the end of it. Will braced himself. "Did she happen to mention our recent date?"

Will opened his mouth, then closed it. *Janine, please*, he thought. *Throw the coffee in my face, anything.*

Janine did not look back at him.

"She did not mention a date, no. We only talked about my unit." He thought of Nora and her recent laughing admission over this word, and shifted uncomfortably on his feet. "My rental property, I mean."

"Ah, yes. On our *date*," Abraham said, really leaning into his preferred conversation topic, "Sally mentioned that it's gone more smoothly for you recently."

I can turn this around, Will thought, seizing on Donny's apartment like it was a lifeline. The irony did not escape him. "Very smoothly. My next tenant is actually a fourth-year medical student from—"

"Sushi," Abraham said. "That was Sally's choice."

Will suppressed a sigh. "Good idea, to let her choose."

"I thought so. However."

Janine had forsaken him entirely. Maybe she threw away his mug back there. He would never look at his telephone in line again.

"I have asked her to dinner tomorrow, and she said she's still deciding."

"Right, well—"

"Usually, when Sally says she is deciding something, she has already decided that the answer is no."

Janine approached the counter with Will's now-full mug, and he tried not to leap forward in relief. But when he turned back, Gerald Abraham was standing in the exact same spot, waiting.

And then he reached up and smoothed his lapel.

Damn, Will thought.

"Dr. Abraham," he said quietly, though it wasn't as if the volume of Abraham's own voice indicated a desire for discretion on the matters of his of his marital problems. "I'm not sure I'm the best person to be talking to about this. I've never been married, and—"

"You will be," said Abraham, because he never let Will finish a sentence. And also because he always interrupted him with deeply uncomfortable statements.

"No, I—"

"You're the type people want to marry," Abraham interrupted again. Still uncomfortably.

"Gerald," Will said, taking a chance that this never-before-attempted first-name deployment would either prevent further interruptions or make his boss mad enough to end this conversation. "Given that you have in fact been married I'd say you're the type, too."

"Yes, but I'm divorced. The point is, even if you're not married yet, I assume you date frequently."

Will's phone chimed in his pocket, and Abraham raised his eyebrows. If that was Nora, she had the worst timing in history. But his hand still twitched to check it.

"I don't re—" he began, but honestly, this time, he was glad to be interrupted. What the hell was he going to say to Gerald Abraham about his dating history, which functionally did not exist? Had he... ever really been *on* a date? He shifted on his feet, that phone feeling suddenly heavier in his pocket.

"I believe I miscalculated, asking Sally to another dinner, even though sushi went well."

Will stared. This tone. This was a *let's debrief the appendix removal situation* tone. "Okay," he said.

"I think there are two problems," Abraham said, and then, in a familiar move, he turned to walk away, still talking. "The first is, during our marriage, I did not take Sally on dates."

"Okay," Will repeated, because now it was like he was in it, with this tone. It at least made him feel like he was on the job. "So you're treating—" *Jesus.* He cleared his throat. "So you're dealing with this by asking her on dates."

"Yes, but this brings us to the second problem, which is that Sally has always felt I am too devoted to routines."

Will cocked his head, nodding. He guessed that explained the white coat. The constant talk of protocol. The thing was, Gerald Abraham *was* a good doctor. What he lacked in bedside manner he absolutely made up for in precision, in the kind of careful, repetitive follow-through that meant he hardly ever missed a thing.

"Sally, as I am sure you have observed, prefers more spontaneity." He looked sideways at Will. "And so in asking her to dinner again, what have I done?"

Will blinked. "I mean it's only the sec—"

"Established a routine!" Abraham said, stopping.

Will stopped too, turning to face his... huh. Didn't feel right to think of him as a boss right at this moment, even though this was basically the time in the debrief when Will was being asked to solve a problem. Abraham had done the diagnosis, and now he wanted Will to develop the treatment.

But with a sinking sense of clarity—and a fair bit of shame—Will realized he was even less qualified to help than he would've originally thought, because not only did he not have any meaningful experience dating, he was also currently spending every free moment he had with a woman whom he'd never *actually* taken out.

Whom he'd confined to a very specific routine.

You're not dating her, a familiar, focused part of his brain told him, and he supposed it was true. What he and Nora had, it was...

Something more.

That was another part of him talking.

He reached up, his palm bumping against the edge of the pocket where his phone weighed down the fabric of his shirt.

"Ideas to show I'm *thoughtful*," Abraham said, and clearly he was repeating that last word straight from the mouth of Sally.

Will swallowed, thinking again about Nora behind that tiny desk that she wasn't ready to change. He'd been thoughtful, hadn't he? He'd watched Nora all these weeks—even in the weeks before he'd ever been in her bed—and he'd known, even when he was fighting with her, that her vise grip on the building was about something more than her concern for her neighbors. And now that he knew her better, now that he'd been in her space—he'd tried to be thoughtful, to help her in this project she hadn't even admitted the full extent of to herself. Towel rods, faucets, whatever she wanted. He'd helped.

But he'd also never taken her out. He'd gone over to her place in the dark of night and left before dawn. He'd never lingered, not since that very first time.

He had a feeling Sally would not approve, though he wasn't sure why that bothered him so much.

"Let me think about it," he said to Dr. Abraham. "I'll find you later."

"Fine."

Will watched him go, leaning a shoulder against the wall beside him. Taking Nora out, that'd be good. A break from routine. Giving her a little relief from her place, where work and home were the same spot—that was helping, too. It's not like he was trying to (re)marry her or something, and anyway, Nora was as clear on the boundaries for this as he was. Hell, she might even say no; she might tell him to come over with a can of paint and to quit asking weird questions.

But it couldn't hurt to ask.

He slid his phone out again, saw her latest message there. *Same time?* it read.

Before he could reconsider, he typed his reply.

Up for a change of plans?

—

Nora had her beach face on.

He hadn't taken her to the beach, not again, because once he had the idea in his head—to take her out, to take her on a *date*— he definitely didn't want to Abraham-botch it and make it some kind of routine. And while he hadn't spent many of his years in Chicago—his residency, first, and then his fellowship, and now his current job—exploring places like this, he'd certainly been around long enough to pick up on what people around here thought was worth doing.

And judging by Nora's smile, the Garfield Park Conservatory was worth doing.

He'd lucked out, getting this idea on the one night a week it was open late, though if he could've helped it he would've gotten here earlier, would've been able to spend a whole afternoon with her, watching her walk through the curved, fragrant pathways, her phone in her hand, the camera app open. As it stood, they had only about a half hour before things shut down for the evening, the sky above them through the panes of the greenhouse glass purple-gray with clouds and the coming night.

Still, it had the feeling of a date, or at least the feeling he thought might be associated with a date—he and Nora for once not dressed for home improvement, not undressed for what always came after. Instead, he'd gone home after work to change, dressing in a version of what he usually wore to the clinic—dark pants, a collared shirt he'd made sure to iron. Nora, of course, looked beautiful—any way he saw her, she looked beautiful—but tonight she'd worn a summer dress, navy and white, a featherlight gold necklace dipping low into the V of her neckline, her long hair down and lightly curled.

When she'd stepped out of her car, he'd almost forgotten to breathe.

Of course that they hadn't come together was a reminder of the ways things were different between them; so, too, was the way they'd both, from the beginning, kept a strained sort of physical distance from each other. Around them, couples strolled with their fingers interlocked, or with hands set gently on one another's backs—casual, natural touches that all of a sudden, Will constantly noticed. He'd wanted to get Nora out; he was glad to get her out. But now that he had her here, he wanted what they had when they were *in*, too. He wanted his hands on her while she moved. He wanted to set his mouth against hers every time she looked up at him, delighted by something she'd seen.

Instead, he kept his hands in his pockets. His mouth to himself.

But even in spite of this restraint, something about being with her here felt undoubtedly loose, freeing. Away from her apartment, he didn't think about the way his footsteps sounded beneath him, or the way his voice carried. He didn't think about the next project they'd use as an excuse, or about what would happen when they finally ran out of them.

"Oh, look at this," Nora said, bending over a sign. "Cycads can live for five hundred years! What a plant, huh?"

Will smiled. Of course Nora would like an old plant.

"Let me take a picture of this for Emily," she said, and lifted her phone. When she finished, she looked down at the screen and gave a tiny, satisfied smile that made Will shift on his feet with longing for her. When she turned, he watched her skirt sway, watched it gently catch at the edges of the ferns that draped lazily over the path. He stayed a few steps behind her, enjoying it—the shape of Nora, surrounded by all this living, breathing green.

When he came even with her again, she was looking up at giant, swaying fronds above her.

"This is so good," she said quietly. "I'm going to do more things like this."

He felt a strange pang at that *I'm*, this imagined future of Nora alone, out exploring places that made her feel good. He thought idly, aimlessly, recklessly of a routine: meeting Nora here every month, one night after work. A different dress every time. His hands out of his pockets. His mouth ready and waiting.

He cleared his throat. "Yeah?"

She nodded, keeping her eyes up, but he could see something pass over her face, something strained and sad that he knew meant she was thinking of someone specific.

He waited.

"At first when I came back, I was so focused on"—her eyes closed, too long for a simple blink, before opening again—"Nonna, and making sure I took care of things the way she had. The way I knew she would want me to. And then it was winter, and I was pretty sad, and then right when things started to..." She trailed off, lowering her head, her cheeks flushing.

"Donny," he said. "Me."

She looked over at him, her expression embarrassed. "I didn't mean that."

"It's okay," he said, because it actually was. In her apartment, with the rental two floors below, maybe it wouldn't have been; maybe it would've felt strained or maybe it would've fallen silent. But right now, to Will, the past felt safer, more comfortable than the future.

So he stuck with it.

"Did you always know you'd come back here?" he asked. "To live, I mean. For good."

When she stayed quiet at first, he worried he might have misstepped—that what felt safer to him in this moment didn't feel the same for her. But after a second, she cast her eyes upward again, and he could tell she was thinking through her answer.

"When I was younger, I did. I used to talk about it all the time, to my grandmother. And to my parents." She lowered her head again, and they both continued on the path. A slow stroll, unconscious of closing time. "But I don't know. I was always going to do college in California, because I could go for free where my parents teach. I still came back here, but not as often, not for the full summer."

She paused, and he looked over at her, caught her pulling gently at the ends of her hair before she released it and smoothed her hand down the side of her skirt.

"And then I guess I got busy, and I got a job I loved. I kept in touch with everyone in other ways, and visited when I could. My grandmother, she was always so supportive of that."

She shrugged a familiar shrug, the one that communicated the exact opposite of carelessness. Guilt and sadness and doubt, instead.

"I guess I always had two lives, in a way. Maybe I picked the wrong one, back then. Maybe I should've come back sooner."

"Nora," he cautioned gently. "Don't do that."

Even as he said it, he didn't feel all that gentle. He thought about that dark home office, that tiny space she was allowing herself. He thought about going back to her place and shoving everything that wasn't Nora's into one tight, stacked-up corner, so she could see how much room she really had.

But even that was looking ahead, and he'd resolved not to do that tonight.

She sent him a wan smile. "I know." She took a breath, her posture lengthening. "I'm glad I came back when I did. I'm glad I get to be here now."

It was a good reminder, that *now*, and for the next few minutes—while he and Nora and the few remaining patrons made their way around the paths that would take them toward the exit—they only talked about what they saw around them, Nora snapping photos and once asking Will to take one while she stood beneath a gigantic palm, her arms stretched out wide, her mouth opened in an exaggerated O. When he handed the phone back, he joked about how she'd need to make a slideshow of all the photos she'd taken, and instead of laughing she set a finger to her chin and said, entirely without irony, that it was a really good idea.

"I could use my projector," she said. "So I could show everyone at once!"

Don't think about it, Will, he told himself. *Do not think about going to a damned plants slideshow in the backyard of that building. That is not your future.*

When an overhead announcement signaled the conservatory's coming closing time, they made their way up the steps toward the greenhouse's exit, Nora ahead of him, her phone already raised.

"Let me get one more of this one," she said, not even really to him, and so he stood where he was, watching her climb a couple more steps to get the angle she wanted. He smiled as she bent close, by now knowing that this was one of the pictures where she was trying to show something to Emily about spores. He thought of Gerald and Sally, hoped their date—Will had given his boss three different ideas—would go as well as this one had.

"They're gonna kick us out of here," he said, teasing.

"I'll get it done faster if you quit talking."

He chuckled at this familiar ribbing, something they'd practiced during their various feuds early on and perfected during their projects over the last few weeks.

He was looking up at her when it happened—when her brow furrowed, when her lips pulled to one side. When she reached out the hand that wasn't holding her phone to wave away a fly that buzzed lazily around the very leaves she was trying to photograph. When she clucked her tongue and said quietly, "Get. *Get!*" with a familiar trace of laughter in her voice.

When his heart hiccupped.

Like he was fifteen all over again.

"This reminds me," he said, before he could think. Before he could yank himself out of the past he'd lulled himself into thinking was so safe tonight. "Of the first time I ever saw you."

She straightened, turning to face him, to look down at him, and he almost wanted to check his hands for cherry tomatoes. But no—they were where he'd left them, still in his pockets, still in control.

"You mean the morning I knocked my plant over?"

Unbeknownst to her, she'd given him an out with this, and he could've taken it. Of course, it could've been that morning. Of course he could've said, *Yes, when you knocked your plant over.* But for some reason, down here like this, Nora above him like that, he couldn't seem to stop himself.

So instead he said, "No. Not that morning."

She blinked down at him, something seeking and intense in her eyes, and he knew he was going to tell her. He didn't have to tell it all, but he knew he should tell her this, on this night they were breaking their routine.

"The day I came with my mom, when I was fifteen. I saw you, up on your balcony."

"You did?"

From where he stood, he could see her chest rising and falling, quicker than normal.

"'Saw' might be an overstatement." He reached up, touched the edge of his glasses, and her lips curved softly, her eyes still stunned.

"You were trying to get squirrels away from your grand-mother's tomato plants," he added. "Nonna, you called her. I'd never heard that word before."

He watched her throat bob in a swallow. "Yes." And then, "Why didn't you tell me?"

"I wasn't sure at first. Not until that building meeting, when you mentioned you came in the summers," he said, but that wasn't really true. Hadn't he been sure, from the moment he'd heard her say *Hey*? From the moment she'd looked over the edge of her balcony, down to his? "And then…" He trailed off, an echo of Nora before. *Donny*, he could have said again. *Me*.

She shook her head, dropping her eyes to her skirt, smoothing it again. "I wish you would have said something."

"It felt complicated, with the building." Another half-truth. *He* felt complicated. From the second he saw her again, he was all complication.

"I mean back then. When you saw me the first time."

"Oh. Well, I almost did. I almost called up to you."

He could remember it so clearly, all of a sudden—all the things his teenaged mind had run through, trying to think of something to say to her while she rained tomatoes down on his head. *Hey, did you drop something?* That's what he'd settled on, in the end.

He felt an unfamiliar tenderness for his teenaged self.

"I would've wanted you to," Nora said. "I always wanted to meet kids my own age here."

"I would've been a little older, I guess. Two years?"

She nodded and smiled. "That would have made it even better. I would've bragged when I got back to school. The cute high school guy who flirted with me over the summer."

She took a step down, bringing herself closer to him, and it hit him almost as sharp as the moment with her phone and the fly and her laughing frustration. What he would've given, to see her up close that day. What he would've given, for one more selfish summer before everything had gone to hell.

Her smile slipped during his silence, and she paused, two steps away. "Then again," she said, "At thirteen, I was in a pretty awkward phase, so maybe you—"

"I thought you were beautiful," he said fiercely, because he wouldn't let anything else stand.

She reached up, touched the edge of his glasses like he had only a moment ago. "I thought you said you couldn't see me."

Another out, but he didn't take this one, either.

"I could, somehow. Your laugh, your voice. I could see you well enough."

One step down, so now she was eye level. At some point, it seemed they'd become the last ones in the greenhouse, though he hadn't remembered seeing anyone pass them by. He knew they were on short time, that they'd have to go soon. But Nora was looking at him like she was trying to see straight into the past, and he wanted to let her. He didn't want to think about the words that had stopped him from calling up to her that day. He didn't want to think about *rash, reckless, selfish*; he didn't want to think about the future.

He took his hands from his pockets, reached out to link his fingers with hers. When she stepped into him again, he kissed her, like he'd wanted to do all along. Not since this date started.

Since before, since before.

And when the final announcement sounded, when they pulled apart and smiled at each other in sheepish delight, he didn't notice the way he held on to her as she turned away, her cheeks flushed and her eyes bright.

He didn't notice that he kept holding on, right up until the second her fingers trailed away.

Chapter 15

It was possible she'd taken it too far.

In the backyard, Nora stood beside Mrs. Salas, staring down at the six boxes she'd set out this morning, all but one full up, sorted by type: kitchenware, linens, clothing, books, electronics, and decor. In thirty minutes, the time limit she and Mrs. Salas had given to their neighbors would be up, and in an hour a van from a neighborhood mutual aid organization would come by to pick up their contributions for an upcoming charity sale that Nora had read about only a week ago.

"The thing about that lamp is," she said, and Mrs. Salas made a sympathetic noise—a tiny hum that was neither curiosity nor assent. Knowing that Mrs. Salas had heard a lot of Nora's ruminating back and forth today, she tried to quiet herself, but soon enough her unfinished thought swirled inside her like smoke, hot and uncomfortable, until she had to open her mouth again to let it out. "It's from Italy."

Mrs. Salas did the hum again, and Nora sighed.

This was difficult, that's all there was to it, and she had no one to blame but herself.

And maybe also Will.

Nora couldn't pinpoint what had changed since that night in the conservatory, but something absolutely had. Between them, certainly, things had changed—a layer of caution removed from their interactions, a layer of freedom added in. They no longer only saw each other inside the walls of her apartment, no longer made such a production of the secrecy when they did. If Nora's neighbors had noticed Will come back to her place that night after their first real date, when the sun hadn't even gone down fully, no one had said a word. And if they'd noticed that Nora had been going out more than she had in—well, ever—no one said much about that, either.

That she wasn't stressed over this—that she wasn't lying awake, worrying over being disloyal—was the change she saw in herself. It wasn't quite like the smoke that had forced her to declare the provenance of a (actually quite ugly!) lamp she'd inherited from Nonna, but it wasn't all that different. This feeling, too, wanted out, wanted expression. But it found its way to the surface in other ways: ignoring Austin's calls when they came in after eight. Telling Dee about LA. Painting that tiny bathroom all on her own, before Will even had a chance to come over and join her. Packing up her laptop and doing a half day of work at a coffee shop five blocks away.

Reading about a neighborhood charity sale and deciding to let go of a few things.

I guess I always had two lives, she'd told Will that night, and ever since she'd said it, she hadn't quite been able to let go of it. When she'd come back to Chicago, she thought she was settling in to one of them, finally and for good. But everything that had happened since she met Will all those weeks ago now suggested something different to her—that she hadn't so much settled into her own life as she had settled into someone else's. That had been comfortable, and comforting, because it's what all her summers here had always been: patterning out the days like Nonna did, loving all the things Nonna did.

Of course she'd started to know all this before the night at the conservatory; maybe she'd even started to know it sooner, during those lonely golden hours way back in the winter when she'd started to work through her grief. Something about what Will had told her, though—that he'd *seen* her, all those years ago, that there was some alternate version of her summer stories here that might have included Will Sterling—it had crystallized everything.

Two lives wasn't what she wanted anymore.

She wanted one. With more patterns she would make for herself. With more loves she would choose for herself.

But it was easier to want things than it was to *do* them, sometimes.

"Maybe I should keep it," Nora said. "If it seems like no one would buy it."

"Someone'll buy it," said Benny, stepping up to drop a brightly colored throw pillow into the decor bin. "Probably the same kind of person who'd buy this pillow."

"*I* bought you that pillow!" gasped Mrs. Salas. "For Secret Santa, two years ago!"

Nora stifled a laugh. Secret Santa was rarely a secret in this building. Plus that pillow had *There's No Place Like Home* embroidered on it. It could only have come from Mrs. Salas.

"Oh," said Benny quickly, bending down again. "I guess I grabbed the wrong—"

Mrs. Salas interrupted him with a heavy sigh and a hand on his arm. "Never mind. We're keeping everything in the bins. I didn't spend forty-five minutes arguing with my husband so he could come back down and try to get this silly helicopter out of here."

The silly helicopter—remote operated, lots of "horsepower," according to Mr. Salas—was probably the item in the boxes that would fetch the most money. But Nora definitely wasn't going to say that, especially because if he'd given it up he was probably right now upstairs in his workroom building something that Mrs. Salas would find even more annoying.

Nora let her eyes pass away from Nonna's lamp, onto the other gathered items she and her neighbors had brought down. The solidarity—and she had a feeling that's what this was—helped. This was fine! That wasn't even one of Nonna's favorite lamps, even if it had been from Italy.

Behind her, she could hear Marian's muffled raised voice inside the building, and within a minute she too was crossing the yard, shaking her head. "Third time I've shouted up those steps," she said, annoyed. "I know he's up there on his computer!"

"Oh, he's met someone *new*," said Mrs. Salas. "She lives in St. Louis! I don't really approve of that."

"Didn't even meet her on an app," said Benny. "They went to high school together."

"*Ooooh*, what now?" Mrs. Salas said, and Marian rolled her eyes, but she also definitely tuned right in.

Nora might've joined in the gossip—she did like a good story about Jonah's dating life—but almost as soon as Benny started to answer, her attention was pulled away by the familiar sound of gravel popping down the alley. When she looked up, she saw Will's car pulling in to the spot for his apartment, vacated only yesterday by his first tenant.

Her stomach flipped in anticipation, and she pretended to rearrange items in the boxes so she wouldn't get caught staring.

"Dr. Sterling is here!" called Mrs. Salas, waving at Will as he got out of his car. "Nora, did you know he was coming today?"

Nora straightened again, her face flushing. "I think he's got someone new coming Monday," she said, noncommittal, because she *did* know he would be coming. *I'll sneak up after I'm done*, he'd said late the other night, whispering this promise against her skin. *I want to see you before you go on your trip.*

She hadn't so much agreed as she had distracted him, letting her own lips move across his skin, making a set of promises to herself. Will Sterling was someone she wanted to choose for herself, and she was going to tell him so. No more secrets, no more limits, no more projects that she could take care of herself.

Tonight, she was going to tell him.

"I hope it's not a man," said Marian, and Benny nodded solemnly.

When Will came over, he was holding a bucket filled with a new roll of paper towels and some extra cleaning supplies, his smile in that easy, charming register that Nora had come to recognize not so much as false but as *particular*. Public-facing, practiced. It wasn't her favorite expression of Will's, but it delighted her that she could read it so well.

"Well, now," he said, looking over the assembled boxes. "What's been happening here?"

"Nora's got us doing a charity drive," Benny said, and Will looked to her, his public smile transforming, briefly, into something private.

"Have you come here to clean your apartment all by *yourself* ?" said Mrs. Salas, obviously impressed.

Marian clucked her tongue, because she did not approve of grade inflation in any form.

"Sure am. Took the day off."

For this, Nora sent back her own private smile, an acknowledgment of Will having taken it a bit easier the last few weeks, not doing extra clinic shifts on his days off from the hospital.

"You won't need the whole day," said Marian. "That woman and her child, they were tidy people. Emily and I went in there twice, you know."

Will looked at Marian. "Is that right?"

Mrs. Salas answered for her. "Oh, I went in there once, too! The daughter, she's quite the young baker! Probably you'll want to spend extra time on that oven."

"Of course," Marian said, "we told them they could come back for the next poetry night."

Will nodded seriously. "Of course."

But Nora could tell he was... proud, maybe. Proud and relieved, to get this tentative seal of approval from her neighbors. Suddenly she wondered if she'd even bother waiting until tonight to tell him. Maybe she'd follow him right into his apartment and tell him in the bright light of day, windows open. Who cared who heard it?

"Oh, here's the beanpole," came Jonah's voice behind her. "I've got a bone to pick with you, now."

Nora stiffened as Jonah approached, a paper grocery bag of stuff held against his chest. He set it down on the grass and put his hands on his hips, like he was ready for a confrontation. "I read that article you sent me."

Nora looked over at Will, whose face was still in that practiced register. "Yeah?"

"I don't see how you want to take something like pepperoni away from an old man," he said, and Nora let out a relieved breath.

Will shook his head. "It didn't say you couldn't have pepperoni," he said. "It said you should have less. And more fiber."

"This is about my diver—" He broke off in the middle of this announcement to the full group. "What's it called again?"

"Diverticulitis," Will said, and then automatically looked to Nora. "It's very mild."

Mrs. Salas made a little fanning gesture beneath her chin. "He's talking medicine!" she said to Marian quietly.

"It's about my colon, Corrine," Jonah said, annoyed.

"Are you being his doctor now?" said Marian, a note of suspicion in her voice. "Giving him medicines or something?"

"Not at all," said Will, because now he knew you answered Marian's questions. "We email a bit."

He looked back to Nora, something sheepish in his eyes. That night they'd first been together, Will had told her he'd done what he had about the apartment—the longer stays, the more careful selection of tenants—for her. But Nora had a feeling he'd done it for everyone else, too, even if he hadn't admitted that to himself. Somewhere between poetry night and cats in his apartment and taking care of Nora, he'd gotten to know her neighbors.

"Did he tell you about the woman from St. Louis?" asked Benny.

"That's enough of that," said Jonah, but his face might've gone a shade pinker as he set down his bag. "It's a good thing you're around, Beanpole. I found another book that belonged to your uncle."

Once again Nora went tense. Bringing up Donny was worse than picking any bone, a tender spot she and Will still stayed away from.

But when she looked at him, she could see that his unbothered expression was authentic, his posture loose. When Jonah passed the paperback his way—the pages wrinkled and yellowed, the cover halfway torn off and faded—Will didn't flinch, didn't tense. He set down the bucket and took it. He looked down at it, not quite with curiosity, but not with pained indifference, either. The hold Donny had on Will seemed, at least lately, to have loosened.

"Were you going to try to donate this torn-up book to charity?" Marian said to Jonah.

"Someone would've taken it," said Benny. "Like this—"

"Bernard, if you say something about my *Wizard of Oz* pillow..."

Nora stopped listening, though, because she was watching Will, who'd gently opened the book's damaged cover to look inside, and something he saw there transformed him, made his jaw harden and his brow lower. He ran his thumb along the side of the pages, a flash reveal of text that Nora could see had been underlined, annotated. Blue pen, loopy cursive.

He cleared his throat. "This was my mother's," he said quietly, but she wasn't sure if he'd meant to.

"Now that explains it," said Jonah. "A whole box of books about some detective with an alcohol problem and then this one! Definitely didn't seem like Donny's type of thing."

Will didn't respond. He closed the book again, bent to pick up his bucket, and Nora's stomach clenched in sympathy for him, this surprise intrusion of something painful.

"Thanks for passing it along to me," he said lightly, but she could tell that this was strained. "I guess I'd better get to work. I'm sure I'll see you all soon."

"Oh, wait," said Mrs. Salas, as Will was turning away. "I think this must've fallen out." She reached down to a white rectangle that had landed on top of the kitchenware box, and even before she turned it over, Nora had a sick, sinking feeling that the surprise intrusion was about to get a whole lot worse.

—

"Well now, these *have* to be your parents!"

Nora winced inwardly as Mrs. Salas stared down at the photograph she'd revealed—flat and glossy and well-preserved from the pages of the book it'd been tucked inside, bright with vivid color. Immediately, her neighbors had tucked in, getting closer to peer over Mrs. Salas's shoulders, their expressions warm and interested.

"Golly," Jonah said, looking up at Will. "There's a real family resemblance!"

"All your height from your dad's side, I guess," said Benny. And Mrs. Salas added, "But this smile! Exactly like your mom's. I see a bit of Donny in this smile."

Nora opened her mouth to say something, to *stop* this, but right before she could speak her gaze caught with Will's, his mask of calm marred by the pained look in his eyes, and he gave a small, warning shake of his head.

It doesn't do any good for them to know, he'd told her, that night when they'd called off their feud, and this look said the same.

At the moment, though, Nora thought it would do some good. It would do some good if they would stop this, if they could read Will like she did, if they could know that this was hurting him.

"Baby faces," Marian chimed in. "These two don't look much older than my eighth graders."

Nora was gripped with concern, with embarrassment, with—and this one, she was ashamed of—curiosity. But she would not look down at that picture. She kept her eyes on Will, and she knew he wasn't looking at it, either, no matter that he had his head tipped in that direction. He'd unfocused his gaze; he was looking somewhere close to but beyond that photograph.

"Did they meet that young, Dr. Sterling?" asked Mrs. Salas, her voice infused with all the curiosity Nora would not allow herself to have.

Will cleared his throat. "First year of high school, I think."

"Jonah!" said Benny, slapping the older man's shoulder. "When did you meet your girl?"

Jonah set his hands on his hips again, tipping his head up to the sky in contemplation. "First year of high school seems early, but maybe…"

Nora breathed a small sigh of relief at the distraction, hoping they could fully move on to Jonah reigniting a flame with a fellow eighty-year-old.

But it didn't last.

"My goodness, they look so in love," Mrs. Salas said, and for a split second, Nora's guard and her eyes dropped, a brief glance at the photograph that showed two young people—baby faces indeed, with their arms around each other, their gazes locked. She snapped her eyes back up, and found Will watching her.

"Do you mind if I take that?" Nora said, reaching out a hand, her patience for this suddenly run completely out. She needed to get him out of this situation, and fast. Every second, she could feel him wilting beneath the heat of it. But either Mrs. Salas hadn't heard her, or she was too preoccupied by everyone else's gathered assessment of the photo.

"You ought to bring them by sometime," Marian said. "I certainly always thought Donny didn't have any—"

"He didn't," interrupted Will, the first overt sign that his control was slipping. Once more, he cleared his throat, the sound weaker this time. When he spoke again, Nora could tell he was making an effort to deliver this piece of news with kindness. "What I mean is, my parents aren't living."

What happened next was something Nora had of course heard before in her life—a collective condolence sound, a tiny, off-key chorus of gentle *awws* and *oohs* and *hmms*. Nora had sung this song before, whenever she'd been in polite company and heard something heartbreakingly final but also wholly separate from herself. But it never sounded so wrenchingly hollow before this moment, no matter that she knew her neighbors truly meant it.

"It's a beautiful photo," said Mrs. Salas gently, holding it out to Will. "You should frame this, put it up somewhere where you can see it."

"They're not the kind of people you'd want a memorial to."

In the brief, painful seconds of silence that followed, Mrs. Salas, Marian, Jonah, Benny—all of them—might've dropped their eyes in awkward, embarrassed surprise. But Nora didn't know, because Nora couldn't look away from Will. She watched as his expression transformed: fierce, pushed-to-the-limit defensiveness to blinking, *Did I say that out loud?* shock.

And then to shamed, desperate regret.

"I guess I'd better get to work," he repeated, and it *sounded* like a repetition, a robotic sort of malfunction, like these were the only words available to him. He didn't take the photograph; he didn't look anyone in the eye. He simply turned and walked away, and Nora and her neighbors watched him go, no one uttering a word until the door closed behind him.

Jonah was the first to break the silence. "You sure stepped in it there, Corrine."

"In fairness," Marian said, "I stepped in it first, I'm pretty sure, saying he should invite them over."

"We should apologize, or—"

"I'll go talk to him," Nora said, reaching out to take the picture, and it was strange, what happened next—each of her assembled neighbors asking her to convey a message, so different from all those weeks ago.

Please tell him—

If you could let him know—

I'm sorry I didn't understand—

227

When she finally made her way inside, the picture held gently between her thumb and forefinger, she wondered if she'd have to knock. But she was encouraged by the fact that Will seemed to know she would come, the door to his place left open a crack. When she pushed it open slowly, she saw he was in the kitchen, his back to her as he unloaded supplies from his bucket, his shoulders set with tension.

"Will?"

He stilled briefly and then turned, his eyes going immediately, unerringly, to the photo she held at her side. When he looked back at her, she could tell the effort he was making—every line of his face, his body, looked so carefully arranged.

"Sorry about that," he said. "I overreacted, I know."

"You didn't." She knew he didn't, even if she didn't know all the details about his parents. She knew enough. She knew that whatever he saw in that photo represented everything painful to him about the way they'd been together, about the way they would've let him go.

He nodded toward the couch, where the battered book rested. "You can go ahead and put the photo back in there. I'll take care of it later."

Take care of it, she could tell, did not mean putting it somewhere safe. It had sort of a *Let me tie cement to it and throw it in the lake* energy.

But that wasn't her business, so she did as he asked, not looking at the photograph again as she slid it between the pages, and then she went to where he stood, stepped into him, and put her arms around his waist.

At first, he responded like he'd been waiting for it, like he had an instinct for it—his own arms wrapping around her shoulders, his head lowering to rest against hers, the breath he'd been holding in his chest letting out slowly. She tightened her arms, wanting to hold him like that for as long as it took for him to feel better.

But not long after he'd settled against her, he straightened again, unwrapping his arms and reaching behind him to where she held him. Gently, he loosened her hold, clearing his throat.

"Door's open," he said quietly, stepping back from her.

She ignored the unease she felt at the way he said it, reminded herself that the secrecy had been her idea all along.

"I don't care," she said, which wasn't quite what she'd been planning on telling him today, but she supposed it was on the way to it.

He didn't respond, only resumed his quiet unpacking of supplies. Nora looked around, saw Marian was right—it was pretty tidy in here. Still, she said, "Want me to help? Maybe afterward, we could get out of here, go get something to eat, or—" She broke off, struck with an idea that she thought might make things better, given what that photograph must've brought up for him. "We could go to your place?"

They'd never done that, not in all these days since they'd started to hang out even beyond the building. It didn't seem that Will had any particular hang-ups about it, and it wasn't like Nora had been dying to see it or anything—it just hadn't happened yet. But now felt like the perfect time. Distance plus privacy, which might be exactly what he needed.

"I think I might go in to the clinic later. If this isn't going to take all day."

He wasn't looking at her when he said it, but almost as soon as he'd finished speaking he set down the spray bottle he was holding and rubbed a hand over his face, sighing heavily.

"I'm sorry," he said again.

"It's really okay. I'm sure it's hard, getting surprised by something like that. Something that's painful for you."

He breathed out a quiet huff, a laugh that wasn't at all a laugh.

"It's not," he said, a stubborn note to his voice that he went on to correct. "It shouldn't be. It's a nice picture."

Nora swallowed, uncertain. He didn't like to talk about his parents; she knew that from the few times they'd come up. But all of a sudden, she had the feeling that if he *didn't* talk about them, she'd never be able to tell him what she'd started this day so optimistic about.

She'd never be able to choose him.

"Well, I know, but… I don't know. What everyone said, when they saw it." Her voice tipped up at the end, an unintentional inflection. She wasn't asking him any kind of question, not really. She was just… *confused.*

"They didn't say anything wrong. They *were* young. They *were* in love. I shouldn't have said what I did, about the memorial thing. They weren't bad people."

Nora pursed her lips, frustrated. Not so much at him as *for* him.

"I'm sure they weren't," she said, even though she actually wasn't. "But they seem like they were pretty negligent. So I think it's really fine if you're still a little pissed about it."

"I'm not, though," he said, with such strained, insistent conviction. "I haven't been, not for a long time. They were who they were, and I dealt with that years ago. I hardly thought of them, until…" He trailed off.

"Until Donny," she finished for him, anger at her former neighbor flaring again. She couldn't regret that Donny's last wishes had brought Will back to this building and into her life, but she hated that the apartment he'd been left had made him feel all this pain.

"No," he said, dropping his eyes to the counter. "Until you."

She blinked in surprise, dread settling along the column of her spine. "I don't know what you mean."

He shook his bowed head, resting his hands on the counter, his arms spread wide. A familiar posture.

"You and me," he said. "And what we're doing here."

"What are we doing here?"

A long, awful pause, another shake of his head. "I don't know, Nora. Too much, I think."

"Too much what?" The dread that had settled was transforming into something else—something harder and more

230

defensive. No matter how things had changed between them, it was familiar to her, this stiffening. She'd spent weeks feuding with Will Sterling, with confronting him, and she'd do it again now, if it meant figuring this out.

She tapped a finger against the counter. "Look at me."

When he raised his head, she had the feeling he was doing what he'd done with the photograph. His eyes were on her, but somehow not; somehow it seemed he'd unfocused his gaze.

"I only mean that it's gotten pretty serious, and I'm—" He took his hands off the counter, tucked them into his pockets. "I'm not looking for serious. I never have been. Before, with the stuff we were doing to your place, and…"

"And the sex?" she said, her voice sharp, accusatory, probably overloud. Dee would be proud of this, she thought. But it was so *hurtful*, to hear him say that. Not serious? Not serious, when he'd seen her sixteen years ago? When now it felt to her like fate? When she'd decided to tell him…

"I don't mean that." One hand came out of his pocket, another frustrated swipe across his forehead. "I don't mean any—Nora, listen. I shouldn't be talking right now. I'm rattled."

"It was a *picture*," she snapped, but as soon as she said it, she regretted it, and not only because he winced. Not only because she clearly didn't understand the full extent of what he saw in that picture. But also because she was being the worst kind of hypocrite. The towel rack. The lamp she'd looked at for an hour this morning! Who was she to accuse someone of overreacting to an artifact, when she had a houseful of them upstairs that she was wringing her hands over getting rid of?

And anyway, what was she going to do, stand here and fight with a man to get him to be with her? She surely hoped Marian wasn't hearing any of this. Clinging to that thought kept her chin from quivering in hurt as she stepped away from the counter.

"This is me," he said, his eyes full of the kind of sympathy that made everything feel worse. "I know this is all me."

231

Oh, God. An *It's not you; it's me* speech. She was not going to stick around for that. "I'm going to let you get back to what you were doing."

She turned to go, but he caught her hand gently. "Nora."

She could've turned back to him, could've stepped into arms that she knew he would put around her. But she was afraid of that chin quiver starting up. So she simply stood still, her back to him, her hand held loosely in his.

"I don't want this to be over," he said quietly. "I only need—"

He stepped closer, close enough that she could feel the warmth of his body along her back. But she didn't turn around. She bowed her head, and when he spoke again, she could feel the touch of his breath along her neck.

"A little time to think."

She nodded once, trying to believe that time to think was what Will needed. He'd hurt her, taken the wind right out of her. But the feelings she had for him meant she didn't want him to be hurting, either.

And she could tell he was.

"Sure," she said, trying to draw on all that practiced charm she hoped she'd absorbed from watching him all this time. "We can talk when I get back."

His hand squeezed against hers, a reflex more than an assent, or an encouragement. When he spoke, he sounded reluctant. "I can come up after—"

She shook her head, too desperate to leave, tears threatening. "Everyone's around. Let's wait."

There was a long pause before he finally said, "Okay."

She ignored the disappointment she felt. He was only doing what she'd suggested, after all. She thought about turning around, thought about giving him a kiss goodbye, some more settled encouragement about this not being over.

But she didn't know if she could, not if he only wanted what they'd been doing so far.

So instead she squeezed his fingers back, not sure herself what she was trying to tell him with the gesture. She swallowed a lump of sadness and said, "I'll see you."

And when she walked away, he didn't try to hold on.

Chapter 16

Well, this was a first.

Will walked with Dr. Abraham down the corridor from the workroom toward the exit, his bag over his shoulder and his helmet held at his side. Beside him, Abraham was talking—something about an orthopedic surgeon who couldn't seem to distinguish between the urgency of a broken finger and a possible brain bleed. The case had happened hours ago—an early morning vehicle crash—but Abraham had been seething about it for the entire shift, coming back to it during any break in the action.

"He was trying to splint the finger," said Abraham, shaking his head. "I'd say it's against protocol, but I think you would agree, Dr. Sterling, that this is an understatement. In fact it is against common sense."

"Yeah," Will said, nodding, not bothering to mimic the formality. He didn't have the energy for it, not today.

Not for almost a week.

It wasn't, of course, a first to be walking these hospital corridors with Abraham, nor was it unusual for Will to be a mostly silent participant in Abraham's airing of grievances. But it was a first to have very nearly planned for it, to have hung around the bay until he knew Abraham would basically kick him out. It was a first to be grateful for it, to be dreading the moment they got to the exit doors. Frankly, Will could've listened to Gerald Abraham talk all evening, so long as it gave him an excuse to stay here.

An excuse to avoid going home.

"Orthopedics," Dr. Abraham was saying, "needs to review their practices. I plan to call the chief up there tomorrow."

"Good idea," Will said, even though he knew that guy, and it probably wasn't a good idea. He had an ego as big as the entire state.

When they pushed open the door, the heat and humidity felt oppressive, miserable. But Will didn't much mind that, either. He'd get on his bike, take the long way back to his place. He'd sweat until he was so tired that he'd *have* to sleep tonight.

In fact it is against common sense, he thought, but ignored it.

"Dr. Sterling," Abraham said, right as Will was setting his helmet on his head. "I would like to make note of my concern for you."

Will paused, a hand frozen on one of his chin straps. For the first time, he noticed that Abraham wasn't wearing the white coat. It made sense, he guessed, since the man was leaving, but it still made Will blink in surprise.

"Uh," he said, which was not an approach he typically took with his boss.

"I note, for example, that you have taken two extra shifts this week."

"Dr. Barrett-Goldberg had to take two personal days," he said, by way of explanation, even though it was a cheap one. The scheduler had those shifts covered weeks ago.

"I also note that during those shifts you worked longer than twelve hours and you are, in fact, over the appropriate limit for physicians in our department."

"I'm off tomorrow." A horrible thought. His stomach hurt when he considered it, all those hours free, and no hope of Nora. Even the clinic wasn't an option; he'd maxed out his hours there, too.

"And this is to say nothing of your mood," Abraham added, as though Will hadn't spoken. "Sullen, is how I would characterize it."

Maybe, on any other day, Will would have taken offense. But the truth was, sullen wasn't the half of it.

He was *miserable*.

In hell, exactly as he'd predicted.

Because he'd messed up with Nora, and now she was gone.

He'd known it as it had been happening, had experienced it almost in slow motion, outside of himself. Fragments of it felt clear, acute: his mom's handwriting, youthful even when she'd gotten older. Mrs. Salas's fingers at the edge of that photograph, her nails pink and glossy. His parents' faces—unlined, joyful, intense. Nora's arms around his waist, her cheek against his chest, her hair against his chin. Her hand letting go of his.

But so much of the rest of it felt fuzzy, too fast. He'd seen that picture and it was like smashing straight into a brick wall of everything he was afraid of becoming. And then he'd told Nora he wasn't looking for serious.

Ah, here was another crystal clear fragment: the look on her face when he'd said it. He was pretty sure his hiccupping heart had stopped right then and there, no matter that he was still standing here right now, relentlessly alive.

"I've had a rough few days," he said to Abraham, which was a comically understated understatement. It was like mentioning your broken finger instead of your possible brain bleed. In fact, maybe he and that surgeon had something in common. After all, "splinting the finger" was a pretty apt metaphor for what efforts he'd made with Nora since she'd left him standing, still shell-shocked, in Donny's apartment. A text before he'd left the building to see if she'd changed her mind about wanting to talk. A call the next morning, the day of her flight, which had gone to voice mail. When she'd texted him back a couple of hours later, her message had been brief, kind, tentative. *Got your message. Hope you're okay. Boarding flight. We'll talk when I get back. Xo.*

I love you, he'd wanted to reply, which couldn't make any sense. Sending her a text like that when he'd all but sent her away the day before? Sending her a text like that when he was still reeling from the shock of having had the idea to type it out in the first place?

He'd written *Good luck* instead, and then he'd spent the rest of the day absolutely kicking his own ass for it, much like Gerald Abraham planned to kick the figurative ass of the finger splinter.

The problem was, if what had happened between him and Nora was, basically, a brain bleed, he wasn't even sure if he should try to fix it. What he was going through now—this sullenness, this hell—this was the reason he didn't belong in something serious with Nora. This intensity, this recklessness, this selfishness—all of it, he should've stopped weeks ago. He'd taken it to a place with Nora he knew he wasn't capable of seeing through, not in the way she wanted. Not in the way she deserved.

But damn, he missed her. Like a hole right in the center of himself, a loneliness unlike anything he'd ever felt, and given the way he'd lived his life, that was really saying something.

"I'd like to invite you to dinner," Abraham said, and Will coughed, and then stared.

He couldn't even manage a reply.

"With Sally and myself. Let me assure you, though, that I have not fallen back into a routine."

"Uh," Will repeated.

"This dinner is at my home, and I am cooking, which is not something I often did during my marriage. Sally would enjoy having you with us."

Will cleared his throat, fully aware of how absolutely ridiculous he must look, standing here in his bike helmet, staring down in shock at his boss.

"I don't want to intrude," he said, which he recognized was exactly what people said when they wanted to be told they weren't intruding. And he realized that this was, actually, exactly what he wanted to be told. He wanted to have dinner with Gerald and Sally because he was confused and frustrated and lonely enough that a meal with a possibly reconciling couple sounded absolutely fine, or at least absolutely better than going back to his own place and staring into the void, thinking about how Nora would be back tomorrow night and he still had no idea what to do.

"You are not intruding because I already told Sally you were coming," Abraham said. "I phoned her two hours ago."

"What if I'd had other plans?"

There was a brief pause, Abraham looking up at Will like he'd just tried to splint a finger in the middle of a massive trauma.

"I'm sure you think you're rather mysterious, Dr. Sterling," he finally said, in that clipped, professional-rectitude voice. "But in fact it is very clear that your problem lately is that you have no plans at all."

—

For the first hour or so, it didn't really help.

One problem was that Gerald's place—though larger and in a posher part of town—was disturbingly similar to Will's own, at least in terms of the details. Like Will, Gerald seemed to have missed the memo on hanging artwork or putting furniture in places other than "up against a wall." Also like Will, he seemed to have an aversion to household items that didn't serve any particular function; beyond the couch, chair, and coffee table, the living room had nothing in it except a floor lamp and five shelves of books, most of them related to medicine. Will had two such shelves, and all of a sudden he saw the next three decades of his life built out in front of him: one shelf at a time, more and more books about the only thing he filled his time with.

There was also the problem of Sally's arrival—not in and of itself an issue, since he liked Sally and also welcomed a break from the ongoing talk about the orthopedics department's failures. But when she bustled through the front door—using a key, Will noticed, signaling him to the state of this reconciliation—she was holding a big, blue plastic cat carrier. When she set it down in the entryway and opened the door, Quincy and

Francis ran to Will like they remembered him, and he coped with an outrageous longing for the nights he spent alone with them in Donny's apartment, Nora only two floors above instead of all the way across the country. When they left him to rub themselves across Gerald's shins, meowing until he gave them treats from a package he had on his counter, Will thought seriously about hiding in the bathroom to google (on his *tele*phone) whether there were any hypoallergenic cats in existence. The hairless kind, maybe? Would Nora like one of those? Would that fix what he'd done, what he still couldn't do?

And then there was the problem of watching Gerald and Sally this way, two people he'd known separately who had never really made sense in his mind as being together. Their reconciliation clearly wasn't settled yet, and it was somehow both amusing and stressful to watch them try for it, like they were doing a dance they hadn't quite learned all the steps to. In the small kitchen, a sweating glass of iced tea in his hand, Will could see Sally struggle not to interfere with what Gerald was doing with his roast chicken; at the table, Will could hear the way Gerald worked to acknowledge all the things Sally said, even the digressions—something about a sequined headband in the middle of a story about her book club, something about ankle weights while she talked about the city council campaign she was volunteering for. It was awkward and gentle and fascinating, and that was because, Will realized, he had never seen anything like it. His own parents' togetherness had always seemed effortless, assumed. A default state of being that had been disconcerting in its own way.

Eventually, though, things eased: Will was hungrier than he'd thought, and Quincy and Francis sat on a chair next to him and watched food go from his plate to the mouth like they were at a tennis match. Once he was used to it, Gerald and Sally's conversation became much like Gerald's workday lectures and complaints—background noise that was welcome, at least, for the way it drowned out Will's own thoughts.

But as soon as he set his fork and knife across his plate, Sally looked straight across the table at him and said, "Well, I guess Gerry isn't going to bring it up."

Who's Gerry? Will thought.

"I brought it up," the man Will would never call *Gerry* said. "At the hospital. I mentioned his work hours and his attitude."

Sally rolled her eyes. Will didn't want to be responsible for any friction, so he said, "I have been working a lot. With… an attitude."

Sally put down her own knife and fork and set her elbows on the table, a move Gerald tracked with his eyes and then seemed to—with effort—look away from.

"Is this about the woman from your building?"

Will thought he could feel Quincy and Francis staring at him. "How do you know that?"

"You probably forgot that you went after her like she was a house on fire that day you almost got caught in a public relations disaster!" She looked dreamily toward the chair beside Will. "That was the day I took home my babies."

Will swallowed. "Right. No, I didn't forget."

"I knew you had a thing for her."

At this, Gerald stood and collected plates, and Will had a feeling like he'd had the day Marian and Mrs. Salas had arrived with all their Tupperware. *Sabotage*, he thought, but this time, he supposed he didn't really mind.

"I've got more than a thing for her," he said, because the correction seemed important. "That's the problem."

Sally looked at him with eyes full of sympathy. "So it's unrequited, then. No wonder you look this bad."

He would've been insulted, but he'd seen himself. He *did* look bad. He needed a shave and a good night of sleep, and also probably a few more meals like the one he'd just eaten.

"I'm not sure it's unrequited," he said, which was an embarrassing thing to admit. But also he was sitting at a dining table next to two cats and getting a talking-to from his boss's ex-wife, so.

"Well, what's the problem, then?" She lowered her voice and smiled. "Does she criticize you for putting your elbows on the table?"

"Nothing like that." He shifted in his seat. "I'm not—I don't know that it's a good idea, for me to get serious with someone."

"You're one of those, then. Commitment-phobic!" She threw up her hands. "I've met a bunch like you. When you turn forty and start losing your hair you'll probably want to have a baby."

Will resisted the urge to touch his hair.

"No, that's not it." Or at least it wasn't that particular version of it, not the way Sally meant.

"It's her or it's no one," he added, and as soon as it was out of his mouth he felt the truth of it, right in the aching center of his heart.

Sally had a look on her face like Mrs. Salas when he talked medicine. "So why isn't it a good idea?"

She said it so nicely, so genuinely, that Will thought he probably could've told her the whole thing, and she would've listened.

I've got this fear, he could've said, *that I'm exactly like my parents.* He could've said, *I've got this fear that I don't know how to love anyone any other way.* He could've told her about what had happened to him, when he'd seen that picture: a big, blurry rush of unpleasant memories. He could have told her that seeing his parents so young and in love had only reminded him of where they'd ended up: utterly lost at the prospect of being without each other.

I've got this fear that I'd lose sight of everything else.

But Will's boss was still in the other room and Sally didn't have all night, and anyway, this wasn't as simple as fixing up Donny's apartment or finding a home for the two cats sitting next to him. This wasn't the kind of thing Sally could have a solution for.

So instead he said, "She and I, we're pretty different."

Sally shrugged. "Gerald and I are different."

"You're divorced."

She pursed her lips and cocked her head at him, giving him an exasperated look. "*Obviously*," she said, "we are *working* on it."

He nodded down at his placemat, appropriately chastened.

"Will," Sally said, and he could tell a big, frustrated, *Why are you like this?* sigh was lingering beyond it. "Let me ask you a question."

One of the cats started to climb onto his lap. Quincy, which meant it was fifty-fifty he was about to get peed on, screamed at, or both.

"Why not," he said blandly, pretty much to both Sally and Quincy.

"Do you *want* to work on it?"

Quincy's tail swiped across Will's face like an admonishment, and frankly, it was extremely clarifying. *Of course you try to fix a brain bleed, asshole*, he thought to himself, straightening in his chair. It was like having an anchor dropped in his body, slowing him down enough to see his surroundings, to actually *think* for what felt like the first time in days, maybe since he'd seen that picture. He thought about Gerald in the other room, washing dishes and probably deep breathing through his annoyance over Sally's elbows on the table. He thought of Gerald in the hospital, asking him about purchasing a kitten or a gift card, trying to sort out ideas for nonroutine dates.

God. Suddenly, being more like Gerald Abraham seemed a whole lot better than being himself, selfish and sullen and ruminating. So he'd overreacted to the photograph. So he'd gotten too in his head about his parents, and about himself. That didn't mean he couldn't work on it with Nora; that didn't mean he couldn't find a way to figure this out so that it would be good for them both. He just had to focus. A diagnosis, and now a treatment. *In fact it is common sense!*

"Yes," he said to Sally, gently moving a stiff-legged Quincy back to his chair. "I do."

Sally smiled across the table at him, her expression a mixture of pride and excitement that dampened some of Will's confidence. He cringed, thinking of the *Good luck* text.

"Pretty sure I've dug a big hole here," he said.

Sally might as well have had a tablet and a neon pink binder in front of her when she spoke again.

"I suppose it's a bit like that mess of an apartment you walked into not so long ago! You've got to start somewhere."

-

When Will walked into his own dark apartment an hour later, "starting somewhere" did, admittedly, feel like a dimmer prospect than it had when he'd been sitting across from Sally. After all, Nora was still in San Diego until tomorrow, and his options for starting to fix things were limited. He could've called, but she'd been pretty clear about wanting to wait until she got back, and anyway, he wanted to give this the focus it deserved, didn't want to call her unless he'd really thought about what he wanted to say.

And another *Good luck*–type text message absolutely wasn't going to cut it.

He kept the lights off at first, not ready to see his spare, functional apartment yet, not wanting the reminder that he—unlike… Gerry…? nope, Gerald—might not ever get out of this purgatory. But as he moved through his lonely night-time routine—shower, sleep shorts, brushing his teeth—lights became a necessity, and when he went into the kitchen to get himself a glass of water, he caught sight of his mother's old book on the counter in the spot where he'd left it almost a week ago. The photograph was in there, he knew; he'd seen Nora slide it gently between the pages when she'd come to find him.

One place to start, he supposed, would be taking that photograph out and staring down at it until he could be assured he wouldn't overreact again. But the fact that the book was still there at all, he supposed, was progress of a sort—years ago, months ago, weeks ago, even, he probably would've gotten rid of it, would've put the photograph into the same box where he kept all pictures from his childhood, small and shoved into the back of his closet.

That was Nora's influence, he thought—maybe she held on to things too hard, but she did love an artifact, more like her parents than maybe she realized. Over at her place, she had an origin story for everything, and mentioning them brought a certain smile to her face, always. The teapot that had been an anniversary gift from her grandfather to her grandmother. The painted tile that Nora's mother had made in third grade. The lamp that he'd seen her giving away last week, apparently from Italy.

So even though he didn't much want to look at the book or the photograph yet, it comforted him, somehow, to know he'd held on to them; it gave him hope he could fix this with Nora. Still, for the first time in his life he thought it might be nice to have the kind of artifact lying around that might make him feel like she did—comforted and closer to someone she'd lost.

A thought hit him, and he set down his glass so quickly that water splashed over the back of his hand. He shook it off, wiped it on his shorts, and moved down his galley to the drawer where he always shoved extra pens or rubber bands or those garbage bag ties he never ended up using anyway. He yanked it open, heart hiccupping, and there it was, exactly what he was looking for: a scroll of paper, a number written lightly at the top.

He smiled down at it, the memory like a balm: in his mind was a long green dress, the line of Nora's shoulders, her long braid and her flower crown, the look she'd given him when she'd handed this scroll over to him, mischief in her eyes.

He felt a smile spread over his face.

He took it with him to his bedroom, for the first time in days not dreading the thought of lying down without her. He propped his pillow up against the wall (something to be said for his furniture-arranging) and sat back, tapping the scroll against his palm and thinking about that night—not only Nora, but also Mrs. Salas and her Solo cup, Mr. Salas's food and Benny's beer, Jonah calling him "Beanpole" and Marian and Emily sitting in the front row, their hands joined together. He thought about himself at that microphone, determined to win over the crowd.

When he first pulled it open, it didn't strike him as much more than what he saw that night: a name he recognized, a soothingly short number of lines. "Sonnet 98." Spring, summer, flowers, that sort of thing. He remembered Nora saying it was sad, and Jonah, too. He didn't know if he was up for sad, but he was up for starting somewhere, and a poem that meant something to his story with Nora, that seemed as good as any idea he had so far and definitely better than *Good luck*.

So he started to read.

At first it wasn't easy: words he recognized but that he struggled to make sense of in this context, laid out in an order that seemed unnatural to him. He read it silently twice, all of it swimming together, before he tried it out loud again. One line at a time, making sense of punctuation marks like he never had in his life. He read it and read it, until it got easier, until it got to be like breathing.

"'From you have I been absent in the spring,'" he read, again and again.

A poem about missing someone.

About moving through the world and missing someone all the time. A few days, or maybe sixteen whole years. Living every spring and summer of your life without really noticing it. Everything you looked at that was beautiful you couldn't see quite right: *figures of delight*, all of them an imitation of the person you were missing the most.

"'Yet seem'd it winter still,'" he read, the phrase like a cold wind across his skin, "'and you, away, / As with your shadow I with these did play.'"

Jesus Christ, that *was* a sad poem.

But also... also it felt like a start.

He looked at the clock, realized he'd been reading for a long time. Where Nora was, it wasn't so late. He could have typed it all out right then, probably from memory by now. The next time she checked her phone, she'd find it—this memory of one of the first nights they'd spent together, this written expression of how he'd felt all the time without her. Not since she left.

Since before, since before.

But as he reached for his phone, he had a passing thought for the morning, for the golden hour when Nora would be waking up in California. By that time, he would have already started his day. He'd send it then, he decided, so that she'd know how much he missed her, thought of her, while she was gone.

So she'd know how glad he was that she was coming back.

That, he decided, would be exactly the right start.

Chapter 17

"He's going to fight for you, Nora."

Sitting crisscrossed on Deepa's jewel-blue velvety couch, Nora sipped her wine and shrugged, affecting a posture of nonchalance that did not, perhaps, entirely match the range of feelings she'd wrestled with over the course of this long and stressful week in San Diego. Surprise and frustration, excitement and anxiety, certainty and also a fair bit of sadness. Inside her, it all swirled, a soaking-rain sort of thunderstorm that somehow felt welcome for all the things it was washing away.

"He might," said Nora. "But it won't change my mind."

As of today, Nora had made the decision: she was leaving Verdant, too.

Not right away, not until she'd wrapped up work on all her current build-outs, and not until she'd helped Austin bring on someone new.

But soon.

It wasn't that being back in the office had been awful. In a way, it'd been comforting: friends she hadn't seen in months other than through videoconferences, favorite snacks from the cafe on the building's first floor, two in-person bathroom mirror meeting debriefs with Dee, who was taking all the news in happy stride, given that she had already found a new and better gig at a marketing firm back in Berkeley. Even the time Nora had spent with Austin had been comforting: however frustrating he could be, it was good to remember how well they'd always worked together, how he trusted her expertise and valued her input, even on projects she wasn't all that enthusiastic about.

But it had also been clarifying. In person, there was no denying the way Austin had changed, the way his priorities had shifted. And now that he'd revealed the full extent of his plans—the move to LA, the shift away from sustainability alone, the pivot to celebrity and influencer brands—Nora had known there was a reckoning coming for her and Austin. After the full team meeting in the afternoon, he'd pulled her aside and practically begged her to come back to California. "More money," he'd said. "A new title, whatever you want. But this will go smoother if you're with us in person."

He'd left that *if* there as a concession—not quite telling her that remote work was off the table, but definitely not pledging his ongoing support of it, either. Certainly not if she wanted more money, or that new title.

A few years ago—a few *months* ago, really—she would have felt that tug of loyalty to him, would have genuinely considered it: a move to a city she wasn't overly fond of, an uprooting of her life for someone who'd always been firmly in her corner.

But now, Nora was different. She knew, deep down: she didn't want to leave Chicago.

Not now.

Maybe not ever.

And it wasn't just on account of her loyalty this time. When she'd chosen Chicago last fall, she'd done it because Nonna had needed her, because Nonna had wanted her to stay. She'd known she was going back to a place and to people she loved— the building, Nonna's apartment, her neighbors. But now, something else drew her there; now, she was choosing for herself. She wanted to go back to the building and her apartment and her neighbors, but also to the neighborhood and the city around it; she wanted to go back for the weirdly Midwestern beaches and the sights she hadn't seen, to the big, brutal seasons and the collective attitude of a city that didn't get nearly enough respect.

And she wanted—maybe foolishly—to go back to Will.

"Honestly I can't believe he hasn't called like a million times already," Dee said, and without thinking, Nora answered.

"I *did* basically tell him not to."

Dee furrowed her brow. "Wait, you did? I thought at the meeting you told him—" She broke off and nudged Nora with her foot, obviously clocking the flush Nora could feel heating her cheeks. "*Haaaaaaaaa,*" she said, happy teasing in her voice. "You're thinking about *him* again!"

Nora took another sip of her wine, skipped the shrug this time. No point trying to fake it, since in between the many work rants and resolutions she and Deepa had both participated in over the course of the week, they'd also spent a fair bit of time talking through what had happened between Nora and Will.

"Ice-cold, Eleanora," said Dee, laughing. "About to tell a whole man you're going to leave him, and you're already on to the next one."

"It's not the *same,*" said Nora. "Austin is my colleague. And also, I think we have well established by this point that I am not, in fact, *on* with Will."

She shifted, uncrossing her legs and adjusting so that she and Dee faced each other, both of them now with backs against either arm of the couch, legs stretched alongside each other. Dee wiggled her feet against Nora's ribs, a gentle, teasing comfort that made Nora smile.

"You're going to be okay?" Dee asked. "If he doesn't come around?"

Nora dropped her head back, closing her eyes. Behind her lids the words *Good luck* flashed irritatingly, so she opened them again, staring up at Dee's ceiling and sighing out a disappointed breath. It wasn't fair, maybe, to be upset that Will hadn't reached out, especially not after all the times she'd said it was better to wait until she was back. At first, she'd set that boundary out of fear—fear that she'd cry, fear that she'd blurt everything she felt out into the open air and freak him out forever. Even as she'd

listened to the message he'd left her the morning of her flight—
Nora, he'd begun, in that perfect way, *I wanted to hear your voice
before you left*—she'd still forced herself to finish packing, to get
all the way to the airport before she let herself text back. Some
of it had been that same fear, but some of it had been her belief
that Will really did need the time. That what he needed to work
out—about his parents, about being *serious*—he needed to work
out without her.

Now, though—a day away from heading back—she worried
she'd made a mistake, insisting on the wait. Banishing him to
silence when he'd at least tried to reach out, and all because she
hadn't wanted to take the risk: to tell him she loved him, and
to have him not say it back.

To have him not *feel* it back.

"I will," she said finally, trying to convince herself, trying to
ignore the vise grip she felt around her heart when she thought
about it. "I'm going to tell him how I feel, and if he doesn't
feel it, too, I'll move on."

She paused, lifting her head to look across the way at her
friend. "Not that I have a great track record of moving on from
things in an expedient manner."

Dee smiled sympathetically, patting Nora's shin. "Now,
now," she said. "Give yourself some credit. You forget the
pictures you showed me of that bathroom you redid."

"True," Nora thought, trying not to focus on the fact that
she'd done nearly all of that moving on with Will right at her
side. "And I have plans now."

All week, she'd been thinking about them: changes she
would make once she got back home. Away from the apartment, not so immediately surrounded by Nonna's things, it
had been easier to consider. When she pictured it now—that
jammed-up bedroom she used as an office, that floral couch
she really couldn't stand—she could see how silly she had been
to keep *so much* of it exactly the same. And as she stayed here
with Deepa, helping her friend with the preliminary packing

for her move next month, it'd been easy to see how well Dee's things—her bold, comfortable furniture, her gilt-framed decorative mirrors hung in clever arrangements on the walls, her many, *many* candles—reflected Dee herself.

Nora wanted a chance to have that again in the place she called home.

So. More changes to the apartment. Looking for a new job. That was the plan.

With or without Will.

"Why don't we FaceTime him now?" said Dee, always impatient. "I'll stay out of frame, and I'll leave if it gets weird, I *promise*. Here, I'll get you more wine so you can really lean in to it," she said, moving to swing her legs over Nora's.

"No, no," Nora said, draining the small amount of wine that was left in her glass. "I don't want to have too much before I fly tomorrow. It always makes me woozy."

"*Waaaaaaah*," Dee said dramatically, grabbing at Nora's shins in playful desperation. "You're *leaving* me tomorrow *and* you won't give me anything *entertaining* to watch tonight!"

Nora laughed and bent her knees, gently toppling Dee to the side. "I ought to sleep," she said. "You know me and my early starts."

"I swear to God, Nora," Dee said, standing. "If you make noise before six a.m. again, that's it for you ever being my houseguest in the future. Even when I get a gigantic condo in Berkeley with my new huge salary."

"I said I was sorry about the garbage disposal! I thought it was the light switch!"

For the next few minutes, they laughed and argued as they made up the couch into Nora's bed for the night, Dee eventually giving Nora the same lecture she'd given her for the last several nights, which was all about how Nora didn't take off her makeup at night properly. When Nora finally—after getting yelled at about washcloths a few more times through the bathroom door—settled onto the couch, calling a joking

"Good night, Sleeping Beauty!" to Dee, she felt the fatigue from the wine and from the workday settle over her like a blanket. But even as her mind and body sunk closer to sleep, she still thought of Will, the same way she had every night she'd been away—whether he was okay, whether he missed her, whether he'd ever held his phone in his hand, like she had, and thought of calling. She did it now, too, out of habit—swiped her thumb across her screen, navigated to the text box where Will's *Good luck* sat like a bad omen.

Maybe she should text something—a few words about how it had gone over the past few days? A question about how his week had been?

But no—no. She was too tired, and it was so late in Chicago. She didn't want to take the chance on waking him, and anyway, she'd said they should wait. She'd text him when she landed; she wouldn't force herself to hold off anymore.

She must've fallen asleep before setting her phone back down, and she must've slept deeply, because when she woke again, it was still clutched in her hand, still resting, face down, on her stomach. She blinked into the darkness, unsure at first what had woken her, until she registered that the phone she was holding was ringing. On instinct, she winced and silenced it, thinking of Dee in the other room. She sat straight up to squint down at the screen while her brain tried to wake up enough to figure out what was going on: how long had she been sleeping, who was calling...

Oh.

She smiled down at the screen when she saw: 4:30 a.m., and it was Will. *The golden hour*, she thought, and she could only blame the fact that she had missed him so much for not thinking of anything else at all.

But when she answered, he only had to speak two words before she knew something was well and truly wrong.

"Nora, baby," he said.

The good news was, Will was exceptional at delivering bad news.

He'd told her the important things first: that Jonah was okay—in the hospital but okay, and not in any imminent danger at all. He told her that the fall had been the result of a middle-of-the-night trip to the bathroom and a pair of shoes Jonah had forgotten he'd left in the hallway, and not the result of any underlying balance or consciousness problems. He told her that the largest fracture had been clean—compound, right in the middle of the femur—and that the other three in the hand he'd used to break his fall were, all things considered, not devastating. He told her, too, that Jonah was awake and his mostly regular self, but that he'd need to have surgery soon.

He told her, again and again, that Jonah would be okay.

But the bad news was the bad news: that Jonah had fallen, that he was hurt, that it'd taken about ten minutes for Mr. and Mrs. Salas to wake up when Jonah had used his good hand to thud one of the offending shoes on the floor as a way to call for help.

That Nora had been all the way in California when she'd found out someone she loved was hurt.

"Marian called me from the hospital," Will explained, while Nora's heart pounded in the early-morning dark. "She thought I might be able to help, get additional information where I could. She was going to call you, too, but I—I thought it'd be better to wait, with you so far away. Until I could get more information. I hope that's all right."

"It's all right," she'd said, already scrambling to get her things together. "I'm coming. Tell everyone I'm coming."

By the time she arrived at the hospital hours later—straight from the airport, her luggage hastily packed in order to catch the earlier flight she'd managed to snag with an assist from Deepa, who hadn't once complained about the early hour—Nora was a wreck, nervous and stressed even though her phone was filled with regular, reassuring texts from Will, the limp *Good luck* from before long buried.

When she walked through the front doors, she followed the instructions he'd sent her for where to go, barely registering her surroundings. This was the same hospital Nonna had been in, at the end, and she was grateful that Jonah was on a different floor. Still, her hands trembled with nerves as she rode the elevator up, and she had to shake them out before grabbing the handle of her suitcase again, rolling it clumsily behind her as she disembarked, using her free hand to type a *Here* to Will as she turned out of the elevator bay.

She'd taken only a few steps before she saw him down the corridor, stepping out of the wide doorway that must've opened to the family waiting room he'd already told her about, his phone in hand, his head tipped down toward its screen. When he looked up and over, spotting her, he moved so swiftly and so purposefully that she simply stilled in place, as though all the residual stress from her rush to the airport and her long, tense flight finally caught up to her, filling up her body like concrete, like lead.

She set a hand across her eyes, unbearably relieved to be back, and to have Will here, and with the full force of the chin quiver she'd tried so hard to hide last time she'd seen him, she started to cry.

"Nora," he said, getting close, and then he was surrounding her, his arms encircling her, pulling her close and tight against him.

"He's okay," he said, ducking his head to put his mouth closer to her ear.

"He's okay," he repeated.

She nodded and kept right on crying, because she was glad Jonah was okay and also upset that he wasn't, not in the way she wanted him to be. She cried because she hated this hospital and because she missed Nonna. And she cried because this hug, by this particular person, felt about as good as anything she could imagine, and she hadn't even let herself realize how much— over the course of these past few days—she'd missed being held by him.

"I've got food down there for you," he said softly, and she thought he might've said other stuff before that, too, doctor-type stuff, only she hadn't been paying attention to anything other than his warmth and his strength and his familiar scent for long minutes. "Marian and Emily are here now, and Benny just took Mr. and Mrs. Salas home for the night."

She nodded against his chest, felt his hand slip down the length of her hair, felt him let out an uneven breath as his arms tightened briefly around her. When he loosened them again, she leaned back so she could look at him even through her tears, and almost as soon as she did he moved, too, lifting his hands from her body so he could gently wipe his thumbs across her cheeks.

"Okay now," he said softly, and she closed her eyes at the tenderness of it, a few more tears slipping out as she did.

When she opened them again, she could see him better, her eyes drier and her mind calmer, and she smiled softly as she saw his ridiculously messy hair, his slightly crooked glasses. She reached up and straightened them. She wanted to say, *I love you*, but she also didn't, not when she felt like a throbbing, raw, exposed nerve, not when she felt like she'd be holding him hostage to her current state of emotional distress.

So instead she said, "I'm glad to see you."

"Nora, you've got no idea." He breathed in, his lashes lowering, his head tipping down and briefly shaking side to side. "You've got no idea how I missed you."

"I've got some idea."

"Let me say how sorry I am, about before you left. About that text message. I've been thinking, and—"

"Will," she interrupted, pushing his hair back from his brow. "Let's not talk about it here, okay? Not in a hospital."

Will blinked, his brow furrowing, like he couldn't imagine why a hospital wasn't a perfectly fine place to have any sort of conversation at all, but then he nodded and said, "Right, yeah. That makes sense. You must want to see Marian and Emily, and I can go check—"

"I'm so glad you're here," she blurted desperately, because she *was*, and also because she hated the way he'd looked when he'd said that—cautious and maybe even a little scared. She moved to grab his hand, to link their fingers together, to reassure him in the same way she wanted to feel reassured—not just about Jonah, but about her relationship with Will. Her future with Will.

For hours she hadn't thought about it at all, not really; from the minute he'd called her she could only think about getting back, about Jonah and whether he would be well. She'd clung to each of Will's updates like a lifeline, but she hadn't thought much beyond that, hadn't thought about how they'd left things before she'd gone—Will telling her it was too much, Will telling her he didn't want anything serious.

But now that she was standing here with him like this, she clung to other things: the way he'd called off work, hustling to get information from and about the doctors who were treating Jonah, the way he'd stayed with her neighbors and kept calm and responsible and practical for them all. She clung to the concern etched into every line of his face, to the wrinkles in his shirt and the hospital badge clipped at the waistband of his jeans. She clung to the way he'd done all this for her and her neighbors, the way he'd taken this all so seriously. He'd been so... so *loyal* to her, and to the people she cared so much about.

She thought of Dee last night—*Had that only been last night?*—asking whether she'd be okay, if Will didn't come around. If Will didn't want anything serious.

Now, though, after the day she'd had, after the things he'd done—that question felt ridiculous, insignificant.

Of course he would come around.

Of course he knew this was serious.

"I wouldn't be anywhere else," he said.

"Let me get down there and see this food you brought me. Check in with Marian and Emily."

Will nodded and loosened his grip, untangling their fingers and moving to tuck his hands into his pockets.

Before he could hide them both away, she caught his hand again, relinking their fingers and setting her other hand back onto her suitcase, rolling it to her side. She looked up at him, a question in her eyes, and his eyes softened, his hand tightening around hers again in answer. *There*, she thought, a weight lifting. *There, that's settled.* He kept hold of her as he shifted, gently moving her other hand off her suitcase and rolling it toward himself instead.

"I'm not going to have Marian and Emily see you carrying your own bag," he said sheepishly, and she felt her eyes well again, relief and happiness mixed in with all her worry and nerves.

If Marian and Emily were surprised to see Will and Nora walk into the family waiting room hand in hand, neither of them showed it; in fact, if anyone was surprised, it was Nora herself. Months ago, when Nonna had been here, Emily had visited once, pale and shaken, stressed enough that Nora had reassured her repeatedly that it was okay for her to stay home. Now she sat beside Marian, a circle of needlepoint in her lap, her expression not quite calm but not nearly as tense and scared as Nora would have expected. Nora let go of Will's hand to cross the room to them, greeting them each with a hug and an apology.

"You've got no reason to be sorry," said Marian. "How would you be able to predict when Jonah doesn't pick up after himself!"

Nora smiled, because that was really just like Marian. For however long it took Jonah to heal, she'd be giving him a lecture every single day.

"I wish I would have been here, though."

Emily patted Nora's arm. "He knew you were coming. We told him before they took him to surgery."

"Anyway, I don't see what help you would've been!" said Marian. "You know who helped is that young man across the hall."

Nora furrowed her brow, and Will cleared his throat. She looked over to where he stood, his hands back in his pockets. "My tenant. He's a fourth-year medical student."

"Right," Nora said, remembering now. "I forgot."

"He was very calm for a person so young. I believe he means to be like your Will here. An emergency physician."

Nora flushed at the phrase: *your Will*. Obviously, there'd been the hand-holding, and even before that, Nora and Will's more lax approach to the secrecy of this whole thing. But looking at Marian and Emily now, she wondered if she ought to make some kind of... statement? Saying something out loud, though—was that too much, given that she and Will hadn't had their promised conversation?

But Emily saved the moment, speaking first. "I might've noticed him come by some evenings. I only mentioned it to Marian."

"I mentioned it to everyone else," Marian said, wholly unashamed. "Corrine is thrilled, I'll have you know. It's taken her a lot of effort not to say anything."

Nora cringed, embarrassed. Probably she'd seen them the night they'd come back from Garfield Park. She should've said something sooner.

Emily placidly worked her needlepoint. "I'll tell you he's hard to miss when he's carrying a seven-foot pole up the walkway at almost ten o'clock at night."

From behind her, Will made a noise—sort of a snort-guffaw. Emily had known since the shower curtain rod! That was... a while, then.

The actual whole time!

"I'm sorry!" Nora said, knee-jerk. "I mean, for not—"

"It's your business," said Emily quietly. "There's no reason to apologize."

Nora blinked at them in surprised silence, her brain still catching up to the stress of the last several hours, to the relief of having come back to Will's waiting arms and her neighbors—these two and Mrs. Salas, at the very least—unbothered by the whole entire thing. She knew there was so much stress ahead, knew she still felt a rattle of nerves throughout her body when she thought of Jonah, but it felt good, for now, to have this part feel so easy.

Marian picked up a brown bag from the seat beside her and held it out to Nora. "Come on and eat your food. This man brought you a muffin that's as big as a baby's head."

Nora took the bag, extremely wishing Marian had not compared its contents to a head of any kind, and then turned to look at Will, who was watching her, his expression a mixture of amusement and concern. When she moved to sit on one of the small couches across from Marian and Emily, he stayed standing, the lightness falling away from his expression.

"I'm going to go check at the nurse's station," he said. "To see if—"

"Will," she said, patting the seat beside her, wanting him to feel as settled about things as she did. "Come on."

"I tried to be careful," he said quietly, when he sat down. "When I came over, I mean."

She shrugged and opened the bag, the smell of sugary goodness wafting up, and her mouth watered. "It's okay," she said, reaching in. "I'm relieved they know. I was going to tell them anyway, if…"

She trailed off, focusing on her head muffin. *If you'd said you wanted to choose me, too.* She was glad to have something to stuff in her face for the time being.

He set a hand on her thigh and checked his phone. "We should hear something pretty soon, I'd guess, judging by how long this surgery usually takes."

Nora nodded and chewed, watching Marian and Emily across the way, watching as Will easily joined into their conversation—asking Emily about the plant in the corner ("It's not a real plant," Emily said, and Nora had a feeling Will already knew that but wanted to give Emily a laugh), talking to Marian about the next poetry night ("I've been getting into poetry," Will said to her, and Marian gave him a look like he was 100 percent lying). She thought about all the things she'd feared that day Will had crashed the building meeting—all the ways she thought she was letting Nonna down, all the ways she thought she was letting her neighbors down.

But right now, in this bland, uncomfortable waiting room, Nora watched Will make conversation with two of her toughest-crowd neighbors, all the while waiting for a health update on the man who was, no doubt, the third toughest. She thought about Nonna and how she liked good manners and pleasant conversation and anyone who liked marinara sauce, and also anyone who liked Nora. Nonna would have been charmed, for sure. Real estate feuds aside, Nonna would have liked having Will as part of this little family.

He's come around, she told herself firmly, and with a small sigh of relief, she finished the last of her muffin, rested her head against Will's shoulder, and settled in to wait.

Chapter 18

Eventually, Marian and Emily went home, too.

The doctor had called around nine, reporting that Jonah was out of the surgery on his leg, doing fine in recovery, no complications. Nora had sagged against Will, already reaching for her phone to call Benny. Marian and Emily had both pressed their hands together and closed their eyes, twin prayers of thanks before they'd turned to hug each other tight. It'd be a while longer before Jonah would be transferred to his room for the night, and Nora had insisted that Marian and Emily go, had promised that she'd stay the whole night through.

"I've got all my things, anyway," she'd said, gesturing toward her suitcase, and Emily and Marian had both turned their eyes on Will expectantly.

"I'm staying," he'd said, and it felt like their official seal of approval when they'd nodded and finally agreed to make their way home.

Alone with Nora, the immediate crisis mitigated, he wondered if it would turn awkward between them—things they hadn't said, but things they'd agreed not to talk about here. But for Will, at least, it was the opposite of awkward. It came so easy to him this way—to get her tea, to help her wrangle things out of her messily packed suitcase so she could go wash her face, to answer every medical question she had about Jonah, who hadn't been brought to a room until after midnight, to arrange his body so she could rest comfortably against him. It all felt so practical, so responsible. So safe.

He recognized her energy from many days and nights he'd spent checking in on families—tired but teed-up, relieved but worried. With her head on his thigh and her legs draped over the arm of the tiny love seat, she told him all kinds of things he didn't know, origin stories for how everyone had ended up in the building. Jonah had grown up nearby, the only child of parents who'd run a small grocery store less than five blocks away; he'd moved in after he married a woman who'd eventually left him (and the apartment) after only three months to move to Maine with a man Jonah worked with. Mr. and Mrs. Salas had moved in after they'd sold their place in Bucktown, only ever intending to stay for a few years but eventually making peace with the fact that their son would be staying for good in Singapore, the place where he'd gotten a job in finance after college. Benny's aunt Alma had lived in the building, and because he'd been her favorite, because he'd stayed with her for long periods when his own mother was ill, he'd taken over the lease way back when Alma had moved into a rest home. Marian and Emily—both from small, somewhat challenging families— had come to the building only two years after they'd graduated from college, the place where they'd met and fallen in love.

Nora's grandmother, for her part, had moved in as a widow, surprising Nora's mother—her only child—by selling her paid-off house in the suburbs and moving into an apartment that she'd always said had something special about it.

"Those little angels in the hallway," Nora said, her feet swinging gently back and forth, "I think that's what sold her. She loved things like that."

Nora thought Nonna had needed a new start, had needed to make a home only for herself after so many years of focusing on making her husband comfortable. "And with my mom so far away, she needed a new family, too, I think," Nora had said.

Will didn't miss that she'd skipped over whatever she might've known about Donny and his history with the building, a kindness that made him love her all the more. Instead, she went right on ahead to the year her grandmother had led the effort to take the building condo, to all the moments where various building traditions were born. Will listened and stroked his fingers idly through her hair, recognizing this for what it was: not only Nora winding herself down but also Nora giving him her full trust, giving him the history of the building that had been the source of their feud. As she spoke, her voice got lower and slower, her eyes closing longer and longer on each blink.

Orphans, kind of, he thought, thinking through the stories she'd told him—grown-ups upended for one reason or another, making their own family unit even amid weird wallpaper and awful wall sconces. For the first time since he got the call from Donny's lawyer, he let himself imagine that his uncle had left him the apartment not as some kind of cross-generational slap in the face but instead as some kind of offering. Some kind of apology, or gesture of understanding. From one orphan to another, maybe. A belated gift Donny—for whatever angry, grudging reason—hadn't been able to give Will sixteen years ago.

He felt strangely, surprisingly grateful to his uncle.

Against his leg, Nora's head felt heavier, her body earnestly sinking into sleep now. "Not gonna drool this time," she murmured. "Because I'm not sick."

"You can if you want," he told her, which he wasn't sure made sense, but it'd been a long day for him, too. He leaned his head back against the wall behind him, grateful that the lights above had dimmed automatically, grateful that he'd slept in far more uncomfortable places, grateful that Nora was home and that he was with her, that he'd gotten to help her. He thought sleepily of that scroll of poetry at home, the one he'd left on his nightstand. Little fragments of it caught at the edges of his brain: *lily's white, deep vermilion in the rose. Figures of delight.*

You, pattern of all those.

He'd have to remember to tell Nora about it, this sentimental start he'd made while she was away. But for now—Jonah's accident aside—this all seemed just as well: the best of who he was, all in service to her.

This is how I'll be with her, he told himself as he drifted off, as sure as if he'd settled on a treatment. *This isn't selfish at all.*

—

He might've known it wouldn't be so easy.

Will woke at the shift change, noises familiar: the more frequent elevator dings, the rattle of dining carts, the greetings of the morning crew and the goodbyes of those finishing up. His head was thudding from leftover tension and from the awkward position he'd dozed in, but on his lap Nora slept soundly, at some point in the night having compacted herself, knees pulled up almost to her chest so she could fit her whole body on the love seat, her cheek—she *had* drooled a little—on his thigh. The room was still empty of other visitors, so Will guessed it'd been a slow overnight around here. As carefully as possible, he slid his phone from his pocket and sent a text to Gerald, an activity he absolutely could not have imagined ever doing only a few months ago.

Were you able to find coverage for my shift today? he typed, checking for typos before he pressed send. He wasn't going to be caught sending Gerald Abraham an accidental, autocorrected *We're* for *Were*.

He set down the phone and closed his eyes again, knowing Gerald was not a particularly fast texter. But within a minute the reply came: *Yes.*

Will might have been unsettled by seeing Gerald's curtness in text message form, but he could see by the gray bubble beneath that he was still typing, so at least he wouldn't be leaving it at that.

Sally asks how your neighbor is doing.

Will started to type his response, a jargony summary of Jonah's injuries, before he realized that he hadn't told Sally about any of this.

Gerald's third reply came in while Will's fingers still hovered over his screen.

I am currently with Sally, as I slept over at her home last night.

Then there was a *winking* emoji.

"Jesus Christ!" Will said, nearly dropping the phone.

Nora jerked awake. "What happened?" she said, her voice somehow both groggy and deeply alert. "Is Jonah okay?"

Will reached out, settled a hand on her back. "Yeah, everything's fine. I'm sorry. I was—uh. Texting with my boss."

Who had clearly been desperate to inform him about this latest development in his (re)marriage efforts.

Nora sagged in relief, her breath coming quickly, and Will rubbed her back, apologizing again.

"Rounds are probably starting soon, so we might want to try to get into Jonah's room, see if we can be there to catch the doctor."

She nodded, shifting her body, pre-stretches that told him she was feeling the cramped discomfort, too. She turned toward him and set a hand on his thigh, pressing a closed-mouth kiss to his lips that—even in spite of their location—he wanted to take deeper. It'd been so long, after all, and—

"Oh *no*," Nora said, jerking back and looking down at Will's lap, lifting her hand slowly from his thigh before clapping it down again, groaning dramatically. "I did it *again*."

He smiled and caught her hand, giving a smacking, teasing kiss to her palm. "It's no big deal," he said, thinking that he could be perfectly happy waking up with Nora Clarke drooling on him for the rest of his life. "Go ahead and get cleaned up," he told her. "I'll meet you back in the hallway."

She leaned forward and kissed him again, standing to grab her bag. When she started to wheel it away, he felt the squeeze of her fingers around his, and he cleared his throat when he realized he'd been holding on to her. He let go, a wispy, nearly forgotten thread of discomfort winding through him that he shook off.

Focus, Will, he told himself, running through the questions he wanted to ask the surgeon when she came by this morning. He made his own way down the hall to a bathroom, splashing water on his face and brushing his teeth with one of the small, plastic-wrapped complimentary toothbrushes the hospital provided for overnight visitors. He stopped at a vending machine in the hall, got coffees for himself and Nora and a granola bar for her. He went to the nurses' station, glad to see that at least one of the nurses he'd spoken to last night was still there; she greeted him with a big smile and gleefully introduced him to the nurses who'd just come on.

"Your friend's up," she told him, and he straightened, immediately looking down the hall for Nora.

"Can we go in?" he asked.

"I'd say so. He's pretty sharp for the morning after a surgery like that! Kind of a tough guy, huh? Doc Terano should be by soon."

"Great." He took a swig of his coffee, his headache fading as the caffeine kicked in. He saw Nora down the hall and waved her over, not liking how fatigued she still looked. They'd talk to the doctor, visit with Jonah until he needed sleep again. Will could call one of the other neighbors to come sit for a while, get Nora back to her place to rest.

Easy.

But nothing was easy when they got into the room, not once Nora saw Jonah for the first time: the angry purple bruises on one side of his face; the hard, overly large line of his recently repaired leg beneath a thin blanket; the elaborate, mechanical-looking splint and sling keeping his hand perfectly set until his next surgery. She went stiff and she stayed that way, even though she was working to seem calm—greeting Jonah with a big smile and an apology, promising to bring him anything he needed from his apartment, gently arranging the pillows behind his head and looking over the equipment that surrounded him as though she needed to memorize it.

"Nora," Will said, because Jonah had just sent him a look that he could've sworn meant, *Help me out, Beanpole.* "You want to take this seat here?"

She shook her head, taking out her phone. "Let me make this list," she said. "I assume you'll want your tablet and charger, and…"

Will knew what this was, had seen it a hundred times. When you weren't used to being around it all the time, seeing someone like this—banged-up, groggy, the particular sort of pale and weak the hospital made a person look—it was more than simply stressful. It was panic holding you in a loose grip, its fingers forever poised to tighten right around your middle and take the breath right out of you. Some people cried, some people pressed a call button until they found somebody to yell at, and some people, like Nora, tried to take total control.

But it didn't matter so much that Will had seen it before; he hated seeing it on Nora, and he felt panic start to get a hold on him, too, tentative and cruelly teasing. While they waited, he felt useless, impractical, unsure, and unlike with Marian and Emily last night, Nora kept her distance from him in front of Jonah, standing beside his bed and barely looking Will's way.

He felt, suddenly, like he entirely didn't belong.

When the doctor finally came in, Will was suffused with relief: finally, some way he could be useful. Dr. Terano was clearly a great surgeon, delivering information clearly and succinctly, confident in Jonah's odds for a full recovery but straightforward about the challenges ahead. On a sheet of scrap paper he'd snagged from the patient whiteboard behind him, he scribbled notes in his usual way, phrases he hoped would make sense to him later.

When the doctor said the name of a facility he was familiar with, he lifted his head, his brow furrowing. "Is that the only option for rehab?"

Dr. Terano turned toward him, letting out a knowing sigh. "It's got open beds, especially for the length of time he'll need to be in. Obviously we can check again after he gets the hand done, but…" She shrugged in that frustrated, overburdened healthcare system way that Will had done a thousand times himself.

"I could make a call." He had a facility in mind where a former coresident worked. It was farther away but better equipped, a place he thought would be more comfortable.

"Wait," Nora said. "Open beds?"

"At his age," Dr. Terano began, and Jonah made a snort of offense. "And with the injuries he has, a few weeks of residential rehab is the right move. He can do therapy during the day, and have twenty-four-hour care at other times."

"I live across the hall from him." Her voice was high, nervous. "If the therapists could come there, me and my neighbors—"

"It's a third-floor unit," Will said, which was absolutely his first mistake. Nora's eyes snapped to his, her expression hard. He cleared his throat.

Dr. Terano looked to Jonah. "Third floor, huh?"

"How else do you think I keep this physique?" Jonah said, which would've been funny had Nora not been vibrating with tension beside him. Even Jonah seemed a bit nervous when he looked over at her.

"The rehab facility is the best option, really," said Dr. Terano. "After you're out, that's the bigger challenge. How accessible is this building you're in? Is there an elevator?"

Jonah laughed, as though the very thought was ridiculous. Will looked over at Nora, something about her expression tugging at his memory, but he couldn't get a grasp on it, not when Dr. Terano was still talking to Jonah about the building.

"Stairs might be fine for you, eventually, but the thing is, your grip strength will need a lot of work, so railings aren't always going to be reliable assists for you. If the stairs are narrow, or steep—"

Will cringed, thinking of all the times he'd gone up and down those steps over the last few months.

"What about one of those chairs?" Nora said. "The mechanical ones, to go up and down?"

"Won't work," Will answered, without thinking beyond the immediate thing, the practical thing, the thing that he felt like he'd been handling safely for hours. "Three flights and landings in between."

His second mistake. Nora looked at him with such naked betrayal that his stomach cramped.

"He's got a poi—" Jonah began.

"He doesn't live there," Nora said to Dr. Terano, and Will knew, he *knew* he'd messed up. Even Dr. Terano knew. She caught his eye and a silent professional communication passed between them: *Not the best time to look too far ahead with the family.*

"We can figure this out later," Will said, taking a step toward Nora. "No need to rush a thing like this."

"Dr. Sterling is right," she said cheerfully, and while he was grateful, the use of his title made everything feel about ten thousand times worse. "First order of business is getting ready for the hand surgery, then we can think about where Mr. Hajduk heads next."

"First order of business is calling my woman!" Jonah practically shouted, obviously similarly relieved to get a break from this conversation. "Nora, I'm going to need that tablet so I can do a video call." He looked to Will, his grin skewed by his still-swollen face. "Chicks dig scars, and all that."

Dr. Terano laughed, and promised to come by again later, dipping her hands beneath the sanitizer dispenser and rubbing them together on her way out, washing her hands of this whole messy scene.

And then it was only the three of them, and the silence was deafening.

–

"Let's review the facts."

Will sighed and stared down at the pavement of the hospital parking lot, avoiding eye contact with Gerald Abraham, who loomed above him in his white coat and projected a profound energy of disapproval at the state of Will's clothing and also possibly his emotions.

"Sure," said Will, because if he'd been desperate enough to contact Gerald forty-five minutes ago when Nora had basically kicked him out of Jonah's room, he was also desperate enough to do this Gerald's way.

"You spent the night at the hospital with your girlfriend—"

"We ought to get the terminology right," Will said, because there was something *wrong* with him, clearly. His Abraham mimicry was off the charts, though he had not used any emojis in his text message requesting a meeting. "I don't know if she's technically my girlfriend."

"Fine."

Will wondered if the man would take out his notebook and start recording this humiliation in shorthand.

"You spent the night at the hospital with the woman you're involved with."

Also doesn't sound right, thought Will, *but whatever*. He nodded.

"She was there for her neighbor, who is also something like a… what would you say? Uncle?"

"Not uncle," said Will, knee-jerk. "More like grandfather, maybe."

"Fine," Gerald repeated. "And the news is not positive for his return to his current home?"

Will swallowed, shifting on the bench that usually served as a pickup spot for a parking shuttle service. "Hard to say," he lied.

"A metal rod in his femur and delicate hand surgery still to come? Eighty years old? Three flights of stairs?"

Jeez, all right. Gerald really went in for the facts. Pretty good thing *he* hadn't been in the room for Dr. Terano's visit.

"Correct. But I didn't say that. I only—"

"You brought up the third floor."

Gerald was a pretty good listener; that was the thing, even if Will had spent the first ten minutes of this conversation telling a very disorganized version of the events of the last two days. Jonah's fall. Nora's rushed return from San Diego and their seeming reconciliation. This morning's meeting, and Nora's insistence afterward that she would "take it from here." He'd tried to stick to the plan he made: suggested that they call Benny, or Mr. and Mrs. Salas, offered to drive Nora back to her place. But she'd wanted none of it. Wanted none of *him*.

"I'll call you," she'd said, cool and remote, and it'd sounded like San Diego all over again.

"Yes, but only because—"

"The problem is obvious. She's very protective of her neighbors, whom you've said are basically her family. There's been a lot of change in her building, and most of it has been your doing."

"Don't sugarcoat it, Gerald," he said. "But also, that's a little unfair. Her grandmother died, and so did my uncle. Now this, with Jonah. None of that's my doing."

"Hmm." This was the noise Gerald made whenever Will introduced a new complexity to a case. Possible undiagnosed diabetes. A secondary infection that complicated the pharmaceutical plan.

Will felt liked he'd scored the most worthless point.

"I admit, I shouldn't have mentioned the third-floor thing. At that moment."

He'd figured that out even before he'd gotten on the elevator to leave, realizing what that tug of memory had been when he'd seen Nora turn pale and sick-looking at the mention of the building's accessibility. That's what *he'd* probably looked like, that day in the backyard when Mrs. Salas had found his parents' photograph.

I'm rattled, he remembered telling her.

"But things had been going well before that. I was taking care of her. I took care of things for her neighbors, before she got there. I was only trying to—"

"You're making her sound like a patient," Gerald said, and Will straightened, defensive.

"You're one to talk. You got Sally back—with my help, by the way—by planning nonroutine dates and not telling her anything about her table manners."

There was a pause, and Will looked up to find Gerald rocking back slightly on his heels. Should he not have mentioned he knew about the elbows on the table thing, or...?

"Actually," Gerald finally said, "I got Sally back because last night I told her how much I loved her. I told her that the two and a half years I've spent without her have been the most colorless of my life. I made her a list of all the ways I'd failed her during our marriage, along with a list of all the ways I wanted to do better. I intended to read it out to her, but frankly I found myself too emotional."

Will stared at Gerald in dumbfounded shock. He felt right on the verge of a recurrence of static brain. His expression must've shown it, because Gerald clarified.

"What I mean is, I cried."

"I got that, Gerald."

"Have you told this woman you love her?"

"No."

"But you do?"

"It's complicated." *No, it's not*, said his heart.

"Let's say," he corrected, "it is complicated for me to be in love."

"I'll need the history on this."

Will shook his head, tucked his fingers under his glasses and rubbed, certain that Gerald was again rocking back on his heels in disapproval at this disgusting display. Two nights ago Will sat across from Gerald's probably-not-really-ex-wife-anymore and passed on an opportunity to tell her the whole entire thing, and part of the reason why was that the man standing in front of him had been in the next room.

Frankly I found myself too emotional, Gerald had said, and all of a sudden, out in this hot parking lot with his heart half broken, Will thought Gerald Abraham might have the best bedside manner he'd ever seen, because the next thing he knew he was saying it all, everything about his parents that he hated to say. That they were selfish, immature, like they'd never grown out of their teenaged selves. He told him the worst of it: not just his mother trying to leave him with Donny, but also the many months after that. Will like a servant in his own house, trying to stay out of the way while they clung to each other in desperation. Holding his mother up in the funeral home while she wailed for a God he'd never known she believed in to take her, too. Nearly a whole year where she couldn't bear to look at him, where despite his desperate protests, she took up all sorts of rash, reckless behaviors—smoking, drinking heavily, probably worse things he didn't even know about.

"I almost felt relieved when she died," Will said. "For her. It's all she wanted, really. To go back to my dad. I know that makes me sound terrible."

In the silence that followed Will felt half relieved, half sick to have said it. He stared down at the pavement some more, thinking about how Gerald was really on to something with the no eye contact thing.

Finally, the man cleared his throat. "Let me express my sympathy," he said. "For the loss of your childhood."

Will blinked up at him. No one had ever put it like that before. "Thank you."

Oh no. Was *he* going to cry?

Gerald kindly pretended not to notice. "I gather you are afraid of turning out this way yourself. With whomever you become involved with."

"Not whomever," he said. "With her. I've only ever felt this way about her."

For a long time, Gerald didn't say anything, and Will supposed that was fair enough. There was really no solving this one, when it came down to it.

But then he said, "You know, my own father and I are very similar. He was also a doctor. Sally used to say that I only ever learned to love someone the way my father loved me. Discipline, improvement, opportunity. That's the way he showed me he cared."

Will swallowed, nodding. He could see, of course, how growing up like that would produce a man like Gerald. But he also thought it sounded pretty nice. All the discipline and improvement and opportunity that Will had in his life, he'd given to himself. It had been hard and lonely and entirely thankless.

"This was a problem in my marriage. To use a relevant example: it isn't necessary to tell someone you love about a mostly harmless flouting of proper table manners. You can simply let them put their elbows on the table and be quiet about it. You don't have to love people the way you learned to love at first."

Will stared. *WHAT*, the static signal seemed to say.

"I would say the same is true for the woman you're involved with. It seems to me that the first person who showed her a love that she understood was a person who offered her a lot of stability. A lot of loyalty."

"Gerald," Will said. "What the *hell*?"

He felt like he'd had his whole brain rearranged.

You don't have to love people the way you learned to love at first.

"I'm not sure why you're so surprised. Of late I'm very successful in matters of the heart."

Will stood from the bench, heedless of Gerald's general discomfort with his height. He paced back and forth in front of it, running his hands through his hair.

"I've been trying to..." He trailed off, shook his head. "I've been trying to keep it so *safe* with her. To just... fix things for her. To put limits on how I am with her. So I wouldn't—"

"You won't," Gerald interrupted. "You are a different person than your parents were people. I feel quite assured of this."

Will stopped pacing, put his hands on his hips. "I *am*," he said, and for the first time, he actually believed it. He thought of Nora in her bathroom, her lit-up eyes every time they put in a new bathroom fixture. The pleasure she took in new things, when she let herself. "And she is, too. I mean, different from how she—"

"Obviously, I'm keeping up," Gerald deadpanned.

In spite of his shitty night of sleep, Will suddenly felt alive with energy, his head swimming with this revelation, this perspective. He loved Nora, and it wasn't rash, or reckless, or selfish to feel it. To *say* it. To live it for the rest of his life, if she'd let him. He was not his parents. He didn't have to love the way he'd seen love at first.

"Gerald, I absolutely have to go. I've got to make a list of my failings, or something."

"Don't do that. It is very clear that your problems aren't mine."

"Right," Will said, momentarily deflated. "Right."

Gerald looked down at his watch. "A bit longer than the ten minutes you requested," he said.

Will couldn't help but laugh. "Of course. I've kept you too long. I appreciate you—"

Gerald waved a hand in dismissal. "No need," he said, looking flustered. "I'll certainly expect to see you back at work to-morrow."

Will nodded, somehow comforted by this return to Gerald's particular brand of professional rectitude. "Certainly," he echoed.

"Very good," Gerald said, and turned on his heel to head back inside.

But watching him go, Will had an impulse—sudden and sharp, the kind of feeling he'd trained himself to ignore for years and years, the kind of feeling he'd long told himself he ought to avoid. He wondered how many opportunities he'd missed in life like this, all because he was afraid of being rash or reckless or selfish.

Hell, he thought. *Why not?*

"Gerry," he called, and waited to get fired.

His boss stilled, and Will held his breath.

But then Gerald turned around, his eyebrows raised. "Yes?"

"I'm sure this isn't very professional," he said, pausing to clear his throat. "But I think you might be my best friend."

There was a long, painful second of silence across the parking lot, during which Will thought he might die of embarrassment, right at the moment he'd finally gotten his life figured out.

And then Gerald Abraham reached up and smoothed his lapel.

"Well, Will," Gerry answered, moving to tuck his hands into the pockets of his perfectly pressed, pristine white coat, "since we're out here in the parking lot, I think it is fine for me to say that the feeling is entirely mutual."

Chapter 19

Nora hadn't expected the blood.

Inside Jonah's apartment, she stared down at the dried patch of it, a circle that probably wasn't any bigger than her hand. Still, it chilled her, seeing it there, bringing to mind the way Jonah had looked this morning, as though he'd taken a terrible beating. She'd wanted to ask Will about that—the darkness of the bruising, the way it'd seemed to take up so much space even though Jonah had sworn he'd only struck the edge of his brow when he'd gone down.

She shook her head, frustrated with herself. It didn't matter. She should clean this up, pack Jonah's bag, get moving so she could get back there. She knew Mrs. Salas would want to go with her, could smell the aroma of her baking all throughout the building, and thought she must've been making Jonah's favorites. Benny, too, was planning to head back today; she'd seen him in the hallway on the way up, had ignored the quizzical look he'd given her as she'd insisted on dragging her suitcase up the steps entirely by herself.

Within minutes she was on her knees, scrubbing gently at the stain and blinking back the tears that kept stubbornly pressing behind her eyes. When she thought she'd mostly handled it, she stood, dumping the bucket of water into Jonah's tub, averting her eyes even when she rinsed her sponge. She stripped off her gloves and looked around. Should she try to tidy up? Make his bed so that when he came back—

She swallowed, flushing with heat.

It's a third-floor unit, Will had said to the doctor, so plain and so technical, and it had felt like having the wind taken out of her once again, when she wasn't even recovered from seeing Jonah there, and like that. The worst of it was, she'd spent the next few minutes trying to get her breath back, trying to remind herself that Will was only saying what was true, even if she'd hated the way he'd said it.

Even if she'd hated *when* he'd said it.

But it'd been beyond her, to breathe right again, to think straight again. *I'm overreacting*, part of her wanted to say, the same way he'd said to her last week, but she'd locked up, her mind like a thunderstorm: Nonna gone, Donny gone, Donny not even the nice man she'd always thought he'd been. Deepa leaving Verdant, Austin leaving San Diego. Nora's bathroom not like it'd always been; Nora thinking she might leave Verdant, too. Jonah in rehab. Jonah somewhere else altogether. She'd looked across the room at Will and suddenly it was like *he* was the wind that had been taken out of her; gusting through and blowing things apart. It didn't matter that she knew it wasn't really true; it didn't matter that she knew she was being unfair.

She'd still asked him to go.

Stop, Nora, she scolded herself. *You don't have time for this; you can talk to him later.* She needed to pack this bag; she needed a shower and a change of clothes; she needed to figure out what was next. She could deal with Will later. She moved quickly, opening Jonah's closet to find the duffel bag he'd told her about, stuffing in the things he'd asked for, checking off items on her phone as she went along. When she finally had it all, she revisited her first instinct, going back to Jonah's room to quickly make up his bed, hoping she wasn't overstepping.

She was pulling his door closed behind her when she saw Marian on the landing.

"Where is he?" she said.

Nora lowered her brow, concerned over Marian's apparent confusion. "He's in the hosp—"

"Will," Marian interrupted, coming down the hall toward her. "Where is he?"

"Oh, um," she said, hoping she could pull off this lie. "He had to go into work."

"That's not what Jonah said. Jonah said he was there speaking to the doctor this morning, and then you kicked him out."

Nora blinked. "I didn't. How did he—he was asleep when I left."

Marian shrugged. "Guess he didn't sleep for long. He called us once you were gone. Probably he was faking."

Nora sighed, stepped across the hall to her own door. "How did he sound? Mrs. Salas and I are going back soon. If you want to come—"

"What I want is to speak to Will about what the doctor said."

"I spoke to the doctor too, Marian. You can ask me."

"Yes, but Will is a *professional*. I don't trust doctors, you know that."

Nora ignored the jolt of satisfaction she felt at the revelation that Marian had moved Will from the category of "doctors" to "people she trusted." Instead, she huffed in annoyance, opening her door, knowing already Marian—Marian who had once very much disliked Will Sterling!—was going to follow her in.

"I'll give you his number," she said. "You can call him."

"Nora Clarke," Marian said, her tone sharp. "What are you *doing*?"

Nora stilled in place, so effective was Marian Goodnight's classroom voice. When Nora was growing up, this was exactly how she always reacted to it—a total body lockdown that ensured she had stopped doing whatever it was Marian didn't want her doing. But this time, her outward-facing freeze-up was accompanied by something similar on the inside, like the morning thunderstorm in her mind had abruptly ceased entirely.

She set down Jonah's duffel and took a deep breath.

"Go right over there and sit down," Marian said, pointing to the flowered couch that two nights ago Nora had promised herself she'd be rid of. When she sat, one of the upholstered buttons poked her left butt cheek, but she didn't even bother to move.

"Can't make coffee on this contraption," Marian said from the kitchen, obviously referring to Nora's fancy coffee machine, and then she set about filling up the old kettle. "So it'll have to be tea."

"Okay," said Nora, even though she didn't like tea. That kettle was Nonna's.

Once Marian had it on the stove, she came back over and sat on the other side of the sofa, obviously avoiding any upholstered buttons.

"You're just like her, you know," she said. "Your grandmother."

It wasn't the first time Nora had heard this—not even the first time she'd heard it from Marian.

But it was the first time it didn't sound all that much like a compliment.

"Now you know I loved her," said Marian. "She was one of my best friends in the whole entire world, and I don't suppose I'll ever get over her not being here."

Nora nodded, tears springing to her eyes. "Me neither."

"But she was awfully stubborn. Like a mule, about things big and small."

"She wasn't." Even as she said it, though, Nora felt a knot of uncertainty take up residence in her stomach. She'd always thought of stubborn people as people who couldn't admit when they were wrong. But Nora had never really been in a situation where she'd thought Nonna had been wrong about anything.

"Now I think I knew her pretty well," said Marian. "I knew her differently than you did, sure. So believe me when I tell you, she was stubborn. Couldn't get her to budge on that wallpaper, for example. And do you know, thirty years ago there was a man who wanted to take her out, a very nice man whose company I happen to know she enjoyed? But did she go?"

This was a rhetorical question, but also it was Marian, so Nora had to answer.

"No?"

"No! And do you know why?"

Nora shook her head.

"Because she said it wouldn't be the right thing to do to your *grandfather*."

"But…" Nora said tentatively. "He was… dead?"

Marian widened her eyes, pursed her lips, and swept her hands out, palms up, in a gesture that began by encompassing the sofa, and then expanded to what was, Nora assumed, the whole entire apartment. This expression said, *I hope I don't have to waste any more of my time on this.*

"I'm going to change the apartment," she asserted, though she was in fact very surprised to hear Marian's feelings about that wallpaper. "I am. Already I started working on the bathroom."

"Great," Marian said, though she didn't really seem that impressed. "Of course you had *help*. From a very *helpful* person, who also did not want you living in a *tomb* for the rest of your life."

Nora winced. Not so much at the tomb imagery (although that was very unpleasant!), but more at the thought of Will at the hospital—all day yesterday, when she wasn't there. All last night, when she was. *God*, she had been such a *jerk* this morning.

She rubbed her hands over her face. The kettle started to rumble, and Marian stood, returning to the kitchen and making tea while Nora stared down at her lap and thought about calling Will.

When Marian returned, she looked over the lip of the mug and stared at Nora while she sipped. When she pulled it away from her mouth she said, "I didn't say I was making it for you."

Nora shook her head and laughed softly. "I love you, Marian," she said, because she really, really did.

"I love you too, doll. But you were definitely wrong to send that man away." She sipped her tea again. "I can't really believe I said that, but here we are."

She could have let it go there; she could have sat in the silence with Marian and contemplated her stubbornness until she got up the courage to call up Will and apologize for the way she'd acted. Marian was probably going to sit here until she did it, actually.

But telling Marian she loved her, and knowing Marian would say it right back—it reminded her of the bigger problem she didn't quite know how to solve. She could get rid of this couch; she could clear out Nonna's bedroom; she could leave her job. She could maybe even deal with Jonah having to go somewhere else. But could she deal with it if...

"He's not really a sure thing," she blurted. "Will, I mean."

Marian raised her eyebrows. "What's he been doing over here all night, then?"

Nora clapped her hands over her face, groaning. "I don't mean *that*! My *goodness*, Marian!"

"Exactly like her," Marian said, rolling her eyes. "Like what, then?"

Nora dropped her hands, sobering. "I'm in love with him. And he's—I don't know. He's not sure about being serious with someone. That's what he said, before."

Marian clicked her tongue. "A person doesn't do the things Will did over the last couple of days unless they're serious, Nora."

Nora nodded again, because of course part of her believed that, too. It's what she'd clung to last night in the hospital, her desperation to believe that they'd settled things, even without words between them. But thinking of it now, thinking of Will's determined, practical helpfulness, a little clumsier than usual, this morning—she wondered if they had both, in a way, still been hiding. Jonah's accident like a towel rod or a sink faucet or a new can of paint. Some way for them to keep from having to risk themselves.

She thought about Will that day in Donny's apartment—that photograph, that look in his eyes when he told her it was too much between them. She wouldn't break her promise to him, wouldn't tell Marian what she knew about his parents and what their relationship had done to him. But she couldn't set it aside in her own mind, either.

She knew Will would forgive her for this morning if she said she was sorry for sending him away, for not talking to him the way she should have.

But would he forgive her for telling him how she really felt about him?

Or was it still too much?

Would it always be?

"But, Nora," Marian said, cutting through her thoughts, her voice gentler this time. "What are you doing, looking for a sure thing?"

Nora looked over at Marian, and for the first time in her life, she didn't even try to answer one of her neighbor's questions. She simply begged with her eyes to have this one answered for her.

"Not every love you have is the kind like you had with your nonna. Or like the kind you have with me or Emily, or Jonah. Or anyone in this whole place, with the exception of that new man downstairs, I guess. Love can't always be a sure thing from the start."

She thought about that dark morning she'd first talked to Will—that electric, new feeling she'd had, that curiosity and intensity that had carried over even into their silly feuds about the apartment. She thought about his laugh and his way of making conversation with almost anyone; she thought about the secret, tender heart that hid behind his practicality, and she thought about how he pushed her, so gently, in the directions she always wanted to go herself. She thought about the way she wanted him, the way she could be a certain version of herself with him, someone different from who she was with anyone else in her life, ever.

"It's scary," whispered Nora, and Marian reached over and patted her leg.

"I sure know."

Nora took another breath, gathering her courage. No more stubborn waiting and withholding; no more *We'll talk when I get back*, or *Not in a hospital*, or *I'll call you later*. She would tell him she loved him even if he thought Jonah should move, even if he hated the hallway wallpaper (had Marian said she didn't like the wallpaper?!), even if he was as rattled and scared as she was. She'd tell him right now, over the phone, if he'd answer. She'd text it if she had to, which was an awful thought, but she wasn't going to wait anymore. She was going to—

"Now what in the world," Marian said, and that's when Nora turned around to see a small cherry tomato splatter against her balcony door.

–

She heard his voice through the glass first, a muffled, single syllable that sounded like *Hey!*, though she wasn't quite sure. For a second, she stood paralyzed, looking first at the leavings of a tomato sliding down the glass, and then toward Marian, who set down her tea onto the coffee table and said, "I had better get out of here."

"*Hey*," he called again, louder this time, and oh, goodness. The whole neighborhood would hear this. She finally gathered her senses enough to go to the door, and she slid it open just in time for a cherry tomato to hit her squarely (and painlessly) in the face.

"Nora!" he called, because he obviously did not know he'd just struck her with a small fruit. She touched at her cheek, making sure nothing had splattered, and stepped out onto the balcony, avoiding other scattered tomato projectiles as she went to the railing and peeked over.

And there, in the middle of her backyard, stood Will Sterling, squinting up at her through his glasses, one hand poised for another throw, and one holding a small, half-empty plastic container of tomatoes.

"Oh my God," she whispered.

Down below, Will lowered his raised arm and smiled, big and boyish, and Nora felt every single cell of her body get in courageous formation, a little army of *I love you*s lining up for launch. But before she could speak, Will called up to her again.

"I stood here," he said, and for the first time she realized he was standing beside something, a spindly, bright-green-leafed tree that came to his shoulders, still packed with a burlap wrap around its unplanted base. "The tree was bigger, obviously."

She put a hand over her mouth, muffling her wet laugh. "Like that," he said. "You laughed, but it was bigger. You didn't know I was down here. You said *Hey*, and then you laughed, and my heart never beat the same after that. I never forgot the sound of it."

Her hand fell away, her laughter fading as her own heart took off into what felt like a full, forever gallop.

"I thought you were yelling at me, at first—I thought you'd seen me. But really you were yelling at those squirrels, and I"—he took a few steps forward, away from the tree—"I was thinking of something to say, *anything*, really. I was all locked up with nerves."

Anything, she thought. *You could have said anything, and I would have loved it. I would have listened and listened.*

"I was almost ready, but then you started tossing tomatoes off your balcony. The first one hit me here." He reached up, touched his hand to the front of his thick, wavy mass of hair. "You can throw some of those ones back down, if you want to get me again."

She shook her head, unable to speak, caught between more laughter and tears, locked up with nerves now like he'd been all those years ago.

He nodded, shifting the hand he'd put in his hair to shield his eyes for a few seconds, and even from here she could see: whatever story he was telling, it was about to change. He looked at her like he was gathering his own courage for it, and she set

285

both her hands over her heart because that was the place she was listening from; that was the place where all her locked-up words lived for now.

She thought he might have taken a breath, a big one, and then he said, "I picked them up, all the ones you'd thrown." He brought his half-full container in front of him, held it cupped in his hands.

"Like this," he said, and then he crossed the yard, moved to stand right by Donny's—*his*—balcony.

Nora moved, too, peeking over from a different spot.

"I stood right here, so I'd be closer, so I could try to see you better. I was going to say, *Hey, did you drop something?*"

Below, she heard the distinct sound of a door sliding open, and then an unfamiliar voice said, "Listen, could you keep it down?"

Will's head turned to his own balcony and he said, "In a minute," with a flat, inarguable seriousness that was nearly as heart-thumping as this entire scene.

"I sleep during the day, so..."

"I'm your landlord," said Will, and Nora thought she might've heard Benny's laugh from somewhere beneath her.

Will looked back at Nora. "Funny he should interrupt," he called up, the smile on his lips carrying a hint of sadness, and she knew it wasn't going to be funny at all.

"So I was going to say, *Hey, did you drop something?* And I know I didn't tell you this part before, Nora, but I think I ought to tell you now."

"Okay," she said, and she hoped he could hear her, hoped the softness in her voice wasn't too soft.

"And I could hear my mom and Donny talking, and that's how I found out my dad was sick. It's how I found out that my mom wanted to leave me here—"

"Will," she called down, shocked into speech by this admission—out here in public, with everyone *home*. "You don't have to—"

"I don't mind if they know." He paused, lowered his head to look toward Marian and Emily's balcony. "Nora told me last night how you all ended up here. I know why this place matters to all of you, so you might as well know why it matters to me, too."

Nora thought she could hear Mrs. Salas's voice from somewhere, too, though the words were indistinct. Still, Will must've caught it, because he smiled before he looked back up at Nora.

"It's also how I found out what Donny thought of my mom, and my dad, and me, really. Rash, reckless, selfish. That's what he said about us. Like we were all of a piece."

"Will," she said again, tears dripping from her chin now. She wiped them away hastily. "Let me come down. Just wait, and I'll come down."

"Not yet."

She nodded, but she had to grip the balcony railing to stop herself.

"I think the thing is, Donny was probably right about that. I think I probably was kind of a reckless kid, back then. After all, I fell in love with a girl on a balcony just from hearing her laugh."

That was definitely Mrs. Salas. A big, swoony sigh.

"And I think if I would've gotten left here with Donny that day, I probably would have been so selfish with you. I probably would've messed up your life in all kinds of ways."

"Don't say that," she said, but it was hard not to think of how it really would have been—Will, angry and alone and intense; Nora, timid and immature and inexperienced. It probably *would* have been a mess.

"I left here that day and I tried to become someone else, someone more focused and in control, someone more responsible. And I thought I'd done fine out there in the world on my own, but I know now a part of me was missing you the whole time. I know it because sixteen years later I came back here and saw you up on that balcony and I was terrified I hadn't changed at all."

"Nora!" Mrs. Salas called from somewhere below. Will lowered his head and smiled, and Nora realized Mrs. Salas must be on Emily and Marian's balcony, too. "This is so good! I'm sorry; I had to say it!"

Nora nodded even though Mrs. Salas couldn't see her. She kept her eyes on Will.

"I'm almost there, Mrs. Salas," he said, and then he looked back up.

"Nora Clarke, I loved you from the first time I didn't see you, but I don't think that matters half as much as the fact that I love you now. I don't think it matters as much as the way I know I'm going to love you forever."

"Oh *my*," said Mrs. Salas.

"I know it's hard for you to trust new people, Nora, and I know you're afraid of everything that's been changing, and I know there might be hard days ahead. But I came here with this tree and these tomatoes because I want you to remember I'm not as new as you think I am. I want you to remember I've been waiting to come back to this place—to you—for sixteen years. It just took me awhile to figure it out."

She had her hands over her heart again, and her eyes on his when she finally was able to speak. "Will," she said. "*Now* can I come down?"

He nodded, and her neighbors *whooped*, and she ran.

–

Will caught her up in a hug so tight it lifted her feet from the ground, a hug so forceful that he had to spin to take all of her momentum. She'd set free her army of *I love you*s before she'd even reached his waiting arms, but once they were wrapped around each other she whispered them against his neck, into his ear, along his cheek. She said it against his lips, *I love you, I love you*, before he kissed her, before he took her words inside him and gave a soft groan of relief that she could feel rumble between them where their chests pressed together. Behind her, she could hear the continued commentary of her neighbors, a goofy smattering of applause that made her smile against his lips until they had to break their kiss.

"Will," she said, now that she had use of her lips again, "I'm so sorry about this morning. I was—"

"Baby," he said, smiling down at her, smoothing his thumbs over her wet cheeks, "it's okay. I shouldn't have brought up the third-floor thing, or the staircase landings. And I don't know why I said *unit*. Jesus. You *hate* that word."

She laughed softly and shook her head. "No, you were trying to help. I was on my way to call you. I completely overreacted; I know I did."

"You didn't. It's scary, what's going on with Jonah, and you didn't need me doctoring my way through that meeting this morning. But I—look, fixing things for you, I thought that was the best way I could be with you. The safest way, for the both of us."

She nodded, putting her hands over his and moving them so they could press their palms together and lock their fingers together at their sides. Some of the noise behind them had quieted, so either her neighbors had turned silent in their spectating, or they'd given them some backyard privacy.

"Keeping things the same," she said. "Obviously, I've—that's how I try to show people how I love them. Nonna, even though she's gone. Everyone here. And even with us, when I thought you might not feel the same way back… I was just trying to keep myself safe, too. To go back to the things I know are a sure thing. I bolted this morning, and I'm sorry."

"We'll work on it," he said. "Both of us. We'll figure this out."

She nodded and pressed up to kiss him again.

"I love you," he said again, when they finally parted. "I should've told you the first night we were together. It feels so good to tell you, I can't believe it."

"I know," she said, and then, because she could, and because she was so full to bursting with feeling, she repeated it. "I love you, I love you, I love you."

He brought her close again, kissed the words from her mouth like he was hungry for them, then bent to put his lips beside her ear, speaking quietly this time, like he wanted to make sure this was only for them. "You're the first, you know."

She shuddered at the feeling of his breath against her neck, at the memory of that first night they'd had together, when he'd told her that their physical connection had felt like a first for him, too. But something about his hold on her hands, something about the way he held his body, signaled her that he was saying something new. She leaned back so she could see him, searched his eyes and found them more serious than she expected.

"The first person you've been in love with?" She'd assumed that's part of what he meant, when he'd told her he'd fallen for her sixteen years ago, but—

He shook his head, and then corrected. "Yes, you're that, but…" He lowered his head, loosening a hand from hers so he could reach up and straighten his glasses in a move that made Nora's whole body ache with longing for him.

He came close again, and whispered in her ear. "You're the first person to ever say that to me."

God, she was going to be so dehydrated at the end of this day; she felt like she could cry for hours over this one precious, painful revelation. She didn't need to ask if he meant it, because she knew it was true. She knew that the people in Will's life who should have told him first had somehow thought they needed to save all their love for each other, and she felt sorry that they hadn't given themselves the chance to say it to their son, too.

She wrapped her arms around him again, hugging him close. "I'm going to tell you all the time, all over the place," she said. "Every morning, first thing. At night. In bed, at the dinner table, in the grocery store. I'll blow up your phone with texts."

She felt him smile against her hair.

"I'll take it," he said.

"And this might sound sort of funny at the moment, but I'm going to make sure I'm not the only one who says it to you."

The people in the building behind her, they were already well on their way. Mrs. Salas crossed the finish line a long time ago, probably. Nora was going to make sure Will Sterling never wanted for love again.

"I'll take that, too," he whispered, maybe something pleasantly embarrassed in his voice.

"Hey, now!" That was Benny calling, and when Will and Nora turned he was standing by the back door with Jonah's duffel, all her neighbors around him. "We're going to go see the chief. Give you two some privacy."

"Oh, are you two going to—"

"Do not finish that thought, Corrine," said Marian. "We're leaving."

The group filed past, offering knowing smiles or small congratulations, a funny little applause dance from Mrs. Salas before they piled into two cars and went on their way, and then it was only the two of them out in this sunny expanse of backyard, the building suddenly a whole new future behind them.

Will tugged her hand toward it. "Come tell me you love me in a different location," he said, his smile loose, easy, perfect. *Happy.*

She smiled back, teasing in the way she stalled him. "Wait a minute. What are we going to do about this tree you brought?"

"I'm going to plant it," he said simply. "Right where the old one was. When it gets big enough, we can carve our initials into it. Sort of a memorial, right? To the day we almost met."

Her heart skipped, remembering that day in his apartment, after he'd seen the photograph of his parents. After he'd told her he didn't want anything serious.

"You're sure about that?"

He leaned down and kissed her again, his tongue swiping across her bottom lip—brief, hot, full of promise. A forever sort of kiss.

"I'm sure," he said. "I've got a feeling. You and me, we're those kind of people."

Epilogue

Two years later

Nora made it onto the balcony first.

She hadn't been the one to wake first, not today, not with all the restless, nervous energy Will had been carrying with him all week. He first stirred at two, and then three, and then three thirty, each time reaching immediately for his phone, checking the time and holding back a groan of frustration before turning over again, seeking Nora's warm, soft skin with his hands, pressing his body back against her so he could doze again. She slept on soundly, tired from a couple of late nights this past week, work on site redesign for one of the first major clients she'd taken on as a freelancer.

Like clockwork, though, she started to stir around four, her body waking slowly, little murmurs of wakefulness that Will thought were the best alarm clock in the whole world. When she turned toward him, pressing her lips against his bare chest and stroking her soft fingers along his stomach, all the restless energy that had been keeping him awake transformed, his body turning hard and hungry for her in the way it always did. He dipped his head, nuzzling at her neck, listening as those waking noises turned into wanting noises, Nora's hands finding him with more focused attention to all the places he liked to be touched best.

When he pulled her over him, she came easily, smoothly, like they'd done this—or some version of this—hundreds of mornings, and after two years he liked to think they had, though he supposed he hadn't made a habit of counting. But even with the earned familiarity they had with each other's bodies; even though he knew she would start in this position slow, sliding down his length with delicious, torturous control, and end it fast, rubbing herself against him as he gripped her hips roughly, it still always felt like a first. When she came around him, when he let himself go inside her, he would always feel it like new; he would always tell her he loved her, like he'd wanted to that very first time, back when they were both still hiding their feelings.

"I love you, too," she breathed, collapsing against his chest, and then she said it again, the way he always wanted her to. He tucked his hand beneath her hair, up to where her hairline met her nape, and relished the dampness there, a telling tale of her pleasure.

He breathed in deep, some of the nervousness gone, and he kissed the top of her head, silently thanking her for the relief she didn't even know she'd provided. It'd been awful keeping a secret from her this long, and when she climbed over him, giving him another smacking, satisfied, good-morning kiss, he finally allowed himself a few lazy minutes of thinking through the night ahead.

But eventually he, too, got up, sliding on his glasses and stopping by the bathroom before pouring a cup of coffee and joining her outside. He handed over the fresh cup and took hers, already half gone, a familiar routine—he still got most of his coffee midmorning, from Janine. They stood beside each other, waking up slow as the smattering of city-visible stars faded with oncoming daylight.

"It's going to be a good evening for it," she said eventually, when she was about halfway through her new cup, and a little pulse of that nervous energy returned.

"Mmm," he said, reluctant to start talking about it. He didn't trust his poker face around Nora.

"Oh, I see," she teased. "Hardly a full year of living together and you're already done with morning conversation, huh? So much for the golden hour."

He laughed softly, reaching out to tug her close. "Tired, that's all," he lied. "You go first."

When he'd first moved in to the building, they'd done this from across the way—Will over on what used to be Jonah's balcony, in the apartment he'd moved into only a few months after Jonah's accident. He'd eaten shit on his lease, lost his security deposit, but as it'd turned out, the money he'd earned off his first couple of tenants had covered those costs, and even if they hadn't, it would've been worth it. Jonah's old place worked just fine for him—close to Nora, close to everyone—and Donny's old place worked perfect for Jonah, a few easy upgrades to make it accessible as he got stronger and stronger. The bonus was winning a bet: one hundred dollars from Donny's smiling, good-sport attorney, when he'd officially signed over the apartment to Jonah on the very day the will's yearlong condition had run out.

Nora had fought him and Jonah on it at first, clasped-hands anxiety over whether Will felt like he *had* to do this, for her, promises that she'd be okay, if Jonah had wanted or needed to go somewhere else. And Will, too, had been anxious—would she think it was too rash, him living so close, so soon? Would it seem too reckless, too selfish? But they'd worked it out, reassurances going both ways, a slow start that they'd worked out across their balconies, golden hours of getting to know each other in ways they hadn't allowed for before. Even on the nights—the many nights—when they'd slept together, they'd still done it, retreating to their respective spaces, making sure they made things solid both for themselves and for each other before they'd done more.

Ten months ago, on the same night Nora had landed her most lucrative design contract yet, she'd made a gigantic pot of sauce and surprised Will by serving a meal out on the balcony, a new table and two chairs waiting. "*Two* chairs, Will," she'd said, sweeping her hand across the set. "If you'd want to join me for good, from now on."

He'd moved in—officially—a month later.

He shifted behind her, gently caging her between the balcony railing and his body in a way he knew she liked, and listened to her talk about the day ahead, her frustration about the fridge-sharing situation at her coworking space, her lunch date with a couple of the friends she'd made there, a meeting she had with a prospective client. He was glad to have had the memory about the time she'd asked him to move in; it was a good reminder for tonight. Bringing him into her space, into the apartment she'd spent months working so hard on, almost all on her own—that was always going to have been her call, and he was always going to wait to do what he was about to do until after she'd asked.

He'd waited for the right time, and he knew it was now.

"Will," she laughed. "I asked you a question."

He dropped his head to her shoulder, sighing out an apology and fogging up his glasses in the process.

"You scrambled my brain in there," he said, which was absolutely not a lie, even if it wasn't the whole truth. She laughed again and subtly pushed herself back into him, a taunt he deserved and enjoyed and definitely responded to.

"Let's go back in," he said against her neck.

"It's pretty late," she said, but he could feel the skin under his mouth pebbling. He let his thumb tease beneath the hem of her camisole.

"Still early," he said quietly.

"Mmm."

"Oh, I see," he echoed, tickling her side, and she turned to face him, pressing her mouth to his, and he settled again, kissing her deeply. *Better this morning*, he thought, *to avoid conversation*.

When she whispered against his mouth that it was, in fact, still early, he wrapped an arm around her waist and carried her inside, giving himself another break from counting the hours until tonight.

"Goodness, this has turned out to be a real disaster."

Will rubbed a hand across the back of his neck, nodding solemnly at the same sparsely attended party setup that Nora was looking at in near horror. Lanterns hung from the fence, a string of fairy lights on the still-growing tree they'd planted together, chairs lined up in rows, a table in the back laden with unused flower crowns and unclaimed scrolls of poetry.

"It's a shame," he said.

"She's going to be so disappointed. How did this *happen*?"

Will shrugged, feigning ignorance. "Maybe people got the date wrong?"

"It's every *month*, Will," she said, and now he was starting to feel guilty. He didn't want Nora to feel this stressed. He'd kept it small tonight, family only, but he supposed he could've invited some of their newer friends—

"And this one's the *big* one," she added.

"The big one" referred to the larger-than-average annual summer poetry night tradition that had only started because of his unexpected inheritance in this building.

"Well, maybe a few more people will show," he said nonchalantly.

She sighed and shook her head. "Marian wants me to go up and get my appetizer now," she said. "Even though there's only, like, *ten* of us here!"

"Sure," he said, relieved. He sent a grateful look to Marian, who was right on time with her request.

Once Nora had disappeared through the back door, his neighbors descended on him in such a suspicious way that he could only hope Nora didn't happen to look out the window.

"She doesn't know a *thing*," Mrs. Salas said.

"Corrine, lower your voice," Mr. Salas cautioned, and Mrs. Salas cupped a hand over her mouth before dropping it again. "I'm just so *excited*!"

"This is the biggest production I've ever seen, Beanpole," Jonah said. "But I suppose that's only because I missed your big backyard speech way back when."

He huffed in annoyance, still carrying a grudge over being the only neighbor to have missed it. Beside him, Kay—his girlfriend from St. Louis, in for another visit—slapped his arm playfully.

"Benny," Will said, "text Deepa and tell her to come out."

"Done," he said, pulling out his phone. Currently, Nora's best friend was hidden away in Marian and Emily's place, part of the surprise for tonight. For the next week, she'd be staying up in his old third-floor apartment, the place he and Nora now ran as a short-term rental, and he had a feeling his next few days were going to be filled with a fair number of makeup tutorials and face masks.

"Will," said Emily quietly, setting a hand on his arm. "Don't forget to breathe, now."

He nodded, face flushing, but it was difficult to get too embarrassed around this crowd these days. Over the past two years he'd made his own way with them, separate from his relationship with Nora. First of all, he'd put a towel rod in every unit of this place, and he'd taken up his own share of chores—changing the filters on the HVAC units, clearing out the dryer hoses when they clogged, helping Marian when she finally convinced Nora to get that wallpaper down. He watched ball games with Jonah; he made beer with Benny; he even spent one afternoon a few weeks ago flying a drone with Mr. Salas and a group of people who had a whole club devoted to amateur robotics.

"Thanks, everyone," he said. "I couldn't have pulled this much off without you."

"Oh, now stop that!" Mrs. Salas said. "We're honored to help. You know we love you."

He smiled, straightening his glasses. He supposed he'd gotten used to this, too. He supposed he couldn't remember it any other way.

Behind him, gravel popped, and he breathed a sigh of relief that the final guests for the evening had arrived. He went to the back fence, greeting Gerald and Sally. Sally patted his cheek but practically flew by him to get to his neighbors, whom she maintained were "the greatest group of people you'd ever want to meet." He watched as she clutched Emily in a hug, moving right on to Marian after.

He and Gerald hung back, and Will was grateful.

"Nervous?" Gerald said.

Will wiped his palms on his jeans. "Hell yes."

"You think she'll say no?"

"Jesus, Gerry. No?"

Gerald rocked back on his heels. He was wearing a short-sleeved collared shirt with a bunch of brightly colored pelicans printed all over it, and his gold wedding band gleamed on his finger. Will looked at his face and saw he was doing his version of a smile.

"Funny," Will said.

"I don't believe you have anything to be nervous about," which was a nice vote of confidence.

Will cleared his throat. "I don't want to be some asshole doing a big public proposal." He ran a hand through his hair. "Was this a mistake?"

He saw Deepa come out the door, and she waved and winked at him. Despite Nora's many stories about Deepa's inability to keep a secret, she'd been an absolute vault about this one. Still, he figured he was about two minutes away from Nora coming outside with a tray of stuffed mushrooms and— once she caught sight of her best friend, and Will's, to boot—a real good sense of what was about to go down.

"Will," Gerald said, in that permanent stick-up-his-ass voice that Will had come to love. "I'll remind you. You have spent two years getting to know Nora, and all the people and things that are important to her, and she's done the same for you. You've planned all this for her because you know the right way to love each other. And you know the right way to ask her this question. Don't forget that."

Will nodded, swallowed down a press of emotion. "Thanks, man," he said.

Gerald looked straight ahead, lowering his brow. "Now, now," he cautioned. "You certainly know I don't approve of that kind of nickname."

And then, as was his habit, he walked away.

-

Exactly as he'd expected, Nora really did know, as soon as she caught sight of Dee. With her flower crown listing to the side and her arms full of way too many stuffed mushrooms for this small crowd, she gasped and nearly tripped over the long hem of her dress, her eyes bright with moisture already.

"Dee?" she said, but almost immediately her eyes went to Will, beaming a smile that he thought could've lit up the whole night sky.

He stepped forward and took the tray from her before she dropped it, and immediately Nora ran to Dee, hugging and exclaiming in joy, and as Will set down the tray, he figured that alone was worth the price of admission, even if she ended up hating the rest of this whole thing.

She greeted Gerald and Sally, too, her hand against her heart. "I'm so—so this is a small poetry night, I guess!"

He walked over to her, set a hand on her back. "I hope you won't mind. I've been around long enough now that I, too, can use poetry night for my own purposes."

She smiled and flushed, her hands coming up to press against her cheeks, and he caught Gerald's eye.

Not a mistake, he thought, and Gerald gave him a nod.

"Why don't we go ahead and sit?"

She nodded and sat beside him in the front row of chairs, clutching his hand tight, and then the evening he'd been planning for got started.

He hadn't been lying, that night in the hospital when he'd told Marian Goodnight he'd been getting into poetry. Maybe it'd only been one poem, back then, but by now, he'd made something of a habit of it. He went to all of Marian and Emily's monthly readings, even the ones Nora couldn't attend, and in between those, he got Marian's suggestions and studied them. He signed up for an email that sent him a poem first thing in the morning, and he read each one, even the weird, too-long ones that he wasn't sure he understood. Upstairs in their apartment, on a new set of shelves he and Nora had put in together, he had a few collections of his own, sitting in a tidy row beside the framed photograph of his parents. Poems he could say from memory, some of them that he'd ended up picking for tonight.

He hadn't been subtle about it, because that wasn't poetry night's style; the first one he'd ever attended had been poems about summer on an early-summer night. So he wanted every poem tonight to be about love, forever love, and before Marian—the natural first reader of the night—was even all the way through hers, Nikki Giovanni's "You Came, Too," Nora had leaned over to him and whispered, "You know I'm going to say yes, right?"

He'd nodded calmly, his heart hiccupping, and squeezed her hand.

They listened and laughed throughout the readings—Jonah's annoyance not to be reading about baseball, and Kay's accompanying good-natured heckles from the audience. Gerald's and Sally's stilted but charming trade-off of lines from Shakespeare; Mrs. Salas's teary rendition of one of Will's favorites, a James Weldon Johnson poem about beauty that never got old. Emily's quiet but moving recitation, barely audible but deeply genuine, and Dee's follow-up full-throated, contrasting performance.

When it was Will's turn, finally, Nora was dabbing a tissue under her eyes and the masses were getting restless, Benny jokingly calling out for the big finish, Mr. Salas rubbing his hands together in anticipation. Will stood and thanked everyone, and then he looked at Nora and wasn't nervous at all. He saw this one so clearly in his mind; he knew this one by heart. Eight lines, even shorter than the first poem he'd ever read for her.

"This one's by Mary Oliver," he said. "So I'm pretty sure Nonna would approve."

And when he got to the very last line—"no more words now"—he dropped to his knee in front of Nora, and she whispered his favorite words, *I love you*, and followed up with the answer he'd been waiting all night, all his life, to get.

Yes.

Acknowledgments

Something that always keeps me going when I am writing a book is the prospect of getting to write this specific section—a joyful part of the process where I get to express some of my gratitude to the many people who make it possible for me to do this work. The list is long and by necessity incomplete, especially for this book, which I wrote during what I would call a... very difficult time. So before I begin, what I would say is that I end this book with a heart full of gratitude and a head full of names, many of which cannot appear here.

That includes the names of so many readers, bloggers, book-sellers, and librarians—you are always the first! Thank you so much for the pleasure you take in books, and thank you for the work you do to share them with the world. Thank you for your notes of encouragement and excitement, which mean more to me than I can say. I hope you loved Will and Nora, and I am so grateful for the support you have shown to me and to my work.

Every time I finish a project, I send it along to my editor, Esi Sogah, and my agent, Taylor Haggerty, with a happy closing line of "We did it!" Both of these incredible women usually try to correct me, to say that *I'm* the one who did it, but I'd like to state for the record (it's in print now!) that they are both incredibly wrong. In the first place, both of them usually have to spatula me off a parking lot of despair at the halfway point; in the second, both of them are sharp readers and savvy coaches, and I am so grateful to them both. Taylor, thank you especially for your total faith in me and your regular, cheerful reminders that I am, in fact, doing okay. Esi, you belong in many places of this acknowledgments section but I know you'll edit me to keep it all up here, so I'll just say: you're the best "quaranteam" partner a gal could have, and I treasure you as a colleague and as a dear friend.

Friendship and family carried me through a great many rough patches as I finished this book. I offer special thanks to a few who saw this one come together up close. Sarah MacLean and Jennifer Prokop were always a phone call away; Sarah in particular helped in the earliest and latest stages of plotting this book ("You just have to write it," she would say, which is very good advice), while Jen stood at the ready for my weird, highly specific Chicago-related questions and for my weepy moments of insecurity. I love you both so. Lauren Billings was an absolute champion: Lauren, you crash-landed into my life (or I crash-landed into yours?) at a supremely weird time in this world, but it sure does feel like fate, and I hope you know that I couldn't have finished this one without your texts and GIFs and your total belief in me. Therese Beharrie, Alyssa Cole, Olivia Dade, Ruby Lang, Elizabeth Kingston, Kennedy Ryan, and Jill Smith were all generous and patient friends at various stages of the process. My longtime first reader, Amy, was heroic for this one—particularly for the last part of my drafting, reading at all hours and always live-texting her reactions.

Kensington Books has been my publishing home since my debut, and I send my most sincere thanks to the entire team for their support and enthusiasm for my books, and for working on them until they (sometimes literally!) sparkled. I extend special gratitude to Michelle Addo, Lynn Cully, Jackie Dinas, Vida Engstrand, Susanna Gruninger, Norma Perez-Hernandez, Lauren Jernigan, Alexandra Nicolajsen, Kristine Noble, Adam Zacharius, and Steve Zacharius. I also extend thanks to the Kensington team for working with people like Erica Ferguson, who deserves my gratitude for her careful copyediting in the final stage of this book's development. You all have made so many of my publishing dreams come true.

A final word for my husband, for this book especially: how fortunate was I to first see you when we were only fifteen, and how sensible were you to know first that we had something rare and special. Thank you for growing up with me, and for always seeing clearly in me the things I struggle to see for myself.